An intimate history of the Greater Kingdom

SON IN SORROW

This work is published by
Sans Culotte Press
4110 SE Hawthorne Blvd #428
Portland OR 97214

Cover design and illustration by Beatriz González:
http://www.beagonzalez.com/
Original cover and character design by Alice Fox: http://www.alice-fox.net/
Book design by 1889 Labs: http://www.1889.ca/
Editing by Annetta Ribken: http://www.wordwebbing.com/

They are all brilliant and you should hire them right this minute.

Go to MeiLinMiranda.com for information, discussion and even more stories in this series.

Printed in the United States of America
First printing: April 2012
ISBN: 978-1-926959-21-4

For the 138 people who believed enough in this project to back it
via pre-sales at Kickstarter and my website,
my beautiful daughters who put up with my scribbling,
and the husband who has encouraged me every step of the way

AN INTIMATE HISTORY OF THE GREATER KINGDOM
    Book One: Lovers and Beloveds
    Book Two: Son in Sorrow
    Prequel stories: "Accounts" and "The Gratification Engine" (ebook only)

OTHER BOOKS BY MEILIN MIRANDA
    Scryer's Gulch
    The Machine God (Drifting Isle Chronicles), due late 2012

An intimate history of the Greater Kingdom

SON IN SORROW

BY

MEILIN MIRANDA

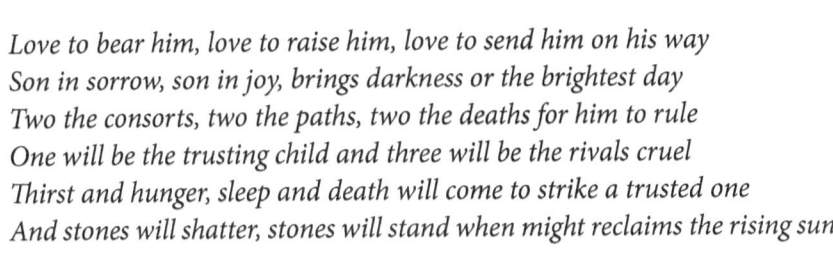

Love to bear him, love to raise him, love to send him on his way
Son in sorrow, son in joy, brings darkness or the brightest day
Two the consorts, two the paths, two the deaths for him to rule
One will be the trusting child and three will be the rivals cruel
Thirst and hunger, sleep and death will come to strike a trusted one
And stones will shatter, stones will stand when might reclaims the rising sun

—Temmin's birth prophecy

ONE

"I do not understand, Your Grace, why so glum the faces," said an enormous brown-skinned man. His long cloak of iridescent feathers covered otherwise unexceptional evening wear; his strong, naturally crimped black hair streamed unfettered down his back, and as he frowned around the ballroom in woozy concentration the blue-black tattoos curling round his nose and eyes furrowed.

"Glum, Your Excellency?" said his light-skinned companion. Anvalt Vonturus, Duke of Litta, was not a short man, but next to the tall ambassador even his stiff military bearing could not overcome an impression of smallness. In contrast with the ambassador's tattoos, a pale scar slashed through his left brow; a black ribbon clubbed his slate-colored hair in a queue that announced he was a conservative.

Litta glanced around the assembly milling about Tremont Keep's Great Ballroom in nervous clumps spiky with the glint of jewels. They winked on countless fingers; in the curls of women's hair; around slender wrists and wrists so fat they nearly hid their bracelets in their folds, and around necks both wrinkled and smooth; and from countless medals—some earned and some Litta knew were given to shut the bearer up. *What a decadent age.*

His eye settled on the musicians, fidgeting on the bandstand. To his approval, all the orchestra's members wore spotless evening attire, their brass and silver instruments polished to a blinding luster. The more careless musicians impatiently tapped violin and cello bows against their chair legs as the more careful ones rosined theirs; fingers ran up and down silent flutes, exercising the valves. Despite the orchestra's splendor, despite the brilliance of the Great Ballroom and its hundreds of inhabitants, a hesitant, uncertain mood hung over the whole.

"I suppose one might call it glum, sir," he continued. "This is not just the Heir's nineteenth birthday, but also his return to the Keep. Some are unsure how he will be received."

"Received, sir?" The Ambassador of the Vakale'le Confederacy, a Pau'an chieftain of birth high enough to match his stature, fidgeted in his unfamiliar suit; his broad, twitching shoulders set the feathers of his traditional cape to whispering. "Who by?"

"By His Majesty King Harsin."

"Happy the father on the birth date of the son, no? In Pau'a, this is so."

Litta allowed himself a smirk. "Oh, it is so here as well. Prince Temmin has been elsewhere for the last year."

"Where the Heir has been?"

"His Highness took religious orders at the Lovers' Temple."

The feathers rustled in shock. "The Heir is a priest?"

"Temporary orders. Supplicancy," muttered Litta. "They end next year at Neya's Day."

The Ambassador nudged the Duke, gently enough that Litta just stayed on his feet. "Ha! My wife hopes we are to be here for the Day of Neya Spectacle. That makes two for us this year. Your Gods Days, they are reversed—your Day of Neya, our Day of Harla. It is fall for us when it is spring for you—Tremont is the far side of the world." The Ambassador's tattoos softened, and Litta realized the man was a bit drunk. "Same Gods the world round, though different names. In strange lands, a comfort. It is said the Embodiments of the Lovers are most beautiful. To take on the Beloved Neya and the Lover Nerr—they must be so beautiful, indeed. They are real twins?"

"Issak and Allis Obby, yes," said Litta; his scar twitched.

The Ambassador pursed his lips. "The Heir is Supplicant, you say? How brave to learn from the Gods, how strange he would have that much skill—no, what word, not skill yet, he learns now the skill—perhaps talent? Talent needs learning to become skill. Oh, to see that deep into someone, to know what he wants. What advantages they could be!" He chose his next words carefully. "The King does not like this?"

"Oh, very much not." Few nobles did. Litta himself feared the prophecy attending Temmin's Supplicancy. He'd helped the King try to stop it, but what had that gotten him but the worst run of luck he'd ever had in his life?

Movement at the top of the ballroom stairs drew everyone's attention upward. On the landing stood a breathtaking pair, a young man and woman each with the same luminous green eyes and loose, thick black hair. The Pau'an hissed, low and soft. "This is them? Real twins, not a matched pair? Have you seen them together on Neya's Day, when the Gods possess them?"

Litta nodded. He'd watched as the Gods borrowed the Obbys' bodies for lovemaking—but not last year. Probably not this year, either. He didn't even bother entering the lottery for tickets, supposing his entry would be "mislaid." When he died, his body would be received into Harla's Hill, but his soul might wander the earth forever, a howling, despairing spirit. Blasphemy always carried such a risk.

In his still-reverent youth, he would have said he'd blaspheme when Nerr got the Heir—though he would never say the phrase aloud. The rather vulgar colloquialism meant "that will never happen." It was the remnant of an old prophecy: when an Heir to the throne became Nerr's Supplicant, the common people would rise to equal the nobility. Of course, no one believed it would ever happen, hence the vulgar meaning.

Commoners believed fulfilling the prophecy meant their prosperity. As Litta grew older, studied more and came into his full inheritance, he'd come to disagree. The Scholars, the priests of Eddin the Wise One, had it right: when "Nerr got the Heir" as a Supplicant, the commoners would revolt and the nobility would fall. When it looked as if Prince Temmin would fulfill the prophecy, Litta blackmailed the Obbys to stop him; it backfired, and now Litta faced damnation. *For nothing.* At least the monarchy hadn't fallen. Yet.

Behind the twins stood an overly-rounded girl he recognized as Anda Barrows, and Temmin himself: the two Supplicants of the Lovers. The lanky young man had put on weight in his year at the Temple—not fat, simply more of a man's stature than a boy's. His beard had finally filled in, and Litta grudgingly approved the proper if short queue curling at the Heir's nape. None of that modern, liberal shagginess that made men look more like dogs, short hair flapping around their temples like a retriever's ears. The Prince seemed relaxed, unruffled and confident. Even when he spotted Litta, his poise never faltered; he twitched one golden eyebrow in recognition and looked away.

Litta shifted his own gaze to King Harsin; his old friend's face was closed, unreadable. Let Temmin and his priests puzzle something out of *that*.

Temmin kept his face as tranquil as he could, though his heart beat so hard against his starched shirt front that its studs must be quivering. Would his father cut him on his own birthday? There'd been more than one royal snub in the last year: no invitations to his sisters' birthdays; careful avoidance at events requiring the attendance of the entire family; communication with the royal family completely blocked—even with his mother.

The Heir's birthday celebrations made contact unavoidable. Every year a countrywide public holiday and fireworks marked the day. Since his coming-of-age the year before, the royal family also hosted a ball. The one last year had been a daunting introduction to life in the City after his peaceful childhood home at Whithorse Estate, to the north and west in the rolling grasslands around Reggiston. How happy they'd all been at home—just him, his sisters, and Mama.

Temmin banished his melancholy and trained his gaze on the twins' glossy heads. Their nearness should have calmed him, but instead it brought more worries to mind. He'd been seeing less of them lately even though they were his teachers as well as his lovers. It troubled him, especially losing regular contact with Allis. In many ways he'd entered the service of the Gods for her sake; first her beauty and then her empathy had knocked him into near-insensibility. She'd instantly known his heart's every secret, and after a year in her company he trusted her more than anyone on earth but for his mother. No comfort could be found in thoughts of the twins; instead, he focused on his father.

Harsin wore his full dress cavalry uniform: a smartly-tailored tunic in the blood-dark hue called Tremontine red, and crisp white breeches tucked into brilliant black riding boots. Several jeweled medals, each one earned, hung in a cluster above his heart. He carried the only sword allowed in the room; it hung at his left hip from a broad black sash across his chest. He appeared invincible, as if he could conquer armies single-handed, though silver had almost conquered his beard and was increasingly invading his near-black hair. Temmin wondered if he'd finally grown taller than his father.

Beside the King stood Temmin's mother, Queen Ansella. She kept her gaze on the Embodiments, though the impatience and excitement twitching at the corner of her mouth told Temmin how much she wanted to embrace him.

Allis and Issak descended into the room's tense stillness to make their bow and curtsey before the King. Harsin took Issak by the right hand and Allis by the left, and raised them to their feet again before kissing each one on both cheeks. A pleased surprise rippled through the crowd.

The twins moved aside to make their obeisance to the Queen. Temmin's fellow Supplicant Anda Barrows flicked her eyes at him in signal, and they started down the remaining stairs to the King. Anda made her curtsey; Harsin raised her up, kissed her round cheeks and released her to the Queen.

The throng held its breath as Temmin and the King came face to face. Temmin concentrated on his training: *Blink little, and slowly, smile little if at all. Face forward, eyes front but not staring, head just bent to show respect but not submission. Mimic his posture and stance, and then subtly start changing it—he will follow. Feel what you are doing, don't pretend. You've beaten him once, you have nothing to prove...Oh, if only that were true...* He waited for his father to break the moment.

Harsin smiled, his white teeth blinding, and clasped Temmin at the elbows; Temmin followed suit, pulling his father close in relief. The onlookers exhaled. Harsin put his cheek against Temmin's and whispered, "I haven't forgiven you, but I can play a part better than anyone in your Temple. Welcome home," he added aloud.

"Thank you, sir," said Temmin, smiling as his insides wrenched. Well, at least he'd get to see his mother and sisters. At a sudden thought, Temmin leaned in again and murmured, "Contrary to your expectations, the prophecy meant nothing. The nobility is still intact and you're still King. All your enmity for nothing, Father."

Harsin's smile hardened as he drew away. "The night is young, son," he said aloud. "Let's enjoy it while we may." He offered his arm to Allis, and she took it.

Temmin moved to his mother, and here his body relaxed; he ignored his training entirely and let delight overtake him. "Good evening, Mother."

"Good evening, my son," all formality until he kissed her on each cheek; she whispered, "Oh, my sweetheart, how happy I am to see you!" He breathed in her familiar scent of roses, lavender and Mama, and allowed himself to close his eyes for a moment.

He released her and saluted his sisters in the same way. First came Sedra Princess Royal, the most like their father of the three siblings—studious, dark and tall. Her chocolate eyes, usually crackling with intelligence and a somewhat biting wit, shone bright and soft tonight as she murmured a welcome.

Ellika was a different matter. The middle child was a near-copy of their mother but for her father's deep brown eyes, and she sparkled with excitement and fun. Where her sister wore a spare, elegant steel-colored dress, Ellika wore an exuberant display of lace and tiny pearls over pale primrose satin. Her golden curls bounced as she pounced on her brother and kissed his furred cheek. "Temmy, you're home!" she chirped in his ear before releasing him.

The King was to dance with Allis, Issak with the Princess Royal, and Temmin with his mother. Who would he give Ellika to for the first dance? Hovering on the crowd's edge stood that loathsome Percet Sandopint— Lord Fennows, the most unwelcome of Ellika's suitors, even if he was the son of the influential Duke of Corland.

Where was the man Temmin had seen earlier? Choosing him would send a clear signal to certain parties present. He led his sister past the glowering Fennows to his sometime enemy, the Duke of Litta, and presented her. "Your Grace."

Ellika, who knew nothing of the history between her brother and the Duke, smiled and offered her hand. "I am honored," said Litta, taking it in astonishment.

Temmin returned to his mother and gave her his arm. The music master shook his black mop of a mustache and his blacker mop of hair; he raised his long, thin arms, the music began, and the dancing pulsed with a cheer no longer forced.

Temmin twirled his mother through the dobla, the simple traditional dance that began all Tremontine balls. As they turned, he took in the room from the corners of his eyes, as he'd been trained. Issak was making the reserved Sedra blush; Ellika was treating the surprisingly graceful Litta as if he were in doddering need of her guidance, luckily to his amusement; and Harsin was entirely too close to Allis. His father wore the intimate, hooded expression that meant far more than polite interest.

Temmin buried his anger and brought his full attention back to his mother, to catch her scanning the balconies; she returned searching eyes to his face. "You look so very well! You've *grown*, my dear! Are you happy? Did you make the right decision?"

"Oh, yes." His mother quirked a brow; no training could hide his heart from his mother. "Mostly," he amended. "It's not quite what I thought it would be. But I'm learning a great deal, and not all what…what most people think goes on there." He blushed; he still couldn't control his blushing reliably.

On the next turn Ansella looked up into the balconies again for a fleeting moment, and when he swung round himself he saw what had fixed her attention, or rather who: Ibbit, priestess of the Temple of Venna the Sister, and the Queen's religious advisor. She'd been Temmin's religious advisor when he was still at home, but they hated one another so much that Ibbit let Temmin skip most lessons: their one shared secret. Ibbit watched the dancing in disapproval until she saw the Queen; her long face broke out into a possessive gloat. She met Temmin's eyes, and her expression changed to contempt.

He spun his mother round the other way and found himself facing the many mirrors lining the hall. One did not reflect the glittering room. Instead, it showed something no one else in the room could see: a slight, androgynous figure, clad in a severe black suit covered in a black robe; its iron-colored hair was pulled back in a tight, conservative tail, and disturbing, silver-gray eyes followed him as he danced. Teacher! It was Teacher.

He smiled at the reflection on his next turn; Teacher's stern face split in a rare grin just before vanishing altogether. Seeing Teacher was almost as great a birthday gift as seeing his mother. He returned his attention to her, giving her a spin that left her giggling like a girl, and let happiness swell his heart.

Harsin spent his time working the crowd and dancing. Balls blended his two favorite pastimes: politics and women. Watching his lords at leisure taught him much. They revealed themselves not only in whom they talked to, but in whom they didn't. It was genuine dislike in cases like Anvalt Duke of Litta and Bornet Duke of Corland, but in the case of Corland and some of the minor lords of his duchy, it seemed to Harsin as if they didn't want to be caught speaking to one another. Interesting.

More interesting tonight were the women. Take Baroness Hawksfield, a blond beauty married to her much older husband not a year and here she was, blatantly carrying on with a handsome cavalry lieutenant. Did Hawksfield care? He couldn't be oblivious to his young wife's dalliances. The Baroness's libido must take after her sister's; Harsin glanced over at Anda Barrows, his son's fellow Supplicant. Baroness Hawksfield received all the beauty allotted to the Barrows girls, but all in all he thought the plainer of the two more honest in her wants, and far more appealing. Judging by the crowd of men around the plump Supplicant, he wasn't alone in his assessment.

Nevertheless, he put the Baroness on his list. Always good to have new faces; he'd gone through so many of the room's beauties already.

In the last year, he hadn't enjoyed his list as much as he had in the past. He chalked it up to the presence of his wife. For most of the last eighteen years she'd been living at her family's estate near Whithorse's ducal capital, raising their children. Her bride price had been simple: In exchange for her coveted hand, she was to be allowed to raise her children away from the Keep. She wanted to give them a normal childhood, she'd said. Harsin's main advisor Teacher had approved; it would ground the Prince in ways the traditional aristocratic education at Parkdale could not. Harsin had agreed; after all, it gave him a free hand with his own…interests.

What a mistake. Temmin grew up too comfortable among commoners, and Sedra grew up too fond of study. He could not complain about Ellika, he thought as his giddy daughter whirled past. Beautiful, happy and addicted to gaiety—a rather frivolous girl he'd have no trouble marrying off to a suitable ally, unlike her overly-serious sister.

Harsin rarely admitted to himself that Ansella's absence had aggravated him the most. Yes, he'd visited her at the Estate, official visits taken by carriage or the new train and secret visits taken there via Teacher's magic, but over the years they'd grown apart. A thousand miles separated them, as did the list. She was unwilling to cross the former, he to cross off the latter.

They'd spent the early days of their arranged marriage struggling against one another in bed and in life. He'd always wanted her, list or no, and before Temmin's birth he knew she wanted him in spite of herself. She might have even loved him. She was porcelain over a malleable metal he never quite shaped to his will. Her resistance thrilled him, aroused him and ultimately frustrated him.

Ansella looked particularly well tonight. She always did in blue. It so suited her porcelain-and-roses skin and golden hair, and it matched the shade of her eyes. The cut of her dress displayed her still-splendid figure without vulgarity, and he once again rued the distance between them. She was squeezing Sedra's hands as if in parting but she was looking over her daughter's shoulder. He followed his wife's gaze up into the galleries to Sister Ibbit.

Harsin was unused to rivals. It galled him. Why must everything always be so complicated with Ansella? Ibbit left the gallery as Ansella left the ballroom with nary a nod his way.

Corland's approach broke into his thoughts. "Dashed impudent of that son of yours to give Princess Ellika to Litta for the first dance," he said. "Belonged to Fennows, I should think. Everyone knows he's first among her suitors."

"'Everyone' does *not* know that, my Lord," replied Harsin, a chill in his voice. "Ellika's marriage is still not settled and won't be until I complete negotiations for Sedra's. I would ask you to remember that."

"Beg your pardon, Your Majesty," said Corland meekly.

"Temmin played the moment well, singling Litta out for the honor."

"Litta and his *honor*. He's dashed unreasonable in council!"

"I share Litta's opinions on your slaves, Borney. I don't want so many Incharis on Tremontine soil, especially under conditions where they might revolt."

"Why would they revolt?" Harsin raised a brow, and Corland grimaced. "Well, yes, there were those damned impudent agitators I had to put down on my plantations in Endar."

"Your 'damned impudent agitators' were three thousand strong."

"The Seventeen Gentlemen of Inchar have had greater rebellions—"

"And the Seventeen have company troops to put them down. Imperial troops had to put your rebellion down, not you."

"I remember. I'm still paying the Treasury," grumbled Corland. "I don't know why you mightn't give me permission to move my own troops to Inchar. My own troops, Harsin, bought and paid for!"

"I need them at the border with the Northern Wastes."

"There hasn't been an incursion in years!"

"And I will keep it that way. It's not negotiable," said Harsin. He cast a restless eye around the room in pursuit of his other interest.

Fennows was talking to a nervous young girl standing away from the dancing. A small circle of men were clustered around her as she blushed under their attentions. Beautiful thing, quite out of her element judging by the way she held her fan. She reminded Harsin of a foal still finding its feet, a foal who'd be a thoroughbred once she got them under her. The girl had astonishing eyes, as large and blue as a spring sky over the mountains, and brown hair the color of mink welled in ringlets over her shoulders. Her cherry dress walked an exquisite line, cut to draw maximum attention to the swell of her breasts, a dress meant for men's eyes and thus unusual; in polite society, women dressed for one another. The dress seemed to make her uncomfortable; her free hand constantly wandered to her neckline, only for her to yank it back down to pluck at her fan.

Harsin had no idea who she was, and rather doubted she was even minor nobility. How had she gotten past his social secretary? Lady Olster made exceptions at more casual affairs for prominent members of the gentility—at the most casual, even for members of the merchant class if they were wealthy enough and not too coarse. Any kind of commoner was not usually on the list for state occasions like the Heir's birthday; the King might make exceptions for a beautiful girl, but Lady Olster would not. "Borney, who is that girl talking with your son?"

"Her? Nice little piece, ain't she?" grinned Corland. "Curves in all the right places. Don't approve of commoners at the Keep, I should think, but it's not up to me, is it?" His small eyes squinted in disapproval. "Ever heard of Shelstone and Sons?"

"The tailoring concern? I believe my man Gram has applied to them for his own needs, and pronounced them quite satisfactory. Is the father Shelstone or Son?"

"Neither—grandson. Elbig Shelstone. Revolting little man. Social climber."

"It is hardly my habit to invite tailors to state occasions no matter how zestfully they climb."

Corland waved a dismissive hand. "Oh, he's not a tailor any more—not any kind of merchant. Sold out and bought himself some gentility. Paid off a relation with a better name to launch his daughter into society. Has hopes for her—if not a brilliant marriage than a brilliant...liaison, shall we say? Recognized only, though. Kept proper."

"Does she belong to Fennows?"

"Not to anyone as far as I'm aware, though not for lack of applicants." Corland noticed his son—the son supposedly devoted to Princess Ellika—flirting with the girl; he blanched and cleared his throat noisily. "Percy was unavoidably introduced to her father—good friends with their relations, d'you see—and he made them known to me for the obvious reason. Might become that brilliant liaison myself if I can manage it. Certainly no other suitor's presented himself who's dazzling enough for Daddy." Corland gave a low, throaty chortle, choked off when he saw his wife across the room, a dry woman covered in a great wave of diamonds breaking in sprays against her desert shore. "I've got the rank, but damned if I can find a way to publicly keep her without hell to pay. Have to keep my girls on the quiet side. Neya bless that little Cosetta of mine. Say, would you like an introduction to the Shelstone chit, old thing?" He jerked his head at his son; Fennows dutifully led the increasingly nervous girl through the throng to the King.

"Your Majesty," said the lordling, "may I make known to you Miss Twenna Shelstone, daughter of Mr Elbig Shelstone of Newtown."

She was even prettier up close—stunning, in fact, with a peach complexion and an unfeigned sweetness suggesting her supposed ambitions were entirely her father's. She made her curtsey. "May I have this dance, Miss Shelstone?" said the King, raising the astonished girl to her feet.

He expected her to giggle, but instead her face lit up in a radiant smile. "I would like it above all things, Your Majesty!" He led her onto the floor.

"Oh, sir!" she burbled as they began the long graceful loops of the dance, "I have lived in the shadow of the Keep my whole life and have *hungered* to be inside and see its splendors! Now that I am here, I am filled with—with—" she stammered, aiming for the right word and missing with room to spare— "with *vehemence*! And I never thought I'd dance with the *King*!" she added.

Usually wide-eyed girls bored him, but Twenna's artlessness extended to an unwitting, innocent physicality. She leaned into his touch like a little animal enjoying its fur being stroked—a natural voluptuary. Harsin found himself increasingly charmed: a beautiful, inexperienced girl ripe for the plucking, uncomplicated and begging to be molded. To take such a girl under his protection might be charming indeed.

Later that evening, The Duke of Corland watched the King and the tailor's daughter disappear within moments of one another. Twenna had caught the royal eye much faster than he'd expected. So much the better. A tremulous voice interrupted his happy musings: "My Lord Corland!"

At his elbow he found an overly elegant little man, his round belly supported on spindly legs. "Oh. Hullo, Shelstone," said Corland; he'd almost forgotten the girl's father was here.

"I do thank you so *very* much for your notice of myself and my daughter."

Corland shifted his weight from uneasy heel to toe. "Not a-tall. One always wishes to see interesting people at these things, I should think."

The former tailor beamed, his smile as pomaded as his hair. "But putting in a word to the royal family's social secretary—!"

The Duke winced. Lady Olster had owed him a great favor; it had galled him to spend such dear coin on Shelstone and his daughter, but it served the greater purpose. The Duke pulled the former tailor to one side. "Listen, old thing. Let's not bandy that about, eh? Just between us. Tell your girl the same. Discretion is the watch word."

"Discretion?"

"In fact, I do not wish to be seen speaking with you."

"Discretion, certainly," said Shelstone, bobbing his head in confusion.

"Nevertheless, I shall always be grateful—"

"Just remember that gratitude. Excuse me." Corland sidled away toward the buffet. As the Crown owned the best vineyards, the King always had the best wine, and the Duke wanted a great deal of it.

Temmin, meanwhile, was enjoying his birthday party immensely; he'd been in society such a short time before Supplicancy. He liked dancing, he liked pretty women whose sole aim was to charm him, he liked sparkling wine, and above all he liked studying Allis and Issak as they sailed through the room's political shoals and depths. He'd learned a great deal about politics in the year he'd been in the Capital, both in and out of the Temple. He escorted his latest partner to the sidelines and her next partner.

Thirst pounced on him, and instead of taking a new partner he went in search of something to drink. Wine was all very well, but it wasn't quenching. Temmin spotted a curtained-off servants' hallway to one side of the room. A year ago there had been water in that hallway for the servants, and he wanted water. He pushed open the curtains and went inside unnoticed.

Temmin's eyes adjusted to the dimmer light. Exactly a year ago he'd danced here with Arta Dannikson, an extremely pretty downstairs maid. In his father's attempts to stop his Supplicancy, Arta had been both human bait and hostage. Temmin remembered the knife at her throat as Harsin tried to force him from the Lovers' Temple. She and her sweetheart Fen were safe at the Estate now; Arta was learning to read and write, and Fen was learning the care of horses. From what their letters told him, especially Arta's painstakingly copied ones, they were busy for the moment, but he'd have to figure out what to do with them longer term at some point.

Temmin drank three dippers of water and strolled back to the hallway's opening to observe the brightly dressed throng. Last year was his first chance to enjoy the company of beautiful women—any women, at least those close to his own age who weren't related to him. Even Mattie. Pretty, hazel-eyed Mattie, the young servant girl he'd almost raped in a drunken haze the night before he left home. Mattie, who'd turned out to be his half-sister. Temmin shuddered. More than once he'd wondered what had become of her, and whether she knew they were related. Letters from home said she and her mother had left Reggiston in a great hurry; he suspected his parents had a hand in that. He wished he knew where she was. He wanted to make amends to her himself.

Temmin sighed. He would find her when he left the Temple next year. For now, duty required him to rejoin the dancers.

Early spring in Corland could hardly be called spring at all, especially in the little city of Arren. It sat far to the north, just on Tremont's side of the border with the Northern Wastes, and winter loved it far too much to leave on time. Downy snow still fell from the sky, determined to smother the streets like an overstuffed featherbed. Mattisanis Ambleson—the former Mattie Dunley of Meadow House, Whithorse Estate—thought it beautiful. The cold rimed everything in brilliant, magical whiteness, hushed, as a breath held. Or perhaps lost. Ever since meeting Adrik Adrikov just after Neya's Day the year before, she had been breathless.

Tonight at the Heir's Birthday celebration in Arren's most modern public ballroom, Mattie's mama sat frowning with the other chaperones, but Mattie sparkled as brightly as the snow outside as she swept down the floor in Adrik's arms. The gaslight gilded her dark hair and shone in her hazel eyes. "How wonderful of you to buy us tickets, Mr Adrikov!"

"How could anyone deny you such a pleasure—anyone knowing how you love to dance," he smiled, his Corrish accent silky and rich as good chocolate. Mattie loved it when he smiled; his large, deep brown eyes turning down at the outside corners gave his face a melancholy cast otherwise. When he smiled, his eyes took on a sly kindness, as if he contained happy surprises within surprises like a Corrish nesting doll.

Among the chaperones, Mistress Ambleson's fidgets increased, and Mattie's pleasure wilted round the edges. "Mama could."

Mama could, indeed. There had been quite the argument when Mr Adrikov's invitation arrived. Tellis Ambleson insisted they could not attend such a public event, that "we must keep a low profile, Mattie, I have told you this and told you this!"

"But never *why*, Mama, and until you tell me why we changed our name and moved away from Reggiston, I see no reason why I mightn't go out—oh *please*, Mama, I don't *wish* to be beastly! See? Mr Adrikov has provided you with a ticket as well, there is nothing unseemly about it, *you* will be with us." Mattie's wheedling, and Mama's reluctance to part with the secret, had finally procured her permission, but clearly she was thinking twice.

"Mistress Ambleson is a loving mother," said Adrik. "She worries about letting her beautiful lamb of a daughter out of the fold, where all the wolves might pick up her scent."

Mattie laughed, pleased at flattery she knew was still true: she *was* beautiful. Her mother had been beautiful, and was handsome even at the decrepit age of thirty-eight. Mattie had inherited her heart-shaped face, neat figure and hazel eyes, but Mattie's almost-too-pronounced nose and near-black hair must have come from some unknown ancestor. Her Papa'd had kind if watery pale blue eyes, a button nose and sandy, receding hair that almost blended into his forehead. For a moment, his memory squeezed at her heart; he'd found great joy in music and dancing, and would have loved being here tonight to dance with her mother. Mattie would have loved for him to meet Adrik Adrikov, the love of her life, but Papa was five years gone.

Adrik encircled her waist to guide her up the form; the warmth of his body so close to hers brought her to the present. Warmth bloomed every time he touched her, no matter how slight or decorous the contact. He had not made an offer yet and of course had thus not won the right to kiss her, but in bed at night she thought of little else but Adrik, how it would feel when he finally did kiss her. Would his mustache tickle? Would she like that? She thought she might.

"Miss Ambleson?" his voice interrupted her musings. "I do wonder what you're thinking, your eyes sparkle so."

She returned her attention to the room and laughed. "Some day you'll know!"

Pawl the footman opened the Amblesons' front door, dull-witted and stifling more yawns than usual. "Why did we have to come home, Mama?" said Mattie.

"What d'you mean, *why*? It's two in the morning!" answered her mother.

Mattie trailed upstairs after her. "But everyone was still there! They weren't scheduled to stop dancing until four at the earliest! Mama, why have you taken such a dislike to Ad—Mr Adrikov?"

Tellis paused at the drawing room door long enough to call for tea and aimed herself at her favorite chair by the drawing room fire. Once the two were settled with their tea before them and the door firmly closed, Tellis let out a great sigh. "Oh, Mattie. It's too soon."

"Too soon? Mama, we've known one another since Spring's End last year, and here it's Spring's Beginning—almost an entire year!"

"No, no, not that. It's too soon since we left...*Reggiston!*" she whispered loudly.

Mattie bounced in her chair. "Until you tell me *why*, that will never be explanation enough!"

Tellis tapped her fingers together in her lap, a nervous habit that some-times sent Mattie into exasperated fits; now, it signaled that perhaps she might finally learn the secret. "Mattie...you must believe me when I tell you this is a very great secret, a burden I'd always hoped to carry for you. I never wanted you to know this. You must tell no one, do you understand?" Huge tears pooled in Tellis's eyes; Mattie bit at her lip in alarm. "We are in danger if you tell *anyone*, Mattie, do you understand? Promise me!"

She nodded.

Tellis exhaled and tried to pick up her teacup but trembled so hard she gave up. "You thought you were dismissed from Meadow House last year, because...because of what happened between you and the Heir."

Mattie's stomach clenched at the memory of that night, a year ago almost to the day. She wouldn't have minded the Prince's attentions in a different context. He was quite handsome but he was also quite drunk when he'd discovered her half-dressed in the hedge alley with her sweetheart. If she hadn't done exactly what the Prince said, she knew she'd be cashiered though he'd said otherwise. She'd done what he asked—no more than a few kisses and some fumbling gropes at her breasts before he threw up—but her mother had fetched her home before the spoke was out, just as she'd known would happen. "If that wasn't it, then what was it?"

"They paid me to take you away."

"Who paid you? Why?"

Her mother's trembling increased. "The royal family. Here is the secret, oh my Mattie, my darling girl!" She looked old and frightened, and suddenly Mattie was frightened, too. "Mattie, you are not Mr Dunley's girl. You're the King's."

Mattie let out a strangled laugh. "What?"

"You are an Antremont, not a Dunley. You are the daughter of His Majesty King Harsin. You know I was in service at the Great House, yes? The King saw me there, when Prince Temmin was born. It was only three times, but I got you from it, my precious, precious girl."

She thought of Papa, how he held her hand as they walked home to the tavern after Paggday market, how his laugh rang out when he joked with customers in the taproom, how he always smelled of sweet pipe smoke when he kissed her goodnight. "Papa wasn't my father?"

"He was your father in all the ways that matter, sweetheart! Darwas knew you weren't his, he married me when I was already two spokes gone, but oh, but he *was* your Papa! He loved you so much, Mattie, never, *never* doubt that!" cried her mother. Mattie sat silent, staring at nothing while her mother sobbed. After many sniffs and shudders, Tellis brought her tears under control. "No one knew but your Papa for the longest time, though I think Standfast Jenks always suspected. *He* would never say anything, though, that dear man. He must have spoken out for fear..." She shuddered into her handkerchief again. "He must have been afraid the Prince might send for you, and that would not do."

"No." Mattie's eyes turned hot and heavy. "I'm tired now, Mama. I know you are. Perhaps you and I should turn in."

Tellis hugged her close and whispered love into her ear as they parted on the landing outside their bedrooms. Ianna the parlor maid came to her after attending her mother, helped her out of her gown and then into bed. Mattie blew out the candle. She lay in the dark, her head too full for sleep.

She was Mattisanis Antremont, not Mattisanis Dunley. Prince Temmin was her brother. That made the Princesses her sisters. She had always wanted brothers and sisters. Now she had three. Did this make her a Princess, too? No, all it made her was a bastard. If Adrik found out, he wouldn't offer for her. But could she deceive him? Tears rose into her eyes and throat in a flood, pouring from her heart until she fell asleep.

Temmin danced until the others dragged him away, making up for the spokes spent isolated from society in general and his family in particular. Now he followed Anda and the twins into the staff foyer of the Lovers' Temple and he wasn't tired a bit. "But the musicians were still playing!" he protested, stubbornly bringing up the rear.

"Because *you* were still there," said Anda.

"Have pity, Tem! It's nearly five—they were falling asleep clutching their instruments," said Allis.

Issak rumpled Temmin's already hectic hair on his way to the stairs leading to his suite. "Master Sullo was this close to dropping his baton."

"But I was enjoying myself! It's my birthday! I'm not tired!"

"*I* am," said Anda. "I can't believe you're not exhausted—you danced almost every dance and drank I don't know how much sparkling wine."

"We royals have strong constitutions. Ellika was still dancing when we left!"

"Your sister has feet of steel," Issak called from the landing above them. "Goodnight, Temmin Supplicant!"

Anda kissed him. "Goodnight, Tem. I'm going to sleep. By myself. Don't come near me unless you intend to rub my feet. Unlike your sister's, mine are made of mere flesh. Very sore flesh." She hobbled through the back door of the Supplicants Chamber.

"Hmf," said Temmin, scratching his chin. "I'm still not sleepy!"

"Good," smiled Allis.

He swiveled, surprised to see she hadn't followed her brother upstairs. "Good?"

"Good." She twined her arms around him, stood up on her toes and kissed him.

He'd never gotten used to her kisses; the hair on his nape still bristled, warm shivers still shook him. He never got as many as he wanted, either. Though he'd come here in no small part for her, they spent only limited, official time together—never more so than lately. Temmin bent over to let her feet rest on the floor, and the kiss ended, their foreheads touching. "Is this a kiss goodnight?"

"Not unless you want it to be."

He kissed her again. "I never want to say goodnight to you."

"Then you are a rude young man." She took his hand and led him up the Embodiments' stairs. At the top stood two doors; the red with white carvings led to Issak's suite, the white with red carvings led to Allis's. She opened her door and pushed him inside, laughing.

Temmin caught her by her slim waist. "So *this* is my birthday present."

She stiffened. "I am not a present."

Her abrupt change in mood startled him. She was usually so hard to read, keeping all but the most professional, compassionate parts locked away, and when she let down her guard he didn't know what to do. "No, you are a gift," he began. "That's different from a present, isn't it? Presents are things. You are not a thing, but you are still a gift, at least to me."

"I'm sorry." She held him close, resting her head on his chest with a small tremor.

He stroked her black hair. "What brought this on?"

"Perhaps I'm more tired than I thought."

He kept himself from drooping. "Shall I go back downstairs?"

"No, no, please don't go," she said, tightening her grasp on him. "Sometimes it feels like...like you and Issak are all I have. Sometimes it seems like you're the only ones in the world who see me as Allis, and not as the Embodiment of Neya."

"Not even Anda, or the Most Highs? Not even Teacher? He told me once you and Issak are the closest he'll ever have to children."

"I love Teacher. He's our sponsor—he's our father, for all intents and purposes. But..." She burrowed into him deeper. "There are times when it feels as if Issak and I are simply means to an end, like the mirrors he uses to go from one place to another. I have no right to feel that way, I know..."

One more thing they had in common, Temmin thought. He was himself now to so few people: his sisters, his mother, Jenks—Alvo, his best friend back at the Estate in Whithorse, knew him inside and out. The last night Temmin spent at home, they'd gotten so drunk. Then there'd been Mattie, and then…then Alvo had said he loved Temmin and begged to suck his cock; before Temmin could even think properly it was done and Alvo had run away, leaving him astonished and confused. They hadn't seen one another since. He needed someone to see him as Temmin, as Alvo always had. What were they now to one another? For that matter, what was Allis to him? Superior? Teacher? Yes, but nothing more?

Temmin kissed the top of her head. "I don't want to think about Teacher, or magic, or Gods or anything tonight. We're alone. We're never alone, and it's my birthday." He moved his hands to her back. His skills in undressing women had blossomed since his arrival at the Temple, and he unbuttoned her bodice and stroked her back at the same time.

She unbuttoned his waistcoat in turn and removed the studs from his shirt, slipping them in his waistcoat pocket. "You'll lose them otherwise, you know you will." She kissed him again, slow and tender.

In time they lay together naked in her wide bed. Allis cuddled in the curve of his arm, her full breasts maddeningly pressed against his side. He resisted tracing the silver sigil on her left hip that kept her from bearing children. No one could see it—not even Allis herself—but he could.

Temmin let her lead; she slid her soft hands along his body and returned no more than brief, gentle touches himself. Her hand traveled down, down into the curly golden hair on his belly. Temmin held his breath until she found the hardness patiently waiting there. Her hand slid lower and cradled his balls; he let out the smallest of groans, afraid to disturb her in the least. "It's all right," she said. "I want to know you're pleased."

"You know already," he said, straining up into the hand now encircling him.

He turned to face her, but Allis pushed him onto his back. "Lie still. We shall follow the Way of Harla."

"I've never cared for the Temple's naming a Way after Death—" Allis straddled him and sank down on his shaft, slow and deliberate. "But this is all right," he gasped.

"Every God has a Way, even Death. Death rides us all, Tem, but tonight I ride you. Be still." She rocked atop him, sighing as if his cock pushed the air from her body. Her hand slipped between her legs, where he wished to put his own hand, her fingers pinched at a nipple he wished to suckle, but he obeyed her and clenched his hands at his sides. Her fingers circled her pearl, dipping down to touch his slippery length as she rose up from him, back to her pearl as she sank down on him.

Even holding still, even letting her set a slow pace, the climax mounted in him. His hands desperately wanted to maul her breasts, pull her down hard on top of him as he thrust up into her. He wished he were tied down; forced passivity would be so much easier than this. "Allis, please let me move, please!"

Her tense, dreamy voice floated down to him. "No."

Temmin dug his fingers into the coverlet and closed his eyes. He could no longer bear to see her body atop him, flushed with desire and untouchable; as Supplicant, he should practice the Patience and delay his release as long as possible. She pulled him in deeper and squeezed until he choked out, "Allis, I am trying, truly I am trying, but you make the Patience very difficult!"

Her low laugh vibrated unbearably against his cock. "I'm not asking for the Patience. No lesson, just pleasure." Allis picked up her pace, swiveling her hips down hard onto him. His breath met the rhythm at first, becoming disordered the closer he came to his crisis. Just when he thought he might faint from the strain of stillness, she convulsed around him; not long after, the world compressed into his balls and exploded outward, lights sparkled beneath his eyelids, and all of his denied movement burst from him in a long roaring arch.

Allis stretched over him, keeping his half-hard cock inside her; her skin against his made him shudder and twitch. Finally free, Temmin brought his hands to her face, his touch soft and feverish as he kissed her cheeks and forehead and eyes and mouth. He felt her smile against his palm, and tenderness overwhelmed him. "I love you," he whispered.

Her hands minutely stiffened against his chest, and he cursed himself. "Ssh," she said, and blocked his mouth with a kiss.

TWO

Allis woke up slowly, her head pillowed on Temmin's shoulder. Just past her nose she could see long strands of her black hair laced among the curly gold ones furring Temmin's chest; she'd neglected to braid her hair the night before. She would have tangles to brush out.

She slipped from Temmin's grasp; he burbled in his sleep and turned over. She smiled at his broad, white back and frowned at his now just-as-white neck. The tan he'd always had from life spent more in the stables and hills than in fashionable drawing rooms had faded in his year at the Temple. It saddened her. The color gave him a common touch; it humanized him. While everyone respected his father King Harsin, few loved him. Temmin would be a king people both respected and loved, she was sure of it. When he ended his Supplicancy next year, she hoped the tan returned. She didn't want to think about next year.

How late was it? Well past dawn; the drawn curtains let in light. It must be blinding in her public rooms. There, the walls were painted soft white, the color of the Goddess Neya, accented with Nerr's red and the entwined rose-pink of the Lovers Joined. Issak's public rooms mirrored hers, all in red with white and rose accents. In their private rooms, the Embodiments could have things as they pleased, an extravagance in lives tradition and service circumscribed into the narrowest of channels.

Allis turned onto her back and gazed up at the blue ceiling. She kept her own rooms in colors of the sky—blue, gray and white. They reminded her of her childhood before Maman died, when she'd sneak up into the brothel's attics and look out over the verdigris rooftops of Ouve, the seaside capital of the duchy of Belleth. The sky there was just this blue, and the clouds all white and gray would float by like the ships leaving the harbor. She would imagine she and Issak and Maman sailing free in one of those puffy ships high in the air, over the city, over the harbor, over the sea far away to some place where Maman would be well and the three of them could live without Maman having to work for Mistress Polls.

When Maman got sick Allis wanted to go to the Sister's Temple to pray to Venna the Healer, but Mistress said a whore's children could never go inside any Temple. Allis found a copper in the gutter and bought a figurine of Venna from a street seller instead of sweets. She prayed and prayed to Venna in her secret attic for Maman to get well so she might finish paying her indenture to Mistress and they could all leave.

Then Maman died, and Issak and Allis had to work for Mistress to pay Maman's debt. No more sneaking up to the attic window. No more windows at all. Just men.

They were ten years old.

Teacher came for them a few spokes later and took them through a mirror to a Mother's House here in the City. One night not long after, the House of Polls burned to the ground. Allis loved the idea of burning down the house where she and Issak had been forced to do things no child should do, and wished she'd set it alight herself—during the day, so that the house's black smoke would rise into Ouve's blue sky. The memories the house contained would sail from their lives forever. The child in her thought perhaps if that cloud ship had sailed, no one would ever have known.

The adult in her knew the King would have found out anyway. When he sent Lord Litta to blackmail the twins, the child in her had wailed in shame and grief, but the grownup Allis remembered her mother. Liddy Obby's sheer force of will had somehow kept her children from anything other than menial work in that house, even as her body withered. Allis could be that strong.

When she and Issak turned the tables on Litta it satisfied almost as much as the brothel's destruction. They paid a great price in some ways for telling their story to the newspapers; now everyone knew. But it bought more than the breaking of Litta's hold on them. As long as the whores paid their fees to Pagg's Temple, prostitution was legal. Child prostitution was not, though enough coin bought anything. In telling the secret, Allis and her brother unleashed a tide of reform that swept through the brothels of Tremont; it freed more than one child kept as they had been. Best of all, Temmin had come to her in spite of knowing, in spite of everything the King had put in his way.

Them. Temmin had come to *Them*, Nerr and Neya, not her. He owed his allegiance to the Lovers, not their Embodiments.

She kissed his shoulder, slipped out of bed, brushed the tangles from her long black hair and pulled on a clean set of the thin linen skirt and tunic she wore within the Temple's confines. The Lovers' Embodiments always wore undyed, undecorated Temple garb and only one color at a time in their other attire; their beauty should be adornment enough. Some day after they retired, she would wear more than one color at a time—patterns, even. She'd put her hair up like other women, and she'd never, never have an all-white room again, nor Issak an all-red one. She walked into her private sitting room, knocked on the door between it and her brother's, and stepped through at the muffled invitation.

Issak's rooms reflected the forests he'd dreamed about as a little boy. Navigating Ouve's stinking back alleys and bustling marketplaces as he carried and fetched for Mistress, he'd imagine himself in the fairy tale forests from the books Maman read to them when she could. "I bet Tremont has lots of forest," he'd said to Allis once after Maman died. "I want to ride the whole country, all the way from Ouve to Greenvale. How far d'you think that is?" She'd always replied that when they'd paid Maman's debt, she'd buy him a horse and he could find out. "Only if you go with me," he'd answer. Issak thus chose greens and browns for his rooms: moss, sage, leaf; bark, rosewood, the amber of sap. He found it restful to the eye after the Temple's relentless parade of pinks and roses.

Issak lounged barefoot on his brown velvet couch as he read the papers; a coffee pot and a tray of pastries sat on the low table before him. "Did you just get up, too?" Allis said.

"No, I was up before noon," he answered, adding in the back-alley Ouve patois they used only when alone, "*Alla time per dem, é no time per we, ehn? Café?*"

Allis accepted a cup of coffee, yawned and settled against him on the couch. "What time is it?"

"Just after two."

"We knew we'd be home late. What could you possibly've had on your schedule the morning after a ball?"

"The Eldest Sister died early this morning and I had to discuss protocol with the senior staff and the Most Highs. It's been a decade or so since the last high official's death. We let you sleep in," he added, kissing the top of her head.

"Wirdun? Hardly unexpected. How old was she?"

"Well into her eighties. I can't remember the last time I saw her but for the Venna's Day Spectacles."

"The Sisters carried her across the Promenade to attend the last two Nerr's Day Spectacles, or so I'm told."

"Can't really say *we* saw her—we aren't exactly ourselves on Nerr's Day," Issak chuckled. "Imvalda is acting Eldest Sister for now, though it looks as if she's going to get a run for her money as far as the official succession goes."

Allis frowned over her cup. "I thought Wirdun made her succession clear. She wanted Imvalda to follow her."

"Oh, she could have engraved it on the Hearth, but the senior Sisterhood still has to vote on the successor."

"But who else—not Ibbit? Oh, surely not Ibbit!" Allis reached for the last pastry on the coffee tray.

Issak snatched it away at the last minute and dangled it just out of her reach before surrendering it with a grin. "Here, eat this for me. Oh yes," he resumed, "The Queen is the Hearth's highest-ranking patron, and Ibbit enjoys the Queen's favor. *The Queen's favor.* One way of putting it. One hesitates to ask Temmin what he thinks of *that* particular affair."

Allis snagged a napkin from the table and wiped the crumbs from her mouth. "I don't think he knows."

"How could he *not* know?"

"They're quite discreet."

"One look and any second-year postulant would know. Tem's a Supplicant!"

"He is also her son. That's always been a blind spot with you—parents and children."

Issak blinked at her. "I suppose to people who grew up the usual way that'd make a difference." He brought his cup to his lips and added casually, "Anda says he wasn't in their room last night, by the way."

"No, Tem stayed with me." Allis slid her eyes the smallest guilty fraction from her brother's. "It was his birthday."

"Allis, you're playing a dangerous game," he murmured. "You know this. *We no per he, he no per we.* Giving him more of yourself than you would any other Supplicant is not a kindness to either of you."

"Spending the night with him on his birthday is hardly special treatment for a Supplicant."

"That's not what I'm talking about."

Allis studied his linen-clad shoulder for a moment. "You're mistaken. In any event," she said, looking back up at him, "is Ibbit a serious threat?"

Issak let her change the subject. "Her influence over the Queen is said to be considerable, and it's swaying a significant number of the Capital's senior Sisters. I don't know what the representatives who'll be arriving from the hinterlands will think, but it wouldn't be the first time a royal connection has swayed the selection of a high priest or priestess."

"But she's suspected of the Annikan Heresy."

"She's never given herself away in public, nor has anyone ever spoken out against her within the Sisterhood. If she is an Annikan—and from her disdain of the male Temples I can only believe she is at the least a sympathizer—she's a very cautious one."

"Considering what happened to Anniki, I should think so," shivered Allis.

Issak frowned. "She and her followers slaughtered every male in the Healer's House at Turus, right down to the newborns."

"Oh, she deserved it, but I would think her head hanging on Marketgate and her body burnt and spread to the winds was example enough to deter anyone from following her."

"Not if you believe Anniki was trying to bring about the return of the One True Goddess and eternal peace on earth. Her followers believe she's a martyr to the greater cause."

Allis snuggled into her brother's side. "I don't see how anyone could believe a single goddess split into many, or that killing all the men would put her together again. Surely Ibbit has to have seen Venna come down into Her Embodiment!"

"Venna is a special case, apparently. Even those who see the Embodiments possessed sometimes don't believe. You know what some say about us."

"'Play-acting whores' I believe is the term," murmured Allis.

Issak put his arm around her. "Mm. Well, if the Queen advocates for Ibbit, she could very well beat Imvalda. Ibbit isn't friendly outside the Hearth, but the Most Highs say within it she is quite the charismatic leader, while Imvalda is seen as...more the administrative type, shall we say. Ibbit has a real chance."

"If she wins?"

Issak shook his head. "It's a bad business. Tensions between the Sister's Temple and the rest of us at the least. If the Sister's Temple leaves the covenant entirely, the destruction of all seven Temples at the worst."

"Do the Most Highs think Ibbit's an Annikan?"

"She was at Turus that day. While not all the Sisters there were Annikans, suspicion still attaches. The Most Highs say Ibbit is smart, but not half as smart as she thinks she is. If she's an Annikan, she'll slip up eventually. But that's not what I want to talk to you about and you know it."

Allis rose from the couch and shook out the folds in her clothing. "Your concern is noted, brother. Now, *na gimme thy grief*. I need a bath, and I want it before Tem wakes up."

His birthday concluded, Temmin reported for duty once again in his role as Lovers' Temple clergy. After a morning spent helping teach Postulants, he went to the petitioning rooms, where Lovers and Beloveds met with worshippers needing private blessings and guidance. Sometimes the petitioners just needed a sympathetic ear or a caring bedmate, but sometimes matters required more delicacy. Such was the assignment Temmin held in his hand. He read it, panicked and tried to calm himself as he walked down the narrow hallways to where he would meet the needy couple.

Temmin opened the door to a tiny room and moved uneasily through it, checking the covering on the low, wide Temple couch, plumping the mound of cushions that served it for a back, making sure the arms would come away if need be. He inspected the room's supplies. Spare towels? Yes. Oil? Yes. Blankets in case of shock? Whose? *This is ridiculous.* "I can't do this."

"Of course you can," said a mellow baritone behind him. Temmin stumbled toward the voice: Barik Lover, the highest among the senior Lovers save their high priest. Unlike most of the Lovers' clergy, Barik kept what was left of his graying hair as closely cropped as the warrior priests of the Brother, leaving only enough hair at his nape to form a small queue. He was over fifty and thus old to Temmin's nineteen-year-old eyes, and he was a good head shorter, but Barik possessed a wrestler's build and the calm assurance of a man who could take down someone twice his size. He entered the room and tweaked the hem of Temmin's red linen Temple shirt, rich with the embroidery that marked him as a Supplicant. "You've worked in the petitioning rooms before."

"This is different. I need help."

Barik stopped Temmin's nervous adjusting of the privacy screen in the corner. The smaller man's hands were as big as Temmin's own, and hairier;

the senior priest gently, firmly scooted Temmin back toward the room's center. "Leave it alone. You know your job, and you're good at it." Temmin still hung back, kicking at the floor like a little boy. Barik gave an exasperated grunt, reached up and grabbed the recalcitrant young man by the ear. "What's gotten into you, Temmin Supplicant? You've not acted like this in some spokes. Do I have to march you down to the schoolrooms and embarrass you in front of the Postulants?"

"No, Barik Lover!" squeaked Temmin.

Barik shook him once. "No, because unlike them you were chosen by the Lovers Themselves. Remember that. I'm going to fetch these petitioners, and when we return you will be calm, cool and professional. Won't you?"

"Yes, Barik Lover!"

Barik took him by both ears, pulled his head down, and kissed him. "Don't let their goal disturb you, Tem. Just give them what they need." Barik gave Temmin's ears a final tug with a little *tchk* and a smile, and strode out the door.

Temmin sighed. He ran his hands through his hair, blanched, and ran to the mirror to straighten the resulting haystack; he had to re-tie his queue, the blasted thing. What he wouldn't give for his manservant Jenks—no, Jenks always turned green in his presence whenever the topic of sex came up. He couldn't imagine the poor man following him around the Lovers' Temple. He'd gotten better at caring for himself at least, and it gave him a sense of accomplishment. He wondered how Jenks was doing back home at the Estate. They'd never been apart this long.

Temmin sank down on the wide, low couch and picked up his paperwork; the Esterills needed help conceiving a child. No notes on the problem, only that they'd married a year ago and no child had come—any number of explanations for that. A Postulant Beloved opened the door and ushered in the two worshippers: a slender young man whose olive skin and dark hair marked him as part Alzehni; and a rosier, chestnut-haired young woman. The woman immediately seized Temmin's attention. While her husband had the excited, eager humiliation many petitioners brought to the Temple, she was impatient, wary and openly mortified. The lines around her mouth were recent, and the pain in her eyes looked out of place in a countenance that favored cheerfulness.

Temmin rose to his feet, schooled himself into unreadable, impartial empathy, and gestured to the couch. "Mr Esterill, Mistress Esterill, please sit down. I am Temmin Supplicant. Yes, that Temmin," he smiled as their expressions changed to astonishment.

"Oh, Your Highness—" began Esterill.

"Please, here I'm just Temmin Supplicant."

He exchanged pleasantries with them, soothing their fear of him until they relaxed, or rather the gentleman relaxed; the wife sat monosyllabic, her hands still gloved and clenched in her lap. Temmin looked down at his notebook. "I see you're petitioning for assistance in conceiving a child. May I ask what the problem is?" The wife's eyelids flickered, but Esterill's eyes caught his. *Ah.* "Mr Esterill, you're a lover of men, primarily?" Esterill nodded; his wife thinned her lips. "Mistress Esterill, you didn't know this?"

"Of course I knew, but..." She squeezed her eyes shut. "Most lovers of men have wives. They have children all the time. Gyors is the oldest son, we have to have children to carry on the name, and to inherit! If we don't, I'll be blamed and he'll set me aside—"

"I won't set you aside, Meggan!"

"Your family will insist, unless you tell them it's your fault, and you won't do *that*, will you? It will be my fault if I can't bring you to it." She turned to Temmin. "I wanted to go to the Sisters, I thought they might give him some sort of medicine, a blessing, *something*—"

Temmin held up a gentle hand. "Mr Esterill, you can't perform with a woman, can you?" Mistress Esterill blushed to her forehead.

"I've tried everything," said Esterill, shaking his head. "My married friends all have children. Some even enjoy their wives as a...a change of pace. But I just can't, no matter what. I've tried closing my eyes, I've tried Meggan—er—facing away from me, but I can't come up to the mark. It's not Meggan's fault," hastened Esterill. "We do quite well together otherwise. I thought I might manage it with a girl I like as well as Meggan—I do like you, Meggan, so very much—but...no, it's entirely my fault."

Temmin nodded, thinking. A barren woman would go to the Mother's Temple for sacrifice and if that didn't work to the Sister's Temple to see if something might be done for her medically, but when the man could not perform, the couple came straight to the Lovers' Temple. The Lovers and Beloveds would do what they could, calling in the Sisters for medical advice. If no solution could be found, the senior clergy would sort through the Lovers without charms against children for close physical matches to the husband, choosing at least two men so that no one could be sure of the father. The wife then discreetly visited the petitioning rooms until she conceived, or until it was plain she could not.

Temmin, with his golden hair and bright blue eyes, looked nothing like the dark-eyed, olive-skinned Esterill. In any event he refused to get a child out of wedlock. It meant nothing but pain for everyone. The instant he ascended the throne, any sons of his would become magically known to Teacher anyway; they'd be pried from their families like a precious jewel from a pot metal ring, for no child of his would ever be called "bastard" or go unacknowledged. Teacher couldn't see daughters; if Temmin hadn't drunkenly assaulted Mattie last year no one but the girl's mother would ever have known she was his half-sister. No, never would he become a father like that.

Temmin glanced at the screened window set high in the wall, leading to the gallery between the ranks of petitioning rooms. Barik probably watched, observing his work for later discussion. He might give up now and tell the Esterills to come back once the Temple had found good likenesses among the Lovers, but first he must suggest another path. "Mr Esterill, you say you and your wife have tried 'everything.' Has that included another man?"

Mistress Esterill murmured in dismay; Esterill gave an apologetic shrug. "Meggan and my *particular friend* do not get along."

"Is what I'm suggesting what you had in mind, Mr Esterill?"

"Oh, no, no! I cannot allow a stranger in my bed!" cried the wife. "I'm married—it *means* something—I'm *married*!"

Her husband tried to capture her fluttering hands. "Meggan, calm yourself."

"The Temple is not your bed, and I'm not a stranger. I'm a Supplicant." Temmin poured sympathy upon her in every way he knew—through his expression, his body language, the tone of his voice, and she began to calm. "Are you a believer?"

"Yes. Yes, of course."

"Do you believe that I am a representative of the Lover on earth?"

"...Yes."

"What we do in these rooms is a sacrament. Would a sacred act be so very bad?"

She looked doubtful. "Will I have to take part—other than, than with Gyors?"

"I will not touch you if you don't wish me to."

For a moment she looked as if she wished he would, but it passed. "If this is what it takes to get a child, then I will do it. But you must promise me something, Gyors."

Esterill took her hands. "Whatever you want—silk gowns—jewels— that smart new silver chocolate pot I saw you sighing after—travel! You once said you wished to winter in Alzeh, we'll rent a villa just before Fall's

End, or stay with my cousins at their country home, they have beautiful orange groves—"

She shook him away. "No, no. You must promise me two things: that you will not shame me in public; and that I may conduct myself as I see fit once I have given you a son."

"As you see fit? Meaning what?" he said.

"For instance, that I may visit the Lovers' Temple for my own sake, or... or take a lover elsewhere, and that if I have another's child you will recognize it as yours. I will, of course, be completely discreet. I will never shame you."

Esterill hesitated. "*Two* sons. Before that, you may come here and only here to...receive care I cannot give you, but only at no risk of a child. After you give me two sons, any lover you take must resemble me enough that I might recognize a resulting child without public ridicule."

Mistress Esterill lowered tear-filled eyes. "I had other offers, but I loved you, Gyors. You told me you loved me." Esterill looked away, shamefaced.

Temmin waited until they regained some composure. "Let us continue. Am I agreeable to you, Mr Esterill?" The man nodded, a small, sly smile springing to his lips. "Mistress Esterill, am I agreeable *enough* to you?" She waved one hand in a small, assenting gesture. Temmin ran through what he'd learned from the Sisters who taught medicine at the Temple. "Is this a time of the moon at which you are likely to conceive? Very good. Would you care to go behind the screen to undress?"

She ducked behind it, coming out moments later minus her coat, hat and gloves but still in her dress. "Have you changed your mind?" said her husband.

"I have removed what clothing I must. More I will not do."

Perhaps keeping her as covered as possible might make things easier, thought Temmin; Esterill would need to be brought to a fever pitch and kept there long enough to disregard his wife's body, poor woman. Temmin turned the lamps down low. "I think it best, ma'am, if you lie with your feet touching the floor—so," he said, gently arranging her legs. "Your skirts should be raised in readiness. Here—" he indicated a small, shallow pitcher he still thought of as a creamer— "is a beaten egg white. I know it seems odd, but the Sisters teach that it helps in conception. No—don't drink it!" He swallowed his laughter. "You must put the egg white inside your vagina. The Sisters say it nourishes the man's seed. Do you need my assistance?" She shook her head, and he turned away to give her what privacy he could.

He fetched a low padded footstool. As he placed it between her feet, he bit back an exclamation of pity. She had drawn her skirts up over her head. Temmin folded them down in concern to find her crying silent tears; she turned her face away. He took a handkerchief from a ready stack by the couch, pressed it into her hand and turned back toward Esterill.

Temmin found the man deeply unattractive. Esterill was handsome enough, but Temmin could not be sympathetic to a man who'd deceive a girl into a loveless marriage. Nevertheless, duty required him to find something about Esterill to desire. "There is always something to desire about a person even if it is only his absence," went the Temple saying. He cleared his mind and focused on Esterill's own excitement, making it his. He opened his thin linen trousers and stroked himself, watching the petitioner for cues.

Esterill dropped to his knees and took the hardening cock into his mouth; he'd done this before, a great deal judging by skill alone. Temmin allowed himself a pleased, sincere groan, and Esterill's own erection twitched in response. *Ah, he likes noisy.* With each stroke, Temmin made sure to make his appreciation known, an easy task until a tiny noise from beneath Meggan Esterill's skirts reminded him how she suffered. She wanted a child enough to consent to this, thought Temmin; he focused on the mouth taking him deeper and deeper.

By now, Esterill was frantically stroking himself as he swallowed Temmin's cock. Temmin fisted a hand in his hair and pulled him off. "Stop," Temmin growled in his best command voice. "You will come when I say." Esterill let out a happily wretched moan, put his hands on Temmin's thighs, and set to work with increased fervor.

A year ago, Temmin would not have been able to hold out this long against such a determined assault. But he'd been learning the Patience, and now he could last for close on an hour of even intense pleasure. He drifted off under the spell of Esterill's mouth, using memories to fan his own excitement: Issak teaching him the Patience, bringing him to the brink over and over again until he wept for release; the enormously endowed Barik driving Allis through climax after climax until even she begged off and he took Temmin instead.

His balls tightened, bringing him back into the room. He pulled Esterill off him; the man's eyes were glazed, and the tip of his erection dribbled. Almost ready. He smacked Esterill's face with his cock, amused as the other man desperately tried to recapture it. When he was sure of his own steadiness and Esterill's desperation he stood up and dragged the other man whimpering to kneel on the footstool. He climbed onto the couch, straddling poor Mistress Esterill, and pulled the man's mouth onto him. A few long sucks, and he removed himself again. "Do you want to come?"

"Yes!" sputtered Esterill.

Temmin reached down between them and guided Esterill's cock into his wife. "Spend for me." Esterill thrust into his wife in an uncaring frenzy, but a nauseous flicker in the man's eyes made Temmin enter Esterill's mouth again; Esterill mewled, instantly focused on him. Would his climax trigger Esterill's? The man was buried in his wife now; it might be enough. Temmin closed his eyes and let himself forget the unhappy woman beneath him and his dislike for the man swallowing him. *Think of Issak sucking me, think of Allis, think of...of Alvo...* The mouth picked up speed, taking him further and further until he scraped the back of the throat, buried to the root and fucking that hot, delicious mouth—

Temmin came in dutiful pleasure. The man screamed around the still-hard cock in his mouth, hips jerking as he came himself, pounding hard against his wife.

When he'd finished, Temmin withdrew and climbed down from the couch, fastening his trousers. The man sunk back on his heels, gasping and shuddering as he stared between his wife's open legs. "I did it. I did it. Will it be enough? Will I have to go through this again?"

Temmin hid his disdain. *Will* you *have to go through this again?* "It's hard to say. Sometimes the once is enough. Sometimes not. There is a basin in the corner, a mirror and towels as well." Esterill began to clean himself and comb his hair. Temmin continued what the Sisters had taught him about conception and turned to Meggan, who lay limp on the couch, feet still on the floor and skirts over her head. "Mistress Esterill? I'm going to touch you now, but just to make you more comfortable, that's all." He gently toweled her mound and thighs dry, and swiveled her unresisting body until she lay fully upon the couch; he smoothed her skirts back down. "I'm putting pillows under your knees, and under your hips as well. You must stay still for a time."

"Will it bring a child?" she whispered to the wall.

"The Sisters teach that it helps."

"Then I will stay like this all day."

Temmin chuckled. "Twenty minutes should be enough." She said no more. Her silence troubled him; he squeezed her hand and rose from the couch.

"May...may I go?" said Esterill, his face a sickly toad-green.

"Would you not wish to stay with Mistress Esterill?"

Esterill fidgeted. "I would prefer to wait in the vestibule if I may."

"If you'd rather. I shall stay here with your wife," said Temmin, just avoiding an edge to the last word. Esterill fled.

Temmin turned up the lamps another notch to dispel the room's gloom and his own, and went to put the towel in his hand into the laundry. In the stronger light, he noticed the blood smears on it and remembered: the Esterills hadn't consummated the marriage. This had been Meggan Esterill's first time. He cursed himself; he'd been taught better. He sat down on the floor beside the couch. Should he call for tea? Or would that make things worse? No, another stranger in the room would be more than Mistress Esterill could bear. He leaned his head back against the couch.

The woman's quiet breathing had almost put him to sleep when her hand on his head brought him back into wakefulness. "Thank you. It would have been worse without your consideration of me," she said.

Mistress, I wasn't considerate enough. "This is what we do here. Next time, you may find all this more pleasant."

"I hope I will not have to return after this."

"I thought you said you wished to come back for your own sake."

"That," she said, lifting her fingers off her stomach in dismissal. "I hoped I might yet provoke Gyors to jealousy. But he does not love me, you see. My body makes him sick. I don't have a—a *member*. We do very well together, but not well enough. I have acquired a brother, not a husband." She pressed her hands to her stomach again. "If I have a child, perhaps the loneliness will end. The last year, all his parents' questioning, knowing he loves another, loving him even as I discovered he lied about loving me…it's been very difficult." Her voice caught.

Temmin turned toward the couch, resting his chin on folded arms. "I shouldn't say it, Meggan Esterill, but you deserve better than this. Come back for your own sake. The Gods love you, even if Gyors can't."

She brushed his cheek. "Has it been twenty minutes?"

"At least."

Mistress Esterill sat up and kissed him on the corner of his mouth. "You've been very kind." With that, she rose and slipped behind the screen. A few moments later, she took her leave.

Temmin plopped himself on the couch and blew out all his breath. The door opened and Barik came in. "That wasn't so bad, was it?"

"How much of that did you see?"

"Oh, all of it."

"Even after Esterill left? *Urf.* I know I shouldn't have said that to Mistress Esterill, but—"

Barik reached up and put his hands on Temmin's shoulders. "No, you did right. She does deserve better than marriage to Gyors Esterill—Gyors himself deserves better than to be forced into marriage when he cannot bear a woman's touch, but that is the way of things for eldest sons who wish to inherit. He won't be unkind to her, but he can't love her. We can."

Temmin grimaced. "I'm very angry at myself even so. She was a virgin. I might have made it easier for her."

"How would it have changed things if you had remembered?"

"I don't know—I might have pleasured her at least a little beforehand in readiness—"

"She would not have let you. We'll make it better for her when she returns."

"If."

"*When.* She is a passionate woman." Barik kissed him. "You did well, Tem."

"I did hope to have children some day, Daddy," complained Twenna Shelstone for the fifteenth time since the old Traveler woman they called their Queen had given her the charm against getting a child. She'd used spit to draw it on Twenna's left hip. Disgusting, but Twenna was an obedient daughter and besides it left no mark. She both hoped and feared the woman was a fraud. The Traveler Queen insisted it was the same spell she used on Lovers and Beloveds; few misbegotten children came from the Lovers' Temple, and so Twenna had to assume it worked.

"It's temporary, sweetheart," said Elbig Shelstone. "You'll have children some day, but the last thing we need right now is you knocked up, even by the King. Now hold still and let the girl pull a little harder." Twenna held her breath while her maid Wendia tugged the laces tighter. "Can you still breathe? Yes? A little more, then."

"He takes the corset off, you know!" complained his daughter.

"Feh. Then look like a cow, I don't care," said her father. At her crest-fallen face, he added, "You don't look like a cow, sweetheart, I'm sorry. I just want you to look your best. You've got him on the hook and I want you to keep him there."

"Oh, never worry!" brightened Twenna. "He loves me!" *And I love him,* she added to herself. She'd been Harsin's favorite ever since the night they met nearly a spoke ago. She'd even made up a little song: *Love at first sight, with him every night, la la!* Though she had to admit that she wasn't with him *every* night. On the nights they were apart, though, he slept alone. Never with his wife. She knew that much. She walked to her closet and pulled out a dress.

"Not the primrose, dear, the blue with the thin white stripes."

"But primrose is the thing, you know, Daddy, ever since Princess Ellika wore it at the Heir's ball—"

"That yellow doesn't turn her complexion all sallow, and it does yours. Mistress Naister should never have suggested it for you—she must've bought too much primrose silk, or maybe she just *wants* you to look your worst—she *is* the royal women's favorite, after all. We're taking our custom elsewhere."

"But Daddy, Mistress Naister is the most fashionable seamstress in the City—"

"I've forgotten more about style than that biddy's ever known. The blue stripe with your long pearls, just falling into your cleavage—so." He helped her tie her skirts and fasten her bodice, and stood back to observe the effect. "Perfect. I should have gone into women's bespoke." He picked up her wrap and gave her a fan and her reticule. "The time for discretion is over. Let it be publicly announced that you are the King's favorite."

"Oh, but Harsin has said I *must* be discreet! How are you intending to announce it?"

"You will be taking the main roads to Foothill Lodge today, not the back ones."

"Through *town*?" Twenna winced. "I shall be much stared at tonight at the theater, then."

"Let them. They'll stare at you anyway—you'll be sitting in the Duke of Corland's box."

"Is that wise?" his daughter fretted. "I'm not sure I can stand the—the *approbation* of the world. Harsin will be angry." The big blue eyes filled with tears.

"That's *dis*approbation. No big words, that's not what he wants from you and you know it. And no crying! I will not have you present yourself at Foothill Lodge with puffy eyes and a splotchy face, not yet at any event. Not until his heart is as engaged as his pecker." Twenna nodded, blinked her eyes until the threatening tears receded, and smiled a watery smile. Shelstone smiled back his approval and patted her cheek. "You've done so very well in such a short time, I'd hate to see it all come to naught, sweetheart. Everyone's already noted the King's interest. Invitations are pouring in! If you play this right, we might end up in the nobility. At the least our creditors have retreated," he added in a mutter. "Speaking of debts! We have a powerful ally in Lord Corland—now, you mustn't speak of His Grace's sponsorship to His Majesty, am I understood? But we owe His Grace a great deal, and foremost among those debts is our discretion."

"But you said—"

"Discretion as to the debt we owe the Duke, little featherhead."

"We owe Lord Corland money, Daddy?"

Shelstone helped her into her wrap. "No, dearest, only our loyalty." He escorted her down the stairs and out the door to their smart—and unpaid-for—open chaise, giving the driver directions to take the most public route to Foothill Lodge.

Twenna hid her blushes as best she could. She was not raised to be brazen. But she was a good daughter; she did as her father told her. She focused on her upcoming tryst to ease her discomfort. Harsin was the most wonderful man in the world! He was handsome and dashing and kind and generous—especially in bed, or so it seemed to her; he was her first lover and she had no basis for comparison, but he always made sure she enjoyed herself, immensely. Then, of course, Harsin was the King! That mattered a great deal to her father, less so to her, but still! To be loved by the King!

Twenna held her head high as she came to Foothill Lodge Road. Behind her, the gossip networks of the City must already be burning as word passed from the streets to the coffeehouses to the parlors and sitting rooms of the gentry, thence to their servants and out into the wider world.

Tonight at the theater there would be a bill to pay; she would have to brazen out whispers, innuendos and open staring as she sat in the Duke's box like a target, but she vowed she would bear up. Her father said it was the right thing to do, that it might lead to elevation to the nobility. Twenna herself didn't care, but she knew her father did. Perhaps being Lady Twenna mightn't be such a bad thing. It sounded nice, and besides, as a noble lady she would certainly be able to hold her head up as high as anyone else, mistress or no.

Twenna settled back beneath the light carriage robe and smiled.

THREE

Ansella lay cuddled beside her lover before her private drawing room fire, Ibbit's arm heavy around her. "You're spending a great deal of time here lately, love. Shouldn't you be more at the Hearth?"

Ibbit squeezed her waist. "I have others helping my cause there. For now, I think it best I should be known to be with you as often as possible."

Ansella frowned, absently running her fingers along the woolen weave of Ibbit's green robes. "Why is it so important that your being here be known?"

"I saw your son today," said Ibbit, playing with a curl escaped from Ansella's hair. "He was paying a mourning call with his senior clergy—and I use the term 'clergy' lightly. When I'm Eldest Sister, there will be an end to visits from the likes of them, I assure you."

Ansella sat up and took Ibbit's hands. "How is he? Did he say anything? Did he look well?"

"He looked the same as he did at his birthday," said Ibbit, jerking her head. "He asked after my health very prettily. I'll say this for that whorehouse, they've taught him impeccable manners."

Ansella dropped Ibbit's hands. "Ibbit, you know I dislike it when you talk about the Lovers' Temple in that way."

"He sent you a message, though." Ansella brightened and brought her hands back to Ibbit's thigh. "He said to tell you he loves you and misses you and hopes to see you as soon as you might come to him now that his father seems to have ended open warfare against him. You won't go, of course."

Whyever not? Ibbit disapproved of her relationship with her son; Ansella never understood why. Ibbit had known him since childhood. True, they had not often gotten along, but as his religious advisor Ibbit had to know what a good boy her Temmin was—so cheerful, so kind. He had grown into a good man, strong and full of conviction, walking in the ways of the Gods, if not the Gods she would have chosen for him. Ibbit preached that men and women were inherently incompatible—certainly true in Ansella's own marriage and her parents'—but that couldn't extend to her only son. When Ibbit got like this, Ansella had learned it was best to nod and be silent. Let her lover think she agreed; it cost her nothing. She would find a way to see Temmin soon without Ibbit discovering it. She returned to the Sister's arms.

"Oh, my sweet girl, I'm so sorry," said the priestess.

"I imagine Temmin and I will run into one another at some state occasion or other."

"Oh no, not for that. No, I meant about the King's current slut openly disrespecting you yesterday."

Ansella blinked. Harsin had promised her he would never bring shame on her, never place another woman above her in the public eye. "What do you mean?"

"Didn't you hear? Twenna Shelstone rode through town bold as brass, straight up to the Foothill Lodge gate for everyone to see—practically a parade. She may as well have worn a sign round her neck with 'King's Whore' painted on it. Then she sat in the Duke of Corland's box at the theater last night. Everyone knows Corland wouldn't have been seen with her except at the King's request. He even came to sit with the Duke during intermission and acted surprised to see her there, but kissed her on both cheeks in front of everyone. Or so I heard."

Ansella choked with rage. "He's acknowledged her publicly?"

"I'm so sorry, my sweetheart, but men betray us. We're better off without them."

Angry tears stung Ansella's eyes, and her heart gave an unexpected thud. "Yes!" she cried. "Yes, we are!" She subsided into silence. *I will not cry over Harsin's faithlessness, I will not cry.*

Ibbit broke the silence. "You have never sounded so sure of it."

"I've never *been* so sure of it," said Ansella into Ibbit's shoulder. "I hate them."

After a pause, Ibbit said, "You support my candidacy as Eldest Sister, don't you, Ansella?"

Ansella blinked away her last unshed tears. "Yes, of course!"

"You will say so when the time comes?"

She snuggled closer into Ibbit's arms. "Nothing could make me happier."

"Then it is time for me to tell you why it is so important, why you must. So very much is at stake. Do you swear you are a true daughter of Venna?"

"Of course I am!"

"Swear it, Ansella. Say, 'I am a true daughter of Venna.'"

"I am a true daughter of Venna," the Queen repeated in some consternation. "I have always been true to Her, above all other Gods. She has been everything to me, my sole support since I began taking instruction with you."

Ibbit stood. "I must go back to the Sister's Temple, but I will leave you with this." She took two books from her apron pocket, one the familiar green-bound Sister's Saga and the other a thin book bound in gray leather. She handed the second to Ansella. "This is one of the last copies. Do not show it to anyone—no one, not even Sedra. She will come to know it in time as she learns the faithlessness of men. Hide it. I have given you almost all the teaching, and would give you this final teaching myself, but there isn't time, and this explains it so clearly, so forcefully! When you've read it, you will know why it is so vital I become Eldest Sister. The old guard, they know nothing. I can bring us back to the True Way of Venna, and help restore the Goddess to Her Oneness." Ansella frowned. *Oneness?* Ibbit pulled Ansella to her feet and kissed her, driving the question from her head. "I need you standing by my side, darling. Will you be beside me?"

"Until I die, Ibbit. I love you."

The priestess smiled and kissed her again. "I love you too, my sweet girl." She straightened her robes, strode from the drawing room into the formal receiving room, winked and shut the door.

Ansella sighed and settled back onto the couch; it was already growing cold where Ibbit's solid body had been. The warmth and security Ibbit brought never lasted long after the priestess's departure. Yet in the last few spokes, especially since Wirdun's health failed and the competition for Eldest Sister began, Ibbit's attentions were more suffocating, her conversation more pointed. Something was not quite right between them, to the point that Ansella had suffered unfamiliar bouts with nerves. She didn't eat when she was out of sorts; she'd taken to wearing tippets to hide her protruding collarbones. Though she still loved Ibbit, she withheld more from her now.

How Ansella loathed the City. It scraped against her soul like a cloak woven of fresh nettles; she wished to throw it off and ride home to Whithorse's rolling hills. How long it had been since she'd ridden. Social obligations overwhelmed her, and Ibbit took up her remaining free time.

She wasn't sleepy, and had no one to call for company. She would have loved to talk with Temmin; though she was proud of him, she wished he were home. Listening to him ramble on in his funny way about the goings-on in the stables and his sisters' foibles was usually enough to banish a dark mood. Sedra's nose was out of joint at present, and she was sulky around everyone. Ellika was never home of an evening; tonight it was a card party in the City. Ansella would die before she called for Harsin.

Harsin's unfaithfulness weighed more on her at the Keep than it had at the Estate. She always knew who his mistresses were; everyone did, though publicly he danced with them now and again and not much more. Never took them to the theater or the opera, never rode out with them, never walked the Promenade with them, always made sure they were never seen going directly to assignations at the Lodge or anywhere else, never brought them into the Keep unless for some event such as a ball, and never kept one under his own roof. Their bargain was this: she would not cause a public scene about the other women, he would not parade them. He'd kept his promise for twenty-three years, but now, just when she'd finally returned to the Keep, just when she needed him to keep that promise the most, he'd broken it. He'd never openly acknowledged a favorite before. Never. Of all his women, sophisticated beauties the lot, why would he flaunt this brainless Shelstone chit?

She looked at the little gray book in her hand. It had no writing on its worn cover. The first two dozen or so pages were a text on beekeeping, but finally she turned to a page that read: "The Truth About the Gods." Ibbit's words about the "oneness of the Goddess" resounded; cold tendrils wound around her chest and squeezed.

Ansella turned the page and began to read.

In the beginning there was the Void, and the Void took form and became the Lady. She was all that there was, and she was beautiful. But the Lady was lonely; She wished for children, and so she took one of Her eyes and one of Her finger bones and made a spindle. She spun Her hair into fine thread and unwound it all around Her in a great cloud, and from it she formed all things—the earth, the stars, the plants, the animals and the people, all spun

from Her hair, woven by Her fingers, enlivened with Her breath.
All were as the Lady. There was no male thing in the world—

Ansella threw the book from her in horror. These were the words of the Murderess of Turus—the heretic Sister Anniki of Litta.

Had she been so smitten not to see it? Ibbit had never come right out and declared men an abomination. She'd said men were so busy thinking about their pricks they had no desire for a spiritual life, and Ansella's experience had thoroughly borne that out—excepting her own son.

But no. Ibbit had said much more, and in her anger against Harsin and love for Ibbit, Ansella had let the priestess's meaning pass over her.

Ansella recalled Sister Anniki's trial nearly twenty years gone. Ansella was heavily pregnant with Temmin then and did not want to be there, but Anniki stood charged of treason as well as heresy; her plans for rebellion had included the murder of the royal family. Harsin was to pass judgment on the woman, but he never got the chance; Venna seized Her Embodiment without warning and passed judgment Herself. Ansella remembered Anniki's bruised purple face as the Goddess squeezed the life from her, how the blood sluiced neatly around Venna's feet, and how She threw Anniki's drained husk down into its own gore. Just before She released Her Embodiment, Venna said the words that reverberated throughout Ansella's life: *Guard your son.*

Ansella had done so; she'd sheltered him from assassins and loose women alike for the first eighteen years of his life, but she'd missed Ibbit completely. Was it possible he'd been given some long-acting poison? The Eldest Sister must see him at once. No, the Eldest Sister was dead—Imvalda. Imvalda was acting Eldest Sister. Temmin might be dying right now, she must do something. Fear, rage and mortification rose up from her stomach; her hand shook as pulled on the bell for her ladies maid.

Miss Hanston served as unofficial gatekeeper to those who might be an annoyance to Her Majesty, including Her Majesty's offspring. To those so deemed, she was as rocky and impenetrable as the Keep itself, but on her royal charge she showered her softest and most beneficent expressions. "Hanston," said Ansella once the boulder-shaped lady was before her, "go fetch Teacher. I need him immediately."

"Teacher?" shuddered Miss Hanston. "Oh, ma'am, he's way up in the Tower Library!"

"Send a footman—I can't wait for Harsin—" Ansella leapt to her feet; she ran through her round receiving room to the hallway, where a duty man waited near her door. "Josip. Run up the Tower stairs and fetch Teacher. And I mean run, not walk quickly!" At the suppressed fear in the young man's face—either of Teacher, the steep climb, or both—she stomped her foot. "Must I find someone properly obedient? *Run!*"

Josip started. "Yes, Your Majesty!" He pelted down the hallway.

Ansella turned to Miss Hanston, who had rumbled through the receiving room after her to the hallway door. "Go find Winmer. Tell him the King must attend to an urgent matter immediately."

"Yes, ma'am," said Miss Hanston, her face creased in worry. She clasped the Queen's shaking hands, a liberty allowed by long acquaintance. "My dear, dear lady, what's amiss? Are you ill? I'll send for a tisane, shall I?"

"No. I shan't be going down to dinner tonight. I want nothing—only send for the King. If he..." *If he is with the Shelstone woman...* "If he is not at the Keep, tell Winmer he must be found. It is most, most urgent. Never worry, Hanston. Find the King and send Teacher to me. All will be well." The maid hesitated, unwilling to leave her mistress in such a state. "Go, Hanston, please, just go!" Ansella begged, squeezing the other woman's hand. Miss Hanston curtseyed and hurried down the hall toward the King's suite.

Ansella returned to her drawing room, fingers steepled against her mouth as she wandered back and forth before the fire. Ibbit, an Annikan. *I will not cry over her, an enemy of my son is an enemy of mine.* But the tears fell no matter how often she repeated it.

Was there *anyone* who could be trusted in the Sister's Temple? Perhaps Imvalda was an Annikan. No, that couldn't be. Ibbit ranked lower than Imvalda. Wouldn't it be easier to take control of the Sisterhood without a fight over the succession? Imvalda was still relatively young, though; if she weren't an Annikan, it would be at least twenty years—perhaps thirty—before an Annikan could try again. Ibbit would need the sponsorship of a great personage to beat Imvalda...someone like the Queen.

She paced and paced, waiting for Teacher. Why hadn't Ibbit killed Temmin, when she'd had five years to do it? No—it made sense. If her only son died, Ansella would be set aside for a younger woman who could bear a new Heir; it had happened in the past. Ibbit needed a Queen, so Temmin lived— until now. She wouldn't need Ansella much longer. No, not much longer at all, the false woman, the woman who'd said she loved her, and why wouldn't she kill Temmin now? Ansella let out a panicked moan.

Teacher arrived quicker than she'd expected, slender, elegant hands clasped before the habitual black robes draping the counselor's slight frame. "Your Majesty, how may I serve you?" said Teacher with a bow.

In her anguish, Ansella ran up and caught the pale hands in her own. "It's Ibbit—you must make sure Temmin is safe, she might do something— might already have done! I don't know where Harsin is, and—"

Teacher tugged on her wrists. "Stop! Calm yourself, ma'am. I can find the King if Mr Winmer is unavailable, but you must tell me what has happened." Ansella retrieved the gray leather-bound book and gave it over. Teacher didn't even bother to open it, silver eyes wide in astonishment. "I thought these were all destroyed when the Scholars burned Anniki's body. Where did you get this?"

"My religious advisor. Sister...Sister Ibbit." Ansella covered her mouth and nose with her hands and turned away.

"Very well," said Teacher. "First we will see to Prince Temmin. I shall go to the Lovers' Temple and alert the Temple's Own immediately. Until this situation is resolved, the Prince should be kept here. The Most Highs will understand. I will bring him back with me, and then I will proceed to the Hearth to speak with the Elder Sisters."

"You will tell me when Temmin is here?" said Ansella, her voice breaking at last.

"Lady, I will bring him directly to you." Ansella followed Teacher into her elegant, bright, circular receiving room where a set of mirrors flanked the fireplace. "I will be back as quickly as possible," said Teacher. "Show me the Supplicants Chamber lavatory." The right-hand mirror flickered. A small, white-tiled room replaced the celadon-walled receiving room's reflection; Ansella's stomach lurched.

Teacher paused, slender fingers half-sunk into the nauseating, fluid mirror, and in a gentle voice added, "Your Majesty, Temmin is alive and well, and will remain so. You have done the right thing, as painful as it is at this moment." Teacher swirled into the mirror until all that was left were the hems of the long black robe; they too passed through, the image in the mirror resolved into the celadon bowl of her receiving room, and Ansella was alone.

She returned to her darkened drawing room and curled into a ball on the couch before the fire. She glanced at the porcelain mantelpiece clock, a blue confection trimmed in gilt and pink porcelain roses. Harsin had given it to her on their first anniversary. He'd said it reminded him of her: the blue of her eyes, the gold of her hair and the blush of her cheek. Where was Harsin? He must be with the Shelstone woman.

Now and then would come a knock at the door and a polite request to see to the fire, trim the lamps, bring Her Majesty a tray, perhaps her bedtime tea? Ansella did not answer. She stared into the flames, hugging her knees. The already-starved fire burned low; a lamp flame fainted.

Sisters, Lovers and Beloveds passed between the Lovers' Temple and the Healer's House all the time. Who knew what might happen before the Sisters rooted out the Annikans? Teacher would see to it. No harm would come to Temmin. *Please, Sweet Venna, let no harm come to him. Guard my son.*

"What do you mean, the kitchen's closed?" said Temmin.

"I mean it's closed," said Anda, lounging on her alcove bed with a book. "Not the cooks' fault you decided to see that hulk of a Postulant instead of eating."

"Mathanus and I've been trying to get some time alone for weeks now!"

"Was it worth missing dinner, oh bottomless pit?"

Temmin considered his stomach, and then the rest of him. "Let me put it this way. Math needs practice with women. You won't regret giving him some." He flopped down on the bed next to her. "You have nothing squirreled away? Not even chocolates?"

"You ate the last of my chocolates, little piggy—oof! *Giant* piggy! Get off!"

"I'm searching you for chocolates!"

"Are you now?" Anda giggled. "I wouldn't hide chocolates there."

"Really? There's plenty of room under here."

"They'd melt."

"I could lick them off."

"Could you now—*Oi!*" yelled Anda. "Where in Harla did *he* come from?"

Temmin rolled away from her and jumped to his feet, ready to fight. "Teacher?" he said, dropping his fists. "What are you doing here?"

"Where did he come from?" repeated Anda.

"The lavatory. Good evening, Miss Barrows," Teacher said to the puzzled Supplicant. "I am glad to see you well, Your Highness."

Temmin swept the slight figure up in his arms. "Teacher! I've missed you so much!"

"And I you—Temmin, put me down, please."

He did so and helped smooth the robes covering Teacher's severe white shirt, black suit and Tremontine red cravat; Temmin wondered if the Tower Library closet contained anything besides. Or perhaps there was just this one set of clothes.

"How're Mother and my sisters? How's Jenks? Is he still in Reggiston? How are *you*? What in Pagg's name are you doing here? Tell me everything!"

"I am here to take you back to the Keep immediately. You are in danger."

Temmin settled back down on the edge of Anda's bed; Anda herself had retreated into its recesses to peer out at the curious pale figure with the iron-colored hair and strange eyes. "I'm always in danger," said Temmin.

After extracting a promise of secrecy from Anda on her vows as Supplicant, Teacher summed up the situation. "This is a more pressing danger than even your uncles' assassins. We do not know who among the Sisters currently in the Lovers' Temple may be trusted, nor do we know if you have sustained any damage from a long-acting poison Ibbit may have slipped you. You must be seen by a trusted Sister, or...or better." Teacher's face clouded over in thought. "I do not think it likely, but all possible threats must be assessed. In any event, you cannot stay here. I must take you back to the Keep until the situation is stable—at the least until Sister Ibbit is taken up and her sympathizers identified."

Anda had scooted across the bed to slip concerned arms around Temmin's neck from behind. "We should get word to the Most Highs, or at least Allis and Issak. Shall I go?"

"The Embodiments are not involved in this. Temmin, on my authority you are excused until such time as we can guarantee your security here. The Most Highs will not dispute this." Temmin rose and tugged at the fastenings of his red linen trousers; Teacher put a restraining hand on his arm. "We have no time for you to change. Your mother is sick with worry. We must go back to the Keep, and I must go to the Hearth to see the acting Eldest Sister. I will speak with High Beloved Malla in the morning."

Anda walked with them into the lavatory and gave Temmin a quick kiss goodbye. "I'll be back soon," he said. "Give Allis and Issak a kiss from me. Don't be scared at what you're about to see, it's harmless, I promise." As Teacher pulled him through the mirror, he looked back into the white-tiled room; a terrified Anda touched her head, her heart and her groin: Amma's Sign, a blessing to protect against the Black Man.

They emerged into his mother's receiving room. Temmin blinked against the room's brighter light, and a chill shot through him. He wore nothing but his thin Supplicant uniform, and the Keep was considerably colder than the Temple. His mother ran to him from her drawing room door. He caught her up in his arms. "I'm all right, Mama, I'm fine, see? Please don't cry. Where's your handkerchief? There, now." He reached into the pocket in her wrapper where he knew she always kept one, awkwardly dried her eyes and dabbed at her nose. He'd done this many a time for petitioners, but comforting the woman who'd always comforted him made him clumsy; she'd never presented such a face to him before, lined with tears and care.

"You're well? Have you had him checked for poisons yet, Teacher?"

"Ma'am, we have just returned. I must be off to the Hearth now to speak with Sister Imvalda. I believe there is time yet before His Highness must be examined. The Traveler Queen is nearby if necessary."

Ansella swallowed hard, fighting back a new gust of tears so fiercely she shook in Temmin's arms. "That is good. Tell Imvalda I will support her as Eldest Sister to the best of my ability."

"Where's Father?" said Temmin.

"On his way back to the Keep, I surmise," answered Teacher. "Mr Winmer has been sent personally for him, and if he has not arrived by the time I am returned from the Hearth I will fetch him myself. Now, I really must go." Teacher turned back toward the nearest of the two mirrors. "Show me Imvalda of the Sister's Temple."

The receiving room mirror wavered into the image of a middle-aged woman sitting in a comfortable if sparsely furnished apartment. Her image was somewhat distorted and to one side; Temmin thought it must be a reflection from something shiny rather than from a smooth mirror. The woman's habit was the Elder Sisters' inky green. Her uncovered hair was black, heavily salted with silver and shoulder-length in the Sisters' style. Her profile was strong but not unkind—a patient, watchful, handsome face. She leaned against a slightly younger woman clad in green a shade lighter, her expression intelligent and filled with humor. They both held books in their hands, and golden light as if from a fire flickered across their faces. The younger woman absently kissed the black-and-silver head against her shoulder.

Teacher swirled through, and the image vanished.

Ansella stumbled against her son, and Temmin grabbed her by the elbows. "Come, Mama, back to your fire." He supported her into the gloomy drawing room and onto the blue tufted couch beside the fire; he propped her feet up on the couch and covered her in a thick shawl draped across the couch's arm. "It's dark as Harla's Hill in here." He made to turn up the nearest lantern and discovered the wick had burned all the way down. He trimmed and relit it, turned up the second lantern on the table opposite, and stoked the fire into a fine blaze again. "You used to sit in the dark and brood at home when you were upset. You haven't eaten, have you?" He didn't wait for her answer but went straight to the bell pull and called for Miss Hanston.

The ladies maid appeared as if she'd been waiting outside the door, already bearing a laden tray and an expression that said she'd spoon it into the Queen's mouth herself if she had to. Her stony facade crumbled into pebbles at the sight of Temmin. "Your Highness! When did you arrive?"

"I snuck in the back door, Hanston, how are you?" he grinned. He took the tray from her, set it on a small table before the fire and shook the maid's hand. "She won't tell me anything, and so I must resort to you. Has she been poorly for long?"

Miss Hanston shook her heavy rock of a head. "She hasn't been eating proper for some spokes, sir—hasn't—" and here her face petrified again—"hasn't since you left us, in fact, but especially this last week." She twisted her hands, spoiling her foreboding walls and crenellated battlements.

"It's all right, Hanston, you may go," said Temmin. "I'll make sure she eats."

Miss Hanston left with a dubious glance and closed the door behind her. Temmin raised the cover on the plate; a fine aroma of roast chicken struck his nose, and his stomach gurgled for its lost dinner. "I'm not hungry, sweetheart, why don't you eat it?" said Ansella.

"No, none of that. You eat this, or it's Nurse's beef tea and custard. I'll bring her here from the Estate nursery if I have to, and then you're in for it." He settled on a footstool and gazed up at her. She frightened him—as pale and transparent as onionskin, so unlike the happy, strong mother he could always depend upon.

She took up her fork and began picking at her food. "Really, Temmy, I can't eat, I can't..." The fork clattered to the tray, and she pressed her hands to her face. "I am not ill, sweetheart," she said, her voice muffled. She dropped her hands. "At least I am not...not bodily ill. I suppose one could say I suffer from an oppression of the spirit."

"But *what* is oppressing your spirit, Mama—or is it a who? I hope it's not me—please tell me it's not me," he said, putting his hands on her knee.

"No, no, though I've missed you and worried for you dreadfully." She cupped his cheek, brushing his golden beard with her thumb. "I am so, so very proud of you, sweetheart."

Her hand was cold. He took it from his cheek and chafed it, willing warmth into her. "You haven't answered me, Mama."

She burst into tears, her free hand shielding her eyes from him. "I hate it here! I want to go home, but I can't!"

"It's Father, isn't it? Is he hurting you?" cried Temmin. Ansella gave a small shrug that said *perhaps, but far from all.* "Then who? Mama, tell me who it is and I will...I will do something, I will make him stop."

"I've stopped her myself!" she sobbed.

Temmin had never seen her like this. She resembled Ellika as a child, shaking in unfeigned, complete grief over some trouble; they were so much alike. An idea crept over him, obvious and uncomfortable enough for him to wish it hadn't. "Stopped who, Mama?" *Her?* He ran through every woman close to his mother. Not the girls, obviously. Hanston? Dear Amma, no. The only woman that might matter this much to his mother was...

Ansella shook her head, still shielding her eyes. "Please—don't ask any more!"

He didn't need to. Every sign he'd been trained to see had been there all along. Anyone seeing her now would know, with no training at all. He swayed inside like a tree with its roots cut. Ibbit—that horrid woman had insinuated herself into their lives at the Estate more than he knew.

When his equilibrium steadied, he moved his mother's legs to sit beside her. He gathered her into his arms as he would any petitioner seeking the most basic human solace and held her close. Ansella calmed and settled against Temmin's side, their roles reversed; her sobs slowed to a few gasps as she swallowed her grief.

When Miss Hanston arrived after a discreet period, he relinquished his limp mother to her maid. He expected a grim remonstrance, but instead, Miss Hanston's rutted face stayed soft: gentle in her dealings with the Queen, near-despairing when she looked up at him. "Get her to bed, Hanston, she's worn to a nub." At this, Miss Hanston hardened into a gray brick wall with *I know my job, thank you* written across it. Temmin gave his mother a last kiss and hug. "Good night, Mama, I will see you at breakfast."

As he strode down the corridor to his old rooms, the thought of the next day's breakfast reminded him he'd had nothing to eat. He would order a tray once he'd changed into warmer clothes. He opened the door to his study.

The fire had been lit, as had the lamps. Everything appeared just as it had the night Teacher had spirited him away to the Lovers' Temple almost a year ago, right from under his father's nose: the moss green velvet sofa; the wing chair he never sat in; the wuisc, brandy and barisha decanters lined up on the sideboard; the tea table by the windows; the heavily-laden book-cases; the globe atop the long library table. One new thing now inhabited the room: a lectern he recognized from the Tower Library, Teacher's own study. Atop it lay a familiar book bound in ancient Tremontine red leather.

The faded gilt lettering on its front cover read, *An Intimate History of the Greater Kingdom.*

The book. The magic book that had changed his life in so many ways.

Temmin's magical sensibilities had grown since he'd first looked in the book; he saw sigils invisible to others—the fertility charms glowing silver on the twins' left hips, the glow of possession when Gods came down into their Embodiments—and when Teacher watched him in a reflection he could see his observer clearly. He couldn't use reflections himself to see or travel without Teacher's assistance, but he wondered if some day he might. Teacher seemed to think so, a prospect frightening as well as enticing.

When he'd first opened it a year ago, the pages were blank. Only when Teacher "read" to him did they come alive. First, words bloomed on the page. Then the words turned to pictures, the pictures began to move, and he was drawn into the story, experiencing it from one set of eyes and then another. Last year the book had told him the story of his ancestor King Warin the Wise and the enchanted Princess Emmae of the Kingdom of Leute—now the Duchy of Litta. It was a story of such erotic passion that he'd had difficulty remembering who he was whenever the book released him. The kings of Tremont still had magic then, magic his family lost some 350 years ago, and though Warin was powerful it wasn't enough to break the curse on Emmae. Instead, she broke it herself.

Temmin learned so much from that story. Leadership. Sacrifice. Servitude. The wages of pride. The hearts of women—or at least the heart of Emmae, his spirited, many-times great-grandmother. How it had helped him see what he had done to Mattie! Would he still consider that moment in the hedge a year ago good fun otherwise? He couldn't say, but it had stopped him from doing the same to Arta Dannikson.

Temmin wondered what the book might still teach him, and if he'd ever be able to read it himself. Perhaps that time had come? He crossed to the lectern, anxiety mixing with anticipation as he opened it.

He peeked at the pages. Still blank. He frowned and said, "Once upon a time...?" Nothing. *Well, it would have been a mixed blessing anyway.*

Temmin shambled through his bedchamber into the gigantic wardrobe, everything as neat as if Jenks were in the next room instead of kicking his heels in Reggiston: clothes brushed, shoes and boots polished, fresh linen and stockings filling the drawers, for all the world as if he were expected back any moment rather than a year from now. He shucked off his uniform, pulled on an old pair of trousers and a shirt over clean undergarments, and shoved his bare feet into his most broken-down, comfortable pair of carpet slippers.

After a tug on the study's bell pull, a footman appeared to take an order for "something edible and plenty of it," and to summon however many of Temmin's sisters who might be flitting about the Keep to his room. In moments, his oldest sister Sedra flung open the door. "What are you doing here?" She ran up and took him by the hands. "Do Mama and Papa know you're here? What's going on? Are you all right?"

He kissed her cheek. "Too many questions before I've eaten! Here, sit. Shall I call for barisha? My decanter's empty."

"Brandy, please. Elly drinks barisha. It's too sweet for me." He raised an eyebrow but poured two fingers from the sideboard decanter into a snifter and handed it over. She warmed the glass in her hand and settled into the wing chair. "One question at a time, then: What are you doing here?"

He laid out the story, skipping the intimate connection between their mother and her religious advisor. "I'm fine as far as I know. Mama's worried I may have some long-acting poison in me or something, but I'm far more worried about her. Seddy, she's come undone!"

Sedra took a breath to speak, but a discreet knock heralded the arrival of Temmin's meal; she sipped at her brandy instead. One footman set the tea table before the fire, while the other laid out the cart's plentiful something edible. Their task completed, they left the room with a visible excitement in their step. They would be popular tonight; none of the other servants had seen the mysteriously returned Prince.

"This is what I've missed the most," said Temmin. "Our kitchens close after a certain hour, but I can always get something to eat here."

"What you've missed most is the food?"

He gave a small, snorting laugh. "No, of course not." He took a huge bite from a cold chicken leg, swallowed, and added, "I've missed you girls and Mama—and Jenks. Have you heard from him? He is an indifferent correspondent at best."

"You of all people haven't any grounds for complaint. Jenks writes to Mama. She says he's doing well, something about training your friend Fen Wallek. Listen, Tem, I don't want to talk about Jenks! I'm terribly worried about Mama. I've tried to get Papa to intervene between her and that Ibbit, but he doesn't care about a *single* thing I say..." She shrugged angrily and took a full enough drink from her snifter that Temmin almost choked from the imagined fumes. "I've been trying to get her away from Ibbit for the last year. Since you left for the Temple. I even wondered if that bitch was poisoning her. I did manage to get Papa to insist she be seen for her lack of appetite and listlessness—he was beginning to worry about her himself. She wanted Ibbit to do it, but Eldest Sister Wirdun said it wasn't proper for her religious advisor to be her healer."

"And?"

"She's fine. At least she's not being poisoned." Sedra rubbed her eyes; how tired and drawn his sister looked, far more than she had at his birthday ball. "I just wish Mama didn't love her so."

Temmin dropped his fork, tried to catch it on the way down to the floor and nearly knocked over his wine glass. "I'm sorry—what?"

"All that fancy training, and you didn't know Ibbit is Mama's lover?"

"I...I grasped it when I came home tonight. How long have you known?"

Sedra slowly shook her head, keeping her eyes on the amber liquid swirling in her glass. "About five years now."

"That's almost as long as Ibbit's been Mama's religious advisor!"

"Oh, she started in on Mama almost immediately."

Temmin sat back against the couch cushions, his supper forgotten. "How did you know?"

"You're not the only one with a talent for observation. And Ibbit left a love letter Mama wrote tucked into a book she lent me," she added sheepishly. "I think she wanted me to know for some reason."

The two siblings stared moodily, Sedra into her snifter, Temmin into his food. He cut a hunk of cheese, topped it with pickled onion and mustard, and ate it while Sedra took another long sip of her brandy. He swallowed and said, "What I don't understand is *why*."

"Why what?"

"Why Mama took a lover!"

"Oh, honestly, she's not just your mother, she's a woman, and still fairly young—Tem, if you don't get that look off your face, I'll slap it off. D'you think it's been enjoyable to know all this about my own mother and have no one to talk to about it?" she snapped.

"You could have told me, or Elly." He ignored her answering scoff, and continued, "But why did she pick a woman? Especially *Ibbit*?"

"Who else could she turn to? She's the Queen! She can't take a male lover—she'd be executed. She can't even go to the Lovers' Temple. Have you learned no history?" In truth, his only tutor who'd ever said anything about the Kingdom's royal women was Teacher, and they'd finished only Emmae's story before he'd left the Keep. His sister continued. "Mama was lonely and vulnerable, and she's too proud to admit she loves Papa, and...and he's a hard man to love." She stifled a sob. Temmin winced inside; seeing Sedra so emotional was like surprising her in her underclothes. "Ibbit found an empty space and filled it. She can be very charismatic and charming when she wants to be, and in the right light is quite attractive."

"I don't think the human eye can see that sort of light. At least mine never have."

"Don't women come to your Temple for comfort in the arms of other women?"

Temmin recalled the many times in the last year he'd seen women make love to one another, thoughts of his mother firmly tamping down any erotic impulse. "Of course. But they come to us because they are at a time of life when they risk pregnancy otherwise, or because their husbands forbid them Lovers but not Beloveds, or because their impulses are childish and they desire women. In time we hope they'll mature, but often they don't, poor things."

"And among the women of your Temple?"

"Well...they do it because they must practice for the petitioners' sakes."

Sedra laughed. "You really believe that? And why, oh servant of the Lovers, are affairs among men tolerated, even encouraged, and not among women? Why do young nobles become Students to older Mentors—why is that partnership honored, revered as the most meaningful, pure and virtuous of all, and two women loving one another is considered childish, foolish, degrading and sordid, even though Neya and Venna both took mortal women as lovers?"

"Because..." Temmin furrowed his brow. He'd never thought about it. No one at the Temple had said anything to him about it all year, and he'd never thought to ask. It was just the nature of things; everyone knew this.

Sedra rose to her feet and hugged him. "It doesn't matter, just something to think about. I'm glad you're here. Mama will be easier with you close."

He slept fitfully that night in the now-unfamiliar bed, wondering how he could have missed something so obvious. A year ago, before he'd become a Supplicant, Allis had said he was quite perceptive when he wanted to be. He must not have wanted to perceive very much at all if his mother had been having an affair right under his nose for five years. Then there was this supposed threat to his life. He just couldn't take it that seriously. His uncles' assassins with crossbows and daggers? Yes. Grumpy, man-hating Sisters? Not really. He finally dropped off, missing Anda's snoring.

Temmin woke the next morning to someone moving through his room. "Jenks?" he called, sitting up and ruffling his hair.

From beyond the bed-curtains came a level voice he recognized as Gram, his father's valet. "No, sir. I'm tending to your needs until my nephew Mr Harbis arrives this afternoon." Gram opened first the bed-curtains then the draperies, letting the gray winter light creep apologetically past the valet's square shoulders into the bedchamber.

Temmin flung himself down on the pillows again. "Harbis? Oh, Pagg's balls," he muttered to himself. He'd had to put up with Harbis as his valet last year when Jenks was called away. The elegant man was irritatingly good at his job, his sole flaw being that he wasn't Jenks—Jenks, the dispenser of advice from fashion to horses, more a father to him than the King. The gravel-voiced ex-cavalryman had been Temmin's personal servant since he could remember. The year they'd spent apart had been busy enough that Temmin hadn't had time to miss him much, but here outside the Temple he felt his old friend's absence greatly. "Gram, your nephew is all very well and good, but I'm not going to be here long enough to need him!"

"As you say, sir. Nevertheless, Mr Winmer has requested his presence. If you do not need him, I am sure there is some further employment for him here."

"Let him be Winmer's valet, then," grumbled Temmin. Harla take Winmer anyway. All the worst things at the Keep seemed to originate with his father's secretary—forcing Arta Dannikson into seducing him, blackmailing the twins, the near-murder of Arta and her sweetheart Fen Wallek, and now foisting an unwanted valet on him. It was enough to put a man in a mood.

Mood or no, he took the bath Gram drew for him and put on the clothes Gram set out for him. "I believe His Majesty expects you at breakfast this morning, sir."

Temmin found his father and sisters already sitting at the breakfast table in the sunny, robin's egg blue morning room; they stood at his arrival. Ellika bounded from her chair, almost overturning it in her eagerness. "I wanted to see you so much I got up for breakfast!" she crowed, hugging him tight.

He kissed her on both cheeks, patted her back toward her chair, and kissed Sedra before he turned to Harsin. Temmin took the King's outstretched hand and shook it warily. "Sir."

"Good morning, son, I'm glad to see you looking well after last night's excitement."

"I'm still not sure it was necessary, sir. The Temple's Own does a fine job."

"They could not protect you against a Sister the Lovers' Temple trusted."

Harsin sat back down, his children followed suit, and his arrival's good feelings evaporated into an uncertain tension. Sedra picked at the corner of the newspaper at the top of her habitual morning stack; Ellika concentrated on spreading apricot jam on toast until she'd covered it in a thick, even coat from crust to crust.

Temmin fidgeted until he could stand it no longer. "What are we going to do about Mama?"

Harsin swallowed a bit of sausage. "We've done it. Ibbit is imprisoned awaiting trial, and the Sisters are purging Annikan sympathizers. I wouldn't go anywhere near the Hearth for the next four spokes for all the tea in Nija," he added in a mutter.

"I mean she's miserable, have you noticed nothing?" said Temmin.

"Have I noticed nothing—of course I've noticed it! Your mother does not do well in the City, it's why she's lived at the Estate all these years. I'd send her back if I could, but we'd both lose face now that you're grown."

"But what can we do for her?"

Harsin had taken on the red beginnings of a fine shade of purple when Sedra murmured, "I've called for Cousin Donnis."

"What?" said Harsin, his ill temper switching to his oldest daughter. "Without consulting me?"

"It seemed more important to bring her here quickly than ask for permission first. You won't deny Mama the comfort of her closest friend, surely?"

Harsin squinted at her in irritation. "Outmaneuvered again. I wish you were one of my generals in Endan. Damned Incharis don't know what's best for them. No, I won't begrudge her Lady Donnis, I've always liked the woman." He tapped his finger on the table. "Temmin, your mother will be better just having you near. I attribute her worry over you more than anything to her indisposition of late. It, ah, it's not too late to withdraw from the Temple. If you're worried about your mother, I'm sure the Most Highs would give you dispensation if you asked—or if I asked for you."

Ellika fumbled her toast; Sedra rattled her newspaper open.

"You're asking me to break a vow, sir, a very serious vow," Temmin said, turning an answering shade of red.

Harsin picked up his fork and pointed it at his son. "Worth a try. But the damage is done, in any event. Coming home now would probably make things worse, now that I think more on it." He tucked into his sausage.

"Well, that's good," said Temmin, "because I'm due back there sooner than later. Neya's Day is coming up."

FOVR

Ansella suffered in ways Temmin didn't understand. Yes, she had loved Ibbit, but Ibbit had proved false. Ibbit wanted Temmin dead. She wanted his father dead. Oughtn't Mama to be more angry than sad? She stayed in her rooms, avoiding both the morning room and the dinner table. Miss Hanston swore she ate, but "Her Majesty is in a kind of mourning, sir, and that's a fact."

Temmin supposed she might well be in the ordinary kind of mourning soon, depending on what the Sisterhood dug up in its investigations. Mama told him she'd been there when Anniki died, and how terrible it was. He hoped she would not be present if they executed Ibbit. He'd never disliked Ibbit enough to want her dead before, but for what she'd done to his mother he wanted to see her horse face looking down its nose from the hooks above Marketgate.

Or did he? He'd seen dead bodies. He remembered the first man he'd seen die a violent death, an assassin at Lord Litta's ball a year ago, and the first to have gotten close to him. Temmin still thought of the blood dribbling from the crossbow bolt in the man's forehead. There'd been several assassins since, but he'd seen only one other die—a pathetic little shopman who'd been forced to attack him. The rest never got near.

He'd seen a great many men killed in Teacher's magical book; the "Intimate History" made him relive the battle his ancestor Warin had fought to take his throne. Seeing the head of someone he knew as well as Ibbit, even if he hated her…he didn't know. Maybe it wouldn't come to that.

Ansella revived in the presence of her children. Without saying anything to one another, on Temmin's second night at home they tried to recreate their cozy childhood evenings at the Estate, sitting together before the Small Sitting Room fire. Even Ellika foreswore her nightly round of parties and brought out her little-seen workbasket. Mama's knitting lay in her lap, but the needles remained silent. She said little; she stroked Temmin's hair as he sat on her footstool, or bent quietly over Ellika's embroidery. Sedra sketched them, singly and together. One study arrested Temmin's eye: Mama staring away toward a dark corner, pressing the tip of a knitting needle into the top of her thigh.

What joy had she had the last few years? Ibbit had reined Mama in for so long, stopped her from doing so many things she'd loved—everything from dancing to reading novels to riding. Temmin's earliest memories of horses involved his mother. She was a true daughter of Whithorse, such a good judge of horseflesh that Jenks said her father the old Duke and her brother Patrin often deferred to her: "His Grace always swore she rode before she could walk, and your Uncle Patrin always regretted having to buy a horse without her advice when we were on campaign. Though he never bought a bad horse in his life." As patrician a lady as any, half the skirts in her wardrobe were riding skirts, divided down the middle.

Mama loved horses. How could she have denied herself one of the great pleasures of her life for so long? Perhaps, Temmin thought, a return to the saddle would help Mama see how wrong Ibbit was—not just in her heresy, but in all things. "Mama, come ride with me tomorrow in the King's Woods. I won't be home long and I'm sure Flor misses you." She demurred, but he detected interest in her voice. He coaxed, and coaxed some more; when she gave in, her smile almost reached her eyes.

The grooms and stable hands were thrilled to see the Queen; she had been a frequent visitor in the past, taking particular care of her little white mare Flor, but a few spokes of the wheel had turned since the stables had seen her shadow. Poor Flor's back more often than not carried a stable boy round the paddock.

Riding Master Cappel came hurrying up from the ring where he'd been working with a promising roan, snatched off his cap, and bowed so low he almost fell over. Ansella took his gnarled hands and helped him up; the old man blushed like a boy. "Yer Majesty! We've miss't you so!"

Ansella mounted Flor. Temmin's favorite, Jebby, had been sent back to the Estate for the duration of Temmin's Supplicancy, and while he missed the big chestnut gelding he enjoyed riding this black half-Inchari mare named LeiLei almost as much. They took off at a brisk walk out of the yards, breaking into a light canter when they reached the War Road leading into the King's Woods. His mother looked as if she'd never left the saddle, more herself than in the entire time they'd been in the City. She moved with Flor as one, giving the white mare little direction beyond the slight shift of her weight, and as they flew over the meadows dotted with blue and red wildflowers and through the dappled, ferny King's Woods her narrow shoulders seemed less bowed; her face relaxed.

They stopped in the Fairy Meadow, high in the foothills where the air was clearest. His mother's aspect altered; a life and vitality informed the way she leaned over and scratched Flor's neck in just the spot to make the little mare shake her head in bliss. "That's what I like to see," said Temmin. "Roses in my mama's cheeks."

"Am I so wan, then?" she said, breathing a little harder than she should.

"Mama, you've had me worried since before—" He stopped himself. No references to Ibbit. "Since before my birthday. Since I saw you at Amma's Day. You're winded. You were never winded after a little canter like this. You must keep riding after I've gone back to the Temple. Mama, you *love* riding. I don't understand why you stopped. You need the air and the exercise. Exercise will improve your appetite."

"I'm eating, sweetheart—"

"Not enough. Cousin Donnis likes to ride. Sedra will instruct her to drag you to the stables if she has to. Promise me you will both ride and eat more, Mama."

Ansella promised, meek as a remorseful child.

For the first time in almost a year, Temmin found himself at loose ends. His ride with his mother took up part of the morning, but they were back by breakfast. He was not allowed to leave the Keep or its grounds. He might go to the stables. At home, the Estate's stablehands welcomed and then ignored him, treating him as a sort of honored comrade. At the Keep he made the men uncomfortable and formal; it turned a pleasure into a pointless exercise. Given time, he could have won them over, but he didn't have time. He would be at the Keep just a week.

An empty day stretched before him, with the annoying, perfect Harbis hovering around for good measure. He could stand his father's Gram; the man had a talent for making himself invisible. But Harbis was always puttering about, making sure everything one needed was at hand from the right change of clothes to a bath at the perfect temperature to the providing of a snack exactly when one wanted it but before one asked for it. Infuriating.

Thus, Temmin greeted Teacher's arrival in his study—and Harbis's brisk, somewhat alarmed departure—with great pleasure. This time he spared the slight figure a crushing hug and instead shook hands. "Just the man I wanted to see! I was so bored I even thought of finding your library again, but it's been some time since I've been up there and I wasn't sure I could find my way."

Teacher smiled. "Your father thought perhaps we might return to our lessons while you are here."

Temmin glanced at the lectern and the old red book. "Lessons? What for? I'm going back to the Temple soon. What kind of lessons are we talking about? Lecturing sorts of lessons, or…?"

"The other sort, if you prefer. I have nothing particular in mind, really, but to begin a story to be finished later. I thought perhaps one of the more exciting ones—well, they are all exciting, your family has a turbulent history. But this story…" Teacher crossed to the lectern for the book and paused, one hand on its Tremontine red leather cover. "You have opened it."

"Oh, well, yes," he blushed. "I've had another birthday, you see, and I thought perhaps…I mean, there's the sigils, and I can see you very clearly in the mirror now. I checked and I still can't use the mirror as you do, so I thought perhaps I might have been given the ability to read the book this year."

Teacher's mouth quirked at its corner. "Of those ancestors who held magic, most saw their abilities begin in a small way at puberty and develop fully at age eighteen. You are the first in 358 years to have any ability at all, and I am not certain how. Though I have my theories."

Teacher picked up the book and brought it to the library table by the windows; Temmin sat down before it. "Which are?"

"I have not come to any definite conclusions, but it would appear the land recognizes you more completely than previous men of the blood. You are the closest in bloodline to the first King in some centuries—perhaps ever. You even look like him."

"You mean Temmin the Great? You knew him? I thought you first served us under Gethin the First."

"I have served from Gethin on, but I knew Temmin the First. Some-times it is hard to look at you and not see him. You are very like, though I did not know him in his youth." Memory, wistfulness and revulsion played across Teacher's face in a rare unguarded moment.

"You didn't like him, did you?"

The expression vanished. "Some day I will tell you the story of the first Temmin and me. Not until you are King yourself may I even try to do so." Temmin nodded; he knew the pain it cost when Teacher got too close to magically forbidden subjects. Teacher perched on the edge of the table as in days gone by. "For now, I can tell you the story of another of your name-sakes: the third Temmin, called Bastard, the only illegitimately born king to date."

Temmin thought of his father's older brothers born on the wrong side of the blanket though raised as potential heirs; Harsin had come late in his own father's life. Even now they plotted somewhere outside the boundaries of the Kingdom to kill both Harsin and Temmin, and thus place the eldest of them on the throne. "Hopefully the only one ever, at least well into my great-grandchildren's lifetimes. All right, let's hear it—or—or whatever you call it when you open this thing." It never seemed to matter which page he turned to, so he spread the book open at random.

Teacher's voice turned hypnotic. "This story is called 'The Bastard.' Once upon a time…"

Words bloomed on the pages, and Temmin's stomach tightened in anticipation. Pictures took the place of words. He looked down as if from a great height at a butte rising high between two rivers converging to its south. The western river sparkled green and light in the sun; the eastern one was wide, and dark as a shadow.

The southern side of the butte sheered off, steep and foreboding; to the north it sloped away into a boundless forest and up into the foothills of a great mountain with three peaks. His viewpoint descended to a stone for-tress built into the butte's highest point. It overlooked a bustling settlement crowding the confluence of the two rivers; smoke from its many chimneys made a cloud. Seven tree-covered hills rose in the city, each topped with what looked like temples in various stages of construction; one had a flat white boulder atop it that Temmin recognized as the Father's Rock, an an-cient shrine to Pagg. The eighth was the largest, a black rise hulking to the south and west, alone in a forest.

A familiar tower rose high above the butte, though shorter than Tem-min knew it now; its base bored into the living rock and thick stone walls with their own towers surrounded it. A road so wide six men might ride abreast cut its way through the snow-covered forest away from the fortress—it was the War Road. This was Tremont Keep.

The sun slid behind the Altenne Mountains to the west, and suddenly Temmin was moving fast through the sky, swooping down and down towards the Keep; he flinched as he passed through its stone walls into the chamber still known as the Great Hall. Though Harsin used the Great Hall now for only the most solemn state ceremonies—there were larger rooms by far to be found in the Keep today—in the book the huge chamber brimmed over with music and dancers. Bright tapestries covered the cold gray walls, servants carried great trays of food to overflowing tables, and everywhere people laughed.

Bright pennants fluttered from the heavy rafters just as they did now—no, some were missing. The green and white of his own dear Whithorse, the russet and gold of Barle, and Tremont's own dark blood red and gold hung beside one another, but where was Corland's pennant? Litta, Belleth, Alzeh, Kellen? The conquered princes of Inchar? Not even the yellow and blue of Valmouth could be seen. Temmin realized this must be a long time ago, longer ago even than the last story he'd been shown—near the kingdom's founding. Teacher's voice began again.

Once upon a time, early in the Kingdom's history, there lived a lady named Lassanna of Whitehorse.

A willowy young woman appeared among the dancers. She wore a dress of Whithorse green trimmed in silver fur, a silver brocade belt slung low on her slender hips. She was slipping through the forms of a dance he didn't recognize, two long lines with the men on one side and the women on the other, bows and curtseys, turn and turn about; the dancers' fingers barely touched. The young woman's straight ash blond hair hung loose to her waist, and ribbons of the same brocade as her belt pulled it back from her face. Her eyes were gray and laughing, and she seemed to be enjoying herself immensely. She seemed to be no older than he was, perhaps younger. He liked her immediately.

The view turned toward an older man with the same gray eyes glowering from the sidelines at the young woman.

Lassanna was the daughter of the Third Duke of Whitehorse, a jealous parent who was not at all sure he'd done the right thing in bringing her to court...

The unhappy man seemed to pull at him, and Temmin's self dropped away.

The first day of Winter's Beginning, 40 KY
Tremont Keep

Gonnor Lord Whitehorse disapproved of modern life—women eating with the men, dancers touching hands!—and never more than right now. His youngest daughter Lassanna danced with Prince Andrin this Eddin's Day night, her collarbones showing above her fur-trimmed neckline, and her unveiled hair fanning to one side whenever she swung round too quickly—he could see her nape! Was honor such a forgotten thing at the court of Temmin the Second? Temmin the Great would never have stood for it. In his days, men knew how to marshal their wives and daughters. But those days were forty years gone, and Gonnor himself had been a child.

Gonnor blamed Sairland. King Temmin had spent his youth traveling in the Sairish territories during the peace, three years in Sairland itself at King Patrig's court. Then his older brother died without a son, and Temmin hurried home to become the Heir. Though skirmishes along the border between Tremont and Sairish-held Valleysmouth had increased lately, the King's love of Sairish customs remained. Now women wore long, dragging sleeves and flashed their napes and ate with the men. He snorted to himself in disgust.

Gonnor kept the old customs alive in Whitehorse. True, he'd been somewhat lenient with his Duchess. Sittenna hadn't been entirely willing to marry him; technically, he'd carried her off from Kellen. He'd kept her bound to the bedpost until she gave in, took up Tremontine ways and settled down to married life, but he had to give her some little things in return, some of the feminine freedoms of her homeland. Perhaps when it came to Lassanna's upbringing he'd given her too much leeway, though he'd spoiled their youngest himself. He should have married Lassa off at fourteen like her two sisters, but here she was, eighteen and unwed—not the most beautiful of his girls but the hardest to give away.

Lassa trotted past him, flashing her bright smile. He tried to frown, but she looked so happy; instead, he reserved his disapproval for the back of Prince Andrin's head. Gonnor would have been delighted at the Heir's interest in his daughter had Andrin not recently married a Leutish Princess in a political alliance. The Duke ground his teeth. Never had he spent such a dismal first day of the year.

Lassanna reveled in her first holiday at the Keep. Real silver stars glittered among the evergreens gracing every beam and arch; the branches' sharp green scent mingled with the hot spiced wine constantly flowing into her cup,

Eddin's Day, with its presents and pranks, was still Lassa's favorite holiday. Farr's Day with its loud, violent tourneys held little attraction; Father didn't think it suitable for women in any event. No one liked Pagg's Day. She always had a kitten or a songbird to be blessed on Amma's Day. She liked giving her brothers presents on Nerr's Day, she supposed. She took Venna's Day quite seriously, for her favorite brother had often been ill as a child. She still made offerings every year in hopes he might stay well; so far, Venna was pleased to keep him so. She dismissed dressing up in costume on Harla's Day as child's play, and as an unmarried woman, she could not attend the Neya's Day celebrations.

Lassa was in no hurry for marriage, for she was just as lively a girl as her father feared. Her mother had explained the barest of the ways of men and women; her lilting Kellish accent made it more of a conspiracy than a lecture. "Once I had your father in better order we enjoyed one another well enow. He thinks he has his way and in most things he does, but not in that way," she'd chuckled. The whole subject made Lassa intensely curious; for this reason alone she looked forward to her wedding night. For now, she would relish her thrilling flirtation with Prince Andrin.

The Heir could not be called handsome. He had inherited his mother's dark complexion rather than his father's fair one, and his nose was a little too hawklike for fashion. But he danced gracefully and spoke well; his eyes were dark and liquid, and he smiled at her as if she were the only woman in the room. His plodding Leutish wife never entered her mind; the woman danced like a cart horse and spoke Tremontine in a horrible, thick accent. No wonder he preferred to flirt with pretty Lassa.

At dawn this morning, Lassa and the other courtiers had climbed the hill to the Wise One's Temple to see Silver-Eyed Eddin descend into His Embodiment. She'd never seen Him before. The God had moved through the crowd offering blessings and whispering secrets in ears. The listeners sometimes clapped with joy, sometimes glared across the room at one another. Eddin always told the truth but delighted in causing mischief, and those singled out often misinterpreted what they heard. Eddin had so favored her, raising her up to whisper in her ear: "Yours will be an exciting life, and you shall be the mother of a king."

Now as she danced with the Heir, Eddin's prophecy fluttered through Lassa's mind like the bright silver ribbons in her hair. She returned Prince Andrin's intimate smile. Perhaps Princess Inglatine would die or be set aside, and Andrin would marry her!

At dance's end, her father pulled her aside, a little too roughly for company. "That was very badly done, Lassanna!"

She laughed. "It's 'Lassanna,' is it, Papa? You must be put out with me indeed."

"It's nothing to laugh about!"

Lassa pulled against his grip. "Papa, you're treading on my sleeve. *Please* let go, people are beginning to stare."

Her father released her arm and raised his offending foot. "Damn these trailing sleeves! We'll speak later, my girl, and you won't be laughing afterwards!"

Gonnor was waiting when she came into her mother's rooms the next afternoon. "I disapprove your sleeping so late, Lassanna."

"The dancing didn't end until dawn, and I was having such wonderful fun, Papa! I don't know how you could stand to go to bed. I suppose when one is old—"

"I'm not old, I'm forty-eight!" He turned to Lassa's mother. "Woman! You should have made her come upstairs much, much earlier. Can I trust you with *nothing*?"

"My lord husband, she's just a girl, she should be allowed her high spirits—"

"High spirits? Girl? She's eighteen!" thundered Gonnor. "What's more, I forbid you to wear these new-styled dresses! Your mother knows well how I feel on this matter—you will not bespeak such another, madam!"

"Oh, don't be angry at Mama! Prince Andrin gave it to me."

Gonnor turned the shade of last night's wine. "You accepted it—and wore it? At *court*? What will people think? Pagg's balls, I know what they think already! Sittenna," he said to his wife, "you are a foolish woman to risk our family's honor so!"

"It was an Eddin's Day present, lord husband. He gave gifts to many here at court."

"Are all the Kells stupid, or just the one I married?" roared Gonnor. "If this is how you both intend to behave I will send you home to Whitehorse—under guard if I have to!"

"It's winter, lord husband," said Sittenna. "There's snow between here and Whitehorse. The Sella Gap must be closed. We won't be able to cross the Altennes until Spring's Beginning at the earliest."

Gonnor closed his aching eyes; she was right. Where could he send them? Sittenna's people were in Kellen, to the far west on the other side of the River Cobb. They might go by ship to Brunsial, her clan's seat on Kellen's coast, but it was no easy journey. No—he would send them to his sister at Summerford, further north on the Feather River and easily reached even now. A fast messenger sent on ahead could make the 150 miles upriver to herald their arrival in four days if the weather held; another four and his daughter would be far from scandal and temptation.

Word spread that Lord Gonnor was sending his women away, and to his surprise he received a summons from King Temmin. The Heir stood next to his father on the dais as Gonnor entered the King's chambers; Temmin looked bored, but Andrin's gaze made Gonnor's scalp prickle. "My Lord Whitehorse," said the King in his drawling Sairish accent, "we hear your wife and daughter are to leave us."

"Yes, Your Majesty," Gonnor answered. "In two days' time, for Castle Summerford. My sister—"

"Yes, yes," drawled the King, "but no. Your daughter is needed here. Lady Lassanna is to serve Princess Inglatine as lady-in-waiting. Her Highness's Leutish women are being sent home, d'you see. It is time she took on our Tremontine ways."

Gonnor blanched. "Your Majesty, your consideration is flattering, but my sister and her husband are expecting my daughter and Lady Whitehorse. A messenger has already been sent."

"We have intercepted him," said the King.

If ever Gonnor had worried for his youngest daughter, nothing matched the fear overtaking him now. "I see. I...I will tell my daughter of her new duties, then. The House of Whitehorse is honored. Your Majesty, Your Highness." He bowed and turned to leave.

"One last thing, Lord Whitehorse," called the King. Gonnor paused. "We sent your messenger onward with new instructions. Baron and Lady Summerford are now expecting you and your wife. We are certain you will enjoy a long visit."

A slow smile spread across the Prince's face. Gonnor's repressed anger racked his limbs. "Yes, Your Majesty. I will inform Lady Whitehorse directly and begin preparations for our journey."

Gonnor stalked from the audience hall to his family's apartments. Ordered to Summerford like a lackey, though on reflection he supposed he was. His family owed its duchy to Temmin the Great, after all, awarded for his great-grandfather's valor some sixty years ago in the conquest of Whitehorse. Giving his Lassanna to the Heir out of wedlock went far beyond fealty. If she got with child, her shame would devolve upon her family as well. Who would take her then? Perhaps the Prince might keep her under his protection for the child's sake. Andrin's grandfather Hildin the First had kept several ill-gotten offspring in the Mother's House. A pious institution for foundlings and destitute women, the Mother's House, but no daughter of Gonnor's would ever end up there. He'd see her dead before that.

When first she heard, Lassanna danced a gleeful little jig until her sleeves knocked over a pitcher. She loved her father and would miss him, but not his old-fashioned notions. Her sisters never got to be young; Papa made them take up husbands not long after they'd put down their dolls. Harla take her if Lassa wasn't going to have all the fun they missed out on.

Now, as she she watched her parents' caravan leave for the War Road, she dreaded their absence. The sharp wind coming through the unglazed window reminded her she now had little protection at court and no real advisors.

"Lady Lassanna," a servant called, "come away to your fitting!"

New dresses! Lassa almost skipped away from the chilly window after the servant, gloomy thoughts banished. *I will have the longest sleeves imaginable and pointed slippers too, see if I don't, Papa!*

Temmin came to himself, still feeling Lassa's delight in fashionable clothes and freedom. "She reminds me of Elly," he said.

Teacher echoed his smile. "Lassanna of Whitehorse could be said to be a spiritual sister to the Princess, yes."

"But why is her story important? It's not real history, is it?"

"The History contains the forgotten stories, especially those of the Kingdom's women—your family's women in particular. Did you know anything about Emmae before you heard her story?"

All the kings of Tremont—Temmin had the entire line memorized all the way back to Temmin the Great. But the queens? No, unless they brought substantial holdings or benefit to the Kingdom. Ilhovin the Peacemaker married a princess of Sairland and cemented the final truce between the colonizer and the once-colonized at last, for instance, but he didn't know her name. In marrying Princess Emmae, Warin the Wise secured Litta for his son Gethin the Third, but Temmin hadn't known her name or her story until Teacher told him last year.

"All right," Temmin admitted, "if you say it's important, then we start with her, and I'll find out what her connection is with Temmin the Bastard at some point, I suppose." He closed the book and began to rise from his chair when a thought took him. "Teacher, is there any news about my sister Mattie?"

"None that I have heard," said Teacher, sliding off the table. "Why?"

Temmin shrugged as if shaking off an irritation. "I feel responsible for her. If you hear anything you will let me know, won't you?"

"Of course. Shall we resume after lunch?"

By now the early spring sun was high in the sky, and Temmin was hungry. Obtaining lunch meant dealing with Harbis, but the big pain was probably already waiting in the hallway with a chafing dish. "If that means getting to the exciting part, I'm all for it."

Teacher nodded and left through the study door, admitting Harbis and his luncheon cart; the valet started back at the sight of Teacher, but once the black-robed figure disappeared down the hallyway, Harbis rolled his cart into the room with nary a rattle. Atop it sat the anticipated chafing dish and inside it was exactly what Temmin wanted: ribbony egg noodles in a thick sour cream sauce, with mushrooms and little meatballs—his favorite dish from home. *How did Harbis always know?*

By the time Teacher returned, Temmin had had about enough and paced up and down his study until Teacher arrived and Harbis beat a somewhat terrified retreat. "Pagg's balls, save me from this valet!" he shouted once the man was gone. "Only one thing ruffles him, and that's you. Don't leave. Ever."

"What a kind invitation," said Teacher.

"Don't leave, or go fetch Jenks from the Estate. Otherwise I'm going to wring this suave bastard's neck with his perfectly tied cravat."

"What is so odious about Mr Harbis?"

"What on earth do you mean?" said Temmin, continuing his pacing.

"He has perfect attention to detail, anticipates your needs, keeps a serene countenance—"

"Not when you're around. You scare him."

"Sir, I scare everyone," said Teacher. "It comes of the terrible parenting habit of threatening children with the Black Man. Apparently I look like this—this bugaboo."

"Oh, don't give me that," Temmin laughed, shaking his head. "You love it. You cultivate it."

Teacher ignored him. "It seems to me that your great complaint against Mr Harbis is that he is not Standfast Jenks."

Temmin gaped, arrested mid-stride. "Well of course that's my great complaint! He's always underfoot, not like Jenks a-tall!"

"Mr Jenks is usually underfoot, sir, and much noisier about it than Mr Harbis has ever dreamed of being. While he is an excellent man on the whole, Mr Jenks is not a touch upon Mr Harbis's professionalism."

"When I'm at the Temple, I'm too busy to miss him, and besides, Jenks in the Lovers' Temple doesn't bear thinking on." Temmin slumped onto the sofa. "When I'm here, though, I miss him terribly." He glanced up at the mirror above his mantelpiece and sat up straighter. "Say, could you do me a favor? Please let me see him. I'd feel better if I could get a glimpse of home."

"Very well." Teacher faced the mirror. "If Standfast Jenks is anywhere in sight of a reflection, show him to me."

The mirror wavered and resolved into a dim, grayed vantage point that moved from side to side in a dizzying manner. A somewhat weathered man appeared, brown eyes intent; a short-cropped beard marched over a strong jaw, and a receding hairline heightened an already great expanse of forehead. The man peered down before a cloth descended and blocked him from sight. After a minute of rigorous scrubbing the man reappeared more clearly than before. He wore a shirt, open at the collar, its sleeves rolled up and a waistcoat over it. The vantage point dipped and swayed again as the man squinted with first one eye, then the other. A satisfied smile broke out on his face. As he stood up the view switched to trousers ending in a pair of carpet slippers; they walked away. The mirror went dark before resolving into Temmin's study.

"I do believe," said Teacher, "that the reflection was from a pair of boots."

"*That's* what I'm talking about!" exclaimed Temmin, leaping to his feet. "He can get a shine on boots—"

"—That I am sure Mr Harbis can match if not surpass." Teacher put a quelling hand on Temmin's shoulder. "Another year. It will pass quickly."

"What's a year to you?" grumbled Temmin. "You have all the years you want."

Teacher took a step back and snapped, "I have not wanted the years I have had."

Temmin started; Teacher rarely displayed such intense emotion. "I'm sorry." He ruffled his hair, dislodging his queue again. "I won't miss him as much once I'm at the Temple, and I'm going back as soon as Cousin Donnis arrives."

"You are going back when it is safe. Which," Teacher amended, "will likely coincide with the Marchioness's arrival. I am sorry too, Your Highness. My sensibilities are difficult for others to understand. A long life is not necessarily a happy one. Let us not dwell on it, for at present there is nothing to be done for it. If you would, please," Teacher finished with a gesture toward the book.

Temmin studied his father's chief counselor, who was under some unknown compulsion to serve the royal family. He knew Teacher hadn't enjoyed serving those like Hildin the Usurper—an evil, troubled man if ever there was one—but surely serving Hildin's brother Warin hadn't been so bad, or even serving Temmin's father. From what he'd heard in his time at the Temple and from Sedra, Harsin wasn't a bad king—merely ruthless in the ways in which a monarch must be from time to time.

Temmin nodded, opened the book, and let it take him away.

Inglatine was just as dull and plodding as expected. She groped for words in her horrendous Tremontine until she lapsed into either Leutish or Old Sairish. Lassanna knew Old Sairish alone of the ladies-in-waiting; her mother had insisted her girls be educated as she was, despite Tremontine custom. Knowing Old Sairish was fortunate, if translating for a lump like Inglatine could be considered so.

Lassa sorted fine wool threads for Inglatine's embroidery, and helped put her to bed at night; the Princess insisted Lassa was the only one who could properly comb out her stubborn, impossibly yellow hair. Lassa soon found herself in the unwelcome position of favorite, but even as tiresome as

Inglatine was, Lassa had to acknowledge her kind, gentle manner.

Court life made it bearable: dancing, feasting, music, entertainments of all kinds, often in the Sairish way even with the two countries on the brink of war. Though the King had spent many years in Sairland and its territories, his chief counselor Teacher insisted the Sairish should not only be opposed but driven back. Land gained was magic gained.

"We'll make merry while we may, Lady Lassanna," smiled Andrin one night as they danced. "Soon enow we'll march to war."

"How sad I shall be, Your Highness, to be deprived of such company," said Lassa, demurely keeping her eyes to one side.

His grasp on her hand tightened. "Who do you watch, my lady?"

Lassa brought her startled gaze back to him. "No one, sir, no one at all."

"I am happiest when you look at no other."

"As you say, sir," she replied, keeping her troubled eyes on him from then on.

That night, the uneasy Lassanna tended to the Princess, unfastening her veil and shaking out the unruly yellow torrent beneath. "What ails you, dear Lassa?" said Inglatine in her heavy Tremontine.

"Nothing, ma'am, nothing at all." She began to comb.

"I wish you to call me Tina," the Princess continued in more comfortable if stilted Old Sairish. "No one knows or cares for me as do you. My husband loves me not, you know."

Lassa cringed but kept combing. "Oh, Your Highness, say not—"

Inglatine stopped her hand. "We are honest with one another, you and I. I am not stupid, though it is supposed that I am because I speak Tremontine little—and badly. Andrin does not often come to me, and when he does he cares not. But it matters not. I am with child." Inglatine removed her hand, and Lassa speechlessly began combing again. The Princess lapsed into silence, her head pulling back in gentle snaps against Lassa's combing. "He likes not women with child," she resumed. "He will leave my bed, perhaps forever if it is a son—I *pray* for a son so he will leave me alone. Yours I think will be his bed now," she added in Tremontine.

Lassa dropped the comb. "Oh, no, Your Highness! I am sure...that is, the Prince certainly..." Flattery evaded her honest tongue. "I wish it not. Were he to ask me—"

"You would say yes," said Inglatine in Old Sairish. "You *will* say yes. I bar not your way, no, I approve."

"But I want my own husband, not someone else's!"

Inglatine bent and picked up the comb. "That is not what Andrin thinks, nor is it what anyone else thinks." She gave Lassa the comb but held onto one end, squinting up at her lady-in-waiting. "Do you know not why you were kept from going to Summerford? I think perhaps you are the stupid one."

Lassa blushed. Any Eddin-inspired thoughts she'd had of the Prince were as a husband not a lover, after some vague unfortunate occurrence to Inglatine. She had no intention of letting any man into her bed unmarried. "My father does not approve."

"Oh, but I think it matters not," Inglatine smiled. She let go the comb with a careless gesture. "Either way, Andrin will not let you go. Finish my hair. I am tired and wish to sleep now."

Inglatine's bluntness kept Lassa wakeful that night; she sat brooding before her fire, watching the flames fall to embers. She decided Inglatine wouldn't know a flirtation from an argument and went to bed.

The court agreed with Inglatine, with reason. Andrin sat Lassa next to him at meals, Inglatine on his other side. He danced almost entirely with Lassa in the evenings. He insisted Lassa call him An, as he was called among family and friends. He came to the Princess's bower but spent his time there flirting with Lassa. Within the week the courtiers began flattering Lassa, the men keeping one eye always on the Heir and the women sneering behind their hands.

Almost a spoke after Lassa's awkward exchange with Inglatine, An appeared in the bower doorway; behind him came a page carrying a pretty lacquer box. "Gifts for my wife and her ladies to celebrate the blessed event to come." The boy opened the box to reveal several small cases. An opened one; it contained a mirror. The ladies-in-waiting each received one, silver chased with patterns in the Sairish style; the Princess's mirror was the same, though decorated with costly mother-of pearl and rich enamel.

Lassa's mirror outshone the Princess's. It had no case; its back formed a stand. Gems inlaid its gold rim. Inglatine didn't seem to care. She thanked her husband and placidly adjusted her veil. Lassa accepted her mirror, knowing she should not but afraid to refuse. An's attentions and gifts must soon be paid for, a thought both frightening and thrilling.

She stayed in her room that night, claiming the headache. The mirror stood on her dressing stand; she kept catching unsettling flashes in the corner of her eye—reflections of flickering candlelight or her own uneasy movement around the room—until she developed a real headache, called for her maid and undressed for bed. When the woman was gone, Lassa reached to snuff out her candle.

The mirror's surface began to ripple; she stared at it, one hand at her mouth, the other at her stomach as the gift's intent became clear. An swirled from the mirror and solidified. "Don't put out the candle just yet, Lassa," he smiled.

Lassa's own father held some small magic, and she'd seen King Temmin and Prince Andrin work magics at court, but never had she seen a royal pass through a reflection. She curtsied, shaking as she did so and holding her chemise against her throat with one hand. He raised her up by the other. "Don't be afraid. Does this displease you? I thought my attentions quite welcome."

She stepped away from him, still shaking. "I hadn't intended, Your Highness…that is, I am rather surprised…your consideration of my family has been most kind…"

"You sound like your father," An laughed. "Your family has nothing to do with this. If I want you, you're mine. You're eager for me, aren't you?"

Lassa flushed so hard she thought she must glow like the fire's coals. "I have not allowed myself to think of it, Your Highness."

"Then think of it," he said, brushing his fingers against her cheek. He stepped closer; his fingers trailed down her neck, tracing her collarbone to the ribbon of her chemise. "Think of it, Lassa." He undid the ribbon.

She grabbed at the cloth as it slipped from her shoulders. *Think of it. No? Yes? Yes.* She dropped her hand and her hesitation. *I will be the mother of a king, he will marry me and I will be the mother of a king.*

Lassanna continued to wait on Inglatine, whose self-confidence grew with her belly. "The Prince has left my bed entirely! Such a relief!" said the Princess in her much-improved Tremontine one night. "You are keeping him amused for me, Lassa dear."

"Your hair is truly beautiful now, Your Highness," murmured Lassa. "Pregnancy suits you."

"Pregnancy suits no woman. Though you are right, my hair grows quickly now. Such a long time it takes you to make the braids, and I must take care not to sit on them when you are through. You had better hurry, my girl. He waits for you and he is an impatient lover. He was with me, anyway. In, out, done." Inglatine stroked her rounding belly. "I wish Teacher might know if it is a son. But he only knows the King's sons, not the Heir's. Ah, you must be a boy, little one! Then it will be you and me, you and me and your father gone from my bed forever. No, I expect he will insist on a second boy. But *then*—then we will be free of one another, the Prince and I! Who will be the happier? I cannot say!"

This was a conversation Lassa did not wish to have ever again.

"You must stay in the Princess's service," said An as they lay in bed that night. "There must be some excuse for keeping you here. It's either service or marriage, and I cannot bear the thought of you married to some minor lordling."

"You're the Heir," pouted Lassa. "Can you not do as you please?"

"Proprieties, darling, proprieties!" He kissed her, and she forgot her frets.

The Princess gave birth to a girl. "Well, now I have *some* little soul to love me," said Inglatine. "The Prince will pester me again, but just when the Sisters deem me most likely to conceive. You will have to do without your lover for seven days a moon, my dear."

"Oh, ma'am, I wish you wouldn't talk to me like this!" said Lassa.

Inglatine patted her hand. "You do not love me. I know this. But you are the closest thing I have to a friend here—yes, I consider you my friend, for you have taken a burden from me and I will be grateful to you whether you would have it or not. You never lie to me, you are as kind as you can manage, and you are not jealous. When you need a friend, you may always turn to me."

How could Lassa be jealous of Inglatine? Here was a woman far from home, unloved, awkward and disregarded at court. An never told Lassa he loved her, but his actions proved he did. Her favorites became An's favorites, in music, in food, in dancing, in people. The ambitious curried her favor, and some even gave her messages to pass to him. Some she repeated. Many she did not, as she pleased. Politics were all one to her.

On Farr's Day Eve, the gardens of the Keep filled with merrymakers, though fall's first knife tip was in the air. Clowns play-acted the tourneys that would fill Farr's Ground the next day, tumbling and beating one another with beribboned sticks, and wherever one walked, music and beauty awaited. An and Lassa wore matching cloth of gold, their huge, scalloped sleeves so long they trailed far behind them. Inglatine was nowhere in sight. The couple walked away from the noise and the torchlight, Lassa pouting at some pretended slight. "No, you do not care for me," she said, suppressing laughter.

"How may I prove it, Lady? Name it, and you may have it. Say it, and I will do it."

She paused, putting a considering finger to one cheek. "Something magnificent. Something very vulgar and very public."

An smiled and faced the gathering behind them. He raised his hands. Balls of flame rose from every torch, shocking the crowd into silence. Bows stilled and pipes fell from lips as even the musicians stopped to stare. The flames climbed into the sky, tails streaming behind them like comets as they rose higher and higher until they all burst into tiny sparks that spelled out "Lassa the Beautiful" before floating back down to earth and rejoining the torches. The revelers burst into applause. Lassa caught a white face, ghostly in the shadows of the arches leading back into the Keep's courtyards; the King's advisor Teacher was frowning up at the sky. Lassa shivered and looked up herself. A few dwindling sparks still lit the night, and she forgot the figure in the shadows in her delight.

Lassa missed her moon. Twice.

She consulted a Sister in secret. "There must be something you can do, some way to stop the child?"

"We do not end pregnancies, especially royal ones," huffed the priestess.

Soon Lassa could no longer hide her blossoming belly from her lover. "You're *with child*? Lassa, you were not meant to be the mother of my children! You were to be everything *but* that! Did you not listen to the Sisters? Had you paid so little attention to their teachings?"

"You insisted even when I told you it was the wrong time of my moon!"

An turned purple. "You *dare* blame me for this! I have no use for you at present—I despise pregnant women. Go home to your father. When your confinement is over you may return."

"What about the child?"

"What do I care?" said An. "Send it to the Mother's House. With luck it will go to the Hill. I'm leaving for a tour of the Sairish reinforcements along the border at Valleysmouth. When I return, you will be gone."

Lassa sent word to her father, not knowing what to expect. Perhaps he would let her come home. But what if he didn't? Would her aunt take her in at Summerford? Not against her father's wishes. She might throw herself on the mercy of the Mothers, but to work like a slave in this new Mother's House—she trembled and waited for the messenger's return.

The messenger did not return; Gonnor of Whitehorse did.

He strode straight into the Princess's bower, scattering servants and ladies alike with the flat of his sword, bellowing, "Girl, did I not tell you I would kill you rather than see Whitehorse shamed?" The Duke deflated at the sight of his daughter cowering in a corner. "Lassanna, my darling, my baby girl, how could you do it? How could you let him do this to you?"

"You yourself know how little choice I had in the matter!" she cried.

"Do not blame me for this state of affairs! I love you, Lassa! Now, be a good girl," said her father, suddenly coaxing. "Come out into the courtyard and I will make your death as painless as possible. Don't make me stain the Princess's chambers with blood."

Inglatine placed herself between them, legs planted firmly on the floor. "This lady is under my protection."

"I am within my rights as her father, Your Highness," growled Gonnor.

"Oh, to be sure, but she is my lady and friend. To kill her you must come through me." Inglatine bounced the baby in her arms. "You would kill a Princess of Tremont—two princesses? To kill *me* would bring more than shame. The King would slaughter your House, to the last girl child."

Gonnor lowered the blade. "You cannot stand in my way forever. Sooner or later Lassanna will leave this room, and I will be waiting." He sheathed his sword and left.

Inglatine gave the baby to another lady. "We have little time." She grabbed the shaking Lassa's arm and dragged her into the Princess's bedchamber. She took a heavy cloak from its hook, threw it into Lassa's arms and ran to a chest; she fished out a purse and thrust it at Lassa as well. Inglatine ripped aside a tapestry on the wall to uncover an opening. "This passage leads to An's rooms. They say you Whitehorsers are born in the saddle, yes?"

Lassa followed her mistress through a narrow passageway to a tapestry-covered door into An's familiar bedchamber; she wondered if Inglatine had heard them making love. "Why are you doing this?"

Inglatine produced a key on what Lassa had assumed was a decorative chatelaine, pushed back another tapestry on the far wall and unlocked a hidden door. "I have told you, you are my friend. You do not love me, but you have never lied to me and have often been kind. An has shown me these stairs to the stables—they are a secret." Inglatine shooed her through the door and shut it behind them; they plunged together into the dark, feeling their way down the stairs as quickly as they could without tumbling headlong. Shame filled Lassa's heart. In many ways the Princess had been her sole friend since her parents' departure, the one person who didn't want something from her other than simple companionship.

A crack of light revealed a door; the faint smell of horses reached her nose. "Hush now," said Inglatine, "I am not sure what we will find. But our choices are limited, yes?" She fitted her key in the lock. The door swung open on silent hinges and they walked through it into the tack room. "Put on the cloak and stay there, Lassa."

Inglatine returned with a reedy young man barely out of boyhood with hair even more yellow than her own. "This is Hanni der Geelt—called Yellow Hanni here. He was once of my escort and has gone on many travels with the King. He will know the way. Where can you go? Summerford?"

"No, that's the first place Papa would look—yes! My mother's people in Kellen! My uncle, Williard ar Sial! I stayed in their holding at Brunsial on the Kellish coast for a whole year with my mother. Kellish ways are different. They will take me in, and it's not too snowy yet to cross the border."

Inglatine said something in Leutish to the reedy groom; he responded with a great gout of words and much gesticulating in Lassa's direction. "Hanni says he knows well the way to Kellen. He is yours now—a good horseman, good fighter, better bowman and so very loyal." The young man rushed off; Lassa took in his flailing arms and legs, and rather doubted his martial prowess. "I have told him to do as you say, that you are his mistress now," continued Inglatine, "but he does not speak much Tremontine yet outside stable talk. That, he knows. Poor Hanni der Geelt, now he will have to learn Kellish, too. I must return the way I came. Stay here until Hanni returns." Inglatine embraced her. "I will miss you, Lassa."

Lassa clung to the Princess. "Oh, how I've misjudged you, ma'am! How kind you are, and how sorry I am!"

"Now, now, yes. When I can set up my own household I will send word and you shall come to me. Perhaps my next two babies will be boys, eh? Then we will both be free." Inglatine hugged her one last time and slipped through the hidden door; the lock shot home.

When they were well away from the Keep, Lassa was stiff from riding and needed to piss. The wind cut through her cloak. They had no food, though Yellow Hanni pointed to his bow and insisted he was a fine hunter. Or at least that's what she thought he said. Hanni was murmuring incomprehensibly to his horse; how would she ever talk to the man? She looked down at her own mount. There was something familiar in the mare's lines, as if she recognized it. "Hanni, which horse is this?"

"To His Highness Lord of Whitehorse has given her," said the groom, "so I for you get. You like? Best mare in stable is!"

"My father's horse is carrying me away from him."

"No worries, Lady. I, Hanni der Geelt, take care of you will!"

Lassa raised her head to the cold sky and burst into tears.

No matter how vivid a dream might be, it could never match the book. It immersed Temmin so thoroughly he could not remember being anyone but a miserable pregnant girl running from her own father. The winter cold faded from Temmin's bones as he came back to himself. He shook out his arms to make his shivering stop. "If I were…*being*…a person in the book, and that person died, would I die too?"

"No, no," Teacher reassured him, "you would simply move to another vantage point in the story. Why, are you concerned for Lassanna?"

"No—well, yes, but it's more that I feel everything so very acutely—I forget I'm *me*. I'd forgotten how disconcerting it is." The shivering stopped to let a different cold creep in. "Could a father really kill his daughter for having a child out of wedlock?"

"Oh, fathers were within their rights to kill a daughter for burning the soup. Children were property. Children still are property, though killing them for one's family honor has generally fallen out of favor. Mother's Houses are somewhat to thank. If a girl in danger of an honor killing makes it to a Temple of Amma she is under its protection—no one can touch her. The Mothers then demand assistance for the girl's upkeep and that of her child in accordance with Pagg's Law, usually from the man who fathered the child. It became such a problem during the reign of Hildin the First that he helped found the first Mother's House here in the Capital. Within a hundred years every larger Temple of Amma had its Mother's House, and honor killings became rare."

Temmin realized he'd been leaning forward in his chair, wedging his hands between his torso and the table edge; he leaned back and flexed his cramped fingers. "I can't imagine it ever being legal for fathers to kill their children."

"It is quite legal now. Wives as well. Both under certain circumstances, of course, spelled out in Pagg's Law—I can find the correct citations for you, if you would care to read them." Teacher crossed the room to the bookshelves. "I believe your Presentation Day copy of the Law is somewhere in this room, though the writing is quite small and the jeweled covers have been removed for safekeeping. Those copies are made more for decoration than use—"

Temmin rose from the library chair. "No, no, unnecessary. What circumstances would make the murder of a wife or child legal?"

"Interpretation of the Law changes with the times, sir. Early in the Law's history a man might kill his wife, unmarried daughter or son not come of age for no reason whatsoever and face nothing more than a fine, the 'blood debt.' It was a fine large enough that a poor man might think twice and abandon a troublesome wife or cast out a pregnant daughter. Even so, I have known many cases over the centuries of men who were indentured for most of their lives to pay off a blood debt. The Fathers currently deem proven adultery as the only pardonable reason to kill one's wife. The blood debt must still be paid, but in all other cases, it is imprisonment or death. As for children, it is disobedience, though a great burden of proof falls on the father and the blood debt is high—higher than for the killing of a wife if the murdered child is a son."

"I suppose that's fair," mused Temmin, "a life still to be lived, worth more than a life that—no, there's nothing fair about it. Can a wife kill a husband or child?"

"Under no circumstances. It is death."

"No blood debt?"

"None. Death and denial of burial rites."

Temmin shook his head. "This is why I never studied the Law in depth. I don't like it." He gazed out the window; the struggling spring sun hovered low in the sky. "I want to go check on my mother—make sure she's eaten. Perhaps you can tell me what happened to this girl tomorrow."

FIVE

Temmin spent another morning dragging his mother out to ride, and in spite of herself, she almost bloomed in the fresh air and sun. Temmin began to wonder if perhaps he should stay, but after breakfast, alone in his study, his vows to the Temple convinced him otherwise. Donnis would be here any day, and with Neya's Day so close he couldn't ask for further leave. When Donnis came he would be easier in his mind. He would make sure she continued prying Mama from her rooms into the wider world.

The mirror above his mantel wavered. He looked up to see Teacher in the Tower Library, hands open in inquiry; Temmin mimed a welcome, and Teacher swirled into the room. "Shall we hear more of the story today, Your Highness? It is our last chance for now. I have seen Lady Donnis. She arrives this afternoon. You may return to the Temple this evening."

"Oh. Well, it's for the best, I suppose."

"You are less enthusiastic than I expected. Are you concerned about your mother, or does another matter weigh on you?" Temmin hesitated. Teacher added, "I have never betrayed a confidence of yours, sir, nor will I ever."

"No, you've always been true to me, even when it's made trouble for you," sighed Temmin. "I'm having difficulty with my vows."

"You wish to leave?"

"No, no, but it's increasingly difficult." Temmin began to pace. "There is someone at the Temple…"

"Someone with whom you are in conflict?"

Temmin laughed. "It'd be easier if I were. I could manage that."

"Oh. Someone with whom you are in love, then. You find this troublesome."

Temmin nodded, eyes on the floor as he paced in slow steps. "It's against our vows and training. Only the love we should hold for everyone is allowed. Loving someone specifically, any exclusivity, jealousy—those emotions are not allowed."

"May I venture to ask upon whom your heart has settled?"

"No," snapped Temmin, "you may not. I will say only that—that it's the worst possible thing that could have happened, with the worst possible person, and I don't know how to make it stop."

"Have you talked with the Most Highs? Senior staff like Barik and Glaes? Allis and Issak?"

Temmin shook his head, loosening strands from his heretofore neat queue; they fell across his eyes and he pushed them back. "I can't tell anyone at the Temple. I don't want any consequences to fall on her—this person." He blushed.

"Ah," said Teacher.

Temmin realized he'd revealed himself and cursed inwardly. "There are times I wonder if I have learned anything at all in that pink heap as my father calls it."

"The Lovers' Temple of all places knows how to deal with such feelings. You must ask for help."

Temmin stopped in his pacing and peered at his counselor from beneath the stray strands once again crossing his face. *I'm not altogether sure I want to deal with these feelings.* He pushed the thought away with his hair. "I'll think about it. In the meantime, take my mind off it. Tell me more about the girl." He crossed to the library table; the old book sat where it had been left the day before. Temmin wondered why Harbis hadn't put it back on the lectern. That accursed valet must have known he'd want it on the table, damn the man. Temmin smoothed his fingers over the cover, opened it, and let himself fall in.

Lassanna and Yellow Hanni arrived at Brunsial, the seat of her mother's clan, after many days' travel; her uncle, his wife, their two sons and their daughter welcomed her as their own. "I will never understand the Tremontines," said Lord Williard ar Sial. "I told my sister not to marry that man. We should have gone into Whitehorse and fetched her back. Threatening to kill you—how is that honorable? Here you are an exile from home, and what of the child's father? I doubt any so-called dishonor has devolved upon *him*. No, you are welcome here, my dear."

"You haven't seen me since my childhood," said Lassa.

"You're the spitting image of your mother and grandmother. I would know you anywhere." Williard embraced her. "I will send word to your family. They must know you are safe. Your father will regret his temper soon enough."

But when the time came for the baby, no word had come from Whitehorse. Had she known how hard the birth would be, Lassa would have let her father kill her. As it was she almost died. "It grieves me to say you will never have another one, ma'am," said the midwife as she washed her hands afterwards.

"*I* am not grieved in the least," mumbled Lassa. She promptly fell asleep, her new little boy swaddled beside her.

Lord Williard gave the baby a name: Tennoc ar Sial. "He'll carry the clan name, none of this no-name business of the Tremontines." Lassa became Lassanna ar Sial after a letter from her mother warned her not to return to Whitehorse; her father had stripped her of his surname.

Lassa spent the first few spokes of Tennoc's life at Brunsial. She exchanged letters with her mother and Princess Inglatine—the former secretive and brief, the latter long and chatty. Inglatine gave birth to another girl. *Alas, dear Lassa,* she wrote, *I am not to be free of the Prince any time soon, it appears! Why could I not have given birth to the son? Then we might live together away from court, you and I, and be comfortable. But no, I will have my own boy soon enough.*

Williard ar Sial's country court at Brunsial was pleasant enough, but Lassa missed the brightness and pleasure of a city court like the Keep; she was still young, mother or no. She confessed to envy when King Dunnoc called her painfully shy cousin Flaryn to serve as lady-in-waiting to young

Queen Hallia. "Oh, do come with me, Lassa!" wailed Flaryn. "Father says I must go to represent the clan, but Mother can't come with me and I can't go alone, I just can't!"

So Lassanna went to Gwyrfal, taking Hanni with her; the man refused to leave her and would have walked the entire way if she hadn't taken him. "My Lady Inglatine said serve you, and protect you I, Hanni, will do with my life!" He brandished the bow he carried whenever they rode out. Though Lassa remained unconvinced of his skill in battle, she had to admit the man was an unparalleled archer in more peaceful settings; if not for him, they might have starved on the journey to Kellen.

Lassa left Tennoc behind at Brunsial; the baby would do fine, everyone was sure. But not a spoke passed before Lassa sent for her son in a paroxysm of longing.

Even with the baby in company, she entered into life at Gwyrfal with a flair her cousin could not muster. Flaryn was the most beautiful woman at court, but so timid and overwhelmed that she faded into the background. Worse: cheerful, busy Queen Hallia made the poor girl nervous.

Not Lassa. Though she had no official position at court, she rapidly became a favorite. King Dunnoc and Queen Hallia set great store by her. Dunnoc was an older man, but Hallia was just Lassa's age and much like her in her love for merriment and music. As it is with so many mothers, though, their sons cemented Lassa and Hallia's friendship. Kenver was a year and a half older than Tennoc; as soon as Tennoc could reliably run, the two boys became fierce companions and the terror of the nursery—a terror briefly interrupted by the arrival of Kenver's little sister Gwynna. They were Kenver-and-Tennoc, one boy with two bodies.

By then Lassa's shy cousin had married an inland baronet and retired to a quiet life within a few days' ride of Brunsial. Lassa officially took her place as first among Hallia's ladies-in-waiting, and Tennoc took his place as companion to the royal children. Though the courtiers accepted and even loved Tennoc, he knew his place even at a young age: he had no father, and as the Tremontine king's bastard he was always suspect.

"So, bread, where's butter?"

Seven-year-old Tennoc squinted up into the sudden shadow over the rose bed where he was digging; the King towered over him, blocking the sun. "Ken? He's lookin' for good rocks—um, h'lo, Your Majesty." Tennoc always tried to remember the formalities, but here in the nursery and its attendant gardens he could not imagine the King as anyone other than the father of Kenver and Gwynna.

Dunnoc squatted down next to him. "Rocks, is it?" The King smelled of fresh sweat, leather and horses, so different from the usual nursery smells of oatmeal mush, wet woolens and chamomile tea. Was that what all fathers smelled like? Tennoc liked it, and the way the King's gray eyes crinkled at the corner when he was interested or amused.

Kenver had gray eyes like his father, and not for the first time Tennoc wondered what color his own father's eyes were. Where they blue like his? He resumed his excavations, suddenly self-conscious. "He should have come back by now. I wish he would. This bird won't bury itself."

"Bird?"

"Aye, Gwynna found a dead bird and cried so much over it that Ken promised her we'd build it a Hill. She's off picking flowers for it or something stupid." Tennoc lifted a worm from his trowel and gently patted it back into the dirt. "D'you suppose Harla takes the souls of birds, sir?"

"Hm. That's a good question, Tennoc, and one better asked of a Friend than myself. But I've always believed animals have souls as good as ours— most of my horses more so. So if you want an old soldier's opinion, yes, I believe She does."

"I hope so, otherwise Ken and I are going through all this for nothing," grumbled Tennoc, though to be truthful he and Kenver were enjoying this morose little pantomime. Kenver had even saved three of the bird's brilliant red wing feathers for their respective treasure boxes—even Gwynna's, though she lost things. Then again, she was five.

The King grinned. "No good deed is for naught, young Tennoc." He stood up, setting the brass rings on his leather tunic to jingling. He pushed his blue cloak back over his shoulder. "Where is the Queen?"

"She's with Mama," said Tennoc, not looking up.

"That would be where, little man?" An edge of exasperation tinged the King's voice.

Tennoc dropped his trowel and sprang up, wiping his hands on his tunic. "I'm sorry, sir, they're drinking wine beneath the willow trees yonder. Mama says Her Majesty isn't feeling well in this warm weather."

"This far along women with child don't feel well in *cold* weather. They're miserable until the child comes, so they make everyone else miserable. But you'll find all that out in due time. Hallia will be right as rain again any day now."

Tennoc stood at near-attention until the King patted him on the shoulder and walked off to find the Queen. When he was sure the King had forgotten him, Tennoc cast about for Kenver—there he was, solemnly approaching the rose bed with his sister, tow-headed Kenver with an armful of rocks, strawberry blonde Gwynna with a little bundle wrapped in a scrap of red cloth and a basket of flowers over her arm.

"We have to do thith right or Harla won't take her," said Gwynna. "I'll thay the words and you thay the other parts."

"Do you even know the words? You've never even been inside a Hill. *I* have," said Kenver.

"What about the bird's final bath?" added Tennoc.

"I cried on her," sniffed Gwynna, adding, "you dug the hole too deep, Tennoc." She lay the little body in the grave, added a few strands of her pale red-gold hair, and got most of the burial ceremony right; the boys gave the proper responses with a seriousness that surprised Tennoc even as he spoke them.

Kenver stacked the rocks atop the red bundle and mounded them up into a satisfying, out-of-proportion monument to the deceased bird; Gwynna arranged her homely little bundle of dandelions, daisies and pinks atop it. "That's that," said Kenver, dusting off his hands.

All three children turned at a cry from the willow trees. Kenver and Gwynna ran to the willow's shade, Tennoc close behind. "What'th wrong, Mama?" said Gwynna.

"It's time for the babe, that's all, sweetheart," said her father.

Queen Hallia leaned against him puffing, a strange look between a grimace and a smile on her face. "Don't worry, my darling," she said when she'd caught her breath. "After the two of you, this baby will come quickly. Then you'll have a little sister or brother."

But the baby did not come quickly, and in the end both the tiny baby boy and Queen Hallia died.

Kenver-and-Tennoc became Kenver. The boy retreated into himself, leaving Tennoc sitting in the garden alone with Gwynna most days. "What did I do? How come he doesn't like me any more?"

"You've thtill got a mama and we don't." Gwynna's lisp had worsened. "I want my mama, Tennoc!"

"Oh, Gwynna, don't cry!" He threw his arms around the little girl. "Look, you can borrow my mama. She can't have any more children, and I don't have a father anyway to give me a brother or sister, so there's lots of her left over and I'm sure she'd like a daughter, so please don't cry!"

"I want *my* mama!" she sobbed. Further persuasion made her cry harder. Tennoc finally took her to her grandmother the Dowager Queen and went in search of his mother.

Mama dressed in black now—everyone did. Tennoc didn't like black. It didn't suit her; it dulled her eyes and made her skin look sallow and pale. He burrowed against her until she let him into her lap. "I don't like it here now," he grumbled. "Gwynna cries all the time, Ken won't talk to me, everyone wears black."

"Well, my sweetheart, we may be going back to Brunsial in any event. I represented Clan Sial in the Queen's court, and with her gone…" Mama grimaced, close to tears. "Now that she's gone we have no reason to be here." She hugged him tight.

Leave Gwyrfal? He'd said he didn't like it there any more, but leaving was another matter entirely. "I don't remember Brunsial. Is it nice there?"

"Oh yes. Lord Williard—our uncle, you know—he's very kind, and your great-grandmother is there. She is very, very old now, and I know she would love to see you. Home is very nice."

"How can you call Brunsial home? Gwyrfal's home, not Brunsial. Oh, Mama, I'm sorry, don't cry! What did I say? Don't cry!"

"I'm sorry, Tennoc!" she sobbed. "Hallia made this place home for us. Now that she's gone I don't know where we belong. We can't go to our real home, ever. That's Whitehorse. Your grandfather…I shouldn't be talking to you like this, I'm sorry, darling. I'll stop." She controlled her tears and wiped her red, puffy eyes.

His mother never said much about Lord Grandfather. He knew from gossip that the Duke had tried to kill his mother before his birth. If Lord Grandfather hated Mama, then he hated Lord Grandfather. He didn't know what to think about his father. If his mother said little about the Duke of Whitehorse, she said even less about King Andrin. The closest he'd ever come to a father was King Dunnoc. "Mightn't the King let us stay if we ask him?" he faltered. "You and he are good friends."

Mama shook her head. "I can't, sweetheart. I really had no business being here in the first place."

Lassanna did her best to adjust to life back at Brunsial. Her grandmother went into ecstasies at their return, and everyone doted on Tennoc. "It is past time and past you got married, niece," said Williard. "The boy needs a father."

"The boy needs a father, indeed," she retorted, "and if I find a man I like who will accept Tennoc as equal to his own children, then perhaps I shall."

Many suitors came to Brunsial just to be turned away, some gently and some not. None would accept Tennoc as his own. The final suitor came at the midpoint of the year: King Dunnoc and his children arrived for a long visit, setting the small castle a-boil as a beehive.

After a brief awkwardness, Kenver and Tennoc became Kenver-and-Tennoc again, tearing through the hallways and raiding the kitchens until the seneschal threw them outside to pester the stablehands and dig up the garden. Two weeks into the royal visit, Lassanna and the King sat in a sheltered grove overlooking the long, rolling grasslands leading to the Western Sea and the white chalk cliffs that gave Brunsial its name. Tennoc, Kenver and an outclassed-but-game Gwynna were fighting among the trees, using fallen branches for swords; Yellow Hanni, long promoted from horse-herder to child-herder, oversaw the matches, pronouncing the outcomes in his comical Kellish.

"It pleases me to see the children so happy again," said Lassanna. "Tennoc has missed Kenver greatly. How…how are they doing now?"

"Since Hallia died? Don't be afraid to say her name, you of all people—her dearest friend. As long as you and I and the children live, she lives. Speak her name. It gives me comfort." Dunnoc shifted on the stone bench. "It gives me comfort just to be near you, to be truthful. You remind me of her, and the good times. It's why I came to Brunsial. Ken and Gwynna miss you and the boy. *I* miss you." He took Lassa's hand, and she turned from watching the children to the man beside her. "Lassa, I want you to come back to Gwyrfal."

Return to Gwyrfal? She wanted nothing more! Lassa's heart expanded, but past experience stayed her immediate answer. "At the risk of presumption, may I ask in what role, Your Majesty?"

Dunnoc laughed. "Older and wiser, eh, my lady?" At her darkening expression he added, "Nay, nay, don't think ill of me. It was a bad attempt at jest. Forgive me. I will speak honestly. I have put great thought to remarrying. I am lonely. Mistresses do not suit me. I never took one while Hallia lived, and I have found no comfort in them since her death though I have tried. As for Beloveds, well, you can't bring one home to warm the bed at night, can you?"

"Are you asking me to marry you, sir?" said Lassa in disbelief.

"I am asking you for permission to court you. I have asked your uncle for his blessing and he has given it, but only if you are willing to consider me."

Lassa stared off toward the sea, glittering in the distance; the children had changed their sticks from swords to horses and were galloping from the grove onto the open sward, Hanni strolling behind them. Their trails through the tall grass wove together in a loose braid, the three paths coming apart and crossing again. "What about Tennoc? What rank would he hold?"

Dunnoc raised his eyebrows. "Rank? Surely you're not asking me to make him equal to Kenver and Gwynna."

"No, of course not." Lassa brought her gaze away from the children and back to the King. "But I want to make sure your lords understand he is to be respected and that he is not to be treated with contempt or as anything less than honorable. He is not to blame for his birth."

"So you will consider my suit?"

"What will be Tennoc's rank?" she insisted.

Dunnoc frowned and released the hand he'd been holding. "I don't understand your concern. Tennoc has always had royal favor and has been accepted in court."

"Tennoc is a sweet-faced little boy right now. In ten years he'll be a man. I don't want your nobles guarding their daughters when it comes time for him to wed, or conspiring to cast him out somehow."

"You know it is less that he is fatherless than that he is the son of the Tremontine king—the only son. How many daughters has Queen Inglatine given Andrin now?"

"Five, poor Tina. Every letter is full of how badly she wishes to be done with him."

"Were she my wife, I'd set her aside and marry again. Send her to the Mother's Temple to be a priestess, preferably a contemplative somewhere praying for our souls. It would make them both the happier, Dear Amma knows. Is King Andrin so very bad, then?"

Lassanna set her mouth; talking about her former lover came hard to her. "Before Tennoc came, he was good to me," she said slowly.

"So were he to set Inglatine aside and call for you?"

"He will never call for me. In Tremont I am damaged goods, as they say. No one would marry me, let alone the King. When I was a stupid girl, I thought he *might*, d'you see. I thought…" She recalled Eddin's whispered words: *You will be the mother of a king.* "My mother raised me more like a Kell than a Tremontine. I was foolish. I thought An loved me. He never said it, but I thought his actions proved it. I believed what I wished to be true. He has never written me, never inquired after his son, never moved to protect me from my father so that I might go home."

Dunnoc let his gray eyes wander over her face in a way they never had before; she blushed. "Gwyrfal is your home, not Whitehorse. Come home, Lassa. Serve as the mistress of Gwynna's household and let us come to know one another better, not only as friends but as lovers. I know I am older by a good twenty years, but I am as ardent as any a younger man. You will be welcome in my court whatever may come. As for Tennoc, as long as he swears fealty to the Kellish throne, I will give him a holding and find him a wife. I swear to both on my honor as King."

"Consider his suit, niece!" said Lord Williard that night. "There's nothing you can bring to a royal marriage from a political standpoint, and you bring more than a bit of trouble considering Tennoc's father. There's many a lord angling to place his daughter in Dunnoc's bed—he must already love you at least a little. Probably a good deal more than a little."

"I remind him of old times, sir, nothing more," answered Lassanna.

In the end, she and an ecstatic Tennoc returned to Gwyrfal. Though Gwynna had rejected a borrowed mother the year before, now she clung to Lassa if not as mother then as a beloved aunt; Kenver, nearly ten years old and his tow hair darkening, held himself a little more aloof but not for long. Lassa was soon a part of the royal family to all its members but Dunnoc, through no fault of his.

Dunnoc made a respectful, determined assault on her. Her favorite dishes appeared on every menu. Music and dancing reappeared now that public mourning for Hallia had ended, and Lassa's favored musicians appeared at Gwyrfal. To Dunnoc's dismay, she kept herself from merriment, preferring to live quietly near the children. This was so unlike her, for while Hallia lived Lassa was the merriest of ladies imaginable, much given to dancing and laughter. That was the Lassa he wanted, and the Lassa he missed.

He took another tack. Gifts began arriving in Lassa's bower with alarming regularity, everything from rare silks from the Western Isles to even more rare incensewood combs from Sairland.

In return, Lassa gave respectful, determined regrets to Dunnoc's invitations to walk with him, dance with him, ride with him, hunt with him, until finally he came to her bower, dismissed the women and children, and thudded into the chair opposite her. "Lady, you give me no chance to press my suit and I grow impatient. Are my attentions so very unwelcome?"

"Your Majesty, may I speak freely?"

Dunnoc leaned forward. "You may always speak your mind, Lassa, I have ever allowed intimacy between us."

"While your gifts are intended with the utmost kindness," she began cautiously, "they are…reminiscent of an earlier time in my life, when luxury blinded me into making unwise decisions."

"What are you saying?"

Lassa lifted her chin. "Do not try to buy me, Dunnoc. I was bought before, and buying myself back cost a great deal."

"Buy you!" Dunnoc stood, his sword sheath banging against his leg. "Lady, those presents were tokens of my esteem alone! To throw them in my face—"

"I'm not throwing them in your face. I have accepted every one of them."

"You reject every attempt I have made at greater intimacy!"

Lassa reached for his hand; he paused, but gave it to her. "I will be more obliging if you stop this shower of goods. I know you mean no harm, but it reminds me of Tennoc's father." She examined the hand in her own. His fingers were long and square-tipped, his hand stiff with scars gained from both war and hunting—quite different from Andrin's smooth, almost girlish skin that had never seen real struggle. "If I come to you, I wish it to be free of past memories and present obligations. Can you understand that?"

Dunnoc sank to one knee, the better to meet her eyes. "Then come riding with me, come walking with me. Talk with me, Lassa, as we used to. I own I have perhaps wooed you the wrong way. I am no sophisticate, merely an old soldier. But when the ghost of that bastard Andrin rises before your eyes, remember this: I have never required your attendance on me, though by rights I could have—I could have required much more of you than that. I hold you in higher esteem than ever he did, or ever will."

Lassa examined the older man's face as she had his hand. Sun and salt wind had tanned his skin and carved lines around his eyes; gray was just beginning to dominate his sandy brown beard. This was a fighting king, hardened in skirmishes against the Tremontines and the would-be Sairish rulers of the continent, and his own sorties across the border into Corland. She wondered if Temmin the Great had been this sort of fighting man; certainly his great-grandson wasn't, though rumor had it that Tremont intended to take the castles along the border with Sairish-held Valleysmouth. Andrin would rely on magic, his own and Teacher's, and stay well away from the fighting. Dunnoc held Kellen's magic, a lesser magic than Tremont's as Kellen was the smaller, but still strong enough that he didn't have to follow his men into the worst of it—and yet he did.

Dunnoc's brows drew together; his expression reminded her of Kenver worrying he'd done something wrong and wondering if he'd be forgiven. Lassa cradled his cheek in her free hand. "You are twice the man Andrin of

Tremont is, Dunnoc."

His face lost its uncertainty and came to abrupt attention. "Then will you dance with me tonight?" he whispered.

"I will," she answered.

They danced every night, rode every day, and hunted in fine weather. In the spring they married. Perhaps, thought Lassa, she might miraculously bear Dunnoc a son and fulfill Eddin's prophecy. No, for it would mean something would happen to Kenver, and she loved the boy almost as much as she did her Tennoc. Perhaps the prophecy meant Kenver—he was her stepson.

She didn't want to think about Tennoc being the prophecy's fulfillment. How could he be? Inglatine had written; Andrin had finally set her aside after the births of two more girls, and she lived comfortably at Marsury Castle in Barley with the youngest four of her seven daughters. The new Queen would surely give him a son.

Despite her own certainty, Dunnoc's lords remained unconvinced. "I don't like it," said young Lord Daevys ar Ulvyn one night not long after the wedding. The men drinking around the fireplace in his Gwyrfal apartments grunted in agreement. "Bad enough she spread her legs for a man before she was properly married."

"Eh, I seem to recall your firstborn arriving into the world a wee bit earlier than is common, Ulvyn," snorted Lord Bryth ar Brennow to general laughter.

Ulvyn glared. "I married her. This boy is the only son of the Tremontine king, and far too close to the Prince."

"You fear for Prince Kenver's life?" said Sian ar Lifris.

"No, no, only the influence the Tremontine boy has over him, and the new Queen has over the King. Tremont wants Kellen, there have been skirmishes between us since before the days of the first Temmin."

"They are far too busy with the Sairish colonies along the Valleysmouth border to worry us," scoffed Bryth.

"Not forever. What if the Tremontine bitch gets her hooks so deeply into the King that he looks to a Tremontine princess as a wife for Kenver?"

"Then perhaps Kenver's son becomes king of Tremont as well as Kellen. We take the country in marriage, since so far Andrin has no Heir but the bastard Dunnoc has taken to his bosom," said Lifris. "There's much to recommend the idea."

"There's nothing to recommend the idea," growled Ulvyn. "Tremontines are barbarians. The children of princesses are not in the succession. Tremont is three times our size, and if they succeed in grafting a Tremontine wife onto Prince Kenver, Kellen will become no better than an occupied territory, with nary an arrow nor spell cast. A hundred years ago, Whitehorse and Barley were independent. Now look at them. Do you want Kellen to fall without a drop of blood? Then sit at your ease while Tremont takes us from within!"

"What should we do?" said one.

"There's nothing we can do but counter their influence as we may," shrugged Bryth.

"There's more, but we must be canny," said Ulvyn, "canny and patient. Individually our power is weak. We each have only so many men, and so little magic. But were we to pool our men and magic... When the time comes, and it will, we must be ready, whether it is to oppose Dunnoc or his son."

"This wouldn't be because you're Dunnoc's cousin and next in line after Kenver?" said Bryth.

"You have said enough among this assembly to hang with me, Bryth. You all have. If you support me, help me in coming years. If you oppose me, go and say nothing." The lords shifted uneasily; a few took long pulls from their wine. None left the room.

Temmin left the book uneasy. "They never leave you alone, do they?"

"Elaborate, please," said Teacher.

"Well, plots and plots and more plots. Is any king ever safe?" He ran his hands through his hair to scratch his scalp; his queue's fastening fell to the floor again. "Pagg damn it, and this thing takes forever to tie. I'm still not used to it, I like my hair shorter."

"The Temples are conservative in all things, sir. And to answer your question, no king is ever completely safe. There are always those vying for power, especially in the days when the Tremontine kings wielded magic directly. Now one might say the competition is for *me*, as strange as it sounds."

"No, I understand what you mean. But this was Kellen, not Tremont."

"Kellen had its own magic then, and not all magic was concentrated in the hands of one man—remember, even Gian of Valleysmouth had his little bit. The lords of Kellen had their little bits as well. Over time Tremont's magic became concentrated in the hands of the King, and now it is wholly mine. I hold it for your family. More than magic drives men to reach for power, though. Women, too, but they must reach for it through their men. There are few outlets now for them."

"Now? Was it ever different?"

"Once, long ago, women had their own power—enough to guarantee many of them an independent place in this world. Those days ended with your—your—" Teacher slipped from the edge of the library table, gripping its edge. Temmin reached out his hands but was waved away. "Too close, I fear. When you are king I may tell you," Teacher wheezed. "I must wish to tell you very badly to risk the pain so often."

Temmin patted his tutor's shoulder, feeling boyish and ineffectual. "You never get the urge to talk with anyone else about…forbidden matters?"

"Oh, I speak with few people in any event—your father, Mr Winmer, the heads of the Temples occasionally. In the past, your sister Sedra. We had wonderful conversations. I wish your father were more liberal in his views on female education," said Teacher wistfully. "You might think after nearly a thousand years I would be more circumspect, but in truth it does not come up very often. The only ones with whom I may speak freely of those times are your father and Connin."

Temmin brushed his loose hair back behind his ears, frowning at the mention of the Travelers. "They are the same as you, aren't they? Connin and his mother, I mean. Immortal. They were in Emmae's story, and that happened some 700 years ago." Connin's mother the Traveler Queen cursed Emmae to return the desire of anyone who wanted her, a horror softened by forgetfulness of her proud past; the Queen granted that mercy when Emmae gave Connin her virginity. "How did Connin end up with a royal name? Was the Traveler Queen one of those ambitious women?" he said, thinking of Lassanna and her initial eagerness to be the mother of a king.

"I can tell you nothing about that."

"How do ambitious women seek power now?"

"They enter the Temples and work their way into positions of authority—Ibbit is an example of such. Those who marry ambitious men help them in their cause however they can. Some women who have married more phlegmatic men goad them into striving for power. Some content themselves with social power. Others pin their hopes on their sons."

"Like Lassanna? But she didn't seem to want her son to be king. Why?"

"She saw it as a dangerous path. As a bastard, Tennoc might face opposition, possibly armed opposition, from all sides unless he showed strength."

Temmin considered the table top, brows raised in thought. "She wanted a title for him, though, and a noble wife." He rose and stretched his long frame. "I wonder what Mama wants for me."

"She wants for you to be happy and safe. There are few mothers as devoted as the Queen."

Temmin thought back on his childhood, living as normal a life as Mama could give him. He'd had no idea assassins had stalked him even then. For the first time he wondered how much she must have worried and suffered on his behalf—and still did. "I'll never be safe," he murmured.

"She knows this, and so she wishes for you to be happy most of all."

He didn't know if that was possible either. "I suppose if Donnis is due any moment I had better ready myself to return to the Temple."

"I have made inquiries, sir. The Temple's Own has secured the building and only Sisters personally vetted by Sister Imvalda are in service at the Lovers' Temple."

Temmin nodded. "All right, then. I'll just have to trust Donnis and the girls to help Mama from here on out. Actually," he considered, "Donnis will do more for her than any of us might."

Lady Donnis Provisa, Dowager Marchioness of Petras, looked nothing like her younger cousin. Her eyes were nut brown, her hair the same color though lightly threaded with somewhat wiry white; her skin less like a dainty porcelain creamer and more like the pottery the cream arrived in from the farmyard; her face broad, ruddy, and good-natured. Miss Hanston muttered that the Marchioness might dress more fashionably now she was in the City, but the lady's own maid retorted that her mistress wasn't stupid enough to follow every ridiculous trend the Capital's dressmakers might invent to gin up custom.

When she arrived, Donnis went straight to Ansella's drawing room still in her traveling clothes after the long journey from the southern Bellesian coast. The moment Ansella laid eyes on her she burst into tears. "What's this?" said Donnis. "Dear cousin, whatever it is, it'll be all right. Come and tell me."

Donnis led her to the soft blue sofa, where she collapsed against the Marchioness's comfortable side; she told all and left nothing out, for Donnis was one of the few people in the world who held Ansella's entire confidence. Donnis encircled her with plump arms. "Oh, Annie, your passions always gallop away with you, don't they? Goodness, you're nothing but bones! We shall amend that." She stood up and rang for tea.

"I'm not hungry, cousin, really," sniffed Ansella, dabbing at her nose with a handkerchief.

"Who said it was for you? I just came from the road and I'm famished!" Donnis ordered tea and a small meal she secretly planned to cajole down her cousin, and said, "I'm going to change, I'll be just a moment." She paused at the door. "Annie, Berto has quite grown into his father's shoes and doesn't need me to help manage things now—and I dare say my daughter-in-law enjoys my absence though we get on well enough. Two women in the same house is never easy, is it? I am here for as long as you need me." She closed the door behind her.

On one side, Donnis exhaled in shock at her cousin's condition; on the other, Ansella breathed easier knowing her oldest and dearest friend had arrived. Each thought things could only get better now.

Temmin returned to the Temple and Ansella gradually rejoined life, faster than anyone expected. In her heart Ansella still grieved, but daily rides with Donnis led to eating with the family and then to making public appearances on the Promenade and in the Temples. Ansella had always been quite observant, but during Sister Ibbit's tenure she'd neglected regular services at the Temples of Eddin, Pagg, Farr and especially the Lovers. Temmin's investiture had been the sole exception to her neglect, though she'd stayed just long enough to let him know she'd been there. The open, shameful disrespect had nagged at her, but Ibbit insisted this was the proper path, and so she'd walked it blind and deaf to her own beliefs.

The equally reverent Donnis now hustled her to all the Temples on each God's name day—to the Lovers' Temple on both Nerrday and Neyaday. "Sometimes we even get to see Temmin there," said Donnis, jollying up her cousin before the trip into town. "Going to Temple every day isn't forever, just until you feel more like your old self. Making strict Temple rounds has anchored you in hard times before. Always turn to the Gods in times of trouble, my dear."

One Paggday in the new regimen's second week, two City gentlemen on the Promenade paused to goggle at a smartly-driven curricle, a light complement of Guardsmen before and behind it. "The Queen's a rare whip hand," said the ginger-haired gentleman. "Drives that pair of grays as well as anyone. Better. Fine-looking woman, too, ain't she?"

"Especially compared to the rawbones next to her," remarked the dark-haired gentleman.

"That's her cousin the Dowager Marchioness of Petras. Shame on you for calling her a rawbones, she's old enough to be your mother. What are you doing looking her over in the first place? Like 'em on the ripe side, do we?"

The dark-haired gentleman ignored the dig. "You don't suppose Her Majesty's decided to compete for the King's affections after all this time, all his women?"

"What d'you mean?" said the ginger-haired gentleman.

"Well, she's been in town for a year but she's hardly seen except at state occasions. Then that Shelstone chit rises to prominence like no royal mistress since the King's father's time, and here comes the Queen, every day on the Promenade."

"She's making her devotions."

The dark-haired gentleman snorted and dug his elbow into his fellow's ribs. "I'll believe it if she shows up at Neya's Day. No, old boy, something's afoot. This is a public challenge."

Whether the Queen intended it or no, Harsin found his wife unexpectedly captivating. Chatting with Donnis and his daughters over the day's events at dinner, Ansella seemed almost happy. Wise Sedra to send for Donnis so quickly.

He might have sent Ansella home to Whithorse Estate. Harsin knew Ansella hated the City, but he couldn't let her go, not without children to keep her there. It would look as if he'd set her aside, and that would cause him troubles however much she might wish to leave. Her departure at this juncture would create a void quite different from her past absences, one of power and position as well as affection. It would stir up more virulent ambitions among the families and hangers-on of his mistresses. Competition to take the Queen's place on her throne as well as in his bed would erupt. The odious Elbig Shelstone came to mind. His naked ambition more than made up for his daughter's complete lack of it. What did the man want, and would Twenna Shelstone be compensation enough to grant it to him?

As charming as she was, Twenna moved to the back of his mind. Ansella looked beautiful tonight in the lamplight, much younger than her 42 years even as pinched as she'd become. The bloom he'd always loved was just returning to her cheek. He'd heard she'd begun riding again; he wondered if she would ride with him now. Should he ask? No, surely she would say no. Things might be different now, though, mightn't they? Ibbit was gone—he should have put an end to *that* when it started. Never again would anyone share his wife's bed but him.

Harsin realized he'd caught Ansella's attention; she turned toward him, a query in her eyes. He smiled. She colored, ducked her head and returned to her conversation with Ellika. How long had it been since he'd made her blush, since she looked at him with anything other than cool disdain? How far might he go on that blush, he wondered.

Ansella returned to her rooms from an evening spent playing crib with Donnis to find him nursing a brandy in her private drawing room. "Hello, Annie."

She drew back until she realized who it was. "How you startled me, sir. I do not like surprises."

"Is it such a surprise to find me in my own wife's apartments? We have not spoken privately in some time. I thought perhaps... Are you well, Ansella?"

She faltered. Her fingers found the pulse point in her throat, a gesture he knew well, and he stepped forward into her softness to pursue his question. She dropped her hand, hardening again before he could reach her. "You are concerned, sir? I find that unusual." She brushed past him, but he caught her arm with his free hand.

"I am always concerned about you."

"Are you, now?" she said, a familiar blaze lighting her blue eyes. "You were not so very concerned about me when you acknowledged Twenna Shelstone in front of every eye in the City."

Harsin released her. Of course she would have heard. The day Twenna took the public way through town to the Lodge, that night Harsin had arrived late as usual to the Duke of Corland's box at the theater to find Twenna there for everyone to see; Corland claimed he didn't know the King had still intended on coming. In Harsin's surprise he'd made a rare slip, greeting her with a kiss on each cheek—the same greeting he gave Lady Corland. Everyone saw him acknowledge her. While they'd had words later on the propriety of her conduct, he'd forgiven Twenna; the fault was her father's. Still, he'd acknowledged her in public, and Ansella had found out.

He put his brandy down atop a nearby console. "Who told you?"

"Never mind who told me. Please leave."

"Annie, it won't happen again," he cajoled, advancing again.

"Oh, you intend to stop seeing her?"

Harsin's blood came up, heating his face. "Do not presume to tell us what to do."

"'Us,' is it?" she laughed. "I suppose it's the royal prerogative to bed every woman in the Kingdom. I am tired of this argument, Harsin." Ansella snatched his brandy off the console, downed it in one gulp and smacked the snifter down so hard the stem broke. She bobbled the snifter's bowl in her astounded hand before putting the remnant next to its stem. She fled to her bedchamber before he could stop her.

"Pagg's balls!" Harsin picked up the broken snifter and threw it into the fireplace; the glass shattered with a satisfying shriek. He stalked back to his own rooms, wondering why everything always ended in shards with his wife.

Ansella had never adored him, even at their passion's height. She had always seen him as he was: worthy of respect, even love, but not adoration. He'd always assumed the respect remained, but perhaps he was mistaken. It galled him. He knew—*knew*—she still wanted him despite everything, but Harla take him straight to the Hill if he would give up his prerogatives.

His thoughts returned to Twenna Shelstone. He needed a refuge, and in Twenna he found one. He wondered if and how he might win back his wife's respect, but in the meantime he would take shelter and solace where he found them.

Embis Winmer was straightening papers on the desk he shared with his master when the King entered their office. "Ah, Winmer. Just when I need you. Might we get Miss Shelstone admitted to the Neya's Day Spectacle?"

"I don't know, Your Majesty," answered the secretary, correctly interpreting the question as a command. "There are several barriers to her guaranteed admittance, not least her unmarried state."

"I find it hard to believe there's anyone in the City who thinks she's a virgin because she's unmarried," chuckled Harsin.

Winmer gave a sliver of a smile. "Oh, most certainly not, sir. I believe she is well known. Perhaps the best known of your intimate friends ever."

Winmer had been Harsin's secretary since before the King had ascended, when Harsin was the eighteen-year-old Heir and he himself was a young clerk of twenty-two. That year Prince Harsin and Lady Ansella married, and a turbulent time it was. The Prince had kept to his new wife's bed, and Winmer had rarely seen him.

Once the Queen had given him a son as well as two daughters, she'd insisted on staying at the Estate full time, with Teacher's support. She'd begun to repeat "We were not a love match," and when the sanctimonious Sister Ibbit arrived, the Queen shut her door against her husband.

To be fair, His Majesty hadn't given up his other women, but did any ruler keep to one bed? And the King had always been quite solicitous of Her Majesty's honor.

Since that night at the theater, His Majesty had been less so. He saw Miss Shelstone in private, intimate gatherings with friends and their own mistresses, but he'd also had Winmer arrange for Twenna to be present at every social event he attended—far more than with other mistresses. True, she might be the most beautiful of the women who'd shuttled through his bed, but still...and then the Queen seemed at her most vulnerable, and Winmer valued her highly.

In this thoughtful mood Winmer said, "Sir, may I ask why? I do not now nor have I ever questioned your choices in anything let alone companionship, but..." His grimace crumpled his neat mustache. "Given recent history between you and the Temple I believe it will require a certain amount of effort to gain Miss Shelstone's rather irregular admittance to the ceremony. Effort that I will of course expend, sir, but..."

"You wish to know what I see in her, eh, Embis?"

Never had His Majesty taken such an unsophisticated girl to his bed for more than a romp. Yet the girl had such an attractive innocence and sweetness that even Winmer wished to protect her. Poor child. Perhaps it lay in her eyes, such enormous eyes and so very blue. "I have no right to ask, sir."

"Nor does anyone, but I'll tell you anyway." Harsin reclined against the partners' desk. "Anyone can see she's desirable—she's beautiful. Flawless skin. Those eyes. But more, she loves me. She loves me with all her heart. No pretense, no plots. Unlike her father. Shelstone is ambitious and I'll tolerate his ambitions to a point. *She* has none beyond my happiness. Do you know how rare that is for a man in my position?"

"May I speak frankly, sir? Her Majesty once did."

A shade passed over the King's countenance. "Not for a long time, Embis, and I don't know if I deserve such devotion from her in any event. No," he said, standing straighter and leaning toward his secretary, "something in me wants to protect Twenna. She's an innocent. She makes me happy. I feel younger when I'm with her. I want her at Neya's Day. Make it happen."

"I will, sir," said Winmer. "How far may I go? The lottery is notoriously hard to influence."

"I give you great latitude, but there's no sense in not using connections if we can. We will start with Temmin and work our way up. I'll spare you the first round and ask my son to procure the invitation myself."

"I thank you, sir. He does not care for me."

"He doesn't much care for me right now, either. I don't expect my request to be fruitful, but the attempt must be made, eh?"

The attempt did not bear fruit. Temmin pruned The King's request so completely, and yet so skillfully, that Harsin wondered just how much training in diplomacy his son might be getting. Perhaps these two years would not be a complete loss.

Up the chain the request went, ending in the laps of the Most Highs. They feigned reluctance, but in the end the first donation the Temple had received from the royal purse since Temmin's investiture, and a promise for a great deal more, conquered all. Twenna Shelstone received a guaranteed place at the Spectacle.

Everyone else, high and low, had to enter the ticket lottery, including Elbig Shelstone. "Infuriating!" fumed the former tailor. "That *I* should have to enter the lottery! Demand that the King procure me a ticket!"

"Papa, I can't do that," said Twenna. "I would give you mine, but it would anger him. *I* really shouldn't be going at all, though, should I?"

"Should you?" shouted her father. "Of course you should! The King is more taken with you than I thought. Your presence there will be the most public declaration anyone's ever seen from him. Every door will open to us. Ha! I wonder that Her Majesty will even show her face this year!"

SIX

THE FIRST DAY OF SPRING'S BEGINNING, 991 KY

Twenna Shelstone stepped down from her father's carriage into the throngs crowding the Lovers' Temple for the Neya's Day Spectacle. An orderly procession flowed from the Promenade to the Temple garden gates, where the Spectacle would be held. Postulants and servants bore hundreds of bright lanterns through the crowded gardens until every leaf seemed illuminated. Twenna fretted to be without even a footman to look after her, but she reassured herself. Harsin had said Winmer would find her there and protect her from unwanted advances.

Many spectators aimed sideways glances and outright stares at her; those who actually knew her greeted her in abstracted familiarity, too absorbed in anticipation of the night's events. What those events might be were in the most vague outlines in Twenna's mind: the Gods would possess their Embodiments, Nerr would chase Neya through the gardens until He caught Her—or until She let Him catch Her depending on how you interpreted the Sagas—and They would make love as the faithful filed past. Witnesses were blessed for the year in all the Gods' activities: music, poetry, performance of all kinds, and of course, love and sex. So blessed, the onlookers then found someone—or someones—to emulate the Gods and ensure the fertility of the earth, at least once on living ground if possible no matter how cold the night.

She pulled her fine wool cloak a little closer and wished she'd brought a muff with a handwarmer hidden inside, but her dresser had put her foot down: "Past the season, miss." Twenna wished someone had told the weather it was past the season.

Once inside the gardens, Twenna looked for her expected escort. Mr Winmer had chaperoned her at more than one event she'd unofficially attended with the King. But he was nowhere in sight, and no substitute came forward. Troubled, she began looking for Harsin. If she could keep him in view, her mind would be easier.

Embis Winmer was having a difficult evening.

First he'd trimmed one side of his little mustache shorter than the other. For one horrifying moment it appeared he'd have to shave his lip bare for the first time since he turned seventeen. After a tense series of snips the little mustache was quite a bit littler, but at least it was still there, and it was even.

Then his tailor sent word his new formal suit would not be ready. His current best was more than adequate for the occasion, but this was the first Neya's Day Spectacle he'd attended in ten years; he had high hopes for the evening once he'd delivered Miss Shelstone to the King for the night. Usually royal paramours who'd won the lottery had husbands to escort them and there was no need for Winmer to chaperone, but the young lady's father, the former tailor, had not won a ticket and Winmer had.

He left in more than enough time to beat the crowds or so he'd thought, but his carriage became snarled in the aftermath of an overturned barouche at the foot of Kingsbridge. By the time he arrived at the Lovers' Temple, he was just in time to see the gates locked. A Temple's Own captain barred his way. "Very sorry, sir. Ticket or no, you're not getting in."

Winmer raised his voice to an unaccustomed shout. "But I am the King's Secretary!"

"I don't care if you're the King himself," said the captain. "The Spectacle is beginning. Opening this gate before the Gods retire is dangerous." Neither cajoling nor threats moved the man. Winmer turned away, his face the color of the Tremontine red livery his coachman wore. Were he not an atheist, Winmer would have sworn the Gods were after him. He rarely failed the King, and tomorrow would be a difficult day in the office. And then there was the girl herself; leaving her alone among the revelers distressed him. He hoped Miss Shelstone had the sense to find a Lover to escort her until the

King fetched her, poor little featherbrain.

Inside the Lovers' Temple itself, the Gods had nearly arrived. Starved, beaten, blindfolded, barely conscious, the twins now hung suspended on frames, each in separate but connected rooms. Barik, Temmin and the terrified Mathanus Postulant attended Issak; in the Goddess's Chamber, Glaes Beloved, Anda and an equally terrified Postulant Beloved named Justinna attended Allis.

Heavy clusters of rubies dangled from clamps on each of Issak's nipples and from his ball sac. He was panting now, head held low and sweat plastering his hair to his head. His erection had lengthened with the pain, seemingly the one unbreakable part of his body and the part the God would use the most mercilessly. His suffering increased his beauty, and Temmin fought the urge to take that length in his mouth and give Issak the release his body wanted, though Issak himself wasn't there any more.

Putting Issak through all this pain still made Temmin nauseous, but at least this time he was prepared for it. Mathanus was not. He wandered into the fumes of the censer at the frame's foot, the smoke's dream-inducing poison disguised in rich amber and woods; Temmin dragged him back, but between the drugged incense and the Embodiment's condition, Mathanus became violently ill. "Never worry, Mathanus Postulant," Barik told him as the big man rinsed his mouth. "It's why we have a basin here. Someone's bound to need it at some point."

Temmin doused the incense at a sign from Barik. The doors to the next room opened, letting in a whiff of Neya's tuberose-and-gardenia incense, and there was Allis, bound, blindfolded and clamped with diamonds. She was weeping, sagging against her restraints. Justinna Postulant and Anda stood at each side of the frame; Glaes knelt between Allis's legs. Barik sent Mathanus to open the doors to the gardens, and the men took up their positions around Issak: Temmin and Mathanus to each side, Barik kneeling between his legs.

At a signal, all six whipped off the clamps and pressed down hard on the tortured flesh with fingers or tongues as the twins screamed and bucked. Then, silence.

Barik and Glaes removed the blindfolds. Suffering fell from the two sculpted figures hanging on the frames. A rosy glow began in the twins' green eyes, growing until it enveloped their bodies. The Gods had arrived.

"Hello, Sister," said Nerr-in-Issak.

"Hello, Brother," said Neya-in-Allis.

They exchanged Their ritual taunts:

"Will this be the year You simply give Yourself to Me, Neya?"

"Why, are You afraid I'll outrun You this year?"

Back and forth, until Neya screamed at the mortals to release Her. Unfettered, She ran into the gardens to the gathered worshippers' roar. Nerr followed close behind Her, Temmin, Anda and the two Postulants after them both.

They ran along the gardens' lit paths, until they came to the wide expanse of lawn between the formal gardens and the grove of trees stretching dark and wild toward the river. Lantern-bearers hurried behind the runners, waiting to stake out a path for the worshippers. Behind them, muscular Lovers loitered with sections of a portable dais; the King and Queen attended the Spectacle this year and would be given a proper viewing platform wherever the Lovers happened to fall.

Fall They finally did, on the lawn near the fringe of the forest, but first Neya and Nerr led them all a chase through the trees, whipping rhododendron branches back into Their followers' faces to Temmin's great irritation. When they assembled the guarding circle round the Gods, they were all breathing hard; Justinna Postulant had lost her vest, the flounce on Anda's best skirt had ripped clean off, and Mathanus's blond hair resembled a haystack more than ever.

Nerr-in-Issak and Neya-in-Allis began Their ferocious annual coupling, rolling in the grass teeth bared and snapping at one another. The Supplicants and the two Postulants formed a loose ring around the Lovers. Other Temple staff caught up and reinforced the circle to keep the Gods in and the crowds safe; there had been lethal interactions in the past between the Lovers and Their worshippers during the Chase.

Lanterns formed a path from the Temple to the Gods' writhing bodies. The worshippers filed past to receive the blessing, some of the men already clutching themselves in arousal. Temmin found it less so. He knew Issak and Allis too well, empathized too deeply with their ordeals, found the Gods' incestuous use of their bodies too disturbing. He thought of the all-too-rare times he'd truly made love with the twins. Last Neya's Day and again on Nerr's Day were the only times they had all three been together, but the Gods possessed the Obbys then, as they did now. Some people, atheists or just the cynical, believed the twins were play-acting—or worse, perverted. Temmin knew better, perhaps because he alone among the worshippers could see the glow of possession about them. A rustling and clatter broke out behind him. His parents were ascending the portable dais. *My happiness is complete.*

Neya was screaming in ecstasy now, Her borrowed breasts bouncing as She straddled Nerr. With no Supplicant to deflower this year, who knew how long They'd be at it. Temmin resigned himself to a long, anxious night on the lawn.

Ansella's attentions were split. She grew agitated watching the Gods coupling and re-coupling on the lawn; she looked away to her son in the Lovers' guard, but that only increased her embarrassment. Where to look? The sooner this night was over, the better.

Harsin, on the other hand, was enjoying himself immensely. Neya's Day was one of his favorite Spectacles.

As a boy he'd waited all year for Eddin's Day as children do, but once he'd started attending the Neya's Day Spectacles at age 14, his enthusiasm for the day of toys and candy had dimmed considerably. Now it was a toss-up between the Farr's Day tournaments and the lovemaking of Neya's Day; he gave himself over to the holiday spirit at them both. He'd missed Neya's Day last year. That Temmin, making a fool of himself and endangering the throne—Harsin couldn't give his approval with his attendance, the commoners be damned. He'd even attempted blackmail by proxy against both Temmin and the Obbys to stop it, at the risk of his soul. No, he would have been allowed in, but he wouldn't have been made welcome. Ansella, on the other hand, had gone against her own inclinations and appeared on the dais last year, alone, to support her son.

Harsin glanced over at his wife. Her lips pressed tightly together, her eyes searched for somewhere to light, her cheeks were flushed. Would she ever admit to even a fraction of her passion? In their youth they'd suited one another in spite of themselves, and an unexpected yearning came over him. He wanted to lay his head in Ansella's lap again, as he had before she'd moved back to Whithorse and left him to his list. Why couldn't things be different between them?

He glanced into the crowd and found Twenna Shelstone there, younger than he was by more than twenty years—younger than Sedra. Her guileless eyes reflected the lantern light as she shifted from foot to foot; he couldn't see Winmer, but he was surely somewhere nearby. Harsin decided on a different outcome to the evening. He would make it up to the girl another time.

Harsin looked back at his wife. They were the same age. Experience lay in the corners of her eyes. A line between her brows had formed since her arrival at the Keep; he wondered if he were its cause, and how he might smooth it away.

Ansella looked up in time to catch a small smile twitching at his mouth. "My Lord?"

His smile widened. "I was remembering when we first were married."

The Queen blushed and pretended to watch the crowds. "That was long ago. What brought those times to mind?"

"The night, I suppose—we haven't attended a Neya's Day Spectacle together in years. I should never have let you go to Whithorse with the children."

"So you have told me many times."

"Ansella, look at me." She lifted her chin but kept her eyes on the nearby trees. "Were those times so terrible for you? We found a solace with each other, didn't we? More than solace."

"We were not a love match."

"Yet we have three children. Had you stayed, there would have been more." He took her hand in both of his, tracing the lines of her palm; he remembered she liked that.

Ansella curled her fingers around his. "What are you doing?"

"I'm seducing my wife. Be one with me tonight. Tell me you will, say 'Be one with me tonight,' say yes, Ansella."

Her hand stiffened in his, her temper radiating into his palm. "You maneuver your current mistress into the Spectacle, and then you try to seduce me," she growled.

Harsin stooped down. "I am asking *you*, not her. I have waited years for you, whether you think it or not. Say yes!" he whispered in her ear. His beard brushed against her skin. She shivered; her blush crept over the tops of her breasts. It still worked, he smiled to himself. "If you were not the Queen, I'd have you right here."

Ansella closed her eyes. Was she picturing it? "But I *am* the Queen."

He cupped her chin in his hand. "Say yes and we will leave right now, you and I, and I will have you the moment we are alone. In the carriage if you will. Say yes, say it, Ansella!"

"Yes," she whispered in a rush. Her voice was awestruck and surprised, her eyes still closed.

He kissed her. "We're leaving." He gave a quick nod to the captain of the Temple's Own, who began parting the crowd. Harsin took Ansella's hand and pulled her down the path to the garden gates. "I wonder if we might secure a room here," he murmured to her as they hurried along.

"Harsin!" How good to hear her say his name with laughter in her voice.

"I don't think so, not tonight of all nights!"

"Then it will have to be the carriage!"

Twenna watched them leave in horror. He'd cut her. He'd cut her in front of his wife and hadn't given her a backward glance. It couldn't mean what it appeared to mean. This had to be something about appearances, but why had he gone to so much trouble to have her admitted if he'd intended to leave with his wife? There must be a reason, a reason she wasn't clever enough to understand. He loved her; she took comfort in that certainty. He would send for her later, surely.

The swaying lanterns planted in the lawn took on a cold look, less like soft yellow moons and more like predatory eyes. What would she do now? She knew no one in the crowd who might protect her, no man she might trust not to take advantage of the Neya's Day festivities. She stayed close to the fierce-looking Lovers in armor still standing beside the royal dais, in hopes one of them might have been given instructions to escort her, but the workers disassembled the dais and took it away, along with the Temple's Own and her hopes.

Screams and cries of a less divine origin had long since filled the wood and gardens when the Lovers finally stood, sated for the time being. "Glaes! And Anda!" hooted Nerr, tweaking a nipple on first the one, then the other. "How are two of My favorite mortals? Well, here's someone new!" the God said to Mathanus, and kissed him until his lip bled. The huge young man stumbled unconscious into the arms of his fellows, who came close to dropping him.

"Temmin Heir of Tremont," Neya said, slipping her arms around his waist. The rosy halo around Her seemed to pulse, and Temmin realized She hadn't spoken aloud. "My darling boy, My King, kiss Me." She wrapped herself around him, pressing Allis's breasts against his chest. His discomfort and near-boredom vanished, replaced with the crushing lust She'd drawn from him a year ago. He kissed Her, matching Her moods from gentle to probing to violent, until She reached into his trousers and took hold of him. He closed his eyes and whined into Her mouth. "Look at Me," said the voice in his head, and he obeyed.

A year ago She had shown him many things in Allis's deep green eyes: his mother bloody-handed; Jenks riding hell-bent from Whithorse Estate sword in hand; his father in battle; Sedra protecting a child; Ellika facing down soldiers; finally, Teacher and the Traveler Queen, wreathed in flames.

This time, a woman appeared. Her figure curved in lush abundance, but her huge blue eyes were those of a child. She grew more real until he could even smell her—sweet honeysuckle like the flowers he'd eaten as a boy, crushed dandelions like the ones his sister Ellika used to make into chains, and the soft, musky desire of a woman. "She is yours," said the Goddess. "You will find her tonight. You and no other will have her, and I will give you this." Her fingers closed on him in a single stroke.

The woman in his mind dissolved into fierce white light as he spasmed in Neya's hand. He thought he might be screaming but the light muffled his hearing, obscured everything. He'd spent like this a year ago in Her bed, over and over, and now it pierced him in a spike from his crown down his spine through his cock into the ground. He hung on it transfixed until he crumpled in a heap at Her feet.

The lantern-bearers followed the Gods as they moved back toward the Temple; Twenna did as well, not knowing what else to do.

In the darkness, a man pulled at her arm. "Be one with me tonight, beauty!" He couldn't be Harsin, nor did he sound like Mr Winmer. Was the man angry? Cajoling? She murmured a polite refusal and tried to shake his hand away, but he persisted. "Come now, you wouldn't be here if you weren't looking for someone for the night. You're here all alone, come be one with me, you won't regret it! If you don't like me, I have some friends— you can have any of us—*all* of us! We'll keep you warm all night!" He pulled her close enough to get an arm around her waist. Twenna cried out, knowing no one would pay any attention to her. So many cries echoed through the garden.

Another set of hands brushed against her, the gentle touch striking her like a blow. His friends must have found them, and now she was lost. The hands moved; they fastened onto the first man's wrists and not her own. "Let her go, son," said a deep voice.

"I saw her first. There are plenty of women here, go find your own! OW!" The man dropped Twenna's arm. "Pagg damn you, you nearly broke my wrist—oh! Oh, I'm sorry, Senior Lover, I didn't realize...I'm sorry, I'll just..."

Twenna watched him back away into the night and turned to her rescuer. All she could see in the dark was that he was short and stocky, and he wore Temple garb. "Thank you."

"Never worry, I'm a Lover. No one will hurt you or make you do anything you don't wish to do. May I lead you back to the Temple?" He offered his arm, she put her hand upon it, and they walked back across the wide lawn. "Neya's Day is not about force," continued the priest. "Some celebrants forget that. It's why a good number of the Lovers' clergy—the men, mostly—don't celebrate the holiday until late in the evening."

"For instance, you?"

"For instance, me," he said in an amused, resigned tone. "I've been a Lover for more than thirty-five years now, and for half of them I've patrolled at the Neya's Day Spectacle. I don't mind. Much." She laughed and slipped her arm through his, a burly arm, well-muscled and comforting—fatherly. "Truth be told, I rather like it. Especially when I can help an inexperienced woman left behind to fend for herself." He paused. "I didn't think the King would do that."

"You—you know who I am?" said Twenna in a small voice. The priest nodded. She hadn't thought beyond her pain at Harsin's faithlessness. The King had cut her not just in front of his wife but in public. Word would travel, and when her father heard—oh, she was in more than romantic trouble. "I imagine people saw what happened, didn't they?"

"Not everyone knows you on sight."

"Not everyone has to." The lanterns bobbed ahead of them. They'd almost caught up, and she slowed her pace; on this man's arm, the dark seemed safer. "I wish...I wish life weren't so complicated."

The Lover slipped his arm around her and hugged her against his side. "We have the strength within us to face almost anything, and when we don't, the Gods carry us if we ask them to. If you are confused and heartsore, make the rounds and leave offerings. Go to the Hill and visit your dead—sometimes going there clears my head more than anything. Yes, even as a priest of Nerr."

They were in range of the lights now, and Twenna could see her rescuer was a man in late middle age wearing a Lover's rose-colored clothing; row after row of elaborate embroidery at the hems marked him as high-ranked, very high-ranked indeed and yet he still patrolled on Neya's Day. Close-cropped, graying hair crowned his balding head but for a little curl of a queue at his nape; limitless kindness filled his large brown eyes. "Who may I thank for my rescue?" she asked.

"My name is Barik Lover, and it's customary in the Temple to say 'thank you' with a kiss. May I?"

Twenna kissed him herself. It wasn't an entirely chaste kiss—rather, a surprisingly skillful and thought-provoking one. At its end, she squeezed Barik's arm and walked away to seat herself among the spectators around the main dais where the Gods would make their farewells. Harsin might be faithless, but she was not.

Excitement rustled through the gathering; the Gods had returned from Their wanderings in the gardens. They moved through the gasping crowd, bestowing a touch here, a kiss there. Neya pulled an older well-dressed woman to her feet and kissed her so thoroughly the woman cried aloud and collapsed into the onlookers' arms, swooning and twitching in obvious bliss. She disappeared under a swarm of worshippers eager to share the blessing she'd received, and reappeared in the arms of two men. They carried her half-undressed into the gardens, a scattering of men and women following behind to watch or join in if they could.

Twenna had never imagined such things. She'd seen this quite respectable woman at various social events, though they'd never been introduced. Her husband had been one of those carting her off into the hedges and didn't seem in the least perturbed that other men were undressing his wife at the same time. Harsin had told her something about Neya's Day, but far from enough.

Harsin—how could he have left her here alone with no one, no escort at all, and gone off with his wife, right in front of her? She should go home.

A hand brushed her hair; a shock flowed from the caress, a tightening of her skin, an unbearable, delightful pressure molding her body. She looked up into the borrowed green eyes of Nerr. "Come here, pretty thing." A yearning obedience overwhelmed her, and she stood. Nerr kissed her, moving His hands down her body to her hips. He broke off long enough to say, "This might sting for a moment," and resumed the kiss.

A sharp burning began under one of His hands, focused in a tight circle on her left hip. She whimpered. In her mind He whispered, "Hush now, little Twenna, this is for the greater good. You will find him—" A golden-haired young man, familiar—what was his name?—filled His eyes, growing to take up all her sight. "You will find him and you will be one with him and only him tonight. No one else will touch you, no one else will know. You will burn until you find him, and when you do, this will be your reward."

Twenna's whimpers turned to moans against His mouth as the burning subsided; pleasure rippled from His searching tongue directly to her core. Nerr pushed His knee between her legs and ground His thigh hard against her mound. His cock was hard against her belly even through her clothes, and she struggled as if she might somehow manage to impale herself on Him, single-minded and frantic in her desire. The pressure grew, squeezing and insinuating itself into her every part, dragging her to a terrifying edge.

He ground against her again, sucking on her tongue, and she fell.

Her orgasm flowed up her spine, down her legs, to explode from every finger, every toe, her eyes, her mouth. She saw and heard nothing, stiff and quivering in bliss until she fainted dead away.

Nerr laid her down in the respectful circle of space around them. "You will none of you touch her," He commanded the crowd. "She belongs to one man tonight." Every man, every woman, nodded hazily; they forgot her, and wandered off into the night to find their own blessings among the hedges and trees.

Twenna awoke, her mind clouded. The crowd was flowing around her as if she were a decorative rock: careful not to step on or run into her, but not really seeing her either. She didn't notice them. The vision Nerr had given her filled her head, spilling over into an overwhelming desire that pricked at her skin. She must find the golden-haired man. She must take him inside her. They must become one like the Lovers, and she must enter that promised ecstasy once again. She began searching.

Temmin stumbled through the shadowed gardens, swatting away worshippers eager to be one with him. Where was the girl with the sapphire eyes? He should know her name, but what did it matter? Neya said she was his, he would find her, and when he did—

There! She was running towards him, she was in his arms, she was clawing at him. "Wait—wait," he said. He picked her up and slung her over his shoulder; passers-by cheerfully hooted congratulations. Where could he take her? He shifted her weight with a grunt and headed for a nook few knew about, where the grass grew long and bushes blocked the wind.

Once in the deserted nook, Temmin dropped the woman on her feet and unfastened the ties of her cloak as she did the same to the drawstring of his uniform trousers and took him in her hand. Her hands were warm, almost feverish in the spring night chill. He bit her neck, and she babbled something about Nerr. "You are mine, Neya gave you to me, you will be one with me," he growled in her ear. Far away in the back of his mind came the idea that his voice sounded different, as if it didn't belong to him, and that the woman was no stranger. He ignored these timid thoughts and returned his attention to the hooks closing her bodice. He tore the last few in his impatience and pushed her down.

The woman tossed up her skirts and Temmin fell atop her, rooting among the petticoats until he found her cleft. She worked at her white brocade corset until her breasts spilled from her chemise. He slurped a nipple into his mouth and shoved his fingers inside her, all the exquisite technique he'd learned in the last year forgotten in his haste and need; she made no objection, opening her legs wide for him and pulling at his shirt to feel his skin against her. Neya gave him this woman, ordered him to be one with her, and as he slid into her heat a sliver of the immeasurable ecstasy he'd found in Neya's bed a year ago pierced him. He buried himself deep inside the woman, she cried out, and they rocked together, spending over and over in infinite time.

Stillness reigned at the Keep the next morning. Most of the footmen went through their chores blinking and yawning, for while they'd been out the night before till all hours, work still waited in the morning. The pointedly energetic maids—all unmarried and thus assumed to be stay-at-home virgins—huffed at them to "move it along, you cock's egg, yer blockin' the way!" Just one downstairs maid looked suspiciously sleepy, and the widowed housekeeper Mistress Mannell wore a drowsy, happy smile herself.

Ellika and Sedra had spent a quiet night playing cards with their fellow unmarried ladies. ("It's so unfair I have to stay home!" Ellika had said. "Do be quiet and deal," Sedra had replied.) This morning they breakfasted early, alone in the cheerful morning room.

"Where d'you suppose Mama is? She almost never sleeps in, not even after a Spectacle," said Ellika.

Sedra's voice floated out of the inky depths of *The Tremontine Spectator.* "Don't know, El. There's always a first time."

"No surprise Papa isn't here, he's always out late on Spectacle nights."

"Mmm."

"Oh, *must* you read at the breakfast table?"

Sedra folded back a new page with a rustling flourish. "Must you talk at the breakfast table?"

Ellika threw down her napkin. "I'm going to see what's the matter with Mama."

"You do that." Sedra groped for the toast rack with one hand, peering over the *Spectator* when her fingers ended up in the jam pot.

Ellika trotted up the stairs to her mother's suite and knocked on the door, but Miss Hanston turned her away. "Her Majesty is well but indisposed, Your Highness," said the brick wall. "I will tell her you inquired after her."

In fact, Miss Hanston had no way of knowing whether Her Majesty was well or not; she wasn't there. Ansella herself didn't know, either. She lay staring up at the canopy over Harsin's bed, clutching the covers to her chin and wondering what had possessed her the night before. The Shelstone girl had stood right there in front of her last night, and yet Ansella had gone to Harsin's bed as if all were well between them.

She turned toward her husband; he slept on, his face slack. It had been many years since they'd shared a bed, but asleep he still looked the same as he had on their wedding night—almost innocent, though she doubted Harsin had ever been innocent. He'd probably tried to seduce the midwife the day he was born. Her pride had slipped away with her clothes the night before; now she began gathering it to her like the sheets clutched to her chin.

Perhaps it would be wisest if she left. He would surely wake up wondering how on earth they'd made this huge mistake—she certainly had.

Ansella gingerly folded back the covers and slid from the bed, searching for something to cover her. Harsin's hand stopped her, his grip on her thigh gentle but firm. "Where do you think you're going, lady wife?"

She jumped. "Oh! I—I thought perhaps you'd sleep better were I to leave."

"Ansella, it's morning, I've slept enough. Come here."

She resolutely turned her mind against the hand stroking her thigh into cooperation. "Is that a request or a command, My Lord?"

Harsin removed his hand in surprise. "It's a request. Please, Annie, come back to bed. Just for a little while. Please." She returned to the covers but kept herself apart. Harsin pulled her close, pillowing her head on his chest. "I'm just asking for a little closeness with my wife."

Ansella raised her head. "You will forgive me my confusion."

He stroked her messy blond hair away from her face and drew her back down against him; his heart beat steady in her ear. "Our children are grown. Forgive *me* if this makes me melancholy and nostalgic for my youth."

She laughed slightly. "Harsin, we're hardly old. We're forty-two."

"Even so. I look into your face and I remember a different time."

Ansella paused, remembering their early marriage. She had loved him, though she thought she'd schooled herself out of it by now. She wondered if he'd loved her then or simply wanted her. He couldn't possibly love her now, not after so many years apart. "I'm surprised you're nostalgic for that time. I know I'm not."

"You never think back on our early days?"

"Not in the way you seem to." She moved away from him onto her back to stare up at the canopy again.

Harsin twisted onto his side and propped his head on his hand. "What do you think of?"

She shifted her gaze to his face. "You really wish to know?" He nodded, and she sharpened her tongue on her resentments. "Very well. I think about having no choice but to marry you. No choice but to leave the Estate. No choice in sharing your bed." *No choice in sharing you with other women.* "No choice in—"

"Stop," he almost shouted. He sat up. "Ansella, you've been allowed to do whatever you want!"

"Really? How very odd," she snapped back. "How did I end up here?"

"I do not recall dragging you into this bed last night."

"I—one mistake doesn't mean I've had things my way, quite the contrary."

"'Quite the contrary?'" Harsin repeated, his mouth twisting in disbelief. "You've had *everything* your way! I've let you have your own establishment a thousand miles away, where you've done whatever you pleased!"

"That was part of my bride price," she said, sitting up herself; in her agitation she let the sheet drop into her lap, leaving her breasts bare. "When I conceived an heir I could go home, and the children would come with me. You agreed!"

"Because Teacher said I should!"

"Don't blame me because you listened to that black crow!"

"Ansella, he was on your side!"

She stopped in confusion. Teacher *had* supported her, vigorously. "Well—why do you care where I was?"

"Because I missed my children. I missed my wife."

"You knew where we were."

"Oh, for the love of Pagg." Harsin rolled out of bed and pulled on a robe. "I had a kingdom to run."

"Oh yes, *affairs of state,* I see." She cast about for something to throw on, and finally found her chemise atop a heap of her hastily shed clothes on the floor. "Mustn't let your wife and children get in the way of affairs of *any* kind."

He whirled around. "Is that it? Jealousy? Your part of the arrangement was not to care what I did outside our bed, if I recall correctly!"

"I haven't!" she spat.

"Then why bring it up!"

"I don't know!" Tears stung her eyes, as if she faced into a cold wind. "I don't know! Why are you commanding my presence in your bed when you have a half-dozen hussies under this roof alone?"

"I don't have a single bedwarmer in the Keep, and my mistresses have never had any bearing on my regard for you—you are still my wife and the mother of my children. I didn't 'command' you, you came to my bed of your own free will!" He cocked his head. "A little morning-after remorse and now you're trying to convince yourself you had no choice but to make love with me?"

Ansella drew herself up as regally as she could in a wrinkled chemise and wild hair. "This conversation is ended, Your Majesty."

Harsin crossed the room so quickly she squeaked when he seized her. "For now. We will continue it another time. You will return to my bed. You won't be able to stay away, not after last night. The doors between our rooms are to remain unbarred, and I swear to you that you will be the one to cross the threshold first." He let her go.

She stumbled onto her feet and smoothed out the crumpled chemise as best she could. "Your over-confidence has always been distasteful to me."

"And your prudery even in the face of your own desire is distasteful to me. Leave me now." Harsin turned his back on her.

Ansella swooped down on her clothes, scrabbling them into a huge pile. Why did clothing for state occasions have to be so bulky! She threw the heavy skirts in her arms back onto the heap and decided to have it all returned to her later. She stalked through the concealed door into the narrow private hallway between their bedchambers and slammed into her room, frightening Miss Hanston. "Is the Marchioness awake? Please send her to me." The ladies maid assessed the Queen with a hard squint, gave a landslide of a curtsey and disappeared. As soon as she left, Ansella burst into tears and sank onto her bed, where Donnis found her not long after.

"Ansella? Hanston said you needed me—oh, dear cousin!" said Donnis, wrapping her arms around the queen and pulling out the two large, practical handkerchiefs she carried in her wrapper's pocket. "What happened?"

"I don't know!" she sobbed. "Something—came over me at the Spectacle, and—and—and now—"

"Sssh," said Donnis, rocking her gently. "Oh, cos. Whatever it is, it'll be all right."

"You don't understand!" She told Donnis all, describing it as a religiously-inspired, temporary insanity. "This is how I am repaid for my devotions! I must make Hanston swear she did not see me come through that door!"

"You will do no such thing—you'd break her heart! As if she'd ever tell anyone a jot of your business! Annie, it's perfectly natural for a loving wife to visit her husband."

Ansella's sobs redoubled. "I—have—NEVER—loved him!"

"So you've said, many times." Donnis offered her a third handkerchief from the nightstand.

"What am I going to do?"

"About what?"

"About Harsin!"

"Is it so horrible to be called to your husband's bed—and on Neya's Day? Can't you just take the blessing and leave it at that?"

Ansella wiped her eyes on the last dry corner of her handkerchief. "I'm sorry to fall apart. I've been so emotional since…" She left Ibbit's arrest unspoken. "This is a passing fancy. He'll be back to ignoring me within the day. I thought he was still seeing that Shelstone girl—I saw her at the Spectacle, bold as brass and completely unchaperoned, the hussy. He must be between women. Not that he's ever chosen me over his women before." She sighed and patted Donnis's arm. "Please have Hanston draw me a bath, my dear. I promise I will stop this ridiculous mewling and not mention it again."

Ansella watched Donnis out the door, took a deep breath, and sat down at her vanity to brush the morning tangles from her hair. *Can't you just take the blessing and leave it at that?* she asked herself. Not when she could still feel Harsin's hands on her, not when she could see the marks he left on her fair skin, not when even now all she wanted was to run through the door and beg for him to kiss her. A blessing? More like a curse.

Temmin usually missed having windows in his bedchamber, but this morning—whatever time it was—he was perfectly happy to wake up to nothing but low lamplight. His head was three sizes too big for his body, and his lips were crusted and dry. He flailed his arms in an attempt to get up and hit something warm and lumpy on the outer side of his alcove bed. A deep grunt issued from the lump's closest half: Mathanus. The other half said, "You just hit me in the nose, clumsy boy." Anda.

He was not surprised to find them in his bed—last night was the Spectacle, after all—but why couldn't he remember what happened? Anda and Mathanus at the same time? How could he not remember *that*? "What happened?" he croaked.

"You passed out on the lawn," yawned Anda. "Neya kissed you but good. That's the last I saw of you."

"You went down like a bag of rocks," added Mathanus.

"Last thing I remember, *you'd* fainted, Math," said Temmin.

"Eh, I came to right quick. I'm from hardy peasant stock, Yer Highness."

"Hmf." Temmin went to scratch his belly and discovered he still wore his garb from the night before. "Why'm I still dressed?"

"You got up and just walked off," said the Postulant. "Then things got... busy, I mean, it was Neya's Day, and the next I knew, I found you passed out again near the maze. I brought you back here and dumped you on your bed before someone stepped on you. And then Anda came in and sat down next to me here on your bed, and I think we'd planned on going to *her* bed, but..."

"It was Neya's Day, yes," finished Temmin. He smacked his lips, searching for a trickle of saliva. "Did we get drunk last night?"

"On Neya's Day? On *duty*? Of course not, silly," said Anda. "Anyway, it's time we all got up. Allis and Issak will be awake soon and they'll be ravenous. At least this year they won't have to contend with greedy guts here for their first meal." She reached over Mathanus and poked Temmin in the ribs.

"I like it when you squash your boobs against my chest," rumbled Mathanus.

"Do you, now? I'll do it some more, shall I?" She planted a sloppy kiss on him, and they began to wrestle.

Temmin rolled away from them, groaning. "If it's time to get up, get up! Or at least go to your own bed!"

Twenna Shelstone awoke in her bedchamber. Her headache throbbed in time with the chirps outside her bedchamber window. How had she gotten home? She remembered Harsin leaving with his wife, she remembered the sweet, paternal Barik Lover escorting her to the Temple...and after that, nothing.

She put a hand on her queasy stomach. Her fingers fell on the stiff silk wales of her bodice; she was in last night's dress, and she lay atop her still-made bed. Her headache tried to keep her down, but she rose enough to pull aside her bed-curtains—opposite the windows just in case the draperies were open. She tugged at the bell pull and fell back against the pillows again.

What had she done last night so horrible she couldn't remember? Harsin had smiled down at her as if she were an obedient puppy, and left with the Queen he'd said he hadn't made love to in six years. He'd abandoned her in front of everyone. That kind Lover had escorted her back toward the Temple, and then—nothing. Tears ran down the sides of her face, but she couldn't raise her heavy hands to brush them away.

Her maid Wendia poked her head through the curtains, made a quick assessment, and came back with tea, dry toast, and the promise of a bath.

Twenna pulled herself upright and took a long sip of unsugared tea, burning her tongue a little; the mellow bitterness revived her, and she took a tentative nibble of the toast. Better.

She let Wendia undress her and took ever-bigger bites of the toast as her hunger increased. "You've torn some of the hooks clean off, miss," the girl murmured.

"I..." The toast stuck in Twenna's throat. The blank between Barik and this morning clutched at her heart with terrible white fingers. Had she and Barik...? Surely she would remember *that*, and she doubted the Lover's gentle hands would have torn her bodice. If someone else had taken advantage of her, he wouldn't have left her fully dressed in her own bed. "Yes, I was so tired I had trouble removing my dress last night and just gave up before I did more harm." That must be the truth. "Why weren't you awake to help me?"

"I'm sorry, miss, but you gave me the night off. You, ah, weren't expected last night."

Twenna let the maid lead her to the bath waiting in the fashionably modern bathroom attached to her bedchamber. What did it matter anyway? If she didn't remember it, she shouldn't remember it. She placed her trust on the charm against childbirth the Traveler Queen had placed on her left hip. The thought cleared the toast crumbs from Twenna's throat.

She sipped her tea as she sat in the hot water and tried to think what she might say to her father about the King's behavior. He certainly hadn't acted the besotted lover he'd seemed to be. She needed to remedy that. For the first time in her short career as a mistress, Twenna began to plot.

SEVEN

The tidy little townhouse in Arren was filling up with strangers, unusual at this early hour but then this was an unusual day. Rodder Pawl the footman grimaced at the hallway carpet: one big track of grime. Mistress Ambleson would be very upset were she to see it. The bell rang, and he opened the door to a tall figure wearing the hooded black robes of a priest of Harla. Pawl tamped down his dread and let the priest in.

Once inside, the figure pulled off the hood to reveal a kind-faced older man, hair shorn very short—almost bald—in the manner Friends male and female alike preferred. Behind him followed two men and a woman, dressed and shorn alike. The largest man carried a pair of poles wrapped in canvas; the woman carried a folded white sheet. "Where is she?" said the lead priest.

"This way." Pawl led them from the entryway up the stairs to the room where Mistress Ambleson sat. At first glance, she appeared to have fallen asleep in her chair before the sitting room fire. On closer inspection, her skin was white and waxy as a taper. Her chin listed down and to one side; her eyes were closed. Beside her on her workstand stood a small half-drunk glass of barisha. One hand held a letter. Three bored-looking Guardsmen clustered in one corner chatting in low voices with the fidgeting, anxious cook; in an opposite corner on a footstool sat Ianna the maid, her apron over her head as she rocked and cried.

A green-clad Sister stood looking out the bay window onto the street, hands folded under her gray overdress. She turned and bowed as the group entered. "Siblings, I am Sister Dagmissa," she said.

The lead priest answered her bow. "Friend Hames, Sister. Who was this lady in life?"

"Mistress Tellis Ambleson," replied the Sister. "I've been treating her for nerves lately."

"Mr Pawl," said Hames. Pawl flinched; he'd hoped the priest had forgotten him. "When did you find her?"

"About two hours ago. I called for Ianna—" he jerked his head toward the crying maid—"and she was no help so I went for a Sister right away, and then she sent me for the Guard, and then they called for you, your honor," he said, bowing and nodding.

"'Friend' is enough, Mr Pawl. How long do you think she's been dead, Sister?"

"I'd say about seven hours or so," said Sister Dagmissa, crossing to the corpse. She took Mistress Ambleson's free hand and flexed the fingers. "She's stiff but not completely. D'you agree with that time, Friend?"

"I do. Your guess at the cause of her death?"

Sister Dagmissa flicked her hand at the worktable. "She killed herself. Tincture of poppies in her barisha. I'd prescribed it for her nerves."

Pawl gasped. "But Mistress would never do such a thing! There's Miss to think of, and Mistress always thought of Miss before everything!"

Sister Dagmissa plucked the letter from Mistress Ambleson's stiff fingers. "Did you read this, Mr Pawl?"

"No, Sister, I can't read much, and besides it didn't seem right."

"It says Miss Ambleson has eloped with an 'Adrik.' Do you know anything about this?"

Pawl fingered Mr Adrikov's gold piece in his pocket. "Not as such, ma'am. I know Mr Adrikov and Miss are very much taken with one another. Mistress disapproved, and their running off—well, it doesn't surprise me any."

"Hm," said the Sister.

Pawl wondered if she could see the guilty gold piece through his trousers. What if they blamed him? He'd never imagined Mistress might do such a thing. Mr Adrikov and Miss were so attached, and no one thought Mistress right to keep them apart—it had seemed kind to help, and he knew

Mistress would forgive the couple when they came back. Then there was the gold piece, more than he made in a spoke, with another to follow on the newlyweds' return. "So…so what's to happen now? Who's going to pay me my final wages?"

"Where is the lady's family, Mr Pawl?" said Friend Hames.

"I don't know, sir. She never spoke about where she was from or who her people were. She and Miss have lived here in Arren close on a year, if that helps."

"Not in the least," said Friend Hames. "Captain," he called to the head Guardsman, "with no family to inherit, I believe the contents of this house are now forfeit to the government."

"But I said I didn't know her family, not that she didn't have any—what about Miss?" said Pawl.

"If a relative steps forward, the proceeds from the auction will be given to him, minus the tithe to the Hill and taxes. Miss Ambleson is the responsibility of her new husband, assuming the rascal married the poor girl."

The thought had never occurred to Pawl. What if Mr Adrikov *didn't* marry her? If she came back in shame to an empty house, what would become of her?

The Guardsman motioned to his men. "Thank you, Friend Hames. I'll report back to the Accountsman's office, and he'll send his men round to pay off the servants and begin the inventory. I leave the body to you, then." He bowed to the Friends and the Sister, and left with his men.

The two priests of Harla unrolled the canvas: a stretcher, a red silk tassel tied in black thread dangling from the ends of its black poles. They spread it on the hearth rug as the priestess manipulated the corpse's arm back and forth at the elbow. "Still somewhat bendable, but not for long," she said.

The priests positioned Pawl's Mistress on the canvas as best they could, and the priestess spread the white sheet over her; all four Friends raised their hoods and the two junior priests picked up the stretcher poles. Somehow the tassels' sway and the lump under the sheet broke free the whimper Pawl had been holding back for two hours. Mistress was dead, and he was responsible. If he hadn't helped Mr Adrikov and Miss—but how was he to know this would happen?

"Please," he said, catching at Friend Hames's sleeve. "Please, when it's time to…may I do the final rites for her in the Hill? Miss won't be back in time, and there's no one else."

"There's me, Rodder Pawl!" said the maid in the corner, her wet, somewhat snotty face emerging from her apron. "I was the one combed her hair of a morning, wasn't I? Not you. *I* should comb it at the last." Ianna resumed bawling and threw the apron back over her head. Cook said something lost in Ianna's renewed sorrow that Pawl assumed was a demand to be among the mourners as well.

"Hush now, good Ianna," said the priest. "Save your tears for Mistress Ambleson's final bath. We'll send a messenger for all three of you later to-day." The Friends carried the body from the room, the priestess before and Friend Hames behind; the Sister followed into the hallway with Cook, leaving him alone with the weeping Peg.

Pawl stared at the empty chair, now fouled with the corpse's final mess. He supposed the Accountsman's auditors would have it destroyed. He crept up to Mistress's work stand, where the letter lay forgotten. Beside it stood a miniature portrait of Miss Mattie, and the fatal glass of barisha.

He'd done this. He'd driven Mistress to suicide. He'd have to make it right somehow.

Pawl picked up the letter and the miniature, glancing at the corner; Ianna still had her apron over her head. He slipped the letter and miniature into his waistcoat. He shouldn't take them, but who'd know? He'd watch for Miss's return, make sure Mr Adrikov had done right by her, help her if not. For now, he and Cook and Ianna the maid would help bathe Mistress's body and sew her into her shroud. There was a start, at least, and may the Gods forgive him.

Inside a well-appointed carriage, Mattie woke up, cuddled against Adrik under a huge pile of furs and carriage blankets. The weather had turned bitter cold; the heavy brown velvet curtains were shut tight against the chill. Even so, her breath formed in the air, and the bricks at their feet had long ago lost their heat. How long had she been asleep? They must be approaching Maryakuspa by now, where a friendly, discreet Father Adrik knew would tie their marriage cord. Adrik stirred and tightened his arms around her; the thought left her head, to be replaced by the one that had plagued her all night.

Why hadn't Mama relented? Mattie hated to leave with nothing but a note on her mother's workstand. On the other hand, eloping on Neya's Day could not be more romantic. No one could blame them, not even Mama.

Adrik kissed her. "Second thoughts, darling?"

"Oh, no, not at all! I was just wishing Mama could be at the wedding. I know she won't be angry when we return home, but she's going to worry until we do."

"I left things in a way to soothe your mother's mind."

Mattie settled into his arms again. "You're so good to us."

The final trouble that had dogged her far longer than their plans to elope now took precedence: her parentage.

Mattie should have told him before they left. She'd even tried to tell him; he distracted her, and she lost her nerve. She must do it now, before he tied the marriage cord round her wrist. Nothing could change his mind, she was certain, but what if he did? She was compromised now.

She would tell him she was a child of Farr—that her real father was an unknown rapist. Close enough to the truth, for how could Mama have refused the King? Papa had married her mother and taken Mattie as his own. She'd had his name, at least until a year ago. Oh, she should have told him before they left.

"Adrik," she faltered, "I need to tell you something. Something about... about my family."

Adrik opened his melancholy eyes. "Oh? I know everything about your family I need to know, I'd wager, but if there's something you wish to tell me I shall gladly listen."

"I meant to tell you sooner..."

"Darling, it cannot be as bad as you think it is."

Mattie told him the amended story and watched his face anxiously. He brought his free hand to his mouth to smooth his mustache; had she not known better, she would have sworn he hid a smile. "Oh, my Mattie, how happy I am that you trust me. Shall you confide the last part as well?"

"What last part? There is nothing more to tell."

"Let's start with your name. It isn't Ambleson. It's Dunley."

"Dunley? No," said Mattie, keeping her voice as blank and calm as she could despite her jittering insides. "My stepfather's name was Ambleson. It's the name he gave me."

Adrik laughed. "One of the things I love about you, Mattie, is that you're terrible at subterfuge. Your emotions cover you head to toe. You fell in love with me the first day, when you twisted your ankle, didn't you? My sweet girl, I would marry you no matter what your name is. I don't use my real name either."

Was Adrik in similar circumstances? Not long ago, when she lived in Reggiston and didn't have to lie about her name and didn't know whose daughter she was, she would never have considered the suit of a bastard. She couldn't very well put herself above one now, could she? She burrowed closer to him, and he hugged her tight. "If my name is not to be Mistress

Adrikov, then, what is it to be?"

"I am Adrik Antremont, some day to be styled Adrin of Tremont."

"Adrin? But that's a royal name, surely you mean Adrik—*Antremont*? But you can't be!" A horrible supposition came to her: could he be another bastard of King Harsin's? She pushed away from him, thinking of the night at the Estate with her drunken half-brother. If she hadn't attracted Temmin's attention she'd still be Mattie Dunley of Reggiston, and here she was again with a man who might be her brother! *Neya, why would you send me two of them?*

"I have every right to the royal family's name. You see, you and I are cousins. My father is King Ruvin of Tremont, whose place your father usurped some forty years ago."

He knew! How long had he known? Always? She peered through the carriage curtains. The carriage rolled along a hard-packed dirt track through flat plains. Tough-looking grass poked through a light dusting of late snow. No crops, no houses, no people. Nowhere to run and no one to help her. "Where are we going?"

He smiled, but his downturned eyes did not. "We've already gone. Over the borders into the Northern Wastes, where your father will never find you."

"My father is dead," she whispered.

"Would that he were, sweetheart. Then I wouldn't be skulking about the countryside and *my* father would be sitting on the Tremontine throne where he belongs."

"What makes you think His Majesty is my father?"

"He's not Darwas Dunley, that's certain," he retorted. "Your uncle is a right prick, by the way, throwing you and your mother out of your tavern when your stepfather died. You are Mattisanis Dunley, or were raised as such. Your mother's maiden name was Ambler. She and the King—your father—had a brief affair when he came to the Estate for your brother Temmin's birth."

She fought down shame and increasing panic. "He's *not* my brother— I've even never met the Heir!"

Adrik shook her by the shoulders. "*I* am the Heir, not that whelp. He's still your brother whether you've met him or not. With luck you'll never meet him. He'll be dead."

Whenever Adrik touched her in the past, a warm melting flowed down her body beneath his hands. Now this stranger gripped her arms not quite tight enough to hurt her but tight enough to let her know she wasn't going anywhere, and his hands burned like ice. "You don't love me at all!" she said.

His down-tipped eyes softened; he was her lover once more. "Oh, there you're wrong, my darling, my Mattie. I *do* love you, though I hadn't intended to. I had intended only to woo you by stages safely and quietly, then take you away with me. When we reach my father, I will tie the marriage cord round your wrist just as I said I would. It is no hardship. I love you." Adrik dipped his head to kiss her, but she turned away. He turned her back, fingers firm on her chin, and kissed each brimming eye. "Never worry, you're safe with me. I shall not touch you until the cord is tied, and no one else shall either. I promise you."

"My mother's expecting us back. The note I left said we were coming home after the wedding."

"Don't worry about your mother, sweetheart, I have taken care of it," he answered. He tucked her into the corner of the carriage under a mound of blankets and furs. "It's cold. Now, sleep. We'll be there in another few hours."

Though she closed her eyes, Mattie did not sleep. She cursed her father for being King. She cursed Adrik for his falsity. She cursed her mother for being right about him, and she cursed herself for believing him.

They stopped soon after, but no comforting inn stood nearby; a change of horses waited on the wide, empty plains, alone but for a native groom holding their reins. The man's hair was a white-blond so pale it was almost transparent, his eyes a flat, acid blue that did not leave her even when she crouched a small distance from the carriage to relieve herself. At least Adrik and the coachmen turned away.

Nowhere to run, no one who might help her. No way to return to her mother—at least right now. She would get home to Mama somehow, and then they would go to the King and demand proper protection. He owed her at least that much as her father, and she wished her mother had demanded it from the beginning. It would have saved Mattie from whatever awaited her at Ruvin's outlaw court. *Don't worry, Mama, I'll find my way back to Arren somehow.*

The flat grasslands of the Northern Wastes turned into forests of pine and newly-greened larches and birch, patches of snow purple in their shadows. They traveled miles through these trees until the road burst into in the open, traveling along the shoreline of a lake so large it could fairly be called an inland sea. Islands greater and smaller rose up from its surface, the small crowned with gray stone buildings, the larger with villages. Boats plied the water and clustered on the many docks; how cold it must be on their decks.

At any other time, Mattie might have found the scenery charming and ex-otic. Now she looked only for opportunities to escape—and saw none.

They drove onto what at first she took to be a causeway, though she soon realized it could not have been manmade. A natural ridge rose up from the water, a broad road planed from the top of its steep, forested slopes. It slith-ered this way and that through the lake, ending at a bridge to a large island. An ancient castle took up all of the island's cloverleaf of a rock, its rough, gray stone walls rising from rocky shores sheering into the water. Towers ringed at the top in ruddy stone rose from each of its several corners; their many round windows stared out at the surrounding waters like lidless eyes. Conical roofs of green copper topped each tower.

Adrik pressed against her back and kissed her temple. "Welcome to Gremassem, Princess Mattisanis, and the court in exile of King Ruvin of Tremont."

Great iron gates driven into the rocky ridge blocked the bridge. At the coachman's call, the gates ground up on their winches; the obstinate doors balked on their enormous hinges but eventually obeyed and opened. Over the bridge and into Gremassem went the carriage, and Mattie with it.

Inside the great main courtyard, Adrik handed her down into a bustling world: women carrying laundry to the tubs; chickens scrabbling underfoot; boys running to take the leads of the carriage horses; a man with a whole pig carcass over his brawny shoulder; handcarts with loads of potatoes, turnips, steaming dung.

Mattie could see her breath. She clutched her bandbox, all she'd taken with her. Adrik marched her across the cobbles to a stern-looking native woman dressed in a gray woolen gown and a long quilted vest; she stood in a stone archway leading from the courtyard. A gray knitted lace shawl covered her head, and her strong blue eyes tilted downward at the outside corners. Behind her stood three serving girls, each more stoic than the last, and two men. A beam of sunshine hit one of the men just so, lighting up the yellow of his beard and the array of knives at his belt.

"Ma Kupar," said Adrik with a broad smile, "may I make known to you Princess Mattisanis of Tremont."

Mattie twisted the bandbox cord around her hands. "Please stop, please, Adrik, stop making fun of me. I'm not a princess!"

Adrik ignored her. "Ma Kupar, please show Her Highness a room where she may freshen up."

The woman sized Mattie up; for a moment, Mattie expected her to open her mouth and inspect her teeth. The woman nodded her head and gestured for Mattie to follow. The miserable girl fell in behind her. What else could she do? She was at least two hundred miles from Arren, probably more. After more than two days straight in a carriage with stops just long enough to change horses, she was tired, disoriented, hungry and filthy. When she had recovered some strength, some sense of where she was, she could plan an escape, perhaps. They walked down endless corridors, up stairs, through echoing halls and on and on into the fortress's heart. Somewhere in this enormous place there must be someone who'd take pity on her. She just needed a little help, a foothold—

"Here, Your Highness," said Ma Kupar, opening a thick dark wood door set in an arch. She stepped aside, and Mattie crept into a surprisingly bright room. The three servants pushed their way past her. One snatched the bandbox from her hands; another took a great iron kettle from a hulking brick stove, whitewashed like the rest of the room, and poured its steaming contents into a large basin on a stand; the third twitched Mattie's felt bonnet from her head and her cloak from her shivering shoulders.

"Please to undress here before the stove," said the woman. "You will be so cold but a moment." Mattie had heard this barbaric accent in Arren occasionally; it reminded her of the ridge road, steep R's and T's at variance with a sibilance curving the woman's speech in long arcs. Ma Kupar gestured to the basin, now cooled with water from a silver pitcher standing beside it. Mattie timidly washed her hands.

The woman made an abrupt gesture; the serving girls stripped Mattie to her stockings before she could squeak an objection and started in on her with steaming wet flannels and soap. "T'would be best were you to take the stockings and shoes off as well and be clean all over. We have new for you."

Already half-soaped, Mattie let them have their way. They scrubbed her from the toes up as she turned one side and then the other towards the stove in an attempt to warm herself; the cold raised goosebumps on her skin and puckered her nipples.

The girl who'd taken her hat and cloak returned with clothing. Mattie slipped on thick but finely knitted cream wool stockings, a linen chemise and thin woolen petticoats. The women burned Mattie's old things in front of her.

The new clothing was made of much finer stuff than even Ma Kupar's. The soft, lilac wool shift used the same embroidered high band collar as did Corrish traditional clothing, belted just under the breasts with a wide silk band woven in dark blues and reds. Over it came the long quilted vest Mattie had seen on both men and women, this one of fine slate blue silk brocade with silver thread shot through its borders. For her feet they gave her fur-lined half-boots of the same brocade. They slipped fingerless mitts knitted in a fine slate silk thread onto her hands. Over her hair they spread a filmy lace veil that matched the mitts; though it weighed nothing, it settled a cozy warmth about her head and shoulders.

Looking at herself in the cheval glass was like looking at a picture from a Corrish fairy tale book, as if she'd gone back in time some 700 years. She had to admit she was warm as toast for the first time since they'd left Arren: practical clothes for a cold climate.

"Come now, ma'am. Your King waits," said Ma Kupar.

"He is not my king," said Mattie. "He's no one's king!"

"This is not the concern of the Gremas," the woman answered, taking her by the elbow. "Our Headman has allied with him as kinsman. You are among the Gremas, you are Tremontine, and so here he is your King. Be quiet now, you will stand before the Headman and your King."

Ma Kupar led Mattie past guards set three and three beside a great arched door banded in iron, and left her in a high-vaulted hall; tapestries covered the stone walls, thick carpets the wooden floors. Mattie was the only woman in the room. Men in native costume filled the benches—the Gremas? She had never heard them called anything other than "northern barbarians," but Ma Kupar had used the name "Gremas." Red heads and brown heads sprinkled the crowd, but most were blond. Almost every eye turned toward her was blue.

At the hall's far end, a roaring blaze filled an enormous fireplace hooded in the same verdigris copper covering the turrets. On a dais before it sat two men in ancient, ornately carved chairs. Both wore richer versions of the common clothing—woolen trousers tucked into modern riding boots, and high-necked shirts. Their long quilted vests were silk embroidered in gold. The one on Mattie's left had hair so shot through with white that the blond strands remaining looked like sunlight streaked on snow. The other's hair was as dark as her own, though heavily threaded with silver; his beard, trimmed more neatly than those of the men around him, was almost completely gray. Something about his lean, angular face resembled the King's profile on a five-silver piece.

Adrik appeared at her side, for all his falsity still handsome in a dark blue high-necked shirt and quilted vest. He placed her numb hand on his arm. "Gremas clothing suits you, darling Mattie. Don't be afraid. No one intends you any harm. Quite the opposite. Now, come." He led her to the dais. He said something to the blond man on the left in the native language;

it had the same steep slopes and sibilance of Ma Kupar's accent. She recognized her own name among the unfamiliar words. Adrik turned to her and said in Tremontine, "Mattisanis of Tremont, this is Uole, Headman of the Gremas." To the dark man on the right he said, "Father, may I make known to you Mattisanis of Tremont, your niece. Princess Mattisanis, your uncle, King Ruvin of Tremont." Mattie knew she was expected to curtsey, but she couldn't move. She wanted to go to sleep, she wanted to go home, she wanted away from the man who'd broken her heart and the men who now studied her from atop the dais.

The Headman said something she didn't understand to Ruvin; Adrik's arm stiffened beneath her hand. Ruvin chuckled in response and stood. "Ah, my niece, and aren't you a pretty thing. Welcome home, Adrik."

"Thank you, sir," he replied, putting his hand over Mattie's. "When shall we tie the marriage cord?"

"The day after tomorrow, I think. The bride looks as though she might profit from a day's rest." Ruvin descended the dais and took Mattie's hand from Adrik's arm. He turned her round, inspecting her from every side as if they were dancing. "Never did I think I would marry again, and certainly not to such a lady as my son has brought me," he smiled.

Adrik stifled a gasp. "Excuse me, Father, but I don't understand you. Who are you marrying?"

"Why, the Lady Mattisanis, of course."

Adrik paused, clearly shocked. "She was to be mine. You said so."

"Did I? I said to woo her and win her, something like that. Don't worry. You are my Heir, Adrik, and that won't change even if she bears me sons." He raised his voice and said something in the native tongue, then added in Tremontine, "I have sworn before everyone here."

Mattie snatched her hand away as the conversation sank into her weary mind. "Are you saying *you* intend to marry me?"

Ruvin recaptured her hand and kissed it. "It helps cement my claim to the throne, my dear, to marry a girl of your lineage."

"My lineage? My mother was a housemaid, and my father owned a tavern, that's my lineage. All right, very well, yes, my mother told me I'm a royal bastard—" Mattie spat the words "—a royal bastard like you. I have as much right to the title 'princess' as you do to 'king'—none!"

Ruvin crushed her hand in his grip until she cried out, her legs buckling. "You will speak to me with the respect due your King, woman, and you will never call me 'bastard' again." Adrik stepped forward as if to stop him, but checked himself. "You'd *best* think twice, son," said his father. "Did you come to believe your own lies, Adrik? I'd swear you actually love this girl."

Adrik's down-tilted eyes took on that hard look. "You said she was for me, that my marriage to her would shore up my own claim since my mother was not of the blood."

"I will not accept this!" said Mattie through teeth clenched against pain. "You will never find a Father who will bind a woman in marriage against her will!"

Headman Uole spoke. "You are not in Tremont, Lady. You are among the Gremas, and Gremas women do as they are told. We have no Fathers, or Mothers, Sisters, Friends, Scholars, Lovers or Beloveds—none of them. Only Brothers, only Farr the Warrior, and He does not listen to women's prayers."

"No Fathers? How else is one to marry?"

"We tie the cord ourselves, at knife point if necessary," said Uole. "That is the way of the Gremas. Once it was the way of the Tremontines, to take the woman whether she would or no and tie her to the bedpost as we still do. We have kept the faith they have forgotten, the faith your King Ruvin swears to bring back to your people."

Ruvin shrugged her away. "You're valuable, Princess, but only if I marry you. You're of no value at all otherwise, not even wed to my son. In fact, you're a danger to me. Adrik's tender feelings notwithstanding, I'd slit your throat myself." Mattie's smarting hand crept to her neck. Uole spoke a word to a servant, who left the room and reappeared with the silent Ma Kupar. "Take Her Highness to her room," said Ruvin. "Bring her food and let her rest after her long journey. The day after tomorrow is either a wedding or a funeral."

Ma Kupar led her away. Mattie took a last look at Adrik; his eyes remained the same hard, flat brown, but he was glaring at his father and spared her not a look.

They walked her down numerous hallways to her bedchamber, a grand, whitewashed affair of tapestries, carpets, and a stove tiled in brilliant blue; the room's mullioned windows looked out at the great lake and its hundreds of islands and thousands of boats. They fed her a light meal: oatcakes, salted fish and some sort of dried berry compote with custard. Mattie offered no resistance when they undressed her down to her chemise, nor when they tucked her into bed, pulled shut the bed-curtains and darkened the room.

Her mind did resist. Would she rather die than marry Ruvin? Perhaps if she offered them compliance, they might grow complacent in time and she could make good an escape. As things stood she had no knowledge of the country nor of the language, and not a friend to help her. Adrik looked as if he wanted to come to her defense, but was it because he wanted the advantage marriage to a daughter of Harsin would confer? Or did he love her, and if he did, would he go against his father?

Mattie peeked out of the bed-curtains. Ma Kupar guarded the room, rocking slowly in a chair by the stove but quite awake. "Go to sleep, Your Highness," said the woman without turning her head.

Mattie sighed and settled back among the pillows. She was so tired, so heartsore. She missed her mother when she'd gone to the Estate to work, but Tellis was just down the road in Reggiston then, waiting to see her on her half-day off every Paggday. Now her mother was who knew how many miles away in Arren. Across a hostile country at the least. The tears she'd held back since Adrik revealed himself drenched the pillow. "I tell you, go to sleep," said Ma Kupar from the other side of the bed-curtains. "Tears change nothing for any of us, but for you, very much not. Sleep."

"I don't want to sleep. I want to go home," sobbed Mattie.

"*I* want you to go home. You are one more trouble for me, one more trouble for my Adrik." The woman rocked a few more times. "I am his mother, you know."

Was Adrik illegitimate, too? "Is that why he calls you 'Ma?'"

"It is title for married women here. It will be yours soon. I was Ruvin's third wife. He had two others, both dead. I am set aside long ago, and yet lived. You take my place."

"I don't want to take your place. You can have it!"

"I cried when he set me aside and I tell you again, tears change nothing. Sleep."

Mattie's exhaustion overtook her in time, and she slept straight through till late the next day. She saw none of the wedding preparations when the day came; they kept her to her room, where she wavered between defiance and despair and wore her nerves thin pacing before the stove. At least it was warm there; outside, a fitful late spring snowfall tried the patience of the newly-green trees.

It grew dark. Ma Kupar and the silent serving girls came in bearing candles and another neatly folded stack of clothing. Mattie hesitated, but in the end chose to live in hope. She put on the heavy white silk gown, an overdress of gold brocade replacing the quilted vest. On her head they placed a gold diadem, covered with a white lace cobweb shawl. Around her neck and in her ears hung freshwater pearls and amber, set in intricately worked gold—"very old, among the great riches of the Gremas," Ma Kupar noted. Mattie wondered if Kupar had worn the jewels at her own wedding to Ruvin.

At night's end, once Ruvin had knotted the marriage cord three times round her wrist himself, once Adrik's cold stare devoid of sympathy flickered over her, once she'd been led by the cord to the marriage bed, once Ruvin had tied her wrist to the bedpost and taken her virginity with casual cruelty, once he'd collected the proof of consummation on a length of silk, once she'd been left alone still bound to the bed while Ruvin and his allies feasted in the great hall so loudly she caught echoes of it even through the stone—then, she lost hope. She stared at the bed-curtains, aching in body, dull in mind and bruised in both, and understood the futility of escape attempts. She would never see her mother again. She would die here, alone and friendless. She wanted to die.

Adrik had never loved her—had never existed at all.

Ruvin was standing on a table top, a dressing gown over his long nightshirt. His bare legs stuck out the bottom, and he roared a Gremas wedding song as he waved the bloodied silk over his head and the drunken men around him stomped an accompaniment. Adrik stayed to one side. He kept his face in the cool mask he'd perfected over years of subterfuge, both in his father's service and his own.

He would never have let himself fall in love with Mattie if he'd known she was meant for his father and not for himself—no, of course he would have. One look at her and he'd opened as if she'd been his key, no matter how hard he'd struggled to keep himself closed.

That spring day a year ago in Arren when he'd arranged their little meeting and she'd stumbled into his arms, he'd chalked his awakening up to professionalism; if he had to play the lover, he must allow himself to feel at least a little in love. She was a target, an instrument, a means to an end; marrying her shored up his family's claims. It was just his good luck she was beautiful, passionate, innocent, trusting, kind, loving, funny, cheerful—that she filled his empty, secret heart. He'd had trouble waiting until the appointed time to take her away, but soothed himself that she would be his. In time she would accept her fate as future Queen of Tremont because she loved him. How could she love him now?

Ruvin shouted a greeting to him; Adrik smiled and raised his cup in response.

His father had lied to him—to what end? Adrik had killed for his father, more than once; he'd been the one to deliver the final blows to both his uncles, the other two bastard sons of old King Temmin the Fifth. Adrik had been raised to his father's service and cause above all else, his loyalty absolute. Did Ruvin know Adrik's own ambition so little, or did he think Adrik would do a more thorough job if he believed the prize was his?

Ruvin fluttered the silk, stained with Mattie's blood and his own semen. Adrik imagined snatching the silk from the older man's hands, twirling it into a cord—he'd done it before before with silks much like this one—and squeezing his father's neck until he crushed the windpipe beneath.

His father had been everything in the world. He'd believed in his father's right to the throne, and his own right as Heir. Now his father had betrayed him. On its face, what was his promise to keep Adrik as his Heir, if Mattie gave him sons? They would have more royal blood than Adrik from both sides of their parentage, and thus a better claim.

"Did you come to believe your own lies, Adrik?"

Yes, just as I believed yours.

EIGHT

Twenna didn't know which of her inexpert coquetries had worked—
she'd done little more than pout—but Harsin returned to her bed not two
days after the unfortunate incident at Neya's Day. He showered her with
gifts: shot silk for a new dress; tortoise-shell haircombs from Pau'a; and a
magnificent set of matching sapphire-and-diamond earrings, collar, ring
and bracelets, "the color of your eyes, my dear. You are to keep them forever."

She was back in Elbig's good graces. "Our sponsor would like you to
start dropping little hints in his favor, darling."

"Hints, Papa? What hints?"

"Oh, I don't know. Make sure he's in attendance at all your cozy little
evenings—invite his friends, too. Compliment Corland's address, his ami-
ability, his reasonableness. How much you like him."

"But I *don't* like him, Papa."

"Then lie, you ridiculous girl!" he fumed. "The point is, make the King
look more favorably on His Grace!"

Twenna pursed her lips in confusion. "I'm sure Borney is already one of
Harsin's particular friends. We see him and Cosetta—Mistress Grasian—at
the Lodge quite often. He makes pop-eyes at me."

"Yes, but if the King thinks you see him as amiable—oh, never mind.

I don't know what he wants with us anyway, that Duke of Corland, but his help got us this far. When he asks us for ours, just remember we are to give it."

"The 'little hints,' you stupid tailor, are to put the King in a more receptive frame of mind to our ideas," said the exasperated Corland when they met the next day on the Promenade. "Your daughter inviting me and the members of my faction to her gatherings gives us political capital, not that you'd understand something like that. Have her mention things like the Heir's bad behavior, how much she'd love a set of Inchari house slaves, how insolent the merchant class is getting—"

"I hesitate to remind you—I hesitate to remind myself, but it must be said—that *I* come from the merchant class."

"Not for long," said Corland. "Harsin is quite smitten. I wouldn't be surprised if he elevated you to a baronetcy."

A baronetcy! While Elbig had bought himself a certain amount of gentility, a title, even one so modest as Sir, would give him real countenance, real claims as a gentleman. Perhaps then the young men strolling so indolently about the Temple Green would stop turning their noses up at him. "Tailor—no—more!" he said to himself, each word a step down the Promenade. "Tailor—no—more!"

Twenna's artless contriving of dinner parties to always include Corland and his friends began to irritate the King. "Why does Borney have to be at every card party, every musical evening, every damn dinner we give? And his hangers-on—what on earth do we need with longfaces like Edgins and Hoop?"

Twenna paused in arranging the roses he'd brought to the Lodge for her and fought to come up with a half-truth. In the end she settled for the lie. "I find him quite amiable, don't you, darling?"

"I find him the same lump he was in school," said Harsin, flicking the butt end of his cigar into the empty hearth. "A little of him goes a long way."

"Oh. I thought you were friends." She kept her eyes on the flowers in the vase before her lest he see her trying to think of what to say next.

"After a fashion, I suppose. That loathsome son of his is too presumptuous by half, but that's hardly enough to make Borney my enemy. He's politically influential among the True Conservatives, and I need his men in Inchar. But friend? Old school mate is more accurate. Now, Lord Litta—Anvalt is my friend. Why don't you invite him more often?"

"I invite him every time, Harsin." So she had, but her invitations were always answered with the same curt note from Litta's secretary: "His Grace regretfully declines." Now she thought on it, of all the King's friends he alone never danced with her.

"Well, invite him again. No, I'll have Winmer do it. Anvalt's a curious old thing—conservative in the traditional sense, not the political sense."

Twenna's intimate dinners at the Lodge were the kind to which men brought their mistresses, not their wives. Perhaps His Grace had no one like her or Lord Corland's Cosetta to bring? Lord Litta was older but hardly unattractive even with that dueling scar through his brow, and if he was a lover of men, why wouldn't he just bring his young man? "Is Lord Litta perhaps... uncomfortable at occasions such as our dinners?"

Harsin crossed one leg over the opposite thigh and settling back in his chair. "You know, he just might be now that you mention it. He's never cared for outside liaisons—never has any of his own, keeps himself to his wife entirely—and used to scold me about it when we were younger. Suppose he's given up on me by now," he laughed. "Stop fooling with those roses, Twenna, and come to me."

Twenna began to feel rather green a week after Neya's Day, and now, halfway through Spring's Ending, she felt worse than ever. Certain scents became unbearable. She passed an overly fragrant person on the street as she made her way to Mistress Naister's for a fitting and almost fainted. Cooking smells, particularly fish, took her appetite completely; she progressed to nausea and outright vomiting in the mornings and sometimes during the day. She even begged off meeting Harsin, which finally made her father call for a Sister.

The droopy-eyed healer hovered over Twenna as she lay on her bedchamber retiring couch. She took Twenna's pulses and questioned her closely: Sensitivity to smells? Oh, horrid. Nausea? Very much so. Exhaustion? Quite fatigued. Tender bosom? Why yes, how had the Sister known?

"You've missed your moon, if I may venture a guess."

Twenna tapped her chin, thinking. "I may have miscounted."

"No, miss," said Wendia, her ladies maid. "You were due two weeks ago. Our moons come at the same time, Sister," she added, "and mine has come and gone."

The Sister stood. "Hmm. If you miss your next one, petition the Healer's House and we'll assign you a midwife for the duration." She dug in her capacious satchel and pulled out a flat-sided amber glass bottle. "Take this in water. Eat some dry toast immediately upon awakening, and the tincture throughout the day as needed. If you run out, send someone to the near-est Sister's Dispensary for more. Ask for a bottle of Early Mother's tincture. Keep something on her stomach at all times, however small," she added to the maid. "Mint and ginger tisane, dry toast, biscuits, that sort of thing. No coffee or cocoa. Keep out of overheated rooms. You need fresh air, at least in your first two spokes. It should pass by then."

"Oh, Merciful Amma," said Wendia.

"Why, but what is it, Sister?" cried Twenna. "Am I in any danger?"

"Danger? Just of stretch marks, and your midwife will give you a cream for your belly for those. You're young and healthy. You should pull through a birth with no troubles at all." The Sister turned to leave.

"Birth?" blinked Twenna. "But I have...the Traveler Queen..."

"The Traveler Queen gave you a mark, did she? She'll take your money, but whether you get your money's worth in return is up for debate. The Blessed Maeve's marks seem to work if she likes you. You must not've made much of an impression. That reminds me." The Sister cleared her throat and studied the satchel in her hands. "Do, ah, do you need to arrange for the child to go to a Mother's House? You may wish to speak to the Moth-ers sooner than later. Oh—but then, the King will arrange for anything like that, I'm sure. Good day, now."

"Am I *that* infamous?" Twenna complained to the empty doorway.

Poor Twenna's interview that night with her father was far from a happy one. "Pagg damn you, girl! What have you done?"

"It isn't as if I did this on purpose, Papa!" she wailed. "I'm quite—quite *disambiguated* myself! You said the old woman made it so this wouldn't happen!"

"So she promised," fumed her father. "By gods, if this spoils our chances I'll track down the old bitch and beat her to death with my cane!"

As it happened, the old bitch's particular band of Travelers camped in the King's Woods at present, and so Elbig Shelstone walked to Marketgate the next day to search among the cabbages and lengths of cloth for a sign of them. He found them busking where the whiff of the nearby river mingled with the fragrances of eel pies and sizzling sausages wafting from the food carts. Elbig stood on the edges of the crowd until the Traveler musicians ended their reel and the barefoot, buxom dancing girls finished catching tossed coins in their cupped skirts.

He beckoned to the guitarist, a small, dark, fox-faced man. The man approached, his sharp blue eyes smiling and his hand outstretched for a coin. Instead, Elbig took a fistful of the startled Traveler's shirt and hissed,

"You tell that swindling Queen of yours I will get my money back for the fake charm she gave my daughter or I'll see her hung at the crossroads for a fraud!"

A hand seized the back of his collar and shook him until he released the guitarist. "You will do nothing of the kind," said a hard, amused voice. The hand released him. Elbig fumbled at the waistcoat that had hitched itself over his belly and stumbled round to face the voice, which belonged to a tall, powerfully built, rusty-haired young man with the same sharp blue eyes as the musician. "You are no threat to my mother, but I will not have you soiling Jesper's shirtfront, little tailor man. You will leave off my people, turn around, and go home."

Which the frightened little tailor man did.

A letter from Mr Winmer came, inquiring after Miss Shelstone's health. She answered she felt rather poorly but was recovering. A note in the King's own hand followed later the same day; might she improve enough to attend a private luncheon tomorrow at Foothill Lodge? Elbig dictated her reply: she would.

In fact, she had improved. The Sister's advice and the flat-sided bottle of Early Mother's tincture had combined to conquer her nausea, and she'd gone to the Lodge strong in both spirits and appetite. Now she sprawled comfortably naked atop the coverlet on Harsin's bed; a soft breeze from the open windows dried the sweat from her body, and she stroked her lover's dark head as he lay pillowed on her shoulder.

He smoothed the glossy brown hair between her legs. "Little mink of mine," he said, dipping his fingers just inside her.

She wiggled obligingly. "We just finished, darling!"

"When you are in my bed, Twenna my love, we are never finished." His thumb inscribed circles on the hard little nub at the top of her vulva; lazy waves spread over her, until she remembered.

He was pleased with her, in quite a good mood, he'd just called her his love. Now might be the time. "Harsin, I need to tell you something, and I hope you will be happy."

His thumb and fingers stopped. "Oh? And what might that be, my dear?"

"I...well, Father—we'd taken precautions, you know, and I'm quite surprised, but...I appear to be...I've missed my moon, and..."

Harsin removed his hand. "Pagg's balls." He flopped back onto the bed, one arm over his eyes. "You're sure?"

"The Sister was quite sure. I suppose my moon might still come."

"That's why you were sick," he said in a flat voice.

Twenna winced. "You're angry with me. My father was *quite* angry with me."

"Your father can go to the Hill." Harsin rose from the bed.

"Where are you going?" Twenna quavered. She sat up as he shrugged on a robe, stalked from the bedchamber into the drawing room and closed the door; he and a servant carried on a low, muffled conversation on the other side which Twenna imagined in distraught detail. He was turning her out. He was calling for her carriage and the nearest maid to help her dress. "I'm sorry," she whimpered to the empty room.

The door opened. The King entered, closing the door behind him again; his eyes beneath their heavy lids were hard. "Stop crying, Twenna. I care for crying women even less than expecting women."

Twenna swallowed back her rising nausea and wished she'd brought the amber bottle. "Will you send me to a Mother's House?"

"A Mother's House?" Harsin repeated. He laughed. "Don't worry, my dear. I have a property about an hour's ride from the City, called Middlemont. You will live there from now on." He sat down on the bed beside her and picked up a lock of her hair; he ran it through his fingers in contemplation. "I am done with unclaimed bastards," he resumed. "I will recognize the child and care for the both of you for the rest of your lives. You must live a quiet life, away from the City and my Queen. I will recognize my daughter, but I will not flaunt you both in front of Ansella."

Twenna captured his hand. "You won't leave me, will you? You won't stop loving me? Because I love you, Harsin, with all my heart."

"I will come to see you at Middlemont often."

She kissed him, and as their lips parted she realized what he'd said. "Why do you think it will be a daughter?"

"An educated guess," he smiled. He pushed her down on the bed and rolled atop her.

Her stomach complained, but she didn't care. His cock pressed hard against her, and as he moved to fill her she whispered, "Only you, there's only you and will only ever be you."

On his return to the Keep, Harsin called for both Winmer and Teacher and informed them of Twenna's condition; he ordered his secretary to draw up papers making Elbig Shelstone a baronet. "Find a holding. Something quite small and quite far away."

"Are you sure, sir?" said Winmer, wrinkling his nose.

"He is a loathsome little toad and a rascal, but it must be done. I will elevate Twenna to an earldom after the baby is born, and her father needs some kind of rank. Ready Middlemont for Miss Shelstone's prolonged stay. Send Hallik and his wife to run things—apologize to old Crookman and give him a sop to make up for Hallik's usurpation—oh, what is it, Winmer?" snapped the King.

Winmer stopped bouncing on his toes. "Sir, wouldn't it be more expedient to send the child to a Mother's House? There's one catering to the extra children of the nobility, not far from the capital. Quite the picturesque estate, you'd hardly know it was a Mother's House. The girl would be raised with the utmost propriety and a fine education."

"Do what I have told you." Winmer gave a skeptical, almost critical bow and left. Harsin turned to his advisor, who stood like a sliver of black ice before him. "It won't change my decision, but do you approve?"

"I confess to surprise at the depth of your attachment, sir."

Harsin paused. "All of my mistresses have told me they love me. Some of them might actually have meant it. With Twenna—I *know* she means it, poor girl. I'll do what I can for her, but no, my attachment is to the baby. I will not let another child of royal blood escape my supervision. Not after my brothers, and not after Tellis Ambler's girl. That damned Ansella. She should never have sent the girl away. I need her—I wish to marry her off to Fennows since he's so deuced anxious for an intimate connection to the royal family. I refuse to give him Elly, and there's no question of Sedra whatsoever."

"Dismissing your half-brothers from court when you were born was perhaps the most unwise thing your father ever did."

"We had quite the mess to clean up all around let alone the bastards' claims once I became king, didn't we. My father should have remarried as soon as his first wife died—by the time he married my mother, Perin had convinced himself he was the rightful Heir."

"In the absence of a legitimate son, he would have been king."

"What a mess Father left me. His women kept him too busy to pay attention to ruling."

Teacher bowed. "As you say, sir."

"About that girl—Mattisanis Dunley. I'd meant to search for her over the last year, but haven't had time to spare a thought. The worsening rebellions in Inchar alone have been enough to preoccupy me, let alone Temmin's hijinks. But now with this new child on the way I'm ill at ease. Miss

Dunley and her mother should be under my protection."

Teacher gestured to the mirror over the mantel. "Shall I look for her?" At Harsin's nod, Teacher intoned, "If Mattisanis Dunley is anywhere within sight of a reflection in this Kingdom or its territories, show her to me."

The obstinate mirror let not a flicker disturb the reflection of Teacher's silver eyes and Harsin's own somewhat worn countenance; he absently noted the increasing gray at his temples. "Try again." The second attempt was no more successful than the first.

"A different tack," said Teacher. "If Tellis Dunley is anywhere within sight of a reflection, show her to me."

The mirror resolved into a murky black. After years exposed to Teacher's magic Harsin never blinked, but this time something put the hairs on the back of his arms at attention. The distorted image kept jiggling; the reflecting object must be something someone was wearing. The wavering light suggested that whoever it was carried a lantern. The image rested on a niche in a rough wall—stone or perhaps brick. Within the niche lay a coffin.

The person carrying the lantern moved away from the niche, and the mirror presented Harsin's reflection once again, his face somewhat paler. "That was the inside of a Hill, wasn't it?"

"I fear so," murmured Teacher.

"So Tellis Dunley is dead. I'm very sorry for it. She was a beautiful girl." He knocked his knuckles against his chin. "How concerned should we be that you couldn't find my daughter?"

Teacher considered. "It may be she was not in view of a reflection. It may be she is out of the country. It has been a year, after all."

"Keep looking for her—you know best how to use reflections to find an elusive quarry."

"If I do not find her?"

"If you don't find her within a week, we shall send out agents and make inquiries. No—I'll have Winmer do that right away. Coordinate with him. It may be she's married a foreigner and gone off to Sairland or some such for all I know. Contact the Sairish through back channels and see if they will search for her there, without letting them know what she is—let *none* of our agents know what she is, but that she is to be unharmed in the search. If she's left the Kingdom, Sairland's her most likely destination."

The long, wide strip of parkland running between the two rows of the City's religious institutions was properly called the Temple Green, but it was better known for the broad walk down its middle: the Promenade. Here the upper class and its aspirants strolled, rode and drove, seeing and being seen. The last of the trees had shed their blossoms to the disappointment of the Promenade's regulars; the pink and white petals scattered on their carriages, shoulders and hats were a badge marking the bearers among the Capital's fashionable, genteel, and indolent.

Down the Promenade strolled the overly fashionable, nominally gen- teel and very indolent Percet Sandopint—Lord Fennows. A great golden knob topped the ebony walking stick swinging from one hand, his black silk hat sat rakishly askew, and his lorgnette searched for Princess Ellika, a Promenade regular at this hour.

Instead, Fennows spied a pair of matched grays drawing a shell-like curricle; a Brother led a smartly dressed contingent of Guardsmen in es- cort, and two familiar figures sat within. Lady Donnis Provisa, the Dowager Marchioness of Petras, handled the curricle's ribbons almost as well as the Queen beside her would have, but to Percet's eye the Queen looked not quite the thing: pale, almost green. He caught Lady Donnis's attention and before she could look away he raised his hat.

Neither the Queen nor Lady Donnis would have had to do more than acknowledge most anyone else in their acquaintance, but the Marchioness was his mother's cousin and Her Majesty was Percet's godsmother. One might assume some affection between godsson and godsmother, but the miserable summer twelve-year-old Percet spent at Whithorse Estate with the royal family obliterated any tenderness he might have had toward her. She'd tried to stop Temmin's endless pranks—him and that groom, what was his name, Alvo Nollson—but the Heir and his friend were clever, sneaky and cruel. They always managed to escape hands clean. Temmin always es- caped consequences for his actions, the bastard, but his luck couldn't hold out forever.

Falling in love with Princess Ellika was almost worse than her brother's gleeful cruelty. She'd paid him kinder attention than Temmin, but at almost fourteen she'd dismissed his love as a little boy's crush. She still dismissed him all these years later. Some day she would be forced to reckon with him, even if he had to wait until their wedding night. Some day he'd pay Temmin and Nollson back too, with interest. Let them all hold him in disdain; if the Sandopints played their cards right, some day they would get everything they wanted from the Antremonts.

With such ties among them, Lady Donnis was required to rein in and accept Percet's address; her cordial mien thinly veiled her dislike. No mat- ter; the Provisas were on his list as well. "Your Majesty, Lady Donnis! How splendid to see you on such a lovely day." The ladies were murmuring their greetings when Percet spied the perfect dart, right to hand. "Oh, look, there's Sir Elbig Shelstone. Who would've thought he'd be elevated."

"Elbig Shelstone has been elevated?" said the Queen, turning even more bilious.

Ah, she'd taken the barb straight to the heart. "Only to a baronetcy, but still. Shelstone's done just one notable thing for His Majesty, and that was, oh, twenty-two years ago, I believe. Though that notable thing has amused His Majesty for weeks now, I should think."

"We have an appointment at the Hearth, Percy," snapped Lady Donnis. "Good day to you."

Percet smiled as they pulled away, the Queen's back rigid and her cousin's furious. "Quite a good day so far," he murmured.

Across the Temple Green from the rose marble Lovers' Temple stood the Hearth—the Temple of Venna the Sister, its dark green stone walls marbled in white, with the enormous gray Healer's House beside it. Donnis pulled Ansella's curricle up before it with a fuming flourish, and a groom jumped down from the curricle's back to take the reins. Ansella stepped out with shaking knees; the curricle's sway and the news about Elbig Shelstone had sickened her so much she'd wondered if she'd make it to her destination without vomiting.

She had vomited every morning for the last few days. She didn't seem to be losing weight, but she was so often chilled. Both Donnis and Miss Hanston had urged her to call a Sister. Ansella had refused, but now she wondered if perhaps she *was* sick. "Percet Sandopint's a worm, just a slimy little worm to be trod underfoot," seethed Donnis as she took Ansella's arm.

Ansella seethed herself but kept her composure better. "Hush, Donnie, it's all right and we're in public." They walked up the shallow switch-backs into the Sister's Temple, made so the sick and infirm could more easily enter.

Just inside the Hearth's portico waited the newly invested Eldest Sister Imvalda, tall and twiglike in her deep green habit trimmed in the gray bands of her high office, and the Sister's Embodiment, a gentle, plump woman named Sarra. A woman in lighter green trailed behind them; Ansella recognized her from the brief glimpse of Imvalda's apartments in her receiving room mirror. That night seemed so long ago, but it was no more than a spoke.

Ansella and Donnis bowed to the Eldest Sister and the Embodiment, each touching her forehead to the priestesses' hands; the priestesses kissed the two women on the cheek and led them inside.

Imvalda put her arm through Ansella's as they walked together through the Temple's public hall past Venna's great statue, past the Eternal Hearth, and into the private cloister. The clean white halls here smelled of the chlorinated potash the Sisters used to scrub everything in their purview. "How are you, Your Majesty? I'm so glad you came to see us. You look a bit pale. Are you well?"

Ansella smiled. "I'm fine, thank you, Eldest Sister." They spoke in pleasantries: The King's health? Very good. And the children? Never better. Two Postulant Sisters wielding brooms bowed as they passed; Ansella wondered what there was to sweep.

Imvalda ushered them into her receiving room. "Sister Nadi, tea if you please," she said to the woman Ansella took to be her secretary and probable sweetheart. The woman bowed and left the room, closing the door behind her. The Eldest Sister motioned to a utilitarian but comfortable-looking gray couch, and Ansella and her cousin sat down. "It must be a great comfort to you, Your Majesty, having your cousin with you," said Imvalda carefully.

Ansella took her meaning. "If anything of a delicate nature is said today, Lady Donnis is in my complete confidence." Donnis took her cold hand and squeezed it. "In fact, now that we are in private, I must ask after Sister Ibbit." Donnis squeezed again, harder, but Ansella continued on. "I feel somewhat responsible for her plight."

"The only one responsible for Ibbit's 'plight' is Ibbit," said Imvalda, hard lines forming at the corners of her mouth. "Knowing I may speak freely—" a nod to Donnis— "I must ask if you understand Ibbit's trespass against you—that her behavior was very wrong?"

"Her behavior?" said Ansella, growing colder by the moment.

"We know the nature of your relationship," murmured Sarra. "Ibbit confessed, or should I say bragged. This involvement was very wrong of her—*her*, ma'am, not you. As your spiritual advisor she should never have done such a thing."

Ansella's breakfast skittered in her stomach. "I'm not quite sure I understand you."

Sarra looked to Imvalda; the Eldest Sister said, "She seduced you."

All the anger and despair inside Ansella wanted out, as did her fitful breakfast. Imvalda must have seen the signs, for she snatched a basin from a shelf just in time for the final escape. "I knew it," the Eldest Sister muttered. Sarra went to the room's basin and brought back a glass of water and two damp towels.

"Oh, what a day, I'm sorry, I'm sorry," Ansella wept.

"Sorry for what, my dear?" said Imvalda. She wiped Ansella's mouth with one cloth while Sarra dabbed at her forehead with the other. Imvalda handed her the glass. "Here, rinse your mouth and spit into the basin. Now lay back. Relax." Ansella did as she was bid and closed her eyes. Imvalda and Sarra discreetly checked her pulses, pressing her slack wrists in several different places, and then her neck and ankles; Donnis appeared worried at first, but a growing understanding started at the tip of her nose and spread over her face. She looked at Sarra, Sarra looked at Imvalda, and they all slid their eyes sideways at Ansella. "When did this nausea start?" said Imvalda.

"Yesterday," she lied. "I'm not running a fever. I just assumed I'd eaten something that didn't agree. May I sit up now? Oh—I think I might be sick again—" She vomited into the basin again. "My nerves—something upset me just before we arrived. I'm so very sorry."

Donnis supported her back down on the couch. "Nerves! Oh, you little liar! You've been sick at least a week. Just when you were getting better, too!"

Imvalda helped Ansella clean up again, depositing the towels in the laundry and passing the befouled basin to a waiting Sister outside; every room in the Hearth seemed to be outfitted like a surgery, even Imvalda's receiving room. "Is it all up now, my dear? Yes? Come lie down again." She settled a shawl over Ansella's legs. "Now, you really don't know what this might be?"

Ansella closed her eyes again. "It was just the once. My moon's a little late, that's all. It's something else, it has to be."

Sarra ran a soft hand over the Queen's forehead. "Your pulses tell the story, ma'am," the Embodiment said, "but it's early yet—very early if you've only missed one moon."

Ansella's empty stomach griped and heaved. "Actually, my second moon is due and hasn't come, either." She subsided into silence.

So this was her Neya's Day blessing. She'd loved being pregnant. She loved her children. She would love this one unreservedly—loved her already. It had to be a girl; if she carried a son, Teacher would have known immediately and announced it to Harsin.

What would *he* think? He'd preen and strut, the smug bastard. Pregnancy would give her an excuse to stay away from him. Except pregnancy usually made her...what was an acceptable word? More...*receptive* to him? *Demanding, more like*, said a traitorous inner voice. She might go home to Whithorse and put some distance between them, but she could not leave her three oldest, just before the girls might leave forever. They were all grown and didn't need her any more, but she still needed them. And it would look as if she were running from that Shelstone bitch. She burst into exhausted, frustrated tears. "I don't know what to do. Please don't tell him yet."

No one asked who she meant. "Hush, now," said Sarra. "We are sworn, and there may be nothing to tell in a moon."

Ansella shuddered. "That would be worse, much, much worse." She put her hand on her still-flat stomach.

"Rest, Your Majesty. We'll send you home with a tincture for the morning sickness," said Imvalda. "If this moon doesn't come, we will send a midwife to you. How old are you?"

"Forty-two."

Imvalda nodded. "It's rather late in life, but if your other pregnancies were uneventful, this one should be, too."

"My pregnancies were all easy. A little morning sickness, and then—just easy. Oh, gods. I'm so tired."

Donnis murmured reassuring nonsense until Ansella stopped crying and closed her eyes; her breathing steadied into a deep, monotonous rhythm. She lay in half-sleep, still hearing everything going on around her but unable to open her eyes or respond without an effort she could not muster. "What about Ibbit?" said Donnis in a low voice.

"Her trial is next week," answered Imvalda. "Its outcome is a foregone conclusion. We have found a good two dozen sympathizers among the Sisterhood here, and I have sent trusted investigators to the greater Hearths starting at Reggiston. Even though she had ten years there to infect it, Reggiston may not be as bad off as I fear. Several Sisters followed her here to the City—we may have already captured most of her people."

After a silence, Donnis said, "The Queen needn't be part of this trial?"

"She needn't. We've turned enough of Ibbit's confederates, and then there are the heretical books. We even uncovered a plot to poison me—not to kill me, but to make me look weak and stupid. That, and the Queen's sponsorship, would make Ibbit appear the best candidate to lead the Sisterhood. They'd already slipped me the first dose. Easily reversed, but still..." Imvalda sighed. "I'm glad Wirdun didn't live to see this. Anniki's insurrection was so hard on her. Sister against Sister, so much death, and for what? A madwoman's ravings."

"Do you think Ibbit is mad?" said Donnis.

"Ambition is a kind of madness," said Sarra, "and Ibbit is very ambitious."

"And her attentions to my cousin?"

Silence again. "I think," Sarra finally said, "in her way Ibbit does love her, but whether it's for the Queen herself or for her influence I cannot say."

Lead thumbs pressed down on Ansella's heart.

"You mustn't tell anyone, Donnie," said Ansella as they drove home an hour later. In her lap she carried a small bottle of tincture wrapped in brown paper and string, the amber, flat-sided bottle within it guaranteed to help her through her morning sickness.

"Why didn't you tell me sooner?"

"I wasn't sure. It was just the one time Harsin and I..."

"Well, you'll feel better soon either way, cos. Your pregnancies have always been easy ones, once you get past that first spoke."

"Oh, yes. I'll be fine in *less* than a spoke. I always am." She patted her stomach again, watching the sun peek through snow white clouds as the curricle rolled toward the Kingsbridge crossing over the Feather River. "I'm due in early Winter's Ending. A snow baby." Ansella laughed and shivered. "Maybe that's why I'm so very chilled this time."

An ornate carriage carrying Lord Corland's crest jostled through the nearby traffic, heading toward the Foothill Lodge road. His Grace must be off to one of Harsin's little dinner parties. Elevating Elbig Shelstone! How could he do that to her? Perhaps her pregnancy might be a way to eclipse the newly Honorable Miss Shelstone; perhaps she would tell him sooner than later. Yes, she would tell him the next time they were alone. It might at least spoil his fun a little.

She found him in the family entrance preparing to leave, presumably for the Lodge. "A word in private, my lord," she said, formal before the servants. Donnis hovered near the Residence Wing stairs, uncertain whether to stay or go.

Harsin raised his eyebrow in irritation. "Now, lady wife? I have a dinner engagement."

"Oh, I'm aware." She met his eyes without a flinch.

A slight flush crept over his cheeks; he waved his gloves toward the butler's nearby office. "Very well."

Ansella rarely visited this room; Affton and Mistress Mannell the housekeeper came to Ansella, not the other way round. Affton kept his office ruthlessly tidy; the one place to sit was a single hard chair behind the man's desk. She drew herself up as tall as she could. "I have news for you, Harsin."

"Do you, now? So do I."

"Shall I brace myself?" she said, her lips thinning into a pinched curve.

"Oh, I think you'd better. I'd rather you hear it from me than another."

"If you're talking of Sir Elbig Shelstone, I had to hear it from Lord Fennows in the middle of the Promenade!"

"That?" snorted Harsin. "I meant to tell you sooner. I have my reasons for elevating the little toad."

"I know your reasons, sir!"

"No, madam, you do not."

Harsin waited, watching her, and her temper rose in spite of her resolution to remain calm. "Well?" she snapped.

"Miss Shelstone is expecting a child. Mine."

The air left Ansella's body; she heaved and would have vomited again were there anything left to bring up. When her breath returned, she said, "Is there any threat to my son? Has Teacher—"

"Apparently it is to be a daughter. Teacher has detected nothing."

"You're certain of it. That it's a daughter and that it's yours."

"Completely."

"What do you intend to do about it?"

"She is to be settled at Middlemont if she carries past her first two spokes, and if the baby survives Twenna will be created Countess Middlemont, a courtesy title that will devolve upon her daughter but will die when she does."

Ansella turned away from him. She braced her hands on Affton's empty desk. She wished the man weren't so spare; she would have loved to sweep a deskful of papers, inkwells and lanterns to the floor in a great messy crash. "You love this Shelstone woman so very much?"

"I am done with other people interfering with my offspring. You've had a free hand for too long in those affairs, Ansella, keeping the children from me and sending the Dunley girl away where I can't find her! This daughter is mine and shall be raised *my* way. When she's of age, she'll be useful to me. Sedra is for Sairland, by the way. Thought I should tell you that, too."

"*What?*"

"Nothing finalized. King Bannig is sending his brother to examine her, and if you know what's good for the girl you'll encourage her to work on her social graces, not her studies. Now if you'll excuse me, I am late for my own dinner party." Harsin opened the office door and strolled out, pulling on his gloves. He left the door open. *He thinks so little of me he won't even let me compose myself in private.*

She couldn't tell him about her own baby now. She would keep it a secret as long as she could—perhaps entirely—no, impossible, but damn him!

Telling her about Sedra's marriage as casually as she'd tell him about selling a horse! Though she could not stop Harsin from marrying off her other two, Ansella would not let her new daughter be "useful" to her father. This one was hers.

A whisper ran through the Hearth that night, carried from one sympathetic mouth in the Healer's House dispensary to various sympathetic ears until it reached a young Sister who worked in the kitchens; she nodded, setting her stubborn black cowlick bobbing. When she returned to her work, she picked up a dinner tray and walked the long stairs into the basement to Sister Ibbit's chilly cell. She gave the renegade her evening meal and murmured, "She is with child, Blessed Ibbit," before she turned away.

Ibbit tore her bread into hunks, the hunks into chunks, the chunks into shreds, the shreds into crumbs. She threw them into her soup and ate with deliberate intensity until the same black-haired Sister came back for the tray. "Tell our friend in the dispensary I have a task for her. Carry it out, the both of you, and then flee," said Ibbit.

The next morning, after the black-haired Sister's work ended, she asked for permission to go into the City on a personal errand. She tucked a brown paper package containing a large amber flat-sided bottle into one sleeve and a small bundle of personal items and food in the other. She walked up the Promenade, through the busy streets to Kingsbridge. The Guards let her through the iron gates into the grounds of the Keep, bowing to her reverently. As she walked up the gravel drive, an estate cart stopped for her and gave her a ride to the Keep itself, where it let her off in the kitchen yard. She walked past the more ornate mudroom door to the delivery door that let straight into the kitchens, and knocked.

"Please, come in, Sister," said the answering footman.

"That's unnecessary," she smiled. "I have a package for Her Majesty from Eldest Sister Imvalda." She handed over the brown paper package, the green wax stamped with the Sister's Temple official seal: a bee. "Tell her it is a stronger, better tincture than the one we sent home with her." The footman accepted the package and made a shy request for a blessing; a nasty head cold was sweeping through the Keep's staff. "May Venna watch over you and keep you from illness. May She watch over all who live under this roof," said the priestess, her hand on his lowered head.

"Thank you, Sister." The footman bowed and closed the door. She wiped her hand on her habit, turned and walked out of the Keep's grounds, through the City and out into the surrounding countryside to hide herself.

By the time the black-haired Sister was missed, the Blessed Ibbit was gone. Ancient, secret passages used for smuggling injured people riddled the Hearth, as they did all Sister's Temples; they were sworn to treat anyone who came to them, even fugitives. The Sisters thought they knew every old tunnel in the Hearth, but they had never thought to look for new ones.

Sedra worried over her mother. Cousin Donnis's arrival had revived her initially, but lately she'd worsened, her face taking on a gray cast. Donnis and Miss Hanston thwarted Sedra's every attempt to find out more.

By nature Sedra preferred solitude early in the day, but now she rode with her mother and Lady Donnis every morning. On this particular ride in the foothills, not long before spring turned into summer on Nerr's Day, the dew on the Fairy Meadow sparkled like the ocean; the sharp, sweet green of wildflowers and fresh grass perfumed the clear air. The three women let their mounts wander as they would, cropping the new plants. Having no particular mount of her own, Sedra rode Temmin's half-Inchari horse LeiLei. She was not the horsewoman her mother was, but the sleek black mare's tidy gait and good wind pleased her. She was scheming how she might get LeiLei away from her brother for good when her mother said, "You should know, Seddy, that your father has spoken to me about a possible match for you."

Sedra pulled back on the reins, jerking the mare's fine head up; LeiLei shook her head in irritation, glanced reproachfully at her rider, and went back to her treat. Sedra patted the horse's neck and murmured an apology, adding to her mother, "To whom shall I be sold?"

"Oh, Seddy, don't say that," fretted Donnis.

"*You* were allowed to choose, ma'am. Mama was sold to Papa. I think I might know who's buying me," she retorted.

"I wasn't *sold*, Sedra. I followed my father's wishes, as shall you," said Ansella. "I'm glad, really. I wouldn't have my beautiful girls and that hectic brother of yours if I hadn't. Some day you will look at your children and feel the same way. Amma guides us for our own good, if we but listen to Her."

"Where is Amma guiding me? That's what I want to know."

Ansella flexed her fingers in their fine goatskin riding gloves; her clear blue eyes gauged her daughter's face. "It would appear the King of Sairland is in need of a wife."

"Sairland!" gasped Sedra. So far away? She would almost certainly never see her family again were she to leave the continent for the great island to the east. "I thought...I know I have said some harsh words about His Grace the Duke of Alzeh, and while I have no feeling for the man at least I would still be in the Kingdom!"

"Your father says Sairland is where your country has most need of you," said her mother. "I have heard much good about King Bannig."

"Bannig?" snorted Sedra. "I've heard all he rules over is drinking and dancing."

"Sairland did not come to rule the Amman Ocean by drinking and dancing, my chicken," said Donnis.

"Bannig didn't obtain that ocean himself, cousin," Sedra countered. "His grandfathers did the work for him."

"He maintains it," said Ansella. "Gently, dear, gently."

"I'm sorry, Cousin Donnis," said Sedra somewhat sullenly, though she meant it.

"Bannig is sending his brother to open negotiations in the coming spokes. It is in your best interests to learn all you can about Sairland, its history and its customs," said her mother.

"You're not talking to Elly, Mama," she snapped. "I already know more about Sairland than Papa, I'd wager." She cracked the reins, and LeiLei left the Fairy Meadow at a sharp pace.

"I'm so very glad I had sons," said Donnis after the departing Princess's back.

"Alberto was no easier," said Ansella, "nor Evval."

"Berto and Ev were hectic boys, true, but in the end they grew up and they're still mine. Girls are given away to the families of their husbands, or to the Temples. Rarely are we allowed to keep one, and though it's a solace to us when we can, not having their own household is hardly fair to *them*, is it?"

"I wonder if there is any fairness to women in this world." Ansella turned Flor's head toward the higher hills and gave the white mare's ribs a heeltap. "Come, let's give Sedra her solitude."

Sedra let her horse pick its way down the steep trail back to the main road through the King's Woods, but on the clearer track she urged the mare to a faster pace. Once on the King's Road itself, she tore away at a run, giving free rein to LeiLei's spirits and her own rage.

The King's favorite child, kept in the dark about her own impending marriage! How much worse could it be were she his *least* favorite? She was the firstborn, she should be the one to rule Tremont, she was better suited than her feckless brother!

Sedra sensed the horse's flagging energy between her legs and eased into a walk, her initial anger dissipated for now. Temmin wasn't feckless, she admitted to herself. He wouldn't be a bad king, but she would have been the better. A woman king. "When Nerr gets the Heir," she muttered before remembering He had indeed gotten the Heir. Well, never mind, it still wouldn't happen.

Sedra was by no means ready to return to the Keep; her body still jangled, and she hated to be seen displaying anything other than a cool, intellectual cordiality in public. When a promising side road presented itself, she took it.

The further she walked LeiLei up the unfamiliar road the closer grew the trees, forming walls green and brown on either side. The great canopy of leaves overhead choked out the underbrush. She was far from her usual haunts. She had no fear; these were the King's Woods, after all. No one came here other than her own family…and the Travelers.

An uncomfortable suspicion eyes watched her pricked at her neck and forearms. Sedra brought her horse to a stop, uncertain whether she should continue on. She had just decided to start for home when a tall, rusty-haired, well-built young man stepped from the cover of the trees. His eyes were a sharp blue, and he dressed as a Traveler: sturdy, mud-colored pants tucked into dusty brown boots, a cheap brocade vest in deep gold, and an old linen shirt, its sleeves rolled up and a bandana at the open neck. A gold ring flashed in one ear. She couldn't decide if his handsome face reminded her more of a fox or more of a wolf. "I thought it was time I said hello, Princess. Hello!" A broad grin split his neat beard.

"Time you said 'hello'?" echoed Sedra.

"I know it's hardly a proper introduction, but Travelers can't expect proper anything, can we?"

Already angry, Sedra indulged in a rare display of rank. "Who are you to speak to me?"

"Oh, I've been watching you ramble about in these woods for years. My name is Connin. Your family and my family—let's just say we go back a few centuries."

Sedra blinked as a blush rose to her face. She knew the name, and now recognized the man. "I know who you are."

"Teacher read you a story from the History, eh? Which one, I wonder?" Connin came closer. "How many have you heard?"

"Just the one. That was enough to tell me everything about you. Good day."

Sedra gathered her reins, but Connin caught LeiLei's bridle before she could turn. "What did it tell you?"

"That you're a rapist. Let go my bridle!"

"Ah, Teacher read you Emmae's story! Never worry, despite appearances I don't take maidens against their will. I never really have that problem."

Connin looked just as he had in Teacher's book; his rusty beard was neatly trimmed, but his hair was neither short in the modern style nor long in the conservative style, and it ruffled round his face. She became quite aware how handsome he was, and Emmae's experiences in the book tumbled into her head. Sedra shifted in her saddle and gave herself a tiny shake. "What do you call what you did to Emmae?"

"She was under an enchantment to return anyone's desire. What man could resist a woman so beautiful and so outwardly willing?"

"Warin the Wise did."

"After he used her himself. Tell me, was that king really a better man than I? We both knew what we did. He lied to himself until he finished. At least I was honest, and I was under a greater compulsion than Emmae ever was. I still am."

"What do you mean?"

He'd come round to her left side so stealthily she didn't notice until his hand slipped up her divided skirt to caress her calf. "You say you know everything about me worth knowing. What you know about me is what Emmae knew. True, she knew...a great deal about me," he grinned. Sedra slashed at him with her riding crop; he dropped LeiLei's reins and stepped out of range, laughing. "When you want to make some memories of your own before a loveless marriage, Princess, I'm easy to find and quite discreet."

Sedra wheeled the mare around and tore back down the path to the War Road. Did everyone know about her marriage but her? No, everyone knew her future as a royal bargaining chip; Connin's taunt was a goad, not specific knowledge. How dare some Traveler accost her? True, he was no ordinary Traveler—the son of their Queen, as immortal as his mother, and as Teacher. Still insolent, still insinuating, still as seductive as he'd been in Emmae's day, some 700 years before.

She trotted LeiLei into the stable yards, threw the nearest groom the reins, stalked back through the mudroom to the family's staircase to the Residence Wing, and climbed the stairs as fast as she could without running. Once in her apartments, she began peeling off her suddenly constricting riding clothes. "A wrapper will suffice," she told her ladies maid. "I'm not feeling well, Camma, and wish to spend the day in my rooms."

"Shall I send for a Sister, Your Highness? Or perhaps Her Majesty?" said

Miss Sinsett, her round face creased in worry.

"No, just find something to do elsewhere for a while, dear. I need to be alone." She stayed curled up on the chaise in her bedchamber until Miss Sinsett finished straightening up and left, casting a dubious look over her shoulder as she closed the door.

Sedra picked up her current book beside the chaise, but Emmae's experiences would not leave her, as vivid as the day Teacher "read" them to her: overwhelming desire; Connin's hands and mouth on her breasts; his cock slowly pushing inside her, bringing her to orgasm over and over; humiliation as her bespelled body betrayed her unwilling mind. Sedra reminded herself over and over that these were Emmae's memories, not her own. She'd been so confused and overwhelmed every time she left the story, struggling with desire. Teacher had been so near, an alluring combination of mystery, a dancer's grace and a mind so sharp…but those thoughts led to nothing but bitterness.

Her hand brushed her breast as she considered Connin's offer. Making memories of her own? What good would it do? At best they would haunt her as she lived trapped in Bannig's court, and in his bed. At worst she might be discovered. What would her father do then?

When the King discovered Teacher's illicit lessons, he shut her in her rooms for an entire spoke, meals included. No visitors were allowed apart from the King himself, Ellika and Miss Sinsett; Mama and Temmin still lived at Whithorse. No long walks, no newspapers, no reading more taxing to the mind than books written for the "improvement of unmarried girls," though Ellika smuggled novels in to her. "Here's to fashion crazes," she'd said, pulling two or three volumes from their hiding place among the yards and yards of muslin making up her skirts. "You'll have something *good* to read for a change!" Sedra had to agree Ellika's "thrilling romances" beat anything written for the improvement of unmarried girls, but longed for her prohibited studies. Over time, Harsin looked the other way as Sedra crept back to her old reading habits, but Teacher's lessons remained forbidden.

It was just as well. She closed her eyes and fell into a doze in which the unknown Bannig's coming inspection, Connin's lovemaking and her own frustrated pursuit of Teacher ran together.

NINE

The last days of Spring's Ending turned increasingly pleasant. The icy mountain winds blowing down the City's two rivers mellowed in the strengthening sun: fresh, kind, their edges softly rounded. The City over-flowed in greenery, and the gardeners at the Lovers' Temple proliferated like the flowers they tended. On this late morning, they worked around Temmin in a mild buzz of snipping and pruning as he sat on the lawn, his tunic off and his drawstring trousers rolled up to feel the sun on his skin.

In fact, it was too bright on the grass for him to read his latest missive from Ellika. He shifted into the nearest tree's dappled light, lying flat on the grass and holding the letter over his head. He began to skim what he assumed would be her usual cheerful nattering about what she would wear to this coming Nerr's Day parties—the last of the season—hints as to what his brother's gift would be, and society gossip about people he barely knew. What he read was quite different:

Temmy, please come home and see Mama before Nerr's Day! I know it's a busy time at the Temple, but something is wrong and she refuses to speak to either me or Sedra about it. Cousin Donnie is just as tight-lipped as Hanston, I can't get anything out of either of them no matter how hard I wheedle!

As for Nerr's Day, can you arrange a private meeting for us on the Eve?

I fear this may be Sedra's last Nerr's Day with us, and I don't like the idea of her giving you your brother's gift in public! You know how emotional she gets, it's why she hides behind newspapers. I don't mind everyone looking at me, you <u>know</u> I don't, and I can't wait until you see my new dress, it's the <u>perfect</u> aquamarine to contrast with all that Nerr's Day rose, but Sedra doesn't like it at all—everyone watching, not my dress, she mumbled something about how very pretty it was, but could I get her to call for Naister and have something more fashionable made up for herself? I could not, it was all I could do to coax her into a new dress at <u>all</u>.

Oh, and you've probably guessed why this is likely to be her last brother's gift to you: Papa is increasingly serious about <u>marrying her off</u>!! I heard rumors of everyone from the Duke of Alzeh to that fathead Fennows, but now Sedra tells me it's <u>SAIRLAND</u>!! Merciful Amma, please let it not be <u>Sairland</u>!! She would be a Queen, and there's much to be said for that I suppose, but I do not like the idea of her being so very far away. Alzeh isn't so very far away, and the Duke comes to the City for the height of the season at least, so we would see her, but <u>Sairland</u>! We'd never see her again! Of course I have no idea what King Bannig looks like, but the Duke isn't so terribly bad, even with that dark Alzehni complexion. One good thing I hear about the King is that he does love a good party. So at least she'll be amused in Cordeneen. Come to think on it, maybe not. She's not one for parties, is she? Maybe <u>I</u> should marry Bannig! No, I don't want to move to Sairland, either.

In any event, Mama is not at all well. Cousin Donnis says Mama's stomach is delicate at present, but she is obviously uneasy about it. Mama started turning odd colors at meals and stopped coming downstairs entirely about a week ago. My Iddie tells me the cooks say all she eats is dry toast and mint-and-ginger tisane! And she won't send for a Sister and she won't tell me what the matter is! That <u>odious block Hanston</u> won't let me near her for more than a few minutes!!

Papa is up to his tricks again and has elevated his mistress's greasy little father to a <u>baronetcy</u>! Gave him a holding on the coast of Kellen, some miserable little fishing village in the middle of nowhere, but at least one doesn't have to see him in society at present—he's there now, gloating. And then! Papa put up the Shelstone at <u>Middlemont</u>!! I'm not supposed to know about it, of course, but how do you keep a secret like <u>that</u>? Papa thinks Mama is sulking. Maybe she is, but I don't think so.

I think perhaps Mama might tell <u>you</u> what is wrong, and if it <u>is</u> your absence, I shall be <u>very</u> put out with you for going away like this even if it was for good reason and I suppose a direct invitation from the Gods is a good reason

*but really, it's caused such a great deal more fuss than I ever expected. I should
never have helped you had I known.*

You simply __must__ come home to see Mama!!

Your loving sister,

E

The letter's length alone convinced Temmin that perhaps he should ask
permission to visit the Keep, but the news about Mama…and then Twenna
Shelstone…

From the little he knew, he didn't think his father had ever gone so far
as to elevate a mistress's family. This did not bode well. He rolled down his
trouser legs, donned his shirt and began composing his request to the Most
Highs in his head as he walked back into the Temple.

Two days before Summer's Beginning on a sunny Vennaday, the merciful Most Highs sent Temmin back to the Keep. He shot his cuffs and twitched
under his now-unfamiliar shirt collar in the warm weather; there was much
to be said for the loose, comfortable Temple garb as the temperature rose.

He sought out his younger sister on arrival and found her in her apri-
cot-and-gilt private sitting room, pacing on the needlepointed roses of her
carpet. Ellika pounced on him as soon as he came through the door. "Oh,
I'm so glad you're home, Temmy, it's been the most vexing spoke ever!" She
poured out her sorrows: the odious Elbig Shelstone's elevation, the hussy
Twenna Shelstone's residence at Middlemont, their father's frequent, indiscreet absences, Sedra's impending engagement, and their mother's troubling
indisposition. "You look well at least," she sniffed.

"I'm here," he said, kissing her forehead. "Doesn't that satisfy, you little
baggage?"

"What will satisfy, you vulgar creature, is your going to Mama's apartments and storming Castle Hanston. Go! Off with you, or I shall prick you
with your brother's gift and there's your hint! Go go go!"

Ensconced in a bed full of pillows, Ansella pushed the soft boiled egg
and toast away untouched. "I just can't, Donnie. Please take it away, the
smell is giving me a terrible headache."

"You must let me call the Sisters!" said Donnis. "You're getting worse,
not better."

"It's just the baby, cos. It will pass in a spoke."

"I'm not sure you have a spoke!" said Donnis, taking the tray. "If you can't eat a little something by tonight, I'm calling the Sisters whether you want me to or not!"

"I beg you not to! I don't want him to know about the baby!"

Donnis dropped the tray to her hips in exasperation. "Why, in Amma's name?"

Ansella set her pale face. "I will not compete with that Shelstone woman!"

"Oh, Annie, you can't stay in here the entire six spokes—" A racket rose from the sitting room.

"I'm sorry, Your Highness, but the Queen cannot be disturbed!" Miss Hanston's voice boomed. "Sir, please!" Donnis clanged the tray down on a nearby console; she had specified no visitors.

"Very sorry, Hanston," Temmin's voice came, "but I'm only here for a short visit." What was he doing here at all? "Mama! Fair warning, I'm coming in!" The rangy young man dashed through the door, Miss Hanston rumbling after.

"I did try, ma'am!" she said.

"It's all right, Hanston," smiled Ansella. "He's welcome, as long as he can be quiet and not rattle the teeth in my head." Miss Hanston gave the Prince a stony look that said she very much doubted it, retired to the wardrobe, and closed its door behind her.

"Hullo, Mama!"

"Hullo yourself, antic boy, what are you doing here?" said his mother.

"An impromptu visit at the command of the Princess Ellika. What's on the tray, Cousin Donnis?" sniffed Temmin.

"Ellika? Haven't you eaten, sweetheart?"

"It's been at least an hour, Mama." He examined the untouched plate. "Donnis, is she eating?" he demanded.

"No, she's not," Donnis answered. She took the tray out to Miss Hanston, Temmin eyeing it wistfully even though all it contained was toast and soft-boiled egg.

When she returned, Donnis found him holding his mother's hand at her bedside. "You do not look at all well, Mama."

"It's just a touch of something. I'll be right as rain in a day or two."

"Elly says you haven't been downstairs in a week, that's not a 'touch of something.' Has she been this ill the entire time, Cousin Donnis?"

"She's gotten worse the last day or two." She told him over Ansella's protests about the headaches, the weakness, the vomiting, the vanished appetite. "But she won't let me call the Sisters! I've given her until this evening, and then I'm calling them whether she likes it or not," she finished.

"I'm not giving her five minutes," said Temmin. "We're calling them now, and there's an end to it. Papa will be furious when he finds out you're ill and haven't gotten help, Mama!"

"If your father cared, he would have enquired," said Ansella.

"Elly says he thinks you're having a sulk."

"And don't I deserve one!" she said, high color and her old temper breaking through her lethargy.

"About Miss Shelstone—"

"Don't bring her up, Temmy," warned Donnis.

"*The Honorable Miss Shelstone* can have him!" shouted Ansella, rising off the pillows and then sinking back, shaking. A spasm racked her, and she cried out in pain.

"Right," said Temmin. "Donnis, I'm sorry to order you about—"

Donnis was already on her way to the sitting room. "Hanston, off you go. Find the nearest footman and have him fetch the Sisters. Be quick about it!"

"Past time!" huffed Miss Hanston. She picked up her skirts and rolled from the room.

Breaking glass brought Donnis into the bedchamber at a run. Ansella was panting, doubled over in Temmin's arms; pieces of a drinking glass lay in a puddle on the floor. "I tried to give her some water—I dropped the glass and it hit the edge of the table, don't tread on it—I had to catch her—" Ansella cried out and clutched at Temmin's shoulders. "Cousin Donnie, what's wrong!" Temmin said.

Donnis rushed to the right of the bed to hold Ansella on the other side. "She might be miscarrying," she said. "There, Ansella, let go of Temmy, I have you!" she soothed as another spasm shook the Queen.

"Don't tell him! Don't tell him!" Ansella wept as Donnis rocked her.

"Tell me what?" said Temmin. He stood up and just missed stepping on the glass shards. "Miscarriage? *What?*"

"Not you, Temmy. Go get Mistress Mannell, *right now!*" said Donnis.

Temmin ran out the door to find the housekeeper, nearly tripping on the rug.

"I don't want to lose the baby, I don't want to lose her!"

Clammy, cold sweat stuck Ansella's golden hair to her cheeks and forehead; Donnis reached for a damp cloth on the bedstand. "I know, sweetheart. Let's make you more comfortable. There, now, cos, it's all right." Donnis lay Ansella against the pillows and peeled off the bedclothes; blood already stained the sheets.

Ansella turned on her side and drew her knees up to her chest. "It hurts! Donnie, I feel wet." She put her hands between her legs; she brought them out bloody and began keening in earnest.

Mistress Mannell bustled in, arms full of toweling stacked in a large basin. Behind her stood Temmin, stock still in the doorway, white-faced and staring. "Hanston!" she called. "Get His Highness out of here!" Miss Hanston tugged hard at Temmin's sleeve, but he didn't budge. "Temmy, go find your father!" said Donnis. This had the desired effect; he fled the room, and Donnis turned back to her charge.

She climbed onto the bed and took her cousin into her lap, using a flannel damp with lavender water to clean Ansella's hands. "Mannell's here, now there's my girl!" she murmured. "The Sisters will come soon, now there's my girl!" Ansella lay limp against her, breath shallow.

Mistress Mannell and Miss Hanston flew around the bedchamber, stripping off the crumpled covers, covering the bed in toweling, starting a fire and putting a large copper kettle on to boil. Donnis had miscarried twice before Alberto, both times quite early. It hurt, but not like this, and she hadn't bled like this. By the time Eldest Sister Imvalda and the midwives arrived, Donnis only hoped they might save her cousin's life.

Temmin had a time tracking down his father. He wasn't in his rooms, he wasn't in his office. The council room contained a few Ministers, alarmed and irritated at his headlong intrusion. He finally thought to ask Affton and tracked him down to the servants' hall. "Riding, I believe, Your Highness," said the butler. "May I say I took the liberty of sending a groom to find His Majesty as soon as the call for the Sisters went out, sir."

Temmin slumped against the kitchen archway and let out a shuddering sigh. His eyes burned, and he wiped at his brow with his handkerchief. "Thank you, Affton, I should have known you'd think to find him."

"May I also suggest, sir, that since there's nothing you can do for the moment you might have a cup of tea?" Affton murmured. "I can send a tray up to your room, if you'd like, or the Small Sitting Room."

"If I go upstairs I'll have a hard time staying away...and Lady Donnis made it clear..." he trailed off. Affton glided him back through the kitchens to the Small Sitting Room. Temmin sat in his shirtsleeves drinking tea and eating plain buttered toast, huddled in a corner of the big room.

His mother, her hands covered in blood: the vision he'd had more than a year ago at Neya's Day in the Gods' bed. The image had receded in his mind—who wants to think on such things? Dread radiated through him, pricking from his scalp down his back to his fingers and toes as he remembered them all: Jenks leading a cavalry charge. Harsin on a battlefield. Sedra shielding a child from some unknown danger. Ellika, of all people, facing down a squad of Tremontine soldiers. Finally Teacher and the Traveler Queen, flames all around them. He had hoped perhaps they'd been metaphors of some kind, but now it all seemed possible, almost inevitable. Could he stop any of it from happening?

Neya said he'd be called either Liberator or Magnificent. She hadn't said which path he should take, or even how he could tell them apart. Could he even choose it? Or was it all pre-ordained, like the blood on his mother's hands? Temmin finished his tea and returned to his rooms, where he threw himself on the bed. This was not how he'd intended to spend his day at the Keep.

In time, Miss Hanston's voice in his study called Temmin from his bedchamber. Temmin hurried into the room. "Hanston, is my father back yet?"

"No, sir. He. Is. Not. But the Eldest Sister is in Her Majesty's receiving room waiting for you, Your Highness."

Temmin shrugged into his coat and followed Miss Hanston down the hall into the Queen's incongruously bright receiving room, where Sedra sat listening intently, Ellika huddled against her in misery. "She may be out of danger now," Eldest Sister Imvalda was saying. Dark patches stained her deep green robes; Temmin looked away, unsure if they were water or something worse. "We should have been called much, much sooner."

Ellika raised her head from Sedra's arm. "Did you know, Tem? Did you know she was expecting?"

Temmin shook his head. "I don't think anyone but Cousin Donnis and Hanston knew."

All eyes swiveled to the crumbling Miss Hanston, who said, "Beg pardon, Your Highnesses, Eldest Sister, but if my lady says 'don't tell anyone,' I don't tell anyone! Nor would you if you were me!"

"It's all right, Hanston," said Sedra. "Please continue that policy for now and tell no one. Go downstairs and have a cup of tea." Once she was gone, Sedra fetched a kerchief from her pocket, put her face in her hands for a moment, and wiped her eyes. "How far along was she, Eldest Sister?"

"Less than two moons—not quite a spoke, as the Eddinites would say, miss." Imvalda smoothed a fold in her habit. "Sarra and I have known since she visited us last, but of course we could say nothing ourselves. You shouldn't refer to the baby in past tense," she added. "The Queen may keep her yet. It's still too soon to say. She must be still and in bed for at least a spoke." Though Imvalda didn't say the words aloud, Temmin heard them clearly: *If she lives.*

Ellika burst into fresh tears and Sedra gave her a fresh handkerchief. "It's a girl? How do you know?"

"Teacher would have known if it was a boy, and he didn't say a word to me," said Temmin. "I think he would have."

Ellika opened her mouth to ask another question, but the Eldest Sister interrupted. "There is more." She held up a large, flat-sided amber bottle. "This came to the Keep from the Sisters' Temple not long after Her Majesty visited us, but it came neither from me nor from Sarra Embodiment."

"What is it?" said Sedra.

"The Sister who delivered it claimed it was a morning sickness draught, stronger than the Early Mother's tincture I gave Her Majesty myself. It is not. It's an abortifacient—a slow-acting poison meant to cause your mother a miscarriage, and probably worse."

"Who would do such a thing!" said Temmin.

"Ibbit," said Sedra.

The Eldest Sister slowly shook her head. "We never suspected she would do this to a woman she…forgive me…she swore she loved. All but one of her confederates escaped with her, but rest assured we will be investigating further. We thought we had rooted out the immediate blasphemy. Apparently we still have work to do." Imvalda studied her hands, her face care-worn and guilt-ridden. "As for tonight," she resumed, "My best midwife will remain here. I will send others so she might rest when necessary, and I've sent for my poisons expert. We've given your mother the first dose of the antidote we think is needed, but we have more study to do. I won't lie to you. She is in considerable danger, perhaps mortal danger. She's more comfortable now but she will have no visitors other than the Dowager Marchioness and Miss Hanston to wait on her."

"Not even Papa?" sniffed Ellika.

Imvalda considered, her eyes to one side and a dismayed frown hovering around her mouth. "His Majesty may make a brief—*brief!*—visit, but I recommend he not visit frequently. The Queen must not be agitated. Now," she said in a different tone, "in no case are you to accept any medicine for her, or for anyone in this family, from any hand but mine or Sarra's in future—*directly* from one of us and no one else, however well known to you or trusted." Imvalda called for the Sisters not staying behind and took her leave.

The three siblings sat silent; Sedra stroked Ellika's back. Temmin rose to his feet. "I'm going to find Father myself, since no one else has managed to."

He strode out into the hall, just in time to see Winmer disappear into the King's apartments next door. "I am not going into a sickroom in all my dirt!" his father said as the door closed.

Inside, Harsin was stripping as he hurried into his bedchamber; his valet Gram followed behind, stooping to pick up the discarded riding clothes, and his secretary Winmer brought up the rear. Harsin changed into fresh clothes and washed his face. "This would have to happen when I was at Middlemont. Cancel any appointments for the next three days, Winmer, and send word that while it was a lovely interlude et cetera, I will not be seeing Miss Shelstone in the immediate future. Do not under any circumstances say anything about the Queen's indisposition, to Miss Shelstone or anyone else." Winmer nodded, scribbling in his neat little book, and Harsin stepped through his bedchamber door through the private hallway and into the Queen's bedchamber.

In one corner Miss Hanston was giving a nervous midwife a flinty going-over. The ladies maid bobbed a quick curtsey to him and rumbled into the sitting room, dragging the protesting Sister behind her. Donnis stood up. "I'll give you a moment, Your Majesty."

Harsin took her hand in his; it was damp with Ansella's sweat. "My dear Donnis, stop a moment. How is she? What's happened?"

Donnis breathed in, long and slow, and let it out. "Ansella may be miscarrying, Harsin. She wouldn't let me tell you she was with child." Harsin's heart soared—a baby he could claim as his own legitimate daughter—and just as quickly tumbled down as he remembered his wife's face when he'd told her about Twenna Shelstone. Had he caused this?

"It's worse," continued Donnis. Miscarriage, disguised poison, still in danger, Ibbit—when he found the rebel Sister, he would kill her personally, trial be damned. "I'll leave you," said Donnis, "but do not stay long. She must be still and rest. Don't agitate her, Harsin, I beg you." She closed the door behind her.

Harsin sat down and studied his sleeping wife and her shallow breathing. *Stubborn woman, you have been nothing but trouble.* He brushed away the hair slicked to her cheek, and she fluttered awake.

"Harsin."

He leaned down closer to hear, stroking her jaw with a gentle thumb. "I'm here, Annie."

"Harsin," his name came again in a tiny, dry chuckle. "You came through the door first. *I win.*"

He laughed, a short, soft bark. "You win, sweetheart," he said through tears. "You win."

Meanwhile, Sedra pushed Ellika away and stood up. "Where are you going?" said her sister.

"I have something to do."

"Temmin's doing something, you're doing something, what am *I* supposed to do!" wailed Ellika.

"Go to your room. Wait here for news. I don't know, find something to do! I'll be back later." Ellika burst into tears again, but Sedra didn't spare a backward glance as she went through the door.

Through the Keep's warren of new and ancient corridors and galleries Sedra ran, scattering footmen and maids, until she came to its oldest part: the original tower that had begun the great fortress, its round base carved into the living rock beneath the Keep. To one side, enormous decorated wooden doors led to the family chapel. To the other side rose stairs, winding up the tower walls higher than she could see. Prayer on one side, action on the other. She chose action and began climbing the stairs, grateful for her long walks and the strong legs that went with them.

Sedra lost count how many steps she'd taken by the time she reached the top and the landing's only door for the first time since her father banned her from study. She knocked.

Teacher opened it. "Your Highness! I am surprised—are you allowed to be here?"

"It doesn't matter, I need you, Mama needs you," she said, pushing past into Teacher's library.

"How may I serve you?"

"Have you heard about Mama?"

" I am afraid I have heard nothing. I have been here in the Tower, looking for several wanted personages. What is amiss?"

"I think Mama is dying." Sedra recounted her mother's condition and Imvalda's sobering assessment. "I need your help."

Those silver eyes shone cold as ever, even in Teacher's sympathetic face. "There is little I can do. My power does not extend to women's magic."

"No," she said impatiently, "but you know where the Traveler Queen is. You can convince *her* to help!"

"I cannot take you to her, nor can we speak to one another," said Teacher, "and you know the pain when we are too close to one another."

"But you know where she is," Sedra insisted. "Tell me. I'll go look for her on my own if I have to, but I *know* you already know where she is, even if you can't be near her—you can get me to her more quickly!"

Teacher took her hands in a long, cool grip. "Calmly, Your Highness."

"You used to call me Sedra, not 'Your Highness.' You said you were my friend, even if you could be nothing else, even if I wanted something else."

"You were not alone in that wanting...Sedra," Teacher said, "but I did not choose what I am, and there is another I have waited for a long while now. Of course I will help you, never worry. I care for your mother very much, though she does not care much for me. I cannot take you to the Traveler Queen, but I can bring you quite close." Teacher turned her to face the great mirror hanging from the round room's ceiling. "Show me Mirror Clearing." The mirror's image shifted; a round, irregular window framed forest greenery.

Teacher paused. "Before we go, I must caution you against Maeve's son."

Sedra said nothing about her encounter with Connin. "Will he try to prevent me from taking the Traveler Queen to Mama?"

"No, no, but I cannot stay to bring you back. He must do it—he possesses much of the same power I do, and he is not bound to the King as I am. He will help you, but be aware he is a sly one." Teacher reached to touch her cheek; Sedra reflexively flinched. Teacher's hand dropped hastily away to take her own, and they swirled through the mirror.

Her stomach twisted; just before she became grossly sick, they arrived in a clearing in the King's Woods in an area Sedra avoided on her walks. It was among the Travelers' haunts, and while she knew longstanding if confusing connections existed between the Travelers and the Antremonts, the vagabonds still made her uncomfortable. She looked around for the reflection they'd used; nothing but trees surrounded them. "Thank you," she said, releasing Teacher's slender fingers. "Which way?"

"Straight down that path you will come to their camp. Now, goodbye, Sedra. I hope Maeve can help your mother, but do not expect her to." Teacher paused. "Give her a message from me. Tell her I love her, and that the time may be coming soon."

Sedra let out a small, astonished breath. "Yes. Yes, of course."

Teacher faced an old, gnarled tree. "Show me my Library." The slight black figure became liquid and swirled into a large knothole in the tree; Sedra's nape pricked.

She stared at the knothole. The *Traveler Queen* had been her rival? She liked to think she had long since patched her heart after its girlish disappointment—but Teacher preferred an old woman? She glared down the path. Colorful glimpses shone through the young leaves: red, gold and blue painted caravans, the bright wagons that served as both home and conveyance to Travelers throughout the Kingdom. She picked up her skirts and ran, ran faster, until she bowled into the clearing headlong into a rusty-haired young man.

"Hold, hold!" he laughed, seizing her arms. "Look, everyone! I've caught a pretty girl!"

"Release me this instant!" she huffed.

Connin grinned. "Some day you may change your mind, but for now..." He let her go and swept a low bow. "Your Highness, how may this humble band of Travelers help your family, since you always need us to get your sorry asses out of every scrape you find yourselves in?"

The camp erupted in roars; men, women and children who had been attending to cooking, dandling babies, mending tack, tuning instruments, all laughed at her. She flushed. "I have come for the Traveler Queen's help. My mother was poisoned. The Sisters say she might die."

"Who's here?" came a creaky voice from across the clearing.

"The Princess Royal," answered Connin, keeping his eyes on Sedra. "Her family craves a boon, as usual."

"I have never asked anyone for a boon," snapped Sedra.

Connin turned his head over his shoulder. "Mother? Will you speak with her, or shall I send her packing?"

"Don't be so cruel, Connin, the girl's worried about her mama," said the old woman, toddling across the clearing. Connin grabbed a nearby folding stool and helped her onto the seat.

Sedra had never seen a crone so old. Her pate shone white and mottled beneath grizzled hair. Her clawlike hands worked to tie a bandana over her head, until Connin took the kerchief from her and gently fastened it behind. She cocked her chin at Sedra, and her wrinkled face broke into a grin reminiscent of her son's but for the missing teeth. "Well, now! It's the eldest daughter. I haven't seen you since you were a baby, not this close up at any rate. You've turned out well. What's amiss, child?"

"My mother is ill..." Should she call the old woman *Your Majesty*? *Lady*? "...ma'am. She's with child, and she's been poisoned."

The Traveler Queen listened as Sedra told the story once again, the old crone's face grave and sympathetic. "It depends upon the poison, child. I might not be able to help her."

Sedra's helplessness concentrated into a flare of anger. "Might not, or will not?"

"Have a care, Princess," growled Connin.

"Every moment we stand here my mother is suffering, every moment we stand here could mean the difference between living and dying!"

The crone spoke so softly Sedra bent down to hear her. "Do you know how many people are dying, right now, just in this Kingdom? Child, Harla gathers up Her harvest every minute." She tapped her withered chest. "I can feel every dying breath, but I feel the first breath of every baby born, as well. So many births, and so many deaths, every moment, day and night. You do not understand what you ask."

"She is my mother! She is my mother and she is your Queen. Come and save her!"

A rumble from the surrounding Travelers. A sharp-eyed man who held his guitar more like a club than an instrument started toward her. "We don't recognize your family's sovereignty, girl. We have our own Queen."

"Jesper, stand down," ordered Connin.

"Will you help me or not!" cried Sedra.

"Connin, help me up," said the Traveler Queen. "Girl, your temper matches your wit—both too great to be controlled at times, I fear."

Sedra pressed her lips together and closed her eyes long enough to pray: *Amma give me strength.* "So I have been told, ma'am. I can hide my wit when necessary, but sometimes my temper escapes me. Forgive me. Please, just tell me whether you will come. If you will not, I must go home and hope the Sisters have better news. I'm on foot now and it's something of a walk." She remembered her promise. "I have a message for you, from Teacher. I don't know if it's for your ears alone, or…" She trailed off, embarrassed at feeling put-upon when she was the one asking for help.

"Tell me."

"He says he loves you, and that the time may be soon."

The old woman took in the color burning on Sedra's cheeks. "A difficult message to deliver. Thank you."

Sedra swallowed a humiliated retort that would ruin any chance of the Queen's cooperation. "I ask you—*beg* you—one last time, ma'am: will you come?"

"I will come, though it may not do any good," nodded the old crone. "Connin, take us there."

He frowned as he took his mother's elbow. "But the pain—"

"I'm sure there's no risk. Teacher expects me and so is far away by now—Inchar at best, Oldtown at the worst," she chuckled.

Sedra prepared herself to creep down the path, but to her surprise the Traveler Queen walked as briskly as she herself did. In the corner of Sedra's eye, a much younger, dark-haired woman flickered, superimposed on the withered Queen's figure; when Sedra looked at her directly, the flicker disappeared.

They stopped before a large knothole in a gnarled tree. "You've asked my mother prettily," said Connin, "but you haven't spoken so to me."

Sedra bit back sarcasm and squared her shoulders. "Do you wish me to beg?"

"I wish for you to kiss me."

"Amma give me patience, boy, stop it!" said his mother.

"You must kiss me," he repeated. "Are you too proud to kiss a Traveler? You'd be the first princess among the many I've asked if so."

Passing time scratched at her throat; she might be too late already. "All right, very well." She made to kiss his bearded cheek, but Connin caught her up and kissed her full on the mouth.

Ellika wore her enthusiasm for the opposite sex like a bright, fluttering pennant, but Sedra kept her own passion tightly furled and stowed away. She'd never been kissed though she'd often longed to be, especially after hearing Emmae's story. While she'd experienced her ancestress's memories as if they were her own, she now discovered actual kissing was greatly to be preferred. Perhaps it was as well that Papa married her off soon.

She closed her eyes and enjoyed Connin's beard against her cheek before breaking away in hasty guilt. "Are you satisfied?"

"Oh, not nearly as much as I should like to be," he smiled.

She just had to tolerate him long enough to get through the mirror, Sedra chanted to herself. She took one of his hands, the Traveler Queen the other. "Show me Queen Ansella's..." Connin turned to Sedra. "Where shall I put you?"

"Mama's receiving room."

"Very well, show me Queen Ansella's receiving room."

Sedra couldn't see the mirror that must be in the knothole, but she could feel the nauseating, dissolving displacement as they swirled into it.

They came out the other end into the round celadon room. Sedra led them into her mother's private drawing room. She made to open the door to the bedchamber, but the Traveler Queen stopped her. "I must go in alone. I shall send your mother's attendants out to you." She gave her son a sharp look. "I think it might be best for all concerned."

"Damn," muttered Connin. He threw himself into the nearest chair.

The old woman yanked open the door, to the startled exclamations of the Queen's attendants. In short order Lady Donnis, Miss Hanston and the Sister midwife found themselves marched out of the room and the door closed behind them. The distraught Miss Hanston spotted Connin and almost distracted herself making sure he didn't steal anything. The Sister kept staring in astonishment at the closed door; she excused herself to kneel in a corner and tell the prayer beads she pulled from beneath her habit.

Sedra pulled Donnis aside. "Is it truly the Traveler Queen?" whispered Donnis. "How did you get here so quickly?"

"Teacher helped me find her. I can't explain, it's too complicated, but she promised to help if she could." Sedra took Donnis's hands. "It's bad, isn't it?"

Donnis nodded, her face lined and distraught. "It is, my dear, very bad indeed. Harla take that Ibbit!" Sedra flinched; her cousin had never sworn in her presence before. "Well," sighed Donnis, "there's nothing to do but wait. I need a cup of tea, desperately."

Two hours later a neat stack of little plates that once held cakes and sandwiches sat before Connin on the tea table. No one else seemed to have an appetite, and "I should hate to see such a lovely spread sent back to the kitchen untouched."

Sedra began to wonder whether the Traveler Queen would ever come out. Was it a good sign she stayed so long, or a bad one? The midwife didn't know and mumbled something about the Traveler Queen's sanctity; she seemed both terrified and elated to be near the old woman and had paused her prayers just long enough for a single cup of tea.

Just when Sedra had made up her mind to knock on the bedchamber door, it opened. The Traveler Queen emerged, her face grave. "She's alive," said the old woman, "and for now she will strengthen—she is already stronger, but the poison has done its work."

"She is stronger? Will she live?" cried Sedra. "Will she keep the baby?"

"It's up to her," said the crone. "It's completely up to her. She will be able to eat now. No restrictions—give her anything she asks for. Spoil her. Give her all her favorite delicacies. She will be able to take exercise in a few days, and I recommend she do so. Let her ride as long as she can get into the saddle, and let her drive as long as she can reach the reins. I've told her to go home to Whithorse, but she's refused." The Traveler Queen looked older than ever, her face collapsed into itself. "Connin, take me home. I'm exhausted."

Donnis stepped forward and took the old woman's hands; the midwife gasped, in horror or perhaps envy. "Thank you for saving her, thank you so much! She is my dearest friend and to lose her...oh, thank you so very much!" After a final squeeze of the crone's hands and an acknowledging nod to Connin, Lady Donnis led Miss Hanston and the still-awestruck midwife back into the Queen's bedchamber.

The Traveler Queen peered through her wrinkles up at Sedra. "Wit and temper. Temper and wit. You need to conquer both. Teacher is not allowed to share all the years of knowledge with you, I'd bet." Sedra said nothing but colored again, lifting her head a little higher on her neck. The Traveler Queen chuckled. "Don't be proud. Don't be resentful. When you want to know more, come to me."

Connin snatched Sedra's hand and kissed her knuckles before she could pull away. "Your Highness, perhaps we'll run across each other in the Woods. You know where our camp is. You're welcome any time." He took his mother's hand and faced one of the two mirrors flanking the fireplace. "Show me Mirror Clearing." The greenery framed in the knothole appeared; Connin and his mother disappeared in a swirling mass, and the mirror once again reflected the celadon receiving room. Sedra rubbed the back of her hand where Connin had kissed it.

Laughter seeped out of her mother's bedchamber. Roused from her contemplation, Sedra hurried into the room without knocking. She found her mother sitting up in bed; color had returned to her cheeks. Miss Hanston rumbled past, a grin like a fissure splitting her face. "She's calling for tea and biscuits, miss, tea and biscuits and a slice of cheese!" The happy ladies maid disappeared through the door.

"Seddy!" called her mother, holding out her hands. Sedra ran to the bed and sat down on the edge just long enough to kiss Ansella's hands before she flung herself onto the bed and sobbed into her mother's breast. "Oh, there now, sweetheart, never worry, I'm all right," said her mother, smoothing Sedra's glossy dark hair. "Tsk. What has Sinsett been up to? Your hair's a mess." Sedra cried and laughed as she burrowed against her mother's side.

TEN

Temmin returned to the Temple reluctantly. Though his mother appeared healthier than ever before, he still worried. The first fulfilled prophecy frightened him, but continued good news from the Keep and Nerr's Day preparations occupied his time and mind. He let himself be reassured that the Traveler Queen had performed one of her vaunted miracles; Mama and the baby would be well.

The twins' twice-annual ordeal began again this evening, a necessary suffering that sickened Temmin every time. Issak and Allis stood at the doors to the Gods' Chambers, the senior staff gathered around them. Allis smoothed Temmin's wrinkled brow. "Never worry. Nerr and Neya will be here and gone in a short while, and then we can all rest until next Neya's Day."

Temmin couldn't wait. Nerr's Day was all very well; brothers received homage from their unmarried sisters, and that meant presents. But if he'd known as a boy what the Lovers' Embodiments went through for him to get those presents he wouldn't have liked them half as much.

"This is your last Spectacle as a Supplicant, Anda," said Issak, his arms around the plump girl's waist. "Any grave and sober thoughts?"

Anda put her head on Issak's chest, hugging him tighter. "I can't be flippant about this."

"We'll be all right, we always are." Issak let her go and patted her cheek. "Have you decided your future? Will you stay at the Temple or make a brilliant match? Perhaps Mr Hasty, the banking magnate? I hear Lord Breitborough has been dangling after you as well."

"We'd be cousins if you become Lady Breitborough, Anda," added Temmin.

Anda shook her head. "I'm hoping Our Lord will guide me on Nerr's Day." She moved to Allis and kissed her over and over before clasping the smaller woman to her generous bosom in tears.

Temmin put his hands on Issak's shoulders. He'd grown enough that Issak had to look up to meet his eyes now. For once, vulnerability filled the green eyes that had so mesmerized him a year ago and that had been so closed in recent spokes. Why did it take the prospect of torture for Issak to open to him? Temmin pressed his advantage; he held Issak's head in his hands and kissed him, pouring as much concern and love into the embrace as he could. They rested their foreheads against one another. "Why have you been so distant?" Temmin whispered.

Issak glided away, professional and closed off again. "I'll see you on Nerr's Day, Tem." He strode into Nerr's Chamber, stopping long enough to kiss Barik Lover before closing the door. Barik locked it behind him.

Temmin turned to Allis, who stood half-in half-out of the doorway to Neya's Chamber. He hated thinking of her locked in there alone for two days: no food, no drink, no light, no sound. Bad enough for Issak, but Allis was so small, so delicate. He wanted to scoop her up and run away with her, even though he knew she was as strong as her brother—perhaps stronger. She smiled encouragingly, its intimacy contrasting against her brother's coolness, and slipped into isolation.

Temmin carried Issak and Allis in his heart until Nerr's Day Eve and his brother's gift ceremony. This would be the first time he'd gotten his gifts from his sisters' own hands since Sedra left home for the Capital four years before, and if rumors were true it would be the last. In all the chaos surrounding Mama's illness he hadn't been able to ask about Sedra's impending engagement to Bannig of Sairland. If what Ellika said was true then Sedra would be married and gone by the next Nerr's Day; as a married woman she would never give him a brother's gift again. He teased himself he could do quite well without one, but as he dressed in his best Supplicant's uniform, he knew it wasn't the little trinkets she gave him that he would miss. How much longer could Ellika remain unmarried? Soon enough there would be no trinkets at all, or sisters to give them.

The Temple's gardens and hothouses supplied the flowers for the nosegays tradition demanded brothers give in return for their unmarried sisters' tributes. On Nerr's Day Eve, Anda helped Temmin arrange them and wrap their stems in ribbons—deep rose for Sedra, blush pink for Ellika. He'd never done up his sisters' flowers himself; the Estate's housekeeper did them when they all lived at home, and then the Keep's housekeeper Mistress Mannell did them long distance when the girls moved away. As he carried the flowers to his meeting with his sisters on Nerr's Day Eve, he smiled at them; his results were not professional, but they were quite the prettiest nosegays he'd ever seen. He paused outside the private drawing room, spent a moment untangling the ribbons, and entered.

His sisters were standing before the empty hearth, chatting aimlessly with the beautiful Senik Lover. The girls turned to the door, both smiling, both holding small cases. Sedra dressed with customary restraint in a simple gown of opulent, thistle-colored silk. She wore simple bob earrings, amethysts dusted a long golden chain round her neck, and fragrant white orange blossoms winked in her dark plaits like jewels in a crown. She made no attempt to conceal her height; she stood straight as a dancer and towered majestically over her fair-haired sister, already queen-like.

As promised, Ellika's aquamarine gown contrasted perfectly with the rose marble of the Temple. Soft, creamy gauze trimmed its low neckline and swathed her shoulders; on its bodice, tiny pearls traced the traditional Nerr's Day horn-and-flower pattern woven into the fabric. Ropes of the same pearls threaded through her golden curls. Its extravagance bordered on the ridiculous and suited her utterly.

Senik Lover stood quite close to Ellika, carrying on a flirtation that for anyone other than a Lover would be considered impolitic. Temmin caught Senik's eye; the priest understood his meaning, excused himself and gave a final wink to the giggling Ellika. Temmin laid the two nosegays atop a nearby console. "Thank you for coming," he said, his voice uncertain and boyish to his own ear; Senik always threw him off his stride.

Ellika threw her arms around him. "Where else would we be, silly? Let Seddy go first," she said into his red tunic.

Temmin released his petite blond sister and turned to the regal dark one, but Sedra held back, ducking her head; her bright, liquid eyes seemed afraid to look at him directly. He picked up the rose-beribboned nosegay and almost crept up to her before he pressed the flowers into her free hand. "Sedra," he began, "*as your brother, should you ever lose our father's protec-*

tion *before your husband comes to claim you, I promise to protect you, to give you food and drink, to shod your foot and clothe your back, until—*" he choked on a sudden marble in his throat— "*until you are safely married.*" His eyes watered; he was ashamed until Sedra began crying herself.

She screwed up her mouth into something like a smile and said in a scratchy voice, "*As your sister, I thank you for your protection, and I promise to pray for you every day until you are safely married!*"

She gave him the ceremonial kiss on both cheeks, but Temmin pulled her close and hugged her. "Oh, Seddy!"

"I will pray for you every day even after you're safely married, Tem. No matter where I end up or how far apart we are. Now, here, it's a small thing," she added, handing him a little jewel case. Temmin opened it. Silver cufflinks nestled in its green velvet interior, each one engraved with a rearing stallion, its mane flying—the symbol of the House of Whithorse. Tiny emeralds made up the horses' eyes and decorated the shirt studs displayed beside the cufflinks.

"They're beautiful!" He hugged her close again, released her and retrieved the nosegay beribboned in blush-pink. "Ellika," he said as he gave her the flowers, "*as your brother, should you ever lose our father's protection before your husband comes to claim you, I promise to protect you, to give you food and drink, to shod your foot and clothe your back until you are safely married.*"

She gave the proper response and added in a merry, false tone, "I hope you've started saving up for my clothes, and I imagine you pray I'll get married before you're responsible!"

Inside the jewel case she'd given him nestled a matching stickpin for his cravat, a larger version of the Whithorse stallion. "Thank you, thank you both," he said, kissing each sister again. "I will wear them often."

"Not with *that* outfit," giggled Ellika in between teary sniffs. "I have never seen you in your priestly raiment." She fingered his red tunic sleeve's hem, squinting at it critically. "Very nice. Who does the embroidery?"

"I haven't the faintest. Now, tell me about Mama. Is she well?"

"She seems very well indeed," answered Ellika. "Almost troublingly so."

"How could you be troubled by it?" said Sedra. "She is well and shall remain so. The Traveler Queen has saved her, and there's an end to it."

"Her cures are not always reliable—"

"And they often are," interrupted Sedra. "Besides, what do you know about it?"

"I don't see what you'd know about it either," sulked Ellika.

Temmin sensed now was not the best time to broach the other matter, but when might he get another chance to speak to his sisters alone? "I have heard rumblings about…about a possible match for you, Seddy?"

His sister's face clouded further. "Apparently I'm marrying King Bannig of Sairland. Papa hasn't spoken to me about it, and Mama tells me Bannig's brother Prince Brinnid will be sent to test my wind, check my withers and examine my teeth."

"I do hate it when you talk like that!" said Ellika.

"Does it remind you too much of your own future?"

"I still don't have to enjoy that sort of talk," Ellika muttered, fussing with her nosegay's ribbons. She cheered as the pink silk satin slipped through her fingers. "I do wish you were coming to the Duke of Barle's ball tonight, Tem, it's the last of the season, you know. We're to go up to High Haven next week before the heat gets too beastly here in town, and then it's nothing but little country dances and concerts until we come back to the Keep for Farr's Day. Well, we'll be back for Venna's Day next spoke, but just for a week. I do hope we'll see you then?"

"At least at the Spectacle. I'll be in attendance with the Most Highs and the Holy Ones."

"Of course," Ellika sighed. "I do wish we were allowed at the Lovers' Spectacles."

"We'll be married soon enough," snapped Sedra.

"Best put a blossom from your brother's gift flowers under your pillow, then, and get a glimpse of your new husband in your dreams tonight!" said Ellika.

"Has that ever worked for you?" said Temmin.

"No-o-o, but it might this year! That's enough marriage talk. We're off to the ball, my dear, and here's hoping we see you before Venna's Day. Don't worry about Mama, she's quite well and happy. She and Papa have even reconciled and he's stopped dancing attendance on that horrid Shelstone chit."

"I'll write you from High Haven, Tem," said Sedra as she hugged him one last time. "Don't worry."

Nerr's Day morning brought the climax of the Embodiments' ordeals. Allis and Issak were beaten, hung on frames, tortured and drugged until their spirits buried themselves deep, leaving their hollowed-out bodies for Neya and Nerr to use. Their howls of pain and longing ceased, the rose-colored halo rippled around them, and their attendants removed the blindfolds and restraints. Allis and Issak were gone, Neya and Nerr in their places.

"Hello, Brother!"

"Hello, Sister." This time there was to be no running, no lovemaking in the garden: a day and night of leisurely pleasure. They exchanged a casual, erotic kiss. "What will you give me for my brother's gift this year? Besides this." He slipped His hand between His Twin's legs, and She moved against it before taking His erection in Her grip.

She gazed sideways at Temmin and Anda. "Our Supplicants, as always. Will they suffice?"

Nerr-in-Issak released His Sister and crossed to Anda. "Our last day with you, my little partridge, at least as Supplicant. Are you frightened? Excited? Sad? Ah, you are all those things," He cooed, tracing her nipples through her white tunic. "I wonder if next time I see you, you'll be wearing a Beloved's rosy clothes."

"I—I was hoping you might guide me, Lord," she stammered; a blush mounted high on her round cheeks, and she trembled.

Neya-in-Allis grasped Temmin's hand. "Little Prince," She smiled, "how happy I am to see you." Her erotic, frightening touch glided over the taut front of his thin trousers.

Temmin bit back a groan. He could not avoid Her borrowed eyes, glowing green with terrifying power, but none of the images he'd seen his first Neya's Day appeared.

"I am sorry, you know, for what's already come to pass," Neya said. She released his hand, took up Nerr's and walked away toward the Great Hall, Barik, Anda and the other attendants forming a train behind them.

"Wait! Lady, wait!" he called, striding to catch up. "Can you just tell me..." He tried to force out words, but they stuck in his throat like a hastily swallowed candy.

She patted his face, Her hand warm against his skin even in the Temple's hothouse air. "Oh, sweetheart, you can't stop it. But your part in these events is not pre-ordained. In them, you are the unknown." The Gods were often so cryptic; what did She mean? But he knew that's all he would get from Her.

They entered the Great Hall. Worshippers, all male, filled the immense space before the entwined statues of the Lovers. Temmin gazed in longing at the door leading to his room, hidden behind the huge statues' feet. To serve the Gods was exciting, yes, and frightening beyond words at the same time. Hiding appealed.

High Beloved Malla and High Lover Gan sat upon a dais at the statues' base, the magnificent red throne between them waiting for the God's arrival. Before the dais, racks displayed offerings from the faithful in the thousands: massive bouquets of rare, fragrant hothouse flowers from the rich to humble handfuls of wildflowers from the poor, and everything in between. Rank dictated the display of both the offerings and the worshippers. In the front rows knelt the nobility; Percet Lord Fennows was among them, for his sister Despilla still lived at home. Fennows gave him a lewd wink; Temmin chose to ignore him.

Behind the nobility knelt the gentility, then the wealthiest of the merchant class. All rested their well-dressed knees on elegant bolsters and cushions, supposedly the handiwork of their sisters. At the back the men and boys who worked for their livings knelt on their coats, or if they had no coats, nothing at all. Most were young, though the odd gray or balding head marked men with spinster sisters still at home.

Nerr ascended the dais, kissed Malla and Gan more intimately than one might usually kiss the aged, and settled onto His throne. Temmin and the other attendants settled themselves on cushions at His feet.

An aisle ran down the crowd's center; in it stood a knot of women, all dressed in black or varying shades of green. Neya joined them, and they sank to their knees in respect. She raised two of them and embraced them tightly. One was Trudannis, the young and solemn Embodiment of Harla the Bloody One; the other Sarra, the graying, gentle Embodiment of Venna the Sister. He liked Sarra though he'd seen far too many Sisters lately, and while he'd met Trudannis, he hoped further acquaintance might be put off as long as possible.

Sarra and Eldest Sister Imvalda approached the dais, both in the dark green robes of the high-ranked among the Sisterhood. Behind them streamed a procession of Sisters in lighter green, each bearing a large basket. Imvalda and the other Sisters bowed, but Sarra did not. "I stand in Your Sister Venna's place, Lord Nerr, and bring You Your brother's gift."

Nerr gave Sarra a different blessing than the one Temmin had recited to his own sisters the night before: "*As your brother, I promise to protect you even should you fall from Our Father's favor.*"

Sarra returned it: "*As Your Sister's representative, I thank You for Your protection and offer You all praise. I bring You Venna's gift, the twenty-two herbs of pleasure gathered this morning by tradition.*"

"I thank you," said Nerr. Lovers took the baskets from the Sisters, giving them enormous bouquets in return.

Next came the High Priestess of Harla and Her Embodiment. The blessings were exchanged, but no gifts. Harla's representatives never gave or received gifts on Her behalf; a gift from Death was bad luck, and everyone gave themselves to Her in the end. Temmin wondered if bad luck even applied to the Gods. Did death? He frowned at the black-clad women. The Bloody One had come far too close to his mother for him to welcome Her priestesses, now or perhaps ever.

Then Neya Herself glided up to the dais in all Her nakedness. In a rare display of power, She floated up to Her Brother's side. They joined hands. "Sister," said Nerr in a voice that could not be called loud but that filled the Great Hall's every corner; its force shook the gathering. "*As your brother, I promise to protect you even should you fall from Our Father's favor.*" He gestured to the rows upon rows of flowers. "All of these, I give to You."

"Brother," she answered, "*As your Sister, I thank You for Your protection and offer You all praise.*" She gestured to the two Supplicants at His feet. "Will You accept My gift?"

"Gladly," smiled the God, stroking Temmin's hair. Temmin closed his eyes as bliss radiated from the fingers laced among his unruly locks.

"Then I will be on My way to Our Brothers' representatives, to make My offerings." Jealousy twisted Temmin's insides; Her offerings to the Embodiments of Eddin the Wise One and Farr the Warrior were of Her borrowed body. Farr's priests didn't even like women—who knew how the Brother's Embodiment would use her? Then, she wasn't Allis; She was Neya. No man could hurt Her, not even a great warrior.

Nerr's fingers tightened in his hair and shook him back into the room. "Your allegiance is to Us, little Prince," Nerr growled, "not to the Embodiments We occupy. Mind your manners and your passions. Isn't that what We're here to teach you?"

"Yes, Lord," he stammered. As he and Anda followed the God back to the sumptuous rooms the Lovers shared during Their twice-yearly sojourn in the Temple, he did his best to banish Allis from his mind and keep his thoughts solely on Neya and Nerr.

Lovemaking did the rest; the two mortals fell into the Gods' bed and opened themselves. The golden, rosy haze so familiar from the last times he'd shared the Gods' bed enveloped Temmin, softening his bones and hardening his erection. Everything was so fogged and so clear at the same time. The God's whispering voice in his mind wordlessly planted understanding of the hearts of men and women as he slid his cock into Anda. Behind him, Nerr slicked his ass and without preamble pushed into him, spearing him as he fucked the woman lying beneath him, and all the time the voice swirled through his mind until he lost himself in a soft haze of desire and pleasure, knowing nothing but touch.

At some point in the long day of lovemaking Neya returned from Her offerings, lifting the rosy veil from Temmin's mind. She smelled of other men's semen and sweat, and he fell on Her in a possessive rage. He wanted to fuck away their masculine taint, to replace it with his own. She laughed as he mauled Her breasts, and dragged him down onto the bed beside Her.

The driving need to take Her and make Her his brought the shadowy memory that nagged at him into sharp focus. The Goddess's borrowed face shifted into something more childlike; green eyes changed to wide sapphire blue, and Allis's silken black hair became lush, mink-brown torrents. He knew this woman. Who was she? Flickering Neya's Day torches appeared in the edges of his sight, and he crushed the body now beneath him, clawing at clothes part of him knew were not there. Is this what had happened to him on Neya's Day?

"Gently, sweet Temmin, it is not for you to know yet," the Goddess murmured into his mind. "Now, please Me. Please Me, and forget for now." The wide blue eyes returned to Allis's green, the hair in his fist became black once again. His frenzy shifted from the need to possess the shadow woman to the need to pleasure the Goddess; the rosy fog descended once more.

The next morning Temmin woke up tangled in the sheets on the floor. Anda's odd, musical little snore reached his ears. She'd managed to retain possession of the bed, one arm dangling from its edge. He pulled himself to standing, unraveling the sheets knotted around him. In the center of the bed lay Allis and Issak, her head pillowed on his shoulder. Color had drained from their drawn faces; their breathing was quick, quiet and shallow. The Gods had left them as crumpled as discarded clothing.

Temmin shook Anda awake. "Hzn? Is it over?" she groaned. "Gods, all I want is breakfast and a nice long soak."

"You are of my mind," said Temmin.

Anda rose from the bed and helped him drape the sheets over the exhausted twins. They crept from the Gods' Chamber into its anteroom. On the low, wide couches the two Supplicants found clean uniforms laid out: white for Anda, red for Temmin, and undyed for the Embodiments. The table between the couches contained food for the Embodiments; they would awake from their possession starving and needing immediate nourishment. "Let's go eat and get a bath and a nap in before our watch starts," said Anda.

Once in their own room, the two sipped their morning coffee in silence over a tableful of breakfast. Anda yawned. Her fingers combed her messy brown hair from her face as Temmin demolished a plate of eggs, smoked fish and tomatoes. "Aren't you hungry?" he said as he reached for a fourth slice of toast.

"In a minute. I'm still half-asleep. I'm going back to bed as soon as I'm out of the baths."

"I'll join you."

"Only if you leave me alone. I do believe I am rubbed raw."

"I won't touch you. I think my fingertips are numb anyway."

"Hm." She reached for more toast, slathered it in butter and marmalade, and downed it in three bites. "Gods, now I'm ravenous." She ate two plates piled with sausages, eggs and fried mushrooms, washed down with heavily creamed coffee. Temmin kept pace until they were both sated enough to leave off and waddle down to the mercifully empty baths; neither wished to see or hear another person.

They washed up and soaked in the hot water until their skins were as red as Temmin's tunic; neither said a word. They returned to the Supplicants Chamber, doffed their garb and slid into their respective alcove beds. "I'm almost glad it was my last Nerr's Day," whimpered Anda. "I don't know if I'd live through another."

"So, it's your last one? You've made your decision?" yawned Temmin.

"What? No. Well, yes. I meant the last in the Gods' Chamber. How can something feel like that and leave me like *this*?" she said, waving a limp hand around her.

"What did you decide?"

"That as much as I love you, I'd rather not be your cousin after all. It seems Our Lord wishes me to stay at the Temple. Besides, I've made my point to my mother. I'm not as pretty as Janetta, but looks aren't the only way to success, even for a woman." Anda turned on her side to face him. "Anything you can share from last night?"

Temmin sorted through his memories. "No."

"Secret stuff?"

"No stuff at all. It's just…blank. Not even hazy like last year. Blank."

"Strange," she mumbled. Her eyes closed. Temmin smiled as her body relaxed, her mouth dropping open just enough to let out the tuneful little snore that always made him sleepy himself. He yawned, opening his jaw wide and squinching his eyes closed, and sank down on the pillow.

Temmin numbered among Issak's attendants for the next few days as the twins recovered from two possessions in as many spokes. Anda had once said they treated the Embodiments like glass for a whole spoke after Nerr's Day; the other six Embodiments carried their Gods once a year, and while it took a toll on them all it was doubly so for the Obbys. While the other Embodiments might serve twenty or even thirty years, the twins would last perhaps ten. They did little but eat and sleep for the first week after Nerr's Day, regaining their strength.

Temmin told himself concern for Allis made him wait for the others to leave so that he might sneak through the door between the twins' apartments. Allis's pinched and exhausted face blooming again as she slept touched him in a way that Issak's did not.

It troubled him. It went against Temple practice. He loved others in the Temple—Anda and Issak especially—but he loved Allis in a way he should not; jealousy raged inside him when she spent time with others, and he could not stop nor could he confess, not even when he was sitting with his back against the bed and Allis touched his hair. "Tem, what are you doing here?"

He jumped up and he could feel the guilt on his face. *Control, control.* "I'm…I was just..it was in case you needed anything."

"Anda, Penna and Justinna are on the other end of this bell pull. You shouldn't be here, Tem. Why are you here?"

"I don't know," he mumbled.

"I think you do. I know I do." She sat up, keeping the covers pulled up around her. "Well?"

His face crumpled. "I'm trying, Allis, but I don't know what to do. I've talked to people, I've distracted myself with others and I'm trying not to feel what I'm feeling, but I don't know how not to feel something."

"What are you feeling?"

"I'm feeling…" The knot in his stomach crawled up into his throat. *I can't, I'm not supposed to, I can't! If I say, I'll make it real!*

"Temmin," she began, "when young men first have sex—"

"No! No, don't ever say that, never say that! I'm not most young men, I've had a great deal of sex since then with many others, and that's *not* how it is." Temmin sank on his knees beside the bed. "Why are you avoiding me?"

"I haven't avoided you, I have duties. So do you. What do you want, Tem? You have to name it before you can begin to heal."

The words came out in a rush. "Heal? How can you heal from loving someone? Because I love you, and I can't stop, and I'm not sure I want to. I'm not asking you to belong to me and only me forever. I know it's not possible, for any number of reasons. Just tell me this one thing. Do you love me? Not as a petitioner, or a Supplicant, or a fellow human being—do you love me?

Do you love *me*, Allis? I need to know. That's all I need to know."

She searched his face, her green eyes sad and bright. "Oh, Tem. You'd best go. This is between us for now, but I urge you to speak with Barik or even Most High Gan. Don't ever ask me that again. Please."

A rustle made Temmin twist on his knees to face the door to Issak's bedchamber. "There you are, Temmin Supplicant," said Senik, his face blank. "You're needed in here."

Temmin rose from the floor, flustered and angry. Of all people to catch him, Senik was the last he would have chosen.

Senik appeared a few days later summoning Temmin to the Most High Beloved's chambers.

The old priestess sat on a low, wide couch propped up on pillows. "I'm perfectly able to sit upright on my own, but Senik likes to spoil me, don't you, dear? Well, Temmin Supplicant!" she said once they were alone. Malla took his hands in her own, her skin cool, soft and papery. "We have not spoken one on one in some time. How is your life here at the Temple?"

Temmin bowed his head over her hands and kissed them in reverence. "I'm told I'm progressing well in my studies and I'm enjoying them, Most High." Perhaps there had been a complaint about his work? Still not good, but better than what he was dreading. "Has anyone reported otherwise?"

"In a way," said Malla, sipping at her tea. "Your studies include freeing yourself from possessiveness, Temmin, and I am told you are failing in this regard. I have seen you failing in this regard myself."

"Oh."

"Well?" she said after a pause.

"I'm not sure what you mean. Perhaps you might tell me what the observers have found fault with in my dealings with petitioners."

Malla chuckled. "Never practice on the practiced, sweetheart—you can't evade me. The fault is not in your dealings with petitioners. With them, you are exemplary. With others..."

Temmin gave up. "I think about her all the time, Most High. When she and Issak started avoiding me I didn't know what I'd done to deserve it. I thought, I'm not understanding something, I'll just have to wait until whatever the next lesson is. I was trying to be patient. I really was." He swiped at his eyes. "And I tried to accept the obvious correction, but I couldn't. She said—she said most young men think they're in love with the first girl they lie with, but they're not." He looked up at Malla. "I do love her, Most High. It's not a passing infatuation."

"I believe you, but loving her will make your work here harder, and hers as well. It happens to everyone here at some point, this possessiveness." Malla smiled and rolled the teacup in her hands. "I remember back when the High Lover and I were young. Gan was a Lover before I joined the Temple myself, though we were bedmates before I joined. He was always admonishing me that he could never belong to just me. I served my postulancy apart from him and some years later we both found ourselves posted here, in the Capital. Of course, we immediately became bedmates again and were overjoyed to be together."

The old woman's faded amber eyes looked past the young man before her. "We were both surprised when jealousy struck Gan. We always thought it would be me when it came, but he couldn't bear my being with anyone else. Oh, not petitioners—that was our vocation. He couldn't stand it that I had other bedmates in the Temple. It took time, patience and dedication to the Gods to resolve it, but we did. We've been together in our way now some sixty years. Jealousy struck me down eventually, too, but not with Gan— with another."

"What did you do? How did you work it out?"

"Prayer. Hard work. Talking. A great deal of talking. We were separated for a time—he went back to Barle."

"I've tried talking with Allis. She won't talk to me."

"Then talk to the rest of us. My door is always open, as is Gan's, Barik's, Glaes's—any of the senior clergy." She smiled wistfully at Temmin. "My dear child, Allis can never have a normal life. If you love her, you must love all of her. That means loving her vocation—you must love sharing her. You've seen firsthand what her life is—taking on the Goddess, consorting with your own father, though he's stayed away lately. She and Issak are this Temple's public face. You are going to be the King. She's a commoner, she can't have children, and she's not a virgin. You can never marry her. You know this. The best you can hope for is that she will consent to be your mistress when she is done at the Temple. That won't be for many, many years to come. Your feelings may have changed, and she may very well decide to stay on here when the Goddess finishes with her."

Temmin wiped his eyes again. "Most High, I haven't even thought about any of that. I just want to be with her."

Malla looked into her teacup before meeting his eyes directly. "She can never love you while she is Embodiment. Neya cannot take her if she is in love, do you understand? It can never happen. It will not happen. You will not try to lead her down that path. None of us can love exclusively, but the

Embodiments risk everything to do so. Were you any other clergy we would have you both reassigned to opposite ends of the Kingdom as Gan and I were. We'll help you as much as we can but ultimately the work is yours. You must pray, Temmin, often and hard, and you must learn to seek both pleasure and affection elsewhere."

"Yes, Most High," he mumbled.

"Now, go on. Issak needs you."

"Yes, Most High."

Temmin walked back to Issak's apartments deep in thought. Why would she reassign Allis? Surely the fault was his alone. Did Malla know something he didn't?

Summer ripened, and so did the Queen; her health returned, better than ever. Harsin had planned to stay in town for the summer, but instead accompanied his wife and daughters to High Haven, the royal family's retreat in the mountains above the Capital. To their surprise, Ansella's brush with death rekindled their passion for one another. They spent their nights rediscovering each other's bodies, though long-exposed nerves still ached. Ibbit never left Ansella's mind, but her emotions changed from heartbreak and bewildered anger to implacable hatred—not just for her own sake, but for the unborn baby she carried. Ansella could almost understand it if Ibbit had tried to kill her from jealousy, but trying to kill the baby? For that, Ansella would see the woman dead.

Harsin suggested she return to Whithorse Estate if she wished—"It's your heart's home, after all"—but after everything that had passed she wanted to stay close to her children. Sedra's betrothal was imminent. When she married, Ansella might never see her again. "In truth," Harsin told her as they rode one day in the cool mountain woods, "I'm glad you didn't go back to the Estate, Annie."

She stayed silent and kept a loose hand on her reins, letting her white mare Flor set the pace down a path lined with evergreens, maple and ash trees. The shade was welcome even in the mountains, though the sun was not oppressive; crushed pine needles and sun-warmed wood filled the air. "Are you? I should have thought you'd prefer me to go. I'm surprised you didn't stay in town. You have business to attend to—*affairs of state.*"

"I will not let you goad me," Harsin answered affably. "There is no affair of state or otherwise as important to me as you are now."

"You're sure of that?"

"I'm sure."

She arched her delicate brow. "It's only a daughter, Harsin."

He pulled his gray gelding short. "Do you believe I love sons more than daughters?"

"I believe you consider Temmin more valuable."

Harsin nudged the gray in the ribs, the animal's gait muddling his shrug. "It can't be helped. He's the Heir. I love all three of my children, and the new one to be."

"They're grown—Sedra, Elly and Tem," Ansella mused. "They hardly need me now, but I don't think I'm quite done mothering. I'll rather enjoy this new little one."

Harsin turned in the saddle toward her. "Annie, do you believe now that I love you? Have I proven it to you? I never did stop loving you, however poorly I may have shown it."

"Is this an apology?"

"An apology?" he considered. "Of a sort. Perhaps not the one you might expect. Or want. I cannot help what I am. Whichever bed I spent time in never had any relation to my love and regard for you. What I am sorry for is letting you go, and I'm not speaking of Whithorse. You were never far away from me—you were a step through the mirror—but you seemed so far away in spirit. I convinced myself it didn't matter. You would always be there and besides, you didn't care."

"That was untrue," she murmured.

"So you did care."

Ansella looked down the path. Tiny insects were swarming in a patch of sun, mating she supposed. If she remembered correctly, the poor things had just the one day for it. "I wanted not to care."

"I let that woman walk right into my house—"

"The Estate is *my* house, Harsin—"

"It's *Temmin's* house, he's the Duke of Whithorse not you, and stop interrupting me. I'm trying to say I should never have let anyone take my place in your life."

Ansella thought back to the days when she and Harsin separated, and Ibbit filled the void. She'd been so lonely, so angry, and Ibbit offered her solace. She could talk to Ibbit in a way she never had with anyone before, not even Donnis; frankness between friends is not the same as intimacy between lovers, and Harsin had more than once walked away from her when she'd tried to show him her secret heart. Ibbit knew things about her body, too, that Harsin—for all his pride in his prowess—had merely guessed at.

Ibbit had known both her secret heart and her body, and chose betrayal.

"Oh, Annie. Have we both been very stupid?" said Harsin.

"I think perhaps, yes."

The path ended in a swath of meadow, warm in the sun. The spring flowers were long spent even this high up, and their summer seedheads were forming; the stalks quaked under their weight in the slight breeze. The horses wanted to stop and eat, but Harsin tapped the gray in the sides. "None for you. It's too warm here for my lady—for me too, truth be told. Come." He turned away and set them along a path leading beside a stream.

Up and up they rode, following the sound of water. The trees closed in. Moss and ferns grew heavy on the ground; tall grasses grew in the few shafts of sunlight. A never-ending roll of sound in the distance reminded her this path led to a series of waterfalls; after a first great drop, the stream cascaded over rocks from pool to pool until its course ran smooth again. Harsin led them to a little pavilion built by a long-dead ancestor, overlooking the clear green ribbon of the smallest fall and its rippling pool. They dismounted, looping the reins over a rustic fence near the water; the horses wouldn't wander far.

Inside the pavilion sat a table and a low lounge before it. Glasses, plates and various delicacies covered the tablecloth; Ansella wondered where the servants who'd carted everything up here were hiding, but the falling water would mask any conversation beyond the pavilion itself. Harsin walked to the pool's edge and pulled out a bottle of foamwine, chilled in the icy water. He wiped the bottle with a white towel, opened it and filled their glasses.

The wine was cold and crisp, so young it was almost as clear as the water. Ansella took a long sip. "Beautiful."

"The '90 is a good vintage, even better than the '88."

"No," she smiled, "I meant all of this. The ride here, this place—it's been many years since I was last here."

"The last time we were here, if what you told me at the time was correct, it resulted in Sedra."

Ansella blushed and laughed. "We haven't been back here since." A fish flickered in the shallows of the pool and the smile left her face. "I wonder how many times you've been here in the interim."

"After that day, I could never bring another here. It reminds me of you. When I missed you and thought I shouldn't come to you, I would come here."

"Flatterer."

"Truth-teller."

"You do not long for your mistress's arms?"

Harsin snorted. "I would be lying if I told you I wasn't fond of Twenna Shelstone, but how could I long for her? Sweet, giving and very pretty, but ultimately boring. She is an uncomplicated girl, no depth of character. That's what drew me to her in the first place. I wanted solace and simplicity, and you are not a simple woman, Annie."

She studied the man she'd been married to for the better part of twenty-five years. His hair was graying at a faster clip. The brown eyes that were in youth cheerful, arrogant and mischievous were sober now, but softer than she'd grown to expect.

"Come here." Harsin put his arm around her; for the first time when he talked of his mistresses, a safe calm enveloped her. He kissed her.

How easy it had been to love Ibbit, and how easy now to hate her—easier by far than it had been to either love or hate Harsin. With him, just when Ansella would begin to love him, he would do something to make her hate him, and just when she got the knack of that, he would make her love him again. It was hard to say whether their newfound closeness balanced out another illegitimate child. Why was he always so difficult? She looked away into the bowl of the pool, its sides terraced by running water over thousands of years. "If the Honorable Miss Shelstone is so tedious, why are you making her a countess?"

"It's for the baby's sake. Were I able to find her, I'd do the same for Mattie Dunley. Her mother's dead, you know."

Tellis Dunley, dead? Such a pretty girl she'd been, and so kind-hearted. Even after she'd discovered the maidservant had borne Harsin a daughter, Ansella couldn't bring herself to hate Tellis, though she'd made sure the woman took her daughter far away from Temmin. "Merciful Amma. What happened?"

"Teacher found her body in a Hill, but we can't tell where. Winmer has his agents searching the kingdom for Mattie. I want her found."

"Why doesn't Teacher just watch for the girl? She has to look in a mirror at some point."

"Teacher's been looking since I found out about...about the other child-to-be. I don't want to repeat my father's mistakes—no remonstrances on my dalliances, woman. I mean the way he dealt with my brothers. I will keep my children under closer observation than he did. Even if she's left the country, I'll find her." Harsin shifted on the silken cushions padding the pavilion bench. "As to the Shelstone girl, I could not in good conscience abandon her now, though I have no interest in resuming my attentions. She's quite an innocent thing, really, in a different context you would like her, Annie."

"Oh, I'm sure we would have been the *best* of friends."

Harsin laughed. "She hasn't much in the way of learning or of intellect, I'm afraid—more at home with Ellika than you, I suspect." And closer to her age, Ansella added to herself. "She is on the whole a good and gentle girl. Her fault at present is that she's not you—say, you're taking this conversation quite placidly. You surprise me."

She sighed and closed her eyes. "After recent events I find myself tired of arguing. Tired of pride. Just tired."

"You seem sprightly enough."

"It is an exhaustion of the spirit, I suppose. My recent…illness…I just don't want to fight you any more. Do as you please."

"What would please me is to spend my time with you."

"A morsel for the expecting wife?"

Harsin drew back as if stung. "Not a morsel. The whole man. I find myself wanting your company and no other. I think perhaps I wanted it all along." She kept a doubtful silence; Harsin began again. "Lord and Lady Litta are at Eaglehome for a short visit before they return to Turus. Will you accompany me to a musical evening there tonight? You've always liked Anvalt, despite the unpleasantness surrounding Temmin's investiture."

"That was *your* 'unpleasantness,' Harsin, not Anvalt's."

"He approved of the goal if not the method."

"Well, he's your faithful friend—a true friend. I wish you'd spend more time with him and less with Bornet Sandopint."

"Mm," said Harsin around a mouthful of wine. "I depend on Corland among the conservatives."

"Litta's a conservative, too. So is Lord Barle."

"And Barle, yes, but Corland is in a different faction altogether, these True Conservatives, whatever that means. I can rely on Litta completely, and Barle usually, but not always on Corland. Borney needs a certain amount of cultivating, but that's none too hard. Eats too much, drinks too much and wenches too much. No raised eyebrows, please, he makes me look like an amateur."

"Corland isn't making his mistress a countess."

"Corland isn't an independent kingdom any more, and Borney discards his women."

"And you?"

Harsin threw a strawberry top into the pool. The shadow she'd seen earlier splashed to the surface and snapped at the strawberry top. "I release them."

"Like fish."

Harsin burst out laughing. "I have missed your humor."

"I have missed *you*." She traced her fingers along the laugh lines around his eyes and kissed him, difficult man that he was.

Twenna fretted at the window overlooking Middlemont's grounds and the long, empty drive curving through the park. The royal family had returned from High Haven at Farr's Day, but here she was, still alone. Harsin hadn't come to see her once. Though notes and small presents arrived constantly, they all bore Mr Winmer's hand.

She was supposed to be planning out the week's menus and activities, but she was finding it hard to attend Mistress Hallik's gentle voice. Could Harsin have stopped wanting her? She was hardly a pumpkin—three spokes gone, three more to come before she gave birth to what Harsin insisted would be a daughter, though how he could be so confident about it she didn't know. What would they name the baby? She leaned toward her late mother's name, Deannis; naming a daughter after Mama comforted her. If Harsin had a preference he hadn't said.

When she first moved to Middlemont it had all been so exciting. Sir Elbig was at Menantola, his new holding in Kellen, and for the first time in her life she had her own way. She decorated the house as she pleased, she wore what she pleased, she ate what she pleased—it was a banquet of independence. The kind Halliks helped her in her new role as mistress of an estate, teaching her how to manage the household and how to settle matters to please not just herself but Harsin. Mistress Hallik, the housekeeper, had even hinted that Harsin intended to give her the house once the baby was born. The round of balls, routs, card parties and dinners she'd grown accustomed to in the City—oh, how difficult it was to stay out here by herself! If this was the price for Harsin's love, she would pay it, but it made his neglect harder to bear.

The baby kicked, and Twenna patted her belly. She'd heard the Queen was with child as well and wondered if Her Majesty's baby kicked her, too. Did the royal pregnancy explain Harsin's absence? She couldn't imagine it did, not after he'd turned back to her so fervently after his infidelity with the Queen at the Neya's Day Spectacle. Twenna had persuaded herself the incident was more for appearances than anything. Perhaps she had misjudged.

She looked down at her middle in dismay. He'd said once her growing bump made him want her even more—and he'd proved it. Pregnancy suited her. Her complexion had never been better, and her hair grew in a rush like a spring freshet, thick and flowing. Harsin had always liked her hair. He said it was the color of mink. "'Little mink of mine,'" she murmured.

"Pardon, miss?" said the housekeeper.

Twenna turned from the window. "Nothing, Mistress Hallik. Let's plan this week's menus."

"Are we…are we expecting company, miss?"

Twenna cringed inside. "We should plan for at least one dinner just in case, don't you think?"

"Yes, miss," said Mistress Hallik, daring a motherly little pat on the hand. "Just in case."

ARREN, CORLAND
THE 40TH DAY OF FALL'S ENDING, 991 KY

"Eh Pawl, there's sum'on to see you."

Rodder Pawl looked up from the pile of silver he was polishing in anticipation of the Winter's Beginning parties to find his fellow footman lounging in the pantry door. "To see *me*? Who?"

"Dunno, but Mr Bortle weren't happy, you getting visitors here. He said you should meet 'em at the beer garden on your half-day, but then he seen 'im and put 'im in the front parlor. Mr Bortle's waiting for you there, and ain't he in a mood."

Mr Bortle the butler could stuff his mood, thought Pawl as he put down the silver tray he'd been working on and donned his livery coat; he knew better than to ask a friend to come round his employer's townhouse. Someone visiting him specifically, someone grand enough to be asked to wait in the front parlor, mystified him. He approached the front parlor door, where Mr Bortle stood like a mother waiting to pounce on a naughty child. "And who is this Mr Brown to you, Pawl?" said the butler.

"Begging pardon, sir, I don't know any Mr Brown," said Pawl.

"He knows you. If you're in trouble, be assured I shall turn you away without a reference, young man. No. Reference. At all. This close to Eddin's Day you wouldn't find a new place *with* a reference. You had better thank Pagg Sir Tomis isn't at home, for he doesn't approve of any such goings-on as this."

"But *what* goings-on, Mr Bortle?" pleaded Pawl.

The butler paused. "I don't know, but for the likes of you to be visited by a person of such quality does not bode well." On these ominous words, he opened the front parlor doors not bothering to announce Pawl's arrival.

The person of quality inside rose as the doors closed behind Pawl, and extended a hand. "Mr Pawl, I am very glad to meet you. I've been looking for someone such as yourself."

The man was well-dressed in a fine wool suit, an understated but sumptuous waistcoat, expensive shoes—Pawl added him up from head to toe. The total made for a man who was more than a wealthy merchant, and less than a lord. A gentleman, then, quite a rich one, and from the south judging by his accent. "Such as myself, Mr...?"

"Mr Brown shall do for now. Please, sit." Mr Brown gestured to the chairs pulled close to the roaring early winter fire, and both men sat down, Mr Brown at his ease, Pawl considerably less so. "Now, then, Rodder Pawl. No preambles. You once served as footman to a lady named Tellis Ambleson, is this correct?"

"Oh, sir, are you a relative of hers?" cried Pawl, scooting to the chair's edge. "Because I did the best by her I could, sir, and if I'd known she'd... she'd..." His guilt at accepting Adrik Adrikov's gold piece gnawed at him. He decided to say nothing to that. "I'm happy to take you to where she lies in the Hill, sir, so you might pay your respects and take her bones back to where she's from when the time comes. I didn't know where to find her people, so I made the arrangements myself, sir."

"What do you know about where she's from, Pawl?"

"Well, I knew she and Miss were probably from Whithorse the way they talked." A small hope came to him. "Sir, has Miss come to her family there? She never came back to Arren."

Mr Brown uncrossed his legs and leaned forward; Pawl retreated an inch into his chair. He'd stepped in it now. "Where did she go? And with whom?"

Panic washed over him: panic, guilt and grief in equal measure. He assumed an indignant expression. "Now look here, sir, she loved the young gentleman, and he'd courted her fair for a year! You can't blame *her*, she was innocent as a lamb in it!"

Mr Brown sat back and re-crossed his legs. "I wonder how innocent *you* are, Rodder Pawl," he murmured.

Pawl's face dropped. This man knew. Make a clean breast, or avow blamelessness? He'd done nothing but assist Miss in marrying Mr Adrikov. If it meant a gold piece in his pocket, well, he'd given it all to the Temple of Harla in memory of his poor mistress, and he'd promised himself he'd take care of Miss if Mr Adrikov proved false in his promise to marry her. "I done nothing wrong, sir," he said, raising his hands before him palms-out. "Miss Mattie and Mr Adrikov loved each other, anyone could see that, and why Mistress wouldn't give permission no one in the house understood."

"Did Miss Ambleson ask you to aid them?"

Pawl nodded. "Yessir. And Mr Adrikov...well...he gave me a gold piece." There. It was out.

"I should hope he did," smiled Mr Brown.

"Then she's all right, sir? Did she come to you? Is that why you're here? Does she know about her mother?"

"I don't know. Can you tell me, Mr Pawl, what Miss Ambleson looked like?" Pawl put an unconscious hand on the waistcoat pocket holding Mattie's miniature. Mr Brown smiled. "Would you like to share, Mr Pawl?"

Pawl flushed and produced the tiny portrait. "Please, sir, I didn't steal it. The Accountsman would have just sold it with the furniture—it's all I could save, and I thought I should keep it to give to her when she came back. Except...except she didn't come back."

Mr Brown accepted the miniature and studied it. "This is the girl I've been looking for, which means you are the fellow I've been looking for, Rodder Pawl. Already knew it, but it's always handy to have it confirmed."

"Oh, sir—"

"You're not in any trouble," said the still-smiling Brown. "Though I imagine you do feel some guilt as to Mistress Ambleson's death." Pawl lowered his head. Mr Brown stood in a graceful, powerful movement that reminded Pawl of a dancer—or a Brother practicing his forms. "I thought so. I've done some prior research on you. No family to speak of, nothing holding you here, and you speak the language of the Gremas tribe. Your grandmother was Gremas, I'm told."

Pawl raised his brows in astonishment and strained to see the other man's face without craning his neck. Why had the man bothered learning about *him*? "If you're asking me to go somewhere for some reason, sir, I have to say no. If Miss Ambleson comes back and there's no one here to tell her what's happened—"

"Miss Ambleson isn't coming back."

"She's not—she didn't follow her mother into the Hill, did she, sir?" gasped Pawl.

"In some ways, it's worse. Mr Adrikov is not the man he said he was. I have reason to believe he has kidnapped Miss Ambleson."

"So...you don't know where she is, either."

Mr Brown returned the miniature. "I have an idea. How attached are you to Sir Tomis's household?"

"Attached?" snorted Pawl. "It's just a job. Truthfully, sir, I feel responsible for Miss. I've been watching for her all this time, and I confess I'm worried."

"Will you help me find her, then? It will be dangerous, very dangerous. I'd go myself, but I am known where I believe she is being held. You will be paid, handsomely," he added.

Pawl stood up. He wasn't the bravest man, but he had a debt to pay to the Amblesons. Then there was the mention of money. "What do I have to do?"

"Right now? Give notice to that butler and come with me."

"I have a right to know what you want me to do before I give up my place. They don't hand places out at Paggday market, y'know."

"Even if you say no, I'll make it worth your while, but I cannot tell you anything more in this house." Brown extended his hand. In it were twelve gold pieces, more than Pawl made in a year. "Consider these a retainer fee, with more to come. Take these, and you come with me. Leave them, and I'll still give you one to forget everything we've spoken of. Are you my man?"

Pawl hesitated. Did he care enough about Mattie Ambleson to put himself at risk? But twelve gold just to begin with…and a chance to make things right with the spirit of Mistress… He snatched the gold from Brown's hand before he could change his mind. "I'm your man."

ELEVEN

Vennaday, the 25th day of Winter's Beginning, 992 KY

"The Queen is in labor?" said Anda.

The spoon in Temmin's hand stopped midway to his mouth and he snuck a glance around the dining hall. His last petitioner had taken longer than expected, and by the time he entered the room most of the diners had already finished; near-empty tables and padded benches surrounded them. Satisfied no one might hear their conversation, he answered, "Yes, I got the message just after lunch with the Holy Ones. How'd you know?"

"Allis made a cryptic remark to me in private. Never worry, nothing indiscreet." Anda pushed back her rose-colored sleeve to avoid dragging it in her soup as she reached for the bread basket; Temmin put down his spoon and hurried to hand it to her. "Thank you. I'm glad I was delayed in my dinner, too. I rarely get to see you any more. Are you still having trouble sleeping?"

"I'm hoping the next Supplicant snores."

Anda stuck her tongue out at him and buttered a roll. "It took me some time to get used to my new room, I confess. When d'you think you'll hear about your mother?"

"It's her fourth child, so I'm told it shouldn't take too long." He took another spoonful of soup, mindful he didn't slurp. His manners in the last two years had improved; he almost never dribbled soup down his front in his haste to fill his stomach now. Jenks would be proud.

"Isn't it rather early for the baby?" said Anda. "It's not quite six spokes since Neya's Day—that went by quickly. Well, I suppose it's not too early. I hope so, anyway. Aren't you worried, though? Shouldn't you be there?"

Temmin shrugged. "I don't know what I could do if I were, apart from pacing up and down with my father." He finished the soup and pushed it aside to attack the chicken and rice before him. "They'll send for me once the baby is born, and then I'll go see my new little sister."

"How do you know it's going to be a sister?"

"Educated guess," Temmin grinned.

"Have they picked a name?"

Temmin swallowed his mouthful of chicken. "Anneya. She's a Neya's Day babe, after all!"

Ansella paced her bedchamber, her gait heavy and waddling. Midwives supported her on both sides; when a contraction swelled she stopped and held onto them. Her voice rose high, verging on a shriek. "Low, Your Majesty, low. Ooooo..." encouraged the midwives. Ansella brought her voice down as they urged; somehow the lower pitch brought the pain down, too. She rested for a moment, letting the women hold her up as she regained her breath, and then resumed the slow walking up and down.

She grew tired. "Why is it taking so long?" she moaned.

"It's not so very long, my dear, though it feels long," soothed the lead midwife. "You'll be able to greet her soon, just think of that!"

"I can't!" wept Ansella. "I can't do this any more!"

The midwives exchanged a knowing smile over her head. "Come dear," said the lead, "let's sit you down in the birthing chair for a rest."

Not long after, Ansella needed to push...and push. She pushed far longer than she had for any of her other children—even Sedra, the first. Once her body understood what to do, Ellika and Temmin came easily, but not this little one. She was stubborn, or reluctant—or stuck. It was as if Ansella lost every precious inch when she stopped to rest; an invisible hand pushed the baby back. She was so tired.

The Sister midwives murmured encouragement, no *Your Majesty* or *ma'am,* just *sweetheart* and *dear* and *little mama;* they rubbed her back and supported her as she squatted on the birthing chair. Someone—Donnis?—mopped the sweat from her face with a cool rag. She would have cried from the tiny pleasure, but she was already crying, gasping and moaning as she fought the invisible hand. A black foreboding came over her. *I can't, I'm going to die before I get her out, I'm going to die and take her with me, no, she can't die, take me, Lady Harla!* Ansella gathered her strength to push again. *Anneya, move, come out, please Amma, let her come out!*

By the time the head was crowning she had no further thoughts, reduced to grunting like the animal every birthing mother becomes. A great ring of fire, and she screamed as Anneya's head crowned. "It's out, sweetheart, her head is out!" Donnis cried. The pain retreated, but Ansella remained deep in herself. "One more push and out come the shoulders, dear," said the midwife rubbing her lower back. "Come, one more push!" Ansella pushed.

Anneya slipped from her in a rushing slither. She did not cry.

The midwives quickly set the birthing chair into a recline and lowered Ansella onto it. "Here, here, see, she's here!" one of them murmured in her ear.

The baby lay on Ansella's belly, the cord still attached to them both. Neither moved. The cord pulsed slower and slower as the baby's body began to work on its own, until it stopped. They were no longer one, but two.

Ansella's eyes rolled back in her head, away from the midwives calling her name and muttering to one another about the silent baby. The choice came to her in the dark, in that place of no conscious thought: One life. Two beings.

Her decision was instinctive, instant and irrevocable. The midwives' voices calling to her made urgent fiery arrows in the dark, the baby's sudden cry a beautiful, throbbing cloud of gold; the colors and the sounds drained as Ansella began slipping away. Even the dark retreated. She hung in a void.

The void spoke in a thousand voices as one, dry, whispering and soothing. *It is time, daughter.*

Anguish and fear flooded her. "Time? It can't be time!"

There was life enough for one. You gave it to your baby.

"But my other children—what will happen to Seddy, Elly, Temmin? Harsin, my mother? *The baby*! What will happen to my baby!"

Leave her to the Gods, leave them all to the Gods—your time to worry is ended. They will be all right without you. Come with Me.

"I'm frightened!" No sooner had she said it than the anguish retreated. Peace, acceptance, love took its place in an overwhelming gush. Her brother Patrin's voice was among the thousand, her father's voice too, and she knew the thousand voices spoke the truth.

I am with you. I have been with you since your birth. I am with all things, always—stars, rocks, flowers, ants, humans—all things—and I love you.

Ansella's own voice sang among the thousand now, and the void seemed to form for a brief flash into a black-skinned Woman, compassion shining from Her ruby eyes. "Blessed Harla, You're beautiful!" was Ansella's last thought as she dissolved into Death's welcoming arms.

The chief midwife came into the Queen's sitting room, where Ansella's daughters and husband waited. Her face formed a professional mask, but the moment the woman entered Ellika knew. From the Queen's bedchamber came a newborn's wail and the sobs of women. The midwife cleared her throat. "The Queen...the baby is fine, healthy and whole, but I'm sorry. The Queen is gone."

A shocked silence fell. Ellika's insides dropped to the floor. "Gone? The Traveler Queen said she'd be all right!"

"No, she said it was up to Mama," said Sedra. "It was her choice. I didn't know this is what she meant! Mama chose the baby. How could she—how could she leave me!" Sedra fled from the room, crying.

Ellika stood stock still, her hands over her leaden stomach. "May we see her?" The midwife hesitantly led Ellika and Harsin into the room.

Ansella had been shifted from the birthing chair to the bed. Her golden hair lay over one shoulder, still in a long plait; the strands around her face were drying. Her eyes were closed, and a smile just touched her mouth. Donnis knelt at the bedside, holding her cousin's hand; her forehead rested against the bed and her body shook in grief. In one corner crouched the sobbing Miss Hanston. In another, three midwives were muttering over a large porcelain basin beside a heap of bloodied linen, and a Sister walked up and down, carrying a small wailing bundle.

Ellika stopped the woman's pacing to look at the baby wrapped in swaddling. Her indignant face already favored her father, crowned in a soft cap of black hair. Ellika's heart hadn't stopped pounding since the chief midwife had brought them the news; her grief was so great it kept her tears from flowing. But as she stared at her new sister a purpose gripped her.

"Wouldn't you like to see your daughter, Your Majesty?" asked the Sister. "She's a little early, but she's healthy."

Harsin waved the woman off, his face pale; Ellika saw in an instant what he would look like as an old man. "I don't care if I ever see her in this life," he said. "Take her away."

"Give her to me," demanded Ellika. "And send for my brother."

Temmin sat beside the bed with his father, trying to listen to Eldest Sister Imvalda. Something about the afterbirth—it was blasted, shriveled and black as if scorched. "None of us have ever seen anything like this before, not even the oldest and most experienced among us. My poisons expert tells me in one quite obscure textbook in the Hearth's library there is a description of such a toxin, but it was written five hundred years ago and to anyone's knowledge it had never been used—until now, apparently. The poison should have killed the Queen, but whatever the Blessed Maeve did left her with enough life for one of them. Her Majesty chose the baby." Imvalda cleared her throat. "Ibbit's knowledge and inclinations run more toward death than life, to a degree that shocks me."

"I will take great satisfaction in bringing her face to face with death," said Harsin in a voice so hollow the Eldest Sister gave an involuntary shudder.

Silent tears ran down Temmin's face. Mama was gone. What would he do, how would he go on? Mama had been everything—mother, sometimes father before Jenks came, teacher, solace. Who would he turn to now? Who would love him now? His father? He hardly knew the man, and what he did know disturbed and angered him. His sisters, yes, and he loved them but it wasn't the same. Alvo and Jenks were far away. Allis? Oh, how he loved her, but what did that matter?

Every happy memory of his mother rushed at him—her laughter as they rode over the plains of home, her kiss as she tucked him in at night when he was small, the two of them in the stables as she taught him to take a horse's measure, her sympathetic listening to his troubles boy and man. Worse by far were the memories of every time he failed her. He could love no one like that ever again, and no one would love him like that ever again.

Temmin put his head down on his mother's cold breast and let out a deep, sobbing roar.

Tremontine flags trimmed in black flew at half mast throughout the City, the dark red field and its three golden mountains limp on this cold, still day. Every bell, from the great War Bell in the Keep to the time-keeping carillons at the University tolled, echoing desolate against the City walls as the funeral procession passed through the streets. Harsin walked before it, dressed in severest black but for the Tremontine red sash beneath his coat; his head wore neither hat nor crown. Emsa, the high priestess of the Friends of Harla, and Harla's Embodiment Trudannis walked beside him, their black hoods lowered to show their stubbled heads.

Black horses drew the Queen's bier behind them. A Brother held the reins; his helmet sat next to him on the box. Bare-headed Friends walked four to a side. Commoners lined the streets, hats in hands, ears and noses red with the cold; as the procession passed, they pressed flowers on the Friends to be placed on the bier. The mass of flowers had grown so deep the simple coffin holding the Queen's body could no longer be seen. While Ansella had passed most of her time as Queen outside the City, the people still loved her. The popular press had idolized her as an exemplar of motherhood since Sedra's birth, and never more so than now.

Behind the bier came Ellika, Sedra and Temmin, all in black. Though Ellika ordered new clothes for every possible occasion, when her maid Miss Clommert asked in her gentle way if she should call for Mistress Naister Ellika flew into such a rage that poor Miss Clommert retreated deep into the wardrobe in self-defense. Ellika pulled all the black lace, ribbons and rosettes from the dress her maid chose, a gown first made for the old Duke of Barle's state funeral almost three years prior: "I have no patience for dressmakers and no taste for fashion, Iddie. I may never again. I don't care if I wear a black sack!" She wore her golden hair in a girlish plait hanging down her back to her hips, and no jewelry at all.

For the first time ever, Ellika dressed more severely than Sedra. The oldest sister had also pulled out her dress from the Duke of Barle's funeral. She wore the jet mourning jewelry she'd inherited from their mother, a much more elaborate set than anything she ever chose for herself: ear bobs, a high choker with pearls separating its many strands, a round brooch framing a white, empty space pinned over her heart.

Temmin dressed in his role as Duke of Whithorse and head of his mother's family. He fingered the green silk sash across his chest beneath his coats. He'd been head of the family for fifteen years and he was not quite twenty; heads of families should be older. At his wrists, the horses engraved on the cufflinks Sedra had given him last Nerr's Day flashed their emerald eyes; Ellika's stick pin reared silver against his black silk cravat. In his waistcoat pocket he carried a new gold mourning watch, a gift from his father. His mother's portrait, done in brilliant enamels, had been taken from another decorative piece and fashioned into the watch's cover. Crystal faced the cover's inside; between the two layers would go a lock of Mama's hair. They walked down the Promenade, past Pagg's Temple and through the City gates, where the Promenade became a broad road through the sacred woods leading to Harla's Hill in the southwest.

Once, each of the seven Temples had its own hill, scattered throughout the City. Now, Harla's old Temple was the only one still in use, the others long since moved from the hilltops to the graceful Temple Green, though their old temples still stood as shrines. While the City had grown to surround the other six—indeed, marched up their hillsides—Harla's Hill remained alone outside the old City walls, surrounded by what was left of the original woods once covering the Valley of Three Mountains.

The Temple itself burrowed into the Hill rather than sitting atop it like the others had once done. Smooth, black stone tiled its entrance. A cool wind emanating from the Hill's wide, dark mouth smelled clean and damp, faint incense floating on it.

The Friends collected the flowers onto a cart and took the box containing Ansella's body down from the bier. They carried it through the great archway and into the Hill; Temmin and his family followed behind with Friend Emsa and Trudannis Embodiment.

A natural cave formed the Hill's main hall, its ceiling high above them; from this vault, the Friends had hollowed out the Hill in all directions to make room for the niches where bodies rested long enough to rot to bones, the private chapels of nobility and the wealthy, and the great royal ossuary, the resting place of its kings dating back to Temmin the Great almost a thousand years before.

They followed the Friends bearing Ansella's coffin into a smaller preparation hall, hung with the royal family's Tremontine red and gold, and Whithorse's grass green, white and silver. A stone table stood in its center; a large basin stood at the table's head. The Friends set the coffin down on a nearby bench and opened it. They picked up the edges of the sheet on which Ansella's body lay, lifted her from the coffin and placed her on the stone table.

Emsa approached Harsin. In her hand was a knife, exquisitely sharp, knapped from slick black obsidian. Harsin took it from her and began cutting away the simple white dress on Ansella's body. "*All this is fleeting, all this is lost, all this is unnecessary,*" said the King.

"*All this is ending, all this is beginning, all this is needed,*" answered the rest, Friends and family in gentle chorus. Temmin did his best to follow along. He knew the words but they kept sticking in his throat.

"*Life is fleeting, life is lost, life continues,*" said his father.

"*Her life has ended, her life is beginning, all this is needed,*" came the response.

Mama's body lay naked now on the stone table, pale but for her still-bright hair, and so small, almost childlike. Her belly was flaccid from the

birth, and Temmin flinched, thinking of his new sister. Part of him wanted
to hate the baby for living, but the better part of him loved her as the last
part of Mama left behind.

Harsin cradled his wife's head in his hands; he bent over the stone basin
before him and began to cry in earnest, letting his tears drop into the salt
water filling it. Temmin's tears began again, and beside him Sedra folded
herself into broken sobs. The Friends wiped away the siblings' tears with a
soft cloth, but for Ellika. She remained stoic, face so blank Temmin wondered if she understood.

Emsa took the soaked cloth and dipped it into the basin, spreading the
tears through the water. "*See, our tears are endless as the ocean,*" she chanted.
"*See, our tears make up your bath.*" Emsa wrung out the cloth and gave it to
Harsin, who began washing Ansella's already clean face. Her children took
cloths as well, and the four gave their wife and mother her final bath. The
Friends turned her on her side. They washed her back and laid her down
onto the shroud again; Sedra arranged her mother's long gold plait over her
left shoulder. Harsin picked up the braid and used the black knife to cut it
off; Emsa accepted it from him and wrapped it in a red velvet cloth.

Harsin took up his mourning braid, woven from the hair growing at his
left temple and omitted from the queue at his nape. A flick of the knife severed it, and he placed it on his wife's chest above her heart. Temmin did the
same. The knife tip cut him; he could see his blood on the braid he placed
beside his father's, and he pressed a handkerchief against his temple, swearing to himself. Sedra unfastened the mourning braid at her left temple, cut
it off and laid it next to the others; the dark hair coiled down Ansella's chest
from her shoulders to her navel. Sedra handed the knife to her sister.

Elly set her mouth in a firm line and looped her full braid around her
hand in a tight twist. Sedra cried, "No, Elly, don't!" just as Temmin realized
Ellika had no smaller mourning braid and reached for her himself. Ellika
sawed her entire braid off at the shoulder before anyone could stop her.
Harsin gasped and sputtered something Temmin didn't catch, and his chest
squeezed harder as Ellika laid the thick braid where Ansella's own had been;
its color matched but for a few gray strands among the Queen's. "Oh, Elly!"
choked Sedra.

Ellika pulled a hand through her ragged, newly-bobbed curls. "It doesn't
matter."

"It would have mattered to Mama!" her sister replied through renewed
tears. Ellika shook her head, still dry-eyed.

Harsin folded Ansella's arms over her chest. The Friends brought the shroud around her body; Harsin and the children took turns sewing it closed. Emsa gave Ansella's velvet-wrapped hair to Sedra, who accepted it with shaking hands. The Friends took up the body in its coffin again and returned to the main hall for the walk to the royal section of the catacombs.

A ramrod-straight, barrel-chested man in the dark Tremontine red uniform of a colonel of the Royal Cavalry waited in the hall; the uniform's markings were of the First Cavalry Battalion of the Whithorse Guard, and medals covered its front. Tradition banned weapons from the Hill, and his sword sheath hung empty at his side. The man held his black fur winter uniform hat under his arm. Gray threaded the black hair fringed round his head as well as his neatly trimmed beard, and his weather-lined face flashed a heavy grief before he snapped to attention.

It was Jenks, Temmin's valet since boyhood, the man who'd raised him with his mother, who'd helped teach him to ride, the other male member of the little family that would sit beside the nursery fire at home of a night at the Estate. Temmin resisted the urge to run to him like a little boy.

He took a second look. Why did Jenks wear a colonel's uniform?

Harsin didn't seem surprised to see him and shook his hand. "At ease, Colonel."

Jenks took each girls' hands in both his own—"Miss Sedra, Miss Ellika—Miss Ellika, have you been ill? What happened to your hair?"

"Oh, Jenks!" cried Ellika, pressing her forehead to his hands. She burst into tears, the first Temmin had seen. She recovered herself enough to release him and turned to her sister, who held her while she cried.

Jenks snapped to attention again. "Your Highness," he said to Temmin.

Not knowing what else to do, Temmin followed his father's lead: "At ease." He added, "Jenks, why are you in uniform? I don't understand."

The older man took Temmin's hand in a strong grip. "Later, sir. It's past time for explaining, but not now."

They all walked deep into the catacombs, past sealed and empty niches carved into the walls. *Jenks should have been with us when we gave Mama her final bath.* Technically he was a servant, but Jenks was as much a part of Temmin's family as anyone—but *was* he a servant? Seeing Jenks in a colonel's uniform confused and unsettled Temmin.

The unhappy group stopped at a niche prepared for its new occupant in the section reserved for high nobility; masons waited, bricks and mortar beside them. The Friends slid the coffin inside, and the masons began to seal the temporary tomb closed. "Goodbye, Mama," whispered Temmin.

The family spent the long day's remainder accepting condolences in the Keep's main Receiving Room until Temmin thought he would go mad. The worst was shaking hands with Fennows, that spotted git. The lordling gave Temmin a syrupy condolence, almost snubbed Sedra and clung so hard to Ellika's hand that the princess had to shake him off with unfeigned annoyance. By now, Miss Clommert had insisted on covering Ellika's shorn locks in a black snood. Perhaps she should have let the shaggy mop be seen; it might have thrown Fennows off.

Each condolence bit at Temmin, leaving his soul as bloodied as his temple; a Sister assigned to the Hill had stitched his cut closed, and Harbis had helped him arrange his hair so it hardly showed. When he escaped to his rooms, he found Jenks standing by the hearth, still in the grand red tunic covered in medals. Relief at seeing his dear friend warred with irritation and no small alarm. "Why are you wearing a cavalry uniform?" he demanded as he came into the room.

Jenks fiddled with his hat. "I am in the cavalry, sir."

"Put that down," snapped Temmin. "You know exactly what I mean. You are long retired, and you were never a colonel."

"Oh, but I was, Temmin—I am," sighed the big man. "Forgive me, but will you sit, sir? You look tired and hungry—and I can't sit until you do."

"Of course!" cried Temmin, abandoning his attitude. "Please, sit. May I offer you a drink? How strange to offer you a drink, I'm not used to playing host with you. I'll order dinner. Is that idiot Harbis around? Harbis!"

The annoying, perfect valet emerged from Temmin's bedchamber. "I have taken the liberty of ordering dinner for you and the Colonel, sir, and have laid out your favorite carpet slippers and house jacket. Shall I help you with your attire, sir?"

"Oh, push off, Harbis. I can attend to it myself." He caught Jenks's disapproving eye. "And thank you. You think of everything, really, and as difficult as these few days have been, I have appreciated your service. Truly."

Harbis bowed. "Thank you, sir. I'll...'push off', sir, but I shall stand by if you need me." He glided across the floor and let himself out.

"Thank Pagg he's gone. Oh, Jenks, I'm so very glad to see you! I don't know about you but I need a drink."

Jenks sat down in the rarely used wingback chair before the fire. "I confess I would not say no to a glass of wuisc, sir."

Temmin poured them each a glass from the decanter on his sideboard, handed one to Jenks, and tossed himself on the moss green sofa. "What's this colonel nonsense? Has Father given you an honorary commission?"

"No, no. It's not honorary." Jenks took a deep breath. "It's time you were told, especially now that…" He cleared his throat and began again. "I wasn't a corporal in the cavalry, sir, and I was never your uncle's batman. I was his aide-de-camp—a colonel. I still hold that rank. I'm chief of your security detail and your personal bodyguard, which has made this time apart very worrying indeed after all these years."

"My bodyguard? You're my valet! Brother Mardus heads my security detail when I'm away from the Temple, at least here in the City, and I never had one at the Estate."

"Ah, but you did, and still do. Your mother—" Jenks swallowed hard again and took a long drink to cover his distress. "Your mother didn't want you to know about the dangers to your life until you were old enough to understand. Being with you most of the time made that possible, and being your valet was my most plausible option."

Temmin wondered when the world would stop pulling itself out from under him. "I never—it never occurred to me. When were you planning on telling me?"

"When you finished at Temple. Speaking of which, may I ask how your time there has gone, sir? You have two—no, two and a half more spokes left, don't you?"

Temmin paused. What to say? That he'd fallen in love against both his training and Temple rules? That he had no idea how he would make it through the next two spokes, how he would console anyone else when he himself was near-inconsolable? "It's complicated."

The older man sat back in the wingback chair. "Life's complicated. If you don't want to talk about it, you certainly don't have to, sir."

"What have you been doing at Whithorse?"

Jenks finished his wuisc. "I wanted to come back very badly after that business with Sister Ibbit. I was worried for you, and for Annie…that is, Her Majesty…" He shook his head and leaned forward. "Temmin, you need to know your mother was my very dear friend, more dear than you realize. It was for her sake, and for your uncle's, that I came into your service. I was ready to resign my commission when that old crow, Teacher, came to me. It wasn't long after Patrin died, you see. I felt responsible for his death. I still do. He was my best friend. He and Annie and I, we grew up together rather like you and Alvo—my father was attached to the old Duke's household as Captain of the Whithorse Battalion. I thought once…" He covered his mouth. "I thought once I loved your mother. It's how I got my early commission—to get rid of me so your father might court your mother more easily. We knew it was never possible, Annie and me, but we were young. Patrin took me on as his aide and we rose together. He was the best, the dearest friend I shall ever have in this world. I would never have spoken of it were it not...were it not..." Jenks put his face in his hand; Temmin looked away to the fire, tears rising in his own throat. "I never thought I could bear to go back to the Estate," Jenks continued, his voice rough but more composed. "It contained too many memories of Patrin, but I did it for her sake. Now I don't think I'll be able to return but for *your* sake, Temmin. You are what I have left of them both."

By now tears were running down both men's cheeks unchecked. Temmin rose from the sofa and crouched before his old friend. He took the man's hands. "Then don't return, Jenks. Stay here and wait for me."

Jenks shook his head. "I have work at the Estate to do. When you're through at the Temple, your father will let you come home for a visit, I'm sure. When you return to the Keep, *then* I will return here with you."

The two spent the three days of Temmin's leave riding together, talking of Ansella when they could bear it, but more often of the doings at the Estate. "How is Alvo?"

Jenks pursed his lips. "More taciturn. I'll say this, though. He hasn't gotten in trouble once since you've gone. Make of that what you will, scapegrace. He misses you but won't speak of you unless forced."

"I miss him. I'm bringing him to the Keep, you know, Jenks."

"He may have other ideas, sir."

"I don't really care. How are Fen and Arta?"

"Miss Dannikson is now Mistress Wallek."

"She wrote me," Temmin nodded. "I read my letters even if I'm not very good at answering them. She's gotten the hang of reading and writing very quickly."

"She would make an excellent housekeeper some day in one of your houses, sir."

Relieving news; Temmin had no choice but to take the two young servants into his household once they'd become embroiled in his father's attempts to stop his Supplicancy, and he'd been wondering what to do with them. "Have they forgiven me yet for almost getting them killed on the Temple steps?"

Jenks chuckled. "Forgiven you? They worship you!"

"Oh, dear. How is married life treating them? Well, I hope. I need some good news."

"Their little boy is three spokes old now, and a strapping infant he is, too," said Jenks as they walked their horses back to the stables along the War Road. "Red-haired like his father but looks more like his mother, lucky little chap. The elder Wallek is learning a number of skills."

"Useful ones?"

Jenks gazed at a spot just above his horse's right ear. "Caring for a gentleman's wardrobe, hand-to-hand fighting, and keen attention to potential threats."

Temmin looked over at the older man in surprise. "You're training him to take your place."

"That I am, sir." He glanced at his Prince almost guiltily. "Temmin, I'm forty-four. Still in fine shape, but no longer young. I will serve you till the end of my days, but in a few years I will no longer be the best man to be your bodyguard. I will still direct your security detail, but I want Fen to become your personal bodyguard and valet. He has a sweet, take-no-prisoners street-fighting style that's just the ticket, and he's coming along nicely in the other respects, except I'm having trouble teaching him the proper way to fall off a horse rather than the way he's insisted upon so far."

"That bad a rider?"

"That bad at first. He's coming along, sir."

"Well, if he's got you to teach him, he'll be fine. You taught me everything I know about horses and that's quite a lot. You and...and Mama."

Temmin's heart plunged into blackness again, and the two men entered the stables in silent, shared grief.

A week after the Queen's funeral, Allis handed cups of tea to the Most High Beloved and Most High Lover. The two high priests and the two Embodiments sat together in a room warmer than most Tremontine rooms, but the two old ones held the handleless winter ceramic cups close to their bodies, letting the heat sink in. Allis wondered if she would be cold all the time when she grew old. She dropped a sugar in one cup for Issak and passed it to him. "What are we going to do about Temmin?" she said.

"Do? Nothing," said High Lover Gan. "He will grieve, and we will help if we can."

Allis sipped her tea. The cup felt good in her hands, too, though hers were smooth and young; it must be a colder winter than she'd thought. "He's not doing anyone any good here," she murmured. "He can't concentrate. He's done nothing but help the Postulants clean the petitioning rooms, and he rarely speaks to anyone. Perhaps he should take a longer leave."

"His vows bind him for less than three spokes more. Mightn't familiar routine be a comfort? It has been so for me in troubled times," said High Beloved Malla.

"I am surprised you'd wish to send him away," Issak said to his sister.

"I think only of his utility to the Temple and his own wellbeing," she answered, meeting his eyes steadily. *You will not make me give myself away, brother. Do not make me give myself away!* "Whithorse may be more comforting to him than the Temple."

"It's also a reminder of his mother," said Issak.

"Perhaps he wants to be reminded of his mother," said Allis a little too sharply.

"Gently, Allis, gently," remonstrated Gan. "I don't like the idea of sending him away. It seems unkind."

"He has nothing left for petitioners at present, Most High," said Allis. "Perhaps we should proceed with choosing a new Supplicant to replace Anda."

Issak put his cup down and studied her.

"No, one is quite enough for now," replied Gan. "You don't always have to have two, dear, and oftentimes Temples don't have any Supplicants at all. Look at Ronnul Embodiment at the Warrior's Temple. He doesn't have one at present."

"You seem quite eager to find a new focus either for Temmin or yourself," said Issak.

Allis flushed at last. "I cannot believe you of all people, Issak, would not remember what it's like to lose one's mother. I remember it clearly."

Issak straightened his broad shoulders. "That was cruel."

"It's cruel to keep him here!" exclaimed Allis stubbornly.

"To you or to him?"

"Children!" said Gan. "You are both excused until you compose yourselves. No, your apologies are due to one another. Go away. I'm tired and I still have matters to discuss with Malla."

Allis put down her teacup and rose from the couch, her skirts tangling round her ankles. She kicked them loose, curtsied and stalked from the room, Issak close behind. "I'm not a child, I'm almost twenty-three," she muttered to herself.

"If you think no one knows about Temmin, Allis, you're quite mistaken," Issak hissed as he followed her down the hallway.

"We are not alone," she replied in kind.

"Let's remedy that, shall we?" Issak grabbed her arm and yanked her into an empty receiving room, slamming the door behind them. The rarely-used room was decorated less to the Temple's tastes and more to the general world's in a conservative, restrained style, chairs instead of couches and no warming braziers. No fire burned in the grate. "You have to stop, Allis. Ask for help. This cannot continue."

"*What* cannot continue?"

"You cannot love him. You cannot."

"*Love* him? I wonder, are you jealous? Seeing rivals that aren't there?"

"Rivals?" he exclaimed. "Allis, I'm your brother. Listen to yourself!"

"I seem to recall many tender moments between the two of you."

Issak took one of the few conventional chairs the Temple possessed, spindly and insubstantial, as if it wouldn't bear Allis's weight let alone his, but it didn't complain—much—when he sat on it. "At least you've clarified who it is I'm supposed to be jealous of. In this case I have managed to confine myself to proper emotions. Allis," he coaxed in their shared patois, "*We no per he, he no per we. Tha knowst it!*"

"You're mistaken."

"You love him."

"You're mistaken!" she repeated, keeping her gaze steady and her face relaxed and unsmiling. "I love him as you do, no more."

"Allis, you have got to swallow your pride!" Issak glowered beneath his strong brow, anger mixed with pain. "You know what may happen."

Allis's heart clenched. "*Na gimme thy grief, frer mine!*" she shouted.

Issak's glower turned to a grim smile. "*Na me who givee the grief, ser mine. The grief's a thee.*" He stood; the little chair gave a tiny, relieved squeak as he walked through the door.

Allis hugged herself, cold in the unheated room. She slipped back into the Temple's warm, busy hallways, but the chill lingered.

In the end, Allis prevailed. The Most Highs dismissed Temmin for a few weeks to return to Whithorse and mourn his mother, an extra spoke to be added to his vow; though he was to have left in two spokes he would stay now until Summer's Beginning at Nerr's Day.

Ellika rarely let the baby go, relinquishing her little sister long enough for the hastily-called wet nurse to feed her before snatching her away again. She declared to the family that Anneya was her responsibility: "No one else seems to care, so I'm taking her back to Whithorse with Temmin. Nurse and I will see to her." She even learned to change the tiny girl's diaper, refusing assistance with a savagery once reserved for incompetent milliners and dancing partners who trod one too many times on her toes. Her famous gusts of tears never appeared; her eyes were red but dry. Her soft, shorn curls framed a face displaying few emotions except the smiles she showered down on her baby sister. She took no interest in the mourning clothes Miss Clommert arranged for Mistress Naister to make for her.

Ellika spent her days and evenings in Anneya's nursery, making the customary mementos from Mama's hair with alarming speed and intensity as the baby slept. Sedra's jet brooch now framed a spray of golden plumes. Their father's mourning watch cover carried an intricate knot, Temmin's a simple coiled lock at his request. For Miss Hanston, Ellika planned a framed display of the bright hair fashioned into a bouquet of flowers. Their old Nurse at the Estate, who'd helped raise Ansella as well as the royal children, would get one, too, if Mama's death didn't kill the poor old lady at last. Ellika wrapped her mother's remaining braid in tissue. She would save the delicate work for the Estate.

She and the baby wore bracelets plaited of Mama's hair. A simple four-strand round braid circled the baby's tiny wrist; Ellika wore a flat, many-stranded herringbone pattern as wide as two fingers, its round clasp made of pearls set in gold. She would make an identical one for her little sister to wear when she was grown. *She won't remember Mama, but at least she'll have that.*

To Sedra it seemed as if her childish, giddy sister had aged overnight into a woman—or perhaps gone a little mad. Sedra's own grieving surprised even her. She spent hours in her room, crying until she ran out of tears and stared at nothing. Her books held no interest, nor did her walks. She ate little, talked less, and her chocolate brown eyes took on the darker hue of the jet mourning jewelry she wore every day.

Ansella and Sedra had sometimes argued. They had the same temper, and there were times when they were too much alike. Every petty argument between them stuck in Sedra's heart. Now her mother would not be there to see the marriage cord tied, to give Sedra advice on dealing with a husband just as likely to stray as her father had. Though Mama hadn't dealt with that at all well, had she? Anger towards her father surged inside her, and she pounded a sofa cushion so hard it burst open, scattering feathers all over her sitting room.

Harsin's untouched dinner lay on the partners' desk he shared with his secretary Embis Winmer. He rubbed his tired eyes. Temmin, Ellika, the baby and the rest of the Whithorse-bound contingent had left quite early that morning in the crown's private train, and in spite of his apathy toward his new daughter he'd seen them off at the station after a long, sleepless night.

"What of Miss Shelstone, Your Majesty?" said Winmer. "Her child is due soon, isn't it? I have the paperwork here. Do you still wish to elevate her to Countess Middlemont on the child's birth?"

"Yes," said Harsin. "In time I'll find her a lord's second son or some such and marry her off, but the child will be recognized as mine. If the little one comes of age I will accept her at court. Middlemont will fall to the girl and her husband if she survives and marries, but the title will die with Twenna. Make it so, Winmer."

"Very good, sir. May I ask if you've you chosen a name for the new child?"

"Twenna wishes to name the baby after her mother. Deannis. A bit High Street, if you ask me, but…" He shook his head. "In truth, Embis, I don't care. She can name the baby whatever she wishes. I don't care. I am done with babies." At his secretary's respectful, lowered eyes and gentle throat-clearing, he snapped, "Oh, Pagg's Balls, out with it."

"I merely question whether you should have let the youngest Princesses go back to Whithorse, sir. Your preference to keep your children close by, expressed so recently by the ongoing search for Miss Dunley and your solicitude for Miss Shelstone's child, seems at variance with their departure."

"I suppose so." Harsin scratched his jaw through his thick, graying beard, perhaps harder than the itch demanded. "I just can't…it's too…" Tears formed in his eyes, almost soothing. His eyes hurt so much these days. "I never knew I would miss her so. She was at Whithorse all those years, yes, but she was as close as the next room any time I chose. Teacher could have taken me there in an instant."

"If we are speaking freely, sir, the situation was not all of your choosing. She was a difficult woman at times."

"How much of that was my doing? If I had been more attentive, if I hadn't let Ibbit insinuate herself into the house—" His voice raised in a roar. "I swear, I swear on Ansella's bones, I swear on the Father's Rock, I will kill that woman myself. I let her take Annie away from me and then just as I was getting her *back*—" The roar broke, and he let his tears fall. "Do you remember when we first were married, Embis? I had her then and could have kept her, but I let her go. She pushed me away…or I walked away…and I let her go. I didn't think twice about it. Women surrounded me, and yes, she was more than just a woman to me, but… and just as I saw her, just as we'd begun to really understand one another… I was getting her back, and then…"

Winmer placed a gentle hand on his master's shoulder. "Harsin, I don't believe in the afterlife. *You do*. Take comfort in that if it helps. If it helps, think of her waiting for you in the Hill. Here and now you have the children she gave you, including the new little Princess. That will have to suffice."

Harsin covered his friend's hand with his own and wept.

TWELVE

With the family in mourning all royal celebrations and parties were canceled for the next year, and the City's leading lights of course followed suit; the social season thus ended two spokes early, to the despair of more than a few mothers looking to marry off daughters who were aging by the minute. Ellika, who would normally never hide herself at the Estate at this time of year, didn't care a bit. She spent her time in the Great House's cozy nursery fussing over Anneya with Lady Donnis.

The wet nurse brought from Tremont City lost her milk, to general alarm. "How does one find a wet nurse, Cousin Donnie?" fretted Ellika.

"One looks among your Estatesmen for a mother who's still nursing a babe, or better, one who's just lost one, as sad as that is. Are there any such?"

There were several nursing mothers, none mourning a dead child. Ellika could not stand forcing a babe off its mother's breast, and luck was with her. An especially devoted mother had enough milk for two: Arta Wallek. "Anythin, miss, *anythin* your family asks! Fen an I owe you the world!" Her own freckled cherub Jaddun joined the nursery by day, and keeping both babies fed often kept the poor girl tied to the rocker.

Ellika read to her to help pass the time. It embarrassed the former housemaid to have a Princess "amusin me, it ain'—beggin pardon, it *isn't* necessary, miss, or proper," until Ellika burst out, "Do please let me read to you, Mistress Wallek! My mother read these stories to me—see, this book is hers." She showed Arta the frontispiece of the book of Kellish folktales she held; inscribed on the bookplate in a childish hand was, *Given to Ansella of Whithorse by her Grandmother, Eddin's Day, 958.*

"Doesn't it make you sad, miss?" whispered Arta, squinting sympathically.

Ellika put the book down and took her sleeping sister from Arta's arms. "Nothing of my mother's makes me sad."

A new baby to raise greatly revived the grieving Nurse, who did not welcome an intruder into her affairs. "We don't need this Wallek woman. I raised your mam, I raised you three, and there's still enough in me to raise one more!" the old woman grumbled.

"There's no question: you are the authority to which we will bow on all matters," soothed Ellika, "but you can't actually *feed* her, dear." Even Nurse had to acknowledge the truth in this. She kept a dyspeptic eye on the curly-haired young mother in the rocker all the same, though the baby boy who accompanied her in time was allowed to be "quite the charmer in spite of those dots a-comin' out." Soon Jaddun was elevated to "a dear sweet little thing," and in the end, the old lady lost her heart to his toothless grin and wispy red curls. No more was said about either Wallek's temporary presence in her nursery. Ellika and Lady Donnis breathed a sigh of relief and began looking for a nanny to "assist" Nurse.

Temmin had no such distraction. While Fen Wallek welcomed him with all the enthusiasm of a big red puppy, his childhood friend Alvo Noll-son did not. The young groom had grown in the time Temmin had been away; he was taller, and his already-stocky frame had lost the last of its boyish roundness and turned to solid muscle. The thatch of dark brown hair had been tamed, and his ratty old tweed cap exchanged for a new one that already showed signs of following in the last one's disreputable footsteps. He kept himself aloof, always managing to find ways to avoid being alone with the Prince—indeed, finding ways to avoid being near him at all.

Temmin finally came upon Alvo alone as he mended a saddle pad in the tack room. Alvo looked up as he came in; just before he took on feigned indifference, a flash of pure pain radiated from him that cut Temmin to the heart. Nothing had changed, though they'd been separated for two years;

Alvo still loved him. "Hullo, Alvy."

Alvo pressed a knuckle to his broad forehead, one end of the double-needled thread still in his hand and a leather thimble on his middle finger. "Afternoon, Your Highness. Forgive me for not standing." He returned to his stitching, pushing first one needle and then the other through the stubborn, thick wool felt before pulling the stitch tight.

Never had silence hung this thick between them. "Have you no good word for me, then, Alvy, none at all?" Temmin finally said.

Alvo paused. "I'm sorry about the Queen, sir, awfully, awfully sorry. You know we all loved her. She was always good to me." He dared a sober, sympathetic glance of real grief at Temmin.

"She loved you too," said Temmin.

Alvo blinked hard and returned to his work. "Jebby has done very well these spokes, sir. I've exercised him regularly. Even given him a sugar cube now and again as you used to. He's—" Alvo cleared his throat. "He's missed you pretty badly, sir. He will be happy to see you."

Temmin sank down on the bench beside him. "And you? Have you missed me?"

"I've kept myself busy, sir," mumbled Alvo.

"Don't I know it. You never wrote."

"That's not true, Tem," protested Alvo, stung into raising his head from his task. He met Temmin's eyes and bent down again. "That's not true."

"You wrote me twice in two years and each time you called me 'Your Highness' and acted like you were writing to my father, not me."

Alvo back-tacked over his stitching and clipped the ends short. "Some of us haven't forgotten our station in life." He gathered his tools into his workbox and stood to put the saddle pad away.

"Alvo—"

"With respect, sir, I'm working." He walked away, his broad back stiff and angry.

"Pagg's balls," said Temmin to the empty tack room.

He scratched at the scabbed-over stitches at his temple and then at his nape under the long, nagging queue he'd grown at the Temple. He'd had time to think and still hadn't figured the Alvo dilemma out. The last time they'd been together for any real length of time was almost two years ago, when he'd gotten roaring drunk and pawed Mattie in the hedge. Nausea and guilt shuddered through him, worry chasing close behind. He wished he knew where she was now so he might set things right.

Temmin turned his mind back to Alvo. The occasional sexual play be-

tween them as boys—play Temmin always assumed was practice for girls—
had turned into something different that night: Alvo's declaration of love,
and Temmin's first climax at another's hands. At the Temple he'd learned
how pleasurable sex with men could be, but that wasn't the issue. Did he
want Alvo as a lover?

He loved Alvo, certainly; Alvy was the closest thing he'd ever had to
a brother. What did he want from Alvo now, and how did he want it—by
choice, or by coercion? He knew at least a dozen different ways to bring
Alvo round his thumb, but none he wanted to use. Some ways he now realized he'd used in their childhood; he'd always been able to coax Alvo into
doing anything he wanted. As Heir, he could make anyone do anything he
wanted by simple fiat, but he never pulled rank, especially with Alvo. At
least, he liked to think so. Mama had drummed it into his head that relying
on rank was the resort of bullies and cowards.

Temmin stood up and stuck his hands in his pockets. In the right-
hand one, his fingers brushed the familiar rasp of sugar cubes. He smiled
and walked to into the stables, where a big chestnut gelding stood peering
over the stall door. Above the stall, an impeccably shined brass plaque read
"Jebby"; an Heir's coronet crowned the plaque. The horse whickered and
bobbed his head. Temmin almost ran to the stall, but once there stood relaxed and calm, letting the horse nudge and nuzzle him. "Hey, Jeb, hey, boy,"
he murmured.

Jebby had his fill of whuffling his master and turned away slightly, presenting his mane to be scratched. Temmin obliged and put his arms around
the thick, muscular neck when he'd finished. He hugged the great horse
close, breathing in hay, carrots, apples, oats, molasses, dung and clean
horse—the smells of a well-run stable that said "home" deep in his bones.
Mama had helped him pick out and train Jebby. Temmin hugged the horse
tighter and released him.

The chestnut eyed him sideways and dipped his head several times.
"Oh, all right," smiled Temmin, producing one sugar cube and then another;
Jebby lipped each one from his hand, the velvety muzzle and its paradoxical
whiskers both tickling his palm. They stood leaning into one another, Jebby
careful not to lean into his master so much the fragile human toppled over.

Temmin let his eyes wander around the quiet stable. This is what he
would do. He would simply stay near. He would let Alvo know the approach
was his to make. He would place no barrier between them. He would offer
himself to be leaned upon, even as he wished he could lean upon Alvo himself. Perhaps when they were comfortable again as friends and brothers, he

might make up his mind whether they could be lovers.

Every morning Temmin and Jebby rode out over the rolling grasslands. Every vista reminded him of Mama; they squeezed his heart dry and filled it with her love over and over. Each time he was that much more as one with the enormous animal, and that much more reconciled with his mother's loss, however minutely. But even he could spend just so much time in the stables. He was unused to working with his hands after nearly two years in the Temple, and Alvo's attitude was so provoking Temmin thanked Nerr for his training in patience. "Alvo Nollson," the stable master scolded one morning just before Temmin turned the corner, "what has come over you? His Highness has never stood much on ceremony, but I'll thank you to at least treat 'im with respect, else I'll show you the business end of a riding crop!"

Temmin halted, listening for Alvo's answer. "How exactly have I been disrespectful, sir? Show me where I'm wrong and I'll correct it." The stable master grumbled that Alvo knew very well what he meant and stumped off. Temmin let himself round the corner; Alvo's guilty expression hardened into dull servitude. Temmin gave him a small smile and left him alone.

Walking back up to the Great House, he wondered what to do with himself for the day. Ellika had Anneya, and Lady Donnis was consoling his grandmother the Dowager Duchess at Meadow House. He considered visiting there, but discarded the notion. Grandmama had taken Mama's death hard, very hard indeed; she had outlived all her children and her husband, and Donnis fretted that the old lady mightn't survive her grief. Temmin wished he could be more supportive, but at times he wondered if he'd survive his own grief; he had nothing to offer.

Once he arrived in his sitting room, Temmin called, "Hullo, Jenks, are you here?" No answer. His mother's influence extended to his rooms at the Estate, more to his taste than his grand apartments at the Keep: brighter and more open, the furnishings nimble—lighter and less formal. Few books graced the shelves here, and those that did contained the finer points of equine management, exciting Cavalry stories, or both. Ranged among them were his schoolbooks—most with near-pristine bindings, some with uncut pages.

Luncheon wasn't for at least two hours. Temmin didn't want to go see Ellika, Arta and the baby. He guessed that Jenks was somewhere watching Fen fall off his horse. Temmin preferred being busy; this inactivity made him restless. He walked to the bookcase and fingered the spines in medita-

tion. Books interested him more since Teacher's reading to him from the
Intimate History, though its magical immersion of listeners in the story in-
trigued him far more than the dusty recitations his tutors had offered him.
Perhaps he'd go through the books in the Estate's library. There had to be
something worth reading to pass the time. He picked out a book of old war
stories he remembered from his boyhood.

"Are you interested perhaps in some study?" came a cool voice.

Temmin dropped the book on his foot. "Gah! Ow! Pagg's balls! Teacher,
I swear you wait to come through mirrors until people aren't looking on
purpose!"

"What purpose would that serve?" said the slim black and white figure
standing in the door to Temmin's bedchamber.

"Your own amusement."

Teacher's mouth curved in a shallow bow. "Forgive me. The only mirrors in your suite are in your wardrobe and bedchamber. I did not mean to
startle you."

"The Bloody One you didn't." Temmin picked up the book on the floor,
hobbled back to his sofa and settled on its red chintz cushions. "You may
have broken my foot," he added, stretching his legs out on the sofa.

"I doubt it, and do not blame me for your own clumsiness." Teacher
took an ancient red book from under one arm and placed it on the table
before the sofa. "His Majesty thought perhaps study might be a good diver-
sion."

"He did? I am understandably surprised."

"To be honest, his exact reply to my suggestion was, 'Do as you please,
I do not care.'"

"He's taking Mama's death harder than I expected he would."

Teacher leaned against the mantel corner closest to Temmin. "Whatever you may think, His Majesty loved your mother and always did."

Temmin curled his lip. "I suppose that's why he's so excited about his
mistress's child. He really means to make the Shelstone a countess?"

"For the child's sake, yes. He has no interest in the woman herself any
more. I have never seen him less interested in women."

"You amaze me." Temmin put his feet back on the floor. "The whole
thing is amazing. I had no idea all it took to become a countess was to whore
yourself out to a king."

"I thought you were sympathetic to the plight of illegitimate offspring."

"Not their mothers."

Teacher gestured toward the book. "Do you remember the daughter of this very House I began to tell you about last year?"

"Lassanna of Whitehorse? Yes." Temmin's scowl held on stubbornly. "She ended up Queen of Kellen, though!"

"Not through 'whoring herself out to a king.' Dunnoc of Kellen had to woo her and win her. Her earlier dalliance with Andrin of Tremont almost cost her her life and that of her unborn son."

"I don't see how it's the same."

"It is not the same, at all. My point is this: The attention of kings is not always favorable, even when one is the wife of a king and not his mistress."

Temmin sat up straighter, elbows on his knees. "Why? Did Dunnoc prove to be a bad husband?"

"Shall we find out?"

Temmin touched the book's old Tremontine red cover; the soft, smooth leather seemed warm, as if it were alive. He opened it. The pages were still blank to him.

"Tennoc grew to manhood in King Dunnoc's court at Gwyrfal, and remained the only living son of King Andrin of Tremont."

The words blossomed on the pages as they used to do and changed to images; the images moved and swallowed Temmin up.

GWYRFAL, KELLEN
SPRING'S BEGINNING, 60 KY

Eighteen-year-old Tennoc ar Sial took the stairs to his mother's bower two at a time, bearing a parchment in his hand. "Mother!" he called. "I— oh!" The young man skidded to a halt. Ladies-in-waiting surrounded his mother, at work on their embroideries and sewing; they smiled at him, especially Cariodas. Any other young man would welcome her soft brown eyes gazing at him in worship, but Tennoc blushed and looked away. "Ah, something has come for you, Mother. The messenger said it was for your eyes only, but that it concerned me."

Queen Lassanna set her tambour aside. "Perhaps we should be alone." Her ladies curtsied and filed from the room; one whispered, "Gently, Cariodas—Princess Gwynna will scratch your eyes out!" Cariodas looked back at him anyway and smiled. With the ladies gone, he handed the parchment to

his mother and sat at her feet. "The messenger said it's from Lord Grandfather," he said, switching to the Tremontine they often spoke when alone.

"I'm surprised the messenger dared come to court, with things the way
they are between the kingdoms," said Lassanna. She slowly broke the seal,
read the scroll's contents, read them again, and put the parchment down on
her lap. "It's from your grandfather, all right, but it's really from your father."

"King Andrin?"

Lassanna looked down on her son in grave amazement. "We are re-
stored to grace. The King has given you his name and is calling for you
to come to Tremont Keep. You're still his only son. I am once again Lady
Lassanna of Whitehorse—oh, my name is long enough now without adding
that back on." She rattled the parchment in dismissal, but Tennoc caught
notes of suppressed pride and something akin to grief in her voice. "And
you are now Prince Tennoc, though here—" she rattled the parchment—
"they insist on calling you by your Tremontine name."

"Which is what?"

"Temmin Antremont, styled Temmin of Tremont."

Tennoc wrinkled his nose. "Feh. I have no wish to be Temmin of Tremont, or know either His Grace or His Majesty. They've had no use for us
these nineteen years—I have no use for them, especially Lord Grandfather.
I'm Tennoc ar Sial, and that's all I want to be."

"That's fine," murmured his mother, stroking his fawn-brown curls. "I
don't want you going to Tremont Keep either, my Tennoc, not with all this
tension at the border."

Word of the Queen's letter from the Duke of Whitehorse reached King
Dunnoc's ears before she could tell him. "A secret message from Tremont,
Your Majesty," said Bryth ar Brennow, "and she's told you none of what it
says."

Daevys ar Ulvyn nodded and poured more wine for the men in Dunnoc's council chamber. "She's Tremontine, sir, and the King was once her
lover—the boy's his only Heir! You should send him away—send them both
away. What if Tennoc should turn his hand against Kenver?"

"Then *you'd* be Dunnoc's heir," snorted Sian ar Lifris. Ulvyn glared at
him. "Besides," continued Lifris, "Tennoc would sooner cut off his own
hand than cut a hair from Kenver's head. Never were there closer friends."

"Too close if you ask me," said Bryth ar Brennow. "He's Tremontine. You
know they take after those filthy Sairish in the bedchamber."

Shame-fueled outrage swelled Dunnoc's neck. Magic sparked in his fingers unbidden; of late he'd had moments where he lost control of his power, strange flickerings as disturbing to him as the tremors creeping into his limbs. "Are you accusing my son of being a man-lover?"

"That Tremontine boy might lead the Prince into iniquity in his innocence," hastened Brennow.

"It's past time Kenver married, Your Majesty," said Lifris. "He's almost twenty-two, and there are several suitable ladies here in court—why, my own Cariodas—"

"I have not changed my mind, Lifris. I am giving Cariodas to Tennoc." The lord's face fell.

"Tennoc of Tremont is more dangerous to the Princess Gwynna's chastity than to Prince Kenver's," said Ulvyn. "I've seen the way he looks at her."

And she at him, thought Dunnoc. "I will never allow that match."

"Then send him away," urged Ulvyn. "Send the boy and his mother back to their clan at Brunsial—or lock them up for fear they will betray us!"

Dunnoc stood, drained his cup and smacked it down on the conference room's long table. "You speak of my Queen. She is loyal to Kellen, and why shouldn't she be? The Tremontines turned their backs on her and she's a Kell now, a good woman of Clan Sial, and what's more, I love her. No more of this talk, my lords."

But the seed had been planted. Though Lassanna gave her husband the letter, he wondered if she knew he'd been told and would have withheld it otherwise. She'd said many times she had no love for Tremont, but she missed her mother and sometimes yearned for Whitehorse.

Perhaps the boy should go to his father. He loved Tennoc almost as much as he did his own children, but he never forgot the boy's origin and subtly reminded Tennoc of it now and again. He would have to remind the boy more openly. His daughter's heart belonged to the blue-eyed bastard of the Tremontine King, but both children seemed to accept their futures apart; Tennoc had already informally consented to marrying Cariodas. Dunnoc had never before considered that perhaps Tennoc and Kenver were more than brothers.

As the weeks went on, the King thought he saw knowing sniggers aimed at his son and stepson, and leers directed at his younger wife; he'd taken to sleeping alone, for despite visits to the Sisters and the Lovers' Temple, Dunnoc's potency in bed had left him. Lassa was a passionate woman, and a tiny voice in his mind said one day she must betray him.

For now, Dunnoc turned away from all that. The best cure for his troubles was always battle, though he himself could no longer fight; his neck and shoulders were stiff, and he trembled unless he stood and moved around, though so far no one seemed to notice.

Tremont was testing the eastern border, but his lords there had things well in hand. He would move against the Sairish fortress at Maalig, on Kellen's southern tip in Trefhallyn. Maalig was Sairland's last foothold in the far west. Tremont tried repeatedly to move against the fortress, but Kellen had a strong presence along the southern River Cobb; the Tremontines had to approach Maalig by boat and brave the fort's impenetrable seaward defenses.

Maalig-based raiders swooped down on Kellish merchant vessels far too often for Dunnoc's taste, and he intended to stop them once and for all. Time to push them into the Gulf of Inchar.

"Pirrun, you should have been there!" cried Tennoc, clapping a young man on the shoulder. Music, endless wine and drunken laughter filled Gwyrfal's great hall; Kellen's warriors were home after a long, successful campaign.

"I would've if I hadn't broken my leg," winced Pirrun. "You've been gone so long it's healed! Why did you two not come home on the Royal Road, as the King did? Why come home with your soldiers? You could've been back weeks ago!"

"I don't ask anything of the men I'm not willing to do myself," declared Kenver. "Besides," he added in mock confidentiality, "Tennoc gets nauseous when I take him through a reflection!" The crowd hooted.

Tennoc took the dig with a slight flush and a grin. "Be that as it may, my lords, Kenver took the day! Had his magic not blocked the spring feeding Maalig we'd still be laying siege to it. He just reached down, so—" Tennoc dropped to one knee and put his hand on the floor— "and those Sairish bastards lost their water. They gave up within two weeks!"

Kenver laughed and took a long drink from his goblet. "Not entirely, brother! A few guardsmen surrendered a gate—they were half-dead from thirst. We still had to fight our way through the rest. I couldn't keep the spring plugged and use my magic to fight at the same time. If it weren't for you, I'd've been gutted more than once. D'ye hear, my lords?" he shouted over the music, "Tennoc saved my life ten times ten, and took the fort's commander single-handed!" Kenver put his arm around Tennoc's neck and hugged him close to his side. "Tennoc ar Sial!" he shouted, hoisting his goblet.

"Tennoc ar Sial!" roared the hall in return.

"I did my duty as a Kell," said Tennoc. He glanced to one side; the King was frowning at them both. Beside Dunnoc sat Lassanna, who nodded reassuringly. Tennoc grinned and turned back to his friends. "It's our pleasure and duty to serve good King Dunnoc—all of us!" he cried, raising his own goblet. "The King!"

"The King!" roared the hall even louder. Every cup was emptied, every cup refilled.

The musicians struck up their best dancing tunes. Servants cleared the benches and tables from the floor, and the dancers formed into lines: men in one, women in the other. Tennoc found himself facing Cariodas ar Lifris, Lord Lifris's daughter and one of the maidens who served his mother. She blushed and held out her soft, warm hand to begin the form.

He gave her his most gentle smile. He had no wish to hurt Cariodas. She was a court favorite, a sweet girl, pretty—hair and shining eyes so dark they approached black, unusual among the fairer Kells. She was kind, intelligent, obedient, accomplished in every way a young lady should be. He was expected to take her to wife, and he would. She already loved him, and he could never love her. Further up the line of women was Gwynna, and his heart.

Among the dancers Dunnoc saw his wife and brooded. She was so much younger than he was, still as merry at thirty-eight as she'd been when she'd first come to court. She refused a matronly role and still loved to dance, though he could not. Now a handsome young man bowed to her, took her hand and paraded her laughing up the gauntlet of lords and ladies. Had they danced together before? Dunnoc must watch him. Neya's Day approached, and while Lassa always insisted on sharing the Blessing with him, perhaps this would be the year she slipped off into the dark to bless the fields and forests with another.

Ulvyn approached, bowed and took a place beside Dunnoc. "The lords are calling Tennoc the Hero of Trefhallyn," he murmured. "Some say you should give it to him—let him found a new clan and become Tennoc ar Trefhallyn."

Dunnoc looked for his stepson among the crowd. There he was, dancing with Gwynna. Wine might explain the flush on his daughter's face, but Dunnoc doubted it. Where was Cariodas? There, dancing with Kenver. It was past time and past to marry Tennoc to Lifris's daughter and pack them off to a holding somewhere away from Gwyrfal until he'd found Gwynna the right husband; Trefhallyn lay some 1400 miles from Gwyrfal. "Perhaps

I should," he muttered.

"And hand over the southern tip of Kellen to Tremont?" said Ulvyn. "Your Majesty, all that separates Trefhallyn from Tremont is the River Cobb. We've had the Sairish to thank—in a twisted way—for keeping the Tremontines out of Trefhallyn thus far. With them gone it will take a strong hand there to keep the border safe, and whether the bastard son *and Heir* of the Tremontine King will wish to keep that border safe..."

Dunnoc's left hand trembled. "I must give him some holding, but not that one."

Ulvyn jerked his head; Tennoc's arm encircled Gwynna's waist as the two whirled around one another in a circle of dancers clapping in time to the sprightly music. "You must also give him a wife."

"Not that one either," grunted Dunnoc.

Gwynna darted among the apple trees so quickly Tennoc couldn't get a bead on her; his missile bounced off a tree trunk. She was luckier. The hard little green apple flew from her hand and hit Tennoc square above the heart. "Ow!"

"A fair hit! A fair hit!" she cried, jumping up and down and clapping her hands until her flowing sleeves flapped. "You're dead, sir!" Tennoc clasped his chest, let out a melodramatic shriek and fell down obligingly.

A few yards away, Kenver said, "Can I get up now?" His sister went to both her fallen enemies and helped them to their feet in gracious victory. "How did you become such a good shot?" grumbled Kenver as he dusted off the dirt and picked twigs from his once nearly white hair, now a dark brown.

"It just comes easy to me."

"It's unnatural. You're far too strong for a girl."

"You'd be strong, too if you had to run in heavy skirts. Blame Hanni. He taught me to 'shoot as Leutan.' He says you 'shoot as Tremontine girl.'"

"You're strong but you're not *that* strong—you still can't send an arrow as far as I can."

"What's the use of strength when you can't hit the target half the time!"

"Gwynna's just got better aim, Ken, and that's all there is to it," said Tennoc, smiling at her. Running had brought a flush to her face, and her red-gold braids had tumbled down. The gray eyes so like her brother's sparkled like the sun striking the waves in the bay. "Are you hungry? I am!" They ran laughing toward the castle; Tennoc wished for the courage to take Gwynna's hand, but even here, in no one but Kenver's presence, he didn't dare.

In the courtyard, Dunnoc awaited them; was it Tennoc's imagination, or was he developing a stoop? "You're getting too old for this, all of you. Gwynna, it doesn't become a young lady to run riot with men unaccompanied."

Gwynna gasped. "Papa, I was with my *brothers*!"

"No more of this. You are done with childish romping. Go to your rooms and arrange yourself." Gwynna's mouth dropped in betrayal, and she walked into the castle as if she were going to the dungeons. "Kenver," the King continued, "you will end this sort of play. If you wish for activity, go to the training ground and spar."

"But sir, we only—" began Tennoc.

"I am not speaking to you, I am speaking to my son. Take your presumption to your rooms and stay there." Tennoc exchanged shocked looks with Kenver and did as he was told.

In the archway leading inside stood Daevys ar Ulvyn and Bryth ar Brennow. Tennoc politely made his leg. "Lord Ulvyn, Lord Brennow, how do you do today?"

The older men did not return the bow. "Do as your father King Andrin wishes and go home, Temmin of Tremont," said Ulvyn.

Tennoc drew himself up in angry surprise. "I am Tennoc ar Sial, and Gwyrfal is my home until the King tells me it's not. Good day, my lords."

Ulvyn made no effort to move, and Tennoc brushed past him as politely as he could. "Bastards have no home, Tremontine whelp," the lord called after him.

Brennow watched him up the stairs and turned to Ulvyn. "Why do you hate the boy so much, Daevys?"

"Hate him?" said Ulvyn in surprise. "I don't hate him. I don't hate anyone. Kenver stands between me and the throne, and Tennoc is his right hand. Therefore, I will strike off his right hand."

"What does that gain us?"

"It weakens Kenver and Dunnoc both—it gives the King reason to doubt his Queen, and his own son's loyalties. Andrin's recognition of the boy as his heir is the most perfect weapon we could have been given. Tennoc has turned from a beloved stepson to an enemy with too much influence, and all it took was a few words written on parchment."

Tennoc wanted to go to his mother, but, obedient to the King, he went to his rooms. "Plagues you something, my lord?" asked Hanni, looking up from examining Tennoc's boots.

"It's all right, Hanni, go get your dinner." The Leutan set down the boots, bowed cheerfully and fled the room.

The King's demeanor had changed markedly of late. Dunnoc was all the father Tennoc had, and he loved him as one. Now Tennoc's place at table had been moved a chair away from Kenver, then another; his once-easy association with Gwynna and Kenver had just been ended. What had he done to deserve it? Gwynna was always to be taken from him, but Kenver taken from him as well would be like losing his wind.

Gwynna's father must be preparing a marriage for her. She was almost eighteen, after all, and everyone knew they loved one another. But everyone also knew he was respectful. He would marry the Lady Cariodas, as the King and his mother wished, but he would carry his love for Gwynna to his death bed.

Tennoc stayed in his rooms through dinner, starved as he was. His mother came to him with a tray. "Why did you not come down, sweetheart? Were you not hungry? Are you feeling unwell? Shall I call a Sister?"

"I feel fine, Mama, and I am very hungry," answered Tennoc, eagerly surveying the tray's contents. He took out his dagger and speared at a cold roast pigeon.

"Then why did you not come down?"

"The King told me to stay in my rooms," he said between swallows.

His mother's brows knit in consternation. "He did? He asked where you were. I said I didn't know, and he said you must be sulking again, that you sulked far too much, and that he wouldn't be surprised if you were beginning to think more highly of yourself than you should. I answered that you never sulk and he told me not to contradict him at table." She puckered her pale brows. "He is ill—you must have seen it—but he refuses to see the Sisters."

Tennoc took a quick swig of wine and wiped his mouth. "He's planning a marriage for Gwynna and wants me out of the way."

"But you've never been *in* the way, and Dunnoc's said nothing to me about marrying Gwynna to anyone. He's always planned to marry you to Cariodas—now, don't look like that, I know she's quiet and a bit insipid, but she's a pretty girl, a kind girl, and she's devoted to you. You could do much worse."

"I don't love her."

"You don't have to," retorted his mother. "She will be a good wife to you. She will guarantee you and your children a place in this world, and love will grow, given time."

Tennoc listened to the sounds rising from the courtyard far below. "Should I go to Uncle Williard at Brunsial, Mama?" His heart sank even as he spoke the words. "Just for a time, until he's reassured I intend no disrespect? Perhaps until Gwynna's...married? I would miss you and Ken—and Dunnoc, too, but if he wants me gone..."

Lassanna stood and circled behind his chair to hug him round the neck. "It might be best, as much as I don't want you far from me. He is beginning to worry me. I've stopped dancing—he frowns so when I do, and his shaking gets worse—and he asks me questions about... But that's not for you to worry over. I'll send word to Brunsial and see if they'll have you for a few spokes. Yellow Hanni will go with you."

By the time Dunnoc demanded Tennoc leave court, the plans had already been made; Lassanna told him with some hauteur that her son had been invited to stay at Brunsial, for Williard ar Sial had use for him even if his King did not. The news left Dunnoc in a grimmer mood than he expected. He thought he'd be more at ease, the danger to his children banished, but he hadn't reckoned on driving a wedge between himself and Lassa. Everywhere he began to see signs she grew bored with him, of her flirting and encouraging younger men.

When he told his lords at council the next day that Tennoc would go to Brunsial, the response surprised him: they urged him to kill Tennoc on the way.

"No, keep him here!" urged Lifris, the lone voice against the plan. "Hold him for ransom, Your Majesty. Hold him hostage until the Tremontines pay a ransom and leave the border, but kill him—sire, that's a step too far, you're inviting a Tremontine attack! If nothing else, think of your wife!"

Ulvyn stared down the smaller Lifris. "The Queen will never know. Tennoc will die on the road to Brunsial, ambushed by Tremontine raiders at the Whitehorse crossroads."

Dunnoc placed a small silver mirror before him. "Show me Tennoc ar Sial." The mirror shimmered to display a distorted image of Tennoc, tending to his weapons in the armory, or at least that's what he thought the boy was doing; the reflection must be something convex on the bench beside him—a shield, or perhaps a chest plate. Tennoc pushed his sandy hair from his good-natured face and sighted down the length of his sword. Kenver appeared in the reflection and said something to his stepbrother that made him laugh so hard he had to put the sword down.

Shame at what he contemplated squeezed at Dunnoc's throat. He'd treated Tennoc almost as his own son. He remembered the shimmering day he'd asked Lassa if he might court her, while the children played in the long grass by the sea. How he'd loved her then, and how happy the children had been. He told himself things were different now. Lassanna had schemed to send her son to Brunsial, without consulting him. Perhaps Tennoc wasn't going to Brunsial at all. Perhaps he really was crossing the border into Whitehorse, and thence to Tremont Keep.

As if reading his thoughts, Bryth ar Brennow said, "As things stand now, Tremont will fall into chaos and turn inward when Andrin dies. He has three cousins. Each has as good a claim to the throne as the others. Chances are the Black Man won't know which to choose—who knows how he chooses! But if Tennoc becomes Heir, the succession will become clear. With his knowledge of Kellen, Tennoc will turn Tremont's attention here first as soon as he is recognized as Heir at their Keep—and he'll start at Trefhallyn, where he is known and loved. If you don't kill Tennoc now, you risk losing Kenver his kingdom. You must choose, sire: your wife, or your son!"

"Tennoc loves your daughter, a good reason to invade Kellen and carry her off as his grandfather did his grandmother," said Ulvyn. "Kenver thinks so highly of him that when he becomes King, he may give the bastard Gwynna and bend his knee to boot, unless the cord between them is severed completely."

"Then there are the increasing rumors about Kenver and Tennoc, Your Majesty," added Brennow. "If Tennoc is dead, those rumors die."

A tiny flame leaped from a candle into Dunnoc's fingers, unbidden. He rolled it between his index finger and thumb, round and round as if he were rolling a pill. This wasn't the first time it had happened. He always tried to stop it, but never could. Dunnoc let the flame burn him though he could keep himself safe from it if he chose. As the pain increased so did his control; he banished the flame back to where it belonged as if he'd intended it all along. "Let it be so. Kill him on the road to Brunsial where it divides into the road to Whitehorse."

The decision sat badly with Lifris. Holding the Tremontine Heir hostage was brilliant; killing him gave the Tremontines cause for war. If the choice was Tremont or death he favored letting Tennoc go to his father; it either got Cariodas out of marrying a bastard, however nobly sired, or it would make her Queen of Tremont if Tennoc honored his informal commitment. He considered spiriting Tennoc away to his own holding in the southeast, but abandoned the idea. May as well declare open rebellion against Dunnoc, and that he would not do though Ulvyn and Brennow seemed to be planning it. But he would not stand by while Dunnoc endangered the kingdom. After much agonizing he made his way the next day to Kenver. He found the young Prince in the gardens teasing the ladies, Cariodas among them. Good and good; this favor to Kenver might also make that alliance more likely should marriage to Tennoc prove unwise. No Tennoc in sight, either. Even better. "Walk with me, Your Highness."

"Willingly," said Kenver, taking Lifris's arm.

Once out of earshot, Lifris told him Dunnoc's plans. Kenver dropped his arm to stand stiffly beside him. "Gently, Your Highness, pretend we are doing nothing more than passing the time."

Kenver made a visible effort to relax; he smiled and took up their walk again. "Where is this to take place?"

"Where the road to Whitehorse diverges from the road to Brunsial. They will claim Tremontine soldiers killed him."

Kenver crushed the smaller lord's arm in his grip. "Why are you telling me?"

"Because this is a mistake," grimaced Lifris; he decided to say nothing about the rest of Ulvyn's plans. "I would take him to my holding if you wish it, my Prince."

"No, but I thank you, Lifris, and I will remember your friendship."

Kenver told Tennoc the moment they were alone. He fell on his stepbrother's shoulder and cried. "How could Father turn on you, knowing how Gwynna and I love you!"

Tennoc held Kenver close. "That's why he wants me dead. He was as my father—no more, but you will always be my brother, Ken, always!"

They parted, and Kenver wiped his eyes. "Shall we tell your mother?"

"No, no," said Tennoc, "I want her held blameless."

"I could take you by reflection to Brunsial."

"Then your father will be angry with you, and I'll look guilty. I've done nothing wrong."

Kenver worried the corner of his mouth. "What will you do?"

"I don't know. Let's see if he really means to do this first—I will give him every chance to repent. I'm bringing Hanni, and you know how skillful is his bow, even if he's not allowed to carry heavier arms."

"You must have another. My sworn man Mycal can hold his own in a fight, and he can keep a secret."

"Well then, we'll be prepared, but perhaps your father will have a change of heart and no attack will come."

"Live or die, we may never see one another again in this life," said Kenver.

And I may never see Gwynna again, thought Tennoc, *but perhaps that is a mercy.* "No distance will ever be able to break our friendship, Ken. Not even when I'm in the Hill. I'll love you always, my brother."

The next day Tennoc kissed his mother goodbye in the courtyard; he carried Lord Grandfather's letter hidden in his breast. Yellow Hanni and Mycal were to travel with him, along with three guards—six riders in all to Brunsial. Kenver came to him and kissed him as well, and the two friends clung together. "Mycal is a fine swordsman, and you may trust him as you do me. He would die for you as I would," whispered Kenver. "The guards are my father's, heart and soul—show no mercy if it comes to it. Gwynna says to tell you she loves you." Tennoc tightened his grip on his stepbrother's arms. Aloud Kenver said, "I will miss you, brother. Safe journey to Brunsial." Dunnoc clasped Tennoc's arms but no more and refused to meet his eyes. Gwynna was kept from goodbyes, but she and Cariodas watched from the high tower until the little company disappeared over the green horizon.

Tennoc, Hanni and Mycal kept a close watch on the guards; though equal in number, the guards were better armed. Each carried a shield, sword, long dagger and lance, and they wore light armor. Tennoc carried the same kit, but Hanni and Mycal wore leather armor and carried only a sword, dagger and buckler. Hanni had his bow, too; he exclaimed "Is good for shoot hare for pot!" whenever a guard looked at him. Everyone knew Yellow Hanni was a fool—a talented archer but a fool all the same.

Tennoc kept his eyes open. They could not afford to be caught out. The moment it appeared the guards might attack, they must strike.

Two days' ride from Gwyrfal, they approached the Whitehorse crossroads, riding three abreast. Here the road narrowed just enough that two might comfortably ride together. Two of the guards declared they'd take up the rear, but they exchanged too long a look among themselves. Tennoc braced himself; the time had come. The guard on point pulled his sword, but Hanni nocked an arrow, drew his bow and fired before the man could turn around; the arrow pierced his throat. He fell and lay choking in the road under the horses' hooves.

Tennoc and Mycal wheeled their horses round. Though he couldn't work up a good gallop, Tennoc lowered his lance. They charged before the surprised guards could finish withdrawing their lances from their holsters.

Tennoc's lance knocked his opponent from the saddle; it cracked in two from the blow, and he threw the remaining haft from him. Mycal suffered a glancing lance blow that brought him down beside Tennoc's opponent. The dazed, dismounted men got to their feet and faced one another down.

The remaining lanceman, finally in possession if not full charge of his weapon, bore down on Tennoc. He raised his shield and hoped for the best, but the lance found his horse's neck. The animal screamed; he threw himself clear and rolled just before it hit the ground and lay kicking in the air. Hanni's arrow flew past the lanceman; a string of Leutish curses followed. Steel shrieked on steel; Mycal grunted and cried out in agony, but Tennoc couldn't afford to take his eyes off the rider before him. He staggered to his feet as the rider swung his sword down at him. Tennoc raised his shield and took a numbing blow to his arm. He slashed at the horse's legs and missed.

An arrow hissed again; armor clattered as the guardsman who felled Mycal fell to the ground himself, the arrow through his eye. Tennoc struggled to raise his shield as the remaining guardsman slashed down at him, but the rider was too close; the swing went wide. Tennoc thrust into the horse's belly. The beast fell, taking his sword with it; a flailing hoof grazed his side. He collapsed, the wind knocked out of him and at least one rib broken. To one side he saw Mycal sprawled in the road; to the other the dying horse pinned its screaming rider beneath it. Hanni strode up, slit the horse's throat and then the guard's. Their blood spattered into the dirt as they died.

Hanni helped Tennoc to his feet. "You saved the day," Tennoc gasped.

"For you, my job it is to be saving days."

The broken rib stabbed at the younger man's side, and he leaned on the Leutan servant until he could stand. Hanni helped him to a nearby rock, where he sat as the man checked on Mycal. "Dead, sir."

"I'm heartily sorry for it," said Tennoc. "Some day I hope to tell Kenver his man died bravely."

Hanni bound Tennoc's ribs, and the two gathered equipment and food from the fallen men and horses as fast as Tennoc's injury would allow. They made sure to take the false Tremontine banners the guards had carried to "prove" treachery, and while they didn't have time to bury Mycal, they laid him out in dignity, his arms folded over his sword and his cloak over his body. They left the guards where they died for the crows to pick at them.

Hanni caught an uninjured horse to replace Tennoc's dead mount. "Riding it is time to, sir. Think you to stay in the saddle?"

"I have to," grunted Tennoc as he swung himself up. Pain barbed each breath, and he winced.

"Where to, sir?"

The dead men and horses lay behind them; the fork in the road lay before them. The straight track led to Brunsial. The other led east to the River Cobb—the border with Whitehorse, and so Tremont. "Dunnoc will move openly against me now, and I would not bring him down on Clan Sial and Uncle Williard for the world. As it is I expect Dunnoc will search Brunsial down to the last mousehole. We ride inland, old friend." Tennoc turned his horse's nose to the east, put the sun behind him, and rode at a gallop toward his unknown grandfather's holding.

They approached the Whitehorse border and the River Cobb. Tennoc paused, considering their options. "We'll avoid Crymavon Castle."

"Your mother's cousin is Lady there, no?"

Tennoc nodded, but said, "For all we know, Dunnoc's sent word ahead. If he hasn't, I won't put Lady Flaryn in danger should the King follow us here."

"Cross we at Riverbend Ferry? Supplies at the village we might buy."

"I'd rather not risk the ferry, and we can always forage. A little upstream there's a ford. We'll cross there."

The ford ran deeper than they'd expected, and soon they were soaked to the waist, their horses snorting and holding their heads high. They climbed the bank and entered Whitehorse.

A searing light flooded Tennoc's body. A thousand doors opened at once within him, a terrifying elation rushing through them into his body and mind. His skin tingled and sparked, as if static crawled across it in all directions. He slumped in his saddle.

"Plagues you the rib?" said Hanni. "Stopping for the night, I am thinking."

"No, no, it's not my rib," Tennoc gasped. "It's something else. I can't...I don't know what it is. I'm all right. Give me a moment." The crawling power reached his scalp, and his hair stood on end. Confusing strength filled him—a fiery power beneath his skin. "We can keep going."

"You may, but I, Hanni, cannot." The servant bullied his master into a copse a decent distance from the river, where they made camp.

Hanni unsaddled the horses and collected green wood. "Is best I can do with no leaving you." He got it sputtering and smoking as best he could, and advanced on Tennoc. "Time it is for rib bandage."

"Please don't fuss over me," said Tennoc, wearily sinking down to sit on his saddle before the fire. "I'm all right, I just want to be let alone for a while."

"Nay, nay, flay me alive your mother would, and I since your boyhood have tended to you." Hanni got Tennoc to his feet again and made to remove his wet tunic.

"I said *stop*," yelled Tennoc, wincing as pain crackled in his side.

The little sputtering fire roared up, flames licking high into the sky; the two men leaped back. Tennoc's strange feeling of power diminished and sang at the same time. The fire sank back into its ring of stones to spit smoke at them. They stared. "Did any of those branches have pitch on them?"

"Nay, sir," said Hanni, eyes so wide the crow's feet around them disappeared. "King Dunnoc I have seen do something like, and Prince Kenver."

"That's magic, Hanni. Are you saying Dunnoc's near?" said Tennoc, hand on his sword hilt.

Hanni stared hard. "Nay, sir. I say, we are in Whitehorse."

"What does that have to do with any—" Tennoc broke off. Power had surged into him as soon as they'd crossed the ford onto dry land.

"Tremont is bigger than Kellen. Lots bigger, sir," said Hanni soberly. "More powerful here than King Dunnoc you are even as Heir."

Tennoc dropped back down onto his saddle in shock. "I'm really the Heir."

Hanni eyed the sputtering fire. "Think you to do it again, sir? I, Hanni, damp clothes hate."

"I'm not sure I can do it without setting us both aflame."

"Eh," sighed Hanni, "it is not to rely on magic, then. You I think will be fine. I go find drier wood."

Left alone before the smoky fire, Tennoc rubbed his eyes and steepled his fingers over his mouth. He bore Tremontine magic. Would that he could keep it from killing them both before someone taught him how to use it.

Tennoc's new power crackled in Temmin's hair and skin as he left the story; shadow pain stabbed at his side. "It never occurred to me Tennoc would get magic when he crossed the border."

"It never occurred to him, either. He knew both Dunnoc and Kenver had magic, but Kenver's was limited—blocking the spring at the siege of Maalig took all of it. Dunnoc was stronger, but men's magic is tied to the lands they control. Just the Heirs of Tremont held more even then than the kings of Kellen ever did. Were Dunnoc to ride into Whitehorse, his magic would vanish in any event, just as Tennoc had none in Kellen."

Temmin stood and stretched as Tennoc's pain faded along with his power's disturbing, exhilarating onslaught. "I bruised a rib once, but breaking one feels infinitely worse. Why did Dunnoc turn so quickly against Tennoc? He loved him like a son."

"In politics, there is no such thing as love," said Teacher, still leaning on the mantel. "Dunnoc's fear was not unreasonable—Tennoc was the Heir to a neighboring kingdom that dwarfed his own—but his response was. Had Dunnoc left things alone, fostering the boy would have forged strong bonds between Kellen and Tremont. Had he married Gwynna to Tennoc, or taken one of Tennoc's half-sisters as wife for Kenver, things would have gone much differently. Dunnoc was fifty-nine, not an ancient man but of an age when his strength was failing—and he was falling ill to the shaking sickness. Sick men often grow fearful, especially men who pride themselves on their physical prowess. As their bodies begin to fail, so their belief in their own power begins to fail, and they blame their women, yes, and others around them. Dunnoc was one such. He feared Tennoc, and he feared losing his wife's affection. The two were intertwined in his mind."

"I see impotent men at the Temple all the time," said Temmin. "It's a chore to teach some of them anything—they can't get past the anger. The Lovers say it's shame. We see many women with scars from such men." Temmin looked out the window. Beyond the courtyard he could just see the hedge alley leading to Meadow House, and the outskirts of the stable yard. "I could never treat someone I loved like a thing."

"Never is a long time, Your Highness."

Temmin turned back and smiled over his shoulder. "And I suppose you'd know."

"I suppose I would," said Teacher, but Temmin got no answering smile in return.

THIRTEEN

Meals at the Estate were still catch-as-catch-can; no one seemed up to being in company. Temmin and Jenks sat in his drawing room over a cold luncheon of cheese, fruit, ham, a loaf of good bread and a dish of pickles; the Estate's own dark amber ale foamed in mugs before them. "How is your pupil coming along?" said Temmin.

"Young Mr Wallek I believe has come far enough to spar with you, sir—if you've kept up your form at the Temple?"

"Of course I have. All of the men train with the Temple's Own regularly. We have to be in good shape, and not just for…*that*," he finished. Anything involving the Lovers' Temple made Jenks squirm. He didn't hate sex; he hated talking to Temmin about sex. "It comes in handy. There are times when we have to restrain petitioners," continued Temmin. "The Temple's Own are good fellows by and large. Some were once Brothers—mostly washed-out postulants."

"I shouldn't think they'd be much use in a fight if they washed out of the Brothers."

"Oh, they're plenty useful in a fight. They left the Brothers because they like women."

"Ah." Jenks took a deep, embarrassed pull on his beer.

Temmin watched him in wry amusement; love for the big man filled his broken heart. "Oh, Jenks." He stopped, compressing his lips in hopes of holding back tears. He'd cried quite a bit in the days since his mother's death, some days more, some days less, and tears often surprised him like this. Just as the gruff-voiced cavalryman's companionship helped him bear his sorrow, it also compounded it; his love for Jenks was bound up in his love for Whithorse, and both were bound up in his love for his mother.

Jenks reached across the table and laid a hand on his charge's shaking shoulder. "Eh now, Temmin, eh now," he murmured in a thick voice.

When Teacher returned, Jenks had just finished clearing the table: "Wallek will be attending to this soon—but I refuse to relinquish your wardrobe." The colonel gave the black figure a cautious nod and exited.

Teacher took up the familiar post by the mantel and took in Temmin's red eyes. "It comes and goes, does it not?"

"I look forward to the day when it just goes."

"Will your mother ever fade from your mind?"

"No," said Temmin in a shocked voice. "How could she?"

Teacher nodded. "That is why it will never leave completely. Grief will strike you down at times until the day you die. Something will remind you of her, and it will all come back, sometimes as sharply as the first day. The greatest mercy is that those times will become further and further apart."

Teacher had lived a thousand years, thought Temmin. "Do...do you still cry over your mother?"

Teacher's eyes dropped to the book on the table. "I cannot cry. Else I would never cease."

Temmin wondered if Teacher meant an unwillingness to cry or an inability. "Perhaps we should begin."

Teacher hesitated. "I chose this story some time ago. I had no indication of what would happen between then and now."

"Meaning what?"

"Meaning the story may become difficult for you to hear."

Temmin waved a hand in dismissal, and the book's pages began to fill up.

Tennoc and Hanni rode through forests, over rolling grasslands, past oak groves, ripening grain fields, neatly tended farms and grasslands dotted with sheep, cattle and horses, all sleek on the lush pasture. Tennoc wondered if it was a good year, or if the land was always this rich. His grandfather must be wealthy indeed. "Prime horse country, just as I've always heard," said Tennoc.

"Aye, sir. Once, long ago, when I served my Princess Inglatine, came I here to Whitehorse. Best horse country there is."

They followed the main track, camping at night wherever they could find cover. When he could, Tennoc practiced his magic, trying little things he'd seen Kenver do. If he concentrated, he could snatch a flame from the fire and bounce it in his hand like a ball. He could float good-sized rocks, though the larger ones made his broken rib hurt and he couldn't always make them go the direction he wanted them to. More than once, Hanni unleashed a torrent of Leutish curses at him when a rock went astray and came close to braining the man.

From time to time they passed farmers and peddlers but no one else until they were less than a day's ride from Lord Grandfather's castle. By now, Hanni had hit on using the false Tremontine banners taken from Dunnoc's guardsmen; they fluttered from the lances they'd taken as well: "For the Heir it is right."

Five riders came towards them from the east, wearing the green, white and silver of Whitehorse. None looked over-friendly. "My bow I am thinking, sir," muttered Hanni.

"Stay your hand until we see what's what," answered Tennoc. When they were within earshot he called out in Tremontine, "Greetings, gentlemen! Are we on the track for Whitehorse Freehold?"

The man at their head was ten years or so Tennoc's senior, a barrel-chested man whose face reminded Tennoc of his mother. The stranger ran an eye over the Tremontine banners. "What would you be doing with Tremontine heraldry, asking the way to Whitehorse Freehold, Kell?" growled the man.

Tennoc wished his Tremontine didn't lilt quite so much. "I wish to visit my grandfather, Gonnor of Whitehorse."

"Grandfather, is it?" snorted the man. "I know every one of his grandsons. I don't know *you*."

"Not by sight but perhaps by reputation. I am Tennoc ar Sial. My mother is Lassanna of Whitehorse."

A murmur somewhere between astonishment and contempt rippled through the men. "The King's bastard, eh?" said the leader. "Only one servant—I can see what high esteem the Kells hold you in. No, I peg you for a down-on-his-luck tinker or some such. Or maybe even a Traveler thrown out of his tribe."

Hanni muttered something in Leutish Tennoc knew would have brought all five Whitehorsers down on them in seconds had they understood it. He squared his shoulders and met the man's eyes steadily. "I am told King Andrin sired me, but—" He stopped himself from saying, *Dunnoc of Kellen is my father.* "But whatever my birth," he continued, "your king and my grandfather have bid me come into Tremont, and here I am. I have Lord Grandfather's letter here." He patted his tunic.

The big man held out an autocratic hand. Hanni tensed beside him, but Tennoc gave him a reassuring glance and pulled the parchment from his breast. He rode halfway to the cluster of men and stopped. The other man scowled, but Tennoc smiled patiently. The Whitehorser gave in, tapped his mount's sides and rode grumbling to meet Tennoc, who handed over the parchment as soon as they met.

The man scanned the letter, raising pale eyebrows. "This is Grandfather's handwriting. Where did you get this?"

"From a Tremontine courier sent to Gwyrfal three spokes hence."

"What did he look like?"

"A small man, dark, with a stiff leg."

The Whitehorser eyed him again. "You are like Gonnor," he admitted, "though you cut a figure more like His Majesty's, I dare say." He handed back the parchment; Tennoc tucked it into his tunic again.

A rock from the side of the road levitated and whizzed toward Hanni's head. Tennoc's magic reached out; the rock stopped within an inch of the man's skull and hovered, shaking. "I am not entirely in control of my magic yet, sir," grated Tennoc. "While I am not used to wielding such power I can guarantee as the Heir I have far more of it than you do, whoever you are. I will not let you hurt Hanni, and I cannot be responsible for where this rock might go."

The rock retreated from Hanni's temple and dropped to the ground. The big man nodded his head. "All right, we shall escort you to our grandfather. My name is Fallik. I am Lord Gonnor's heir, and your cousin, Temmin of Tremont."

"My name is Tennoc ar Sial," muttered the young man, but he and Hanni fell in among the riders and cantered toward the east.

Whitehorse Freehold reared up from a flat plain, its ancient earthen and stone fortifications undulating around it in sinuous curves. Rising above it stood a new stone fortress, spectators lining its ramparts; a look-out must have noted the unknown additions to the outriders and spread the word. Though the fortress was huge, the hill fort itself dwarfed it—an old, old place. Across the valley, another hill rolled up from the grasslands surrounding it. Turf had been carved away from the hill to form a rearing horse, white chalk against the deep green grass.

Tennoc, Hanni and the Whitehorsers rode through the first gate and up the winding causeway; the earthenworks mounded on each side hemmed a potential invading force into a single file, perfect targets for boulders and boiling oil. They passed through two more lightly defended gates, up the last curve and into the hill fort. A small city bustled within the walls, tradespeople and craftsmen coming and going; numerous wattle-and-daub thatch-roofed houses huddled between the fortress and the outer ramparts, with plenty of open space for seasonal markets. The houses and Temples looked a bit old-fashioned to Tennoc's eye, but the fortress itself was every-thing a modern military man might want, thick-walled and easy to defend. The earthen and stone defenses included enough room for the people of the surrounding countryside to shelter in times of war—with all their cattle if need be, so great a space it contained.

Fallik led the riders into the fortress's own courtyard, where they dis-mounted. Fallik began calling out orders in a loud voice, speaking so quick-ly in Tremontine that Tennoc had trouble following. While his mother had spoken Tremontine to him his whole life and he considered himself fluent, he'd never been around groups of people speaking it all at the same time. He caught his Tremontine name, and heard himself described as "King An-drin's bastard out of Lassanna"; he grit his teeth and reminded himself he needed these people's help. His cousin's commands ended with an order to find Lord Gonnor.

Tennoc would finally meet his hated grandfather, the man who'd tried to kill him in his mother's belly. His father the King was a coward for not protecting Mama, but Lord Grandfather was a bully, and Tennoc despised bullies. Even so, Tennoc could not afford to anger the man. He was depen-dent on Gonnor's shelter until he could equip himself for the journey to Tremont City.

It never occurred to him that as Andrin's Heir he outranked every man in the castle.

Grooms took their horses; Hanni made as if to follow, but Tennoc stopped him, saying, "I need you close by, Hanni. You're all I have here."

Hanni snorted and waved his hand around the courtyard. "The home of your family. The Heir to the Kingdom. A holder of powerful magic. You, perfectly safe. My horse a fifth shoe needs, more than you need me."

"I need you to keep me from killing my grandfather," muttered Tennoc.

Hanni put his hand on his master's elbow and spoke in the perfect Kellish he used only when dead serious: "You are a smart boy. Let Pagg guide you, for His justice is with *you*, not your grandfather." Hanni snatched his horse's reins from a surprised groom, abusing him in randomly accented Tremontine as he walked the animal to the stables.

Tennoc strode behind Fallik into the fortress itself, thinking on how to behave toward Gonnor. Haughty? Angry? Imperious? No, those smacked of fear. He would be himself. He would speak to Gonnor as he would to Lord Ulvyn—politely, but with reserve. Fallik led him not to the castle's hall, where Tennoc expected to meet Gonnor, but to Gonnor's own rooms; his new cousin ushered Tennoc through the door and shut it behind him.

Gonnor Duke of Whitehorse stood with his back to the door; his hands clenched and flexed at the small of his back in agitation. Tennoc waited. Lord Grandfather knew he stood there. Was disdain to be his greeting?

Gonnor turned to face his grandson and clasped his hands before him. He was still a well-formed man, tall, with the body of a thoroughbred forced to pasture. His eyes were blue, and Tennoc wondered if they were like his own. The expression in them was unreadable—a wariness, but not directed at him. "So you're Lassanna's boy," the old man said slowly. "Did you leave your mother well?"

"Perfectly well, sir," he replied, inclining his head. *Though I'd like to know what business it is of yours*, he said to himself.

"And she is happy in Kellen?"

"Happier than she was in Tremont, sir," he snapped, his rare temper getting the better of him.

Gonnor smiled, a small, weak thing that died on his mouth. "I dare say. Dunnoc is good to her?"

"Yes," he answered more slowly.

"And you? Has he been good to you?"

How to answer? His stepfather had tried to kill him—but so had Lord Grandfather. Dunnoc's betrayal hurt far more, and was of far more import in the here and now. "He…he was, sir, but of late he has turned against me. Your letter to my mother, calling for me to come to Tremont, seems to have convinced him I am a danger to Kellen."

"Are you?"

"It is an unfair charge, sir. Kells are my kinsmen. I would never move against them."

"Temmin—"

"Whatever name my father chooses to list as mine in the rolls of the Tremontine nobility is his concern, but in private my name, sir, is *Tennoc.*" His mother's flight across the border, a tale she never told but one often recounted by Hanni, tumbled into his head. "Clan Sial accepted me as their own and gave me a name when no Tremontine would. I will be Tennoc ar Sial until my dying day."

Gonnor shook his head. "You must accustom yourself to a Tremontine name, Temmin."

"No," said Tennoc, "Tremont must accustom themselves to an Heir with a Kellish name. I have not forgotten why my mother fled to Brunsial, and if you think I ever will, you are greatly mistaken. Forgive me, sir, I have been on the road many days and I am tired." He turned on his heel to go.

"Grandson—!" At the anguish in the old man's voice, Tennoc turned. Tears were rolling down Gonnor's lined face into his white beard, and he'd aged twenty years since the interview's beginning. "I have spent these long years regretting what I did—what I tried to do—"

"You could have given my mother back her name at any point, and yet you did not until your King required it of you!"

"And here you see the results of my pride," said Gonnor, openly weeping. "I knew I'd wronged your mother within the year. Reports came to us over time, you know—we have eyes everywhere. I heard much of you and your valor at Maalig, and much of your mother, too. All of it good, all of it honorable. It made me secretly proud. Lassa was my darling, my favorite, and I have never stopped loving her or missing her. Driving her out was the greatest mistake of my life, and seeing you I realize your mother has not shamed our house but glorified it."

"Because I have the luck to be the only son of your King. You wouldn't hire me as a stall-mucker let alone receive me in your house otherwise."

"No, no!" choked the old man. "No—Temmin—*Tennoc*—you don't understand. You don't understand."

"I don't suppose I do. Nor will I. Good day, sir."

Tennoc left the room much disturbed and ran almost headlong into Fallik. "Do you have a habit of listening at doors, cousin?" said Tennoc.

The cords stood out in the bigger man's neck. "You are a rude, dishonorable cur. I've half a mind to challenge you!"

"By all means!" answered Tennoc; his new power crackled and sang within him. "Name the time and place, if you ever find the other half."

To Tennoc's astonishment Fallik faltered and dropped his gaze. A pursing of the lips, an exhalation, and he raised sullen eyes. "I have more sense than to challenge the Heir in single combat, however deserving he might be of the flat of my sword. Stay here. The seneschal will be along to show you to your room."

As his cousin walked away Tennoc's magic quieted, but his brain boiled: Fallik feared him. Perhaps Lord Grandfather did, too.

Once in his room, Tennoc unbuckled his sword belt and took off his boots for the first time in days; he wiggled his toes and gave a happy groan. He wanted to lie down on the comfortable-looking bed and fall into a deep sleep, but he was starving and a meal had been set for him on a table: a big slice of mutton pie, a small wheel of cheese, a wheaten loaf, a dish of stewed apples and a silver pitcher of wine. Beside it stood a matching cup. Tennoc sat down before it and had just reached for the wine when a face appeared on the surface of the pitcher. Its eyes were the color of the silver, its hair the shade of the iron candleholder. The face was almost delicate, clean-shaven and boyish, the mouth sensitive.

Tennoc jumped back; he knocked the chair over and drew his dagger. The surface of the pitcher distorted; a swirling mass rose from it, forming itself into a black-robed sliver of a figure that bowed as soon as it had a waist to do so. "Your Highness, sheathe your dagger. I could never harm you even if I wished to. I serve you."

"Who are you? *What* are you?" stammered Tennoc. "Are you my father?"

"No," smiled the newcomer. "My name is Teacher."

"Teacher what?"

"Just Teacher. I have been the counselor to the Kings of Tremont since Gethin the First."

"That was sixty years ago. You can't be more than thirty."

"Appearances, as I am sure you are aware, can be deceiving. Trust that your interests are mine, and that I am here to serve your family until...until I am no longer needed. However many years that may be."

"How do you have magic?" Tennoc persisted. "Are you a royal? A noble?"

"I am sorry. I can tell you nothing of myself until you are King."

Tennoc sheathed his dagger, still keeping his eyes on Teacher. "I've heard of you," he admitted. "They call you the Black Man."

"Many call me the Black Man, but I am no fairy tale, nor have I ever carried off a child and eaten it. In fact, I dislike being called the Black Man to my face, please."

"They say you choose the Kings, that you've chosen them all since Temmin the Great."

"I do not choose, I recognize. I sense the bloodline of Temmin the First, and the one closest to direct, preferably legitimate descent is the one I serve. Today that is Andrin. Some day, barring a true miracle from His Majesty's latest wife, it will be you."

Tennoc sat down slowly, dinner forgotten. "So if she bears a son, I am supplanted. The legitimate son comes before the illegitimate one, no matter when they are born?"

Teacher nodded. "But I have not sensed a son in Her Majesty's womb though they have been married these three years, and I doubt I will."

Tennoc leaned forward, curious in spite of himself. "You know the sex of a King's child before it's born?"

"I sense only the sons. I do not know a girl child is coming until she is here—or if one of the King's women is obviously increasing and I sense no son."

Tennoc considered. "Did you know me?"

"Your father was the Heir then, not the King, or I would have. When he ascended, you flashed like a beacon in the west."

"More's the pity. I should have preferred going unnoticed."

Teacher sat on the table's edge. "Is ruling Tremont so repugnant, then?"

"It was not what I expected from my life." Tennoc poured himself a needed cup of wine. "Oh, shall I send for another cup?" he added, offering his own.

"I do not drink, but thank you. I ask again, is ruling so repugnant?"

"I never expected to *enter* Tremont let alone rule it," he said into his wine cup. He took another long sip; the red wine lay thick and complex on his tongue—and strangely unwatered. Not for gulping. He set the cup down and rubbed his face with both hands. "I'm sorry, but I must eat."

"I am not hungry, please do not hesitate," said Teacher, waving a long-fingered hand over the table as Tennoc pounced on the loaf. "What *did* you expect of life?"

Tennoc swallowed a chunk of bread. "A quiet holding a few days' ride from Gwyrfal, marriage to the lady my stepfather chose, and service at Prince Kenver's right hand in combat. That's what I wanted." *Not all*, whispered a traitorous voice in his head. He wanted Gwynna, not Cariodas. Perhaps now he might have her. Dunnoc would never agree to the marriage.

Tennoc would have to take her by force. The King of the Kells might save Tennoc the trouble; he looked to be headed toward war with Tremont already. "I'm not sure how I feel about being a Prince," he muttered. "I left that part to Kenver." He picked up the piece of mutton pie and took a grateful, speech-blocking bite.

Teacher met that night with the nervous Duke, his fidgeting heir and the new Prince. No one in the room seemed at ease around the pale figure in dark robes; Teacher took their fear in stride. When a servant made a furtive sign of Amma—head, heart and groin—Teacher may even have smirked. "We leave tomorrow, Your Grace," said Teacher.

"The boy should rest, counselor, do you not think?" said Gonnor. "It's been a long journey for him…and I would like for Prince Temmin—*Tennoc*," at his grandson's lowering look, "to know his homeland and family. He's been on the road for more than two weeks already, surely a rest before such a long journey—it's the better part of a spoke to Tremont City."

"We will go back the way I came," said Teacher.

Tennoc's skin prickled at the memory of traveling through a reflection with Kenver. He was in no hurry to take to the road again but said, "Mightn't it be better for me to see more of the country, sir?"

Teacher frowned. "Do not call me 'sir.' I dislike it intensely." Tennoc bowed his head in puzzled apology. "You will see your country in time, Your Highness, but your father required me to bring you to his Keep as soon as I found you. Today was my first sighting of you in a reflection."

"We didn't have time to polish my armor," said Tennoc with a faint smile.

"Will you at least accept my hospitality for the night, Your Highness?" said the anxious Gonnor.

Every muscle in Tennoc's body ached and he wanted nothing more than bed. Still, he consulted Teacher with a glance. The counselor lifted an eyebrow; Tennoc took it to mean he might decide for himself. "We will stay the night, Lord Gonnor, and then Hanni and I will leave with Teacher as King—er, as my father desires." Gonnor and Fallick bowed, as did Teacher. He returned it in reflex.

"Princes of Tremont do not bow to their lords," said Teacher.

"I'm not used to being a prince," answered Tennoc. He leveled a gaze at his cousin. "Yet." Fallik frowned uncertainly.

When they returned to Tennoc's room, Teacher said, "Lord Fallik has his grandfather's impetuous temper. Do not hold it against him. He is honorable and would fight at your side to the death were you to need him."

"Whitehorsers hold their honor in too high esteem."

"And you?"

Tennoc sat down to pull off his boots and grinned. "Bastards have no honor in Tremont. Or so I'm told."

In the morning, Tennoc found a polished steel plate the size of a table top set up in the Freehold's courtyard. Teacher pronounced such a large reflection unnecessary, but Gonnor insisted it made transporting livestock easier. Hanni waited with their horses, eyeing Teacher apprehensively. "It's all right, Hanni. You might get a bit sick, but it's a quick journey," said Tennoc.

"Worry not for me to get sick, it is to worry for the horses."

"Horses don't vomit."

"No, but stumble and flatten my foot they can, sir. Big enough is my foot."

"Must you bring the horses?" frowned Teacher.

"Better horses you will not find, not even here! I, Hanni, from Whitehorse stock did breed them—from horse you gave Prince Andrin I stole for Mistress long ago, begging pardon," he added, bowing to Gonnor. "Was fine horse!"

Teacher waved a resigned hand at the steel plate. "Show me Mirror Clearing." The reflection resolved into murk, a round, irregular window at its center revealing trees and greenery as if he were looking through a knot-hole.

Tennoc and his grandfather eyed each other awkwardly. The old man had aged even since the day before; in spite of himself, Tennoc pitied more than hated him, though he could never love him. He offered his arm. Gonnor took it and they clasped one another at the elbow. "Thank you for your hospitality, Lord Grandfather."

"My door is ever open to you, Tennoc," said Gonnor.

Tennoc's heart twisted. "Thank you, sir. Lord Fallik," he said, turning to his cousin, "in time perhaps we may come to enjoy our kinship more than we have so far. I am not too proud to try." He extended his hand.

Fallik hesitated, but in the end they clasped arms. "Safe journey, Your Highness," he grudgingly answered.

"Can you handle both horses, Hanni der Geelt?" said Teacher.

"In my care always are the horses," bristled Hanni.

"You are in *my* care," said Teacher. "I must hold your hand and pull you through the mirror. Hold their bridles firmly."

"And my master?"

Teacher's silver eyes filled with mischief. "Your master can take himself through now." Teacher grabbed Hanni and pulled the man and both horses through the mirror, their bodies flowing like swirling water to appear in the round, framed reflection on the other side. Teacher waved, and the image vanished.

Tennoc stood agape before the mirror. He'd been left behind! But Teacher said he could travel the Highway of the Kings now, like Kenver and Dunnoc. Was it so? He flushed. How had Kenver done it? "Show me…" he faltered. Where had Teacher taken Hanni and the horses? He couldn't remember. No, he didn't need to know the place, just— "Show me Hanni!"

The mirror resolved into the irregular round of light in a plane of darkness, though Hanni's giant eye filled almost all of the round. What held the reflection on the other side? The times Kenver had taken him through a reflection he'd been violently ill, and he worried it might happen again. He glanced at Fallik and Gonnor. *Well, if I am sick, they won't see it.* He swallowed his nausea and put his hand on the mirror. It sank into the surface, and the magic began.

His bones melted into water. The space inside the reflection had no north or south, no means of knowing which way was down, and slivers of light whirled around him. He fought to keep his breakfast—and then he was stumbling into a clearing among young trees. He put his hands on his knees until his head cleared.

"Hello," smiled Teacher.

The Keep was a short ride down a wide, well-tended way called the War Road. "Our armies ride to battle from here, six abreast," said Teacher from a perch behind Tennoc. "These are the King's Woods. Only the King hunts here—and now you, if you please."

"I wish for nothing but a roof over my head at this point."

The trees thinned, giving Tennoc his first view of Tremont Keep, a stone fortress that was new in his great-grandfathers' day built into the living rock that sheered above the confluence of two rivers. Four rounded towers stood at each corner; the side closest to them bowed out toward the forest. A fifth tower rose just behind the bowed wall, higher than the other four. It looked out over the King's Woods and the foothills, and in the other direction, the Capital. Tennoc wondered how it stayed up; he'd never seen anything so tall.

"Never did I think to see this place again," murmured Hanni. "Remembering I am my good Lady Inglatine."

"Your good lady is healthy and happy at Marsury—with your two youngest half-sisters, sir," added Teacher to Tennoc. "When the Princesses are married, Lady Inglatine is considering returning to Leute."

"Will you go back with her, Hanni?" said Tennoc.

Hanni sucked on a tooth. "My Lady to Queen Lassanna gave me, Queen Lassanna to *you* gave me. If give you me back to my Lady, I end up at beginnings, I go. Else, no."

Tennoc faced his father not long after in the Keep's Great Hall. Though his mother had never said, he'd always imagined his father as tall, dark-haired and blue-eyed, elegant and somewhat languid. This man's eyes were hollow and dark; his crown rested on graying hair that hung lank and greasy, and if he had once been tall and elegant, now he seemed diminished, almost shrunken. How old was his father? He knew Andrin was older than his mother, but the King couldn't be more than fifty, and yet he looked older than Lord Grandfather. A man supported him to his throne; he sat down panting, in obvious pain. He beckoned.

"Your Majesty," said Teacher, "may I present to you your son, Prince Temmin of Tremont." Tennoc made a hesitant, respectful bow.

"The Kells do not call you Temmin, though, do they?" said King Andrin in a tired wheeze.

"My Kellish name is Tennoc ar Sial, and I prefer to be called Tennoc, sir."

"Tennoc it is," nodded his father. "In the family they call me An, after all." He examined his son with fierce and hungry eyes, as if he had a brief moment to learn the young man's features before he vanished. "You are very like her. You are very like me in some ways—don't you think, Teacher?"

"He has the shape of your eyes, sire, and your form. Tall and well-made."

"Once I was tall and well-made at any rate," said Andrin. He looked around the hall. "Leave us. Yes, even you, Teacher. You will have time to speak with the boy after. Much time." Andrin's lords and servants bowed low and left the room, Teacher trailing behind. "Come closer. You dislike my looks, hey? Didn't expect a father who looked like this? What did your mother say of me?"

"As little as possible, sir. May we not speak of my mother, please? Doing so can only lead to pain for us both."

Andrin smirked. "Do you believe her memory pains me?"

"Not in the least, sir, for you made your contempt for us quite clear."

"Contempt?" said Andrin in surprise. "Look at you, you're a fine young man. Strong, a warrior. The troubadours sing songs of Maalig even here. Any man would be proud to have you as a son, and I would have welcomed you and your mother at my court at any time."

"You never sent for her. You never even sent word to her. You did nothing to protect her from her father." Andrin kept silent. "In fact, sir," Tennoc pressed on, "you thought nothing about either of us until I became necessary to you."

"Why would I?" said Andrin on a long exhalation of air. "Since you insist on being plain-spoken: You have turned out to be a fine young man, but you are also a bastard. If I had been here I would have stayed Gonnor's hand against your mother, but I wasn't and it was too much trouble to send to Kellen for her. Had she stayed, I would have kept her until I tired of her and then set her up handsomely with some lordling—and I would have consigned you to the Mother's House. I would have done exactly as I have done: tried to sire more sons. But there will be no other sons. I'm dying." His feverish eyes fastened hard on Tennoc's own. "You are necessary to me, but not as Tennoc ar Sial. I need Temmin Heir of Tremont. I cannot leave this kingdom to be picked apart by the Sairs, the Kells, the Leutans—or worse, the barbarians to the north. I *will* not. So I recognize you as my Heir and give you my name, bastard though you may be."

Such speaking was too plain for Tennoc. "Sial is a better name in my books. Why should I care if your kingdom is picked apart? Perhaps I don't want your name or your throne. Perhaps I might encourage the Kells to nibble at your western border."

"You left the Kells and came to *me*. You're no foolish boy who'd reject a kingdom, let alone one as magnificent as Tremont, no matter how much you hated me—and you do hate me, don't you?" Tennoc said nothing, and his father continued, "You are an Antremont. You bear the direct blood of Temmin the Great, on your mother's side as well as mine. The land recognizes you, does it not? Show me."

Tennoc flushed. "I am unused to holding magic."

"Do your best. I do not sit in judgment."

Tennoc cast about the room. He'd been practicing picking things up and putting them back down; sometimes they even stayed in one piece. He settled on a massive bench. His mind reached out and tugged it bit by bit into the air; it rose as if he were pumping up a bladder beneath each leg. Frustrated, he pushed harder. The bench flew into the rafters. Gasping, he stopped it within an inch of smashing into splinters; he brought it down in several lumbering jerks before it hit the floor. Still in one piece: better than usual.

Andrin's mouth twisted into a smile. "You'll improve. Now that you have magic you won't want to be without it ever again. You'll want more of it. Powerful is better than powerless, son." Andrin sat back; sweat beaded on his sickly yellow forehead, his eyes so sunken their sockets stood out in clear relief all round each one. "I am tired now. Call for the servants. The seneschal will take care of you and your manservant. He's familiar. Do I know him?"

"His name is Hanni der Geelt."

Andrin chuckled faintly. "I remember Yellow Hanni." Andrin closed his eyes and said no more. For a moment, Tennoc wondered if he still breathed, but then his chest rose and fell. Tennoc called in the servants, and they tenderly bore his father away.

"The Sisters say he will not last the turn of the wheel," came Teacher's cool voice at his elbow. "Myself, I do not think he will live to see the end of next spoke. We do not have much time, Your Highness. You must master the magic you have before you inherit his as well."

"I have not decided I will take the throne."

Teacher's cold silver gaze flicked over him. "You decided when you crossed the River Cobb and claimed your magic."

"The magic claimed *me*," said Tennoc. "It hadn't even occurred to me what might happen, and I'm not at all comfortable with it." He sighed. "Quite honestly, I wish nothing more than to return to Gwyrfal and have everything be peaceful again."

"You will never be at peace outside Tremont again. Should your feet leave Tremontine soil, your magic will leave you—and when that happens, you will find yourself far less comfortable without it than you are with it. The thirst for magic has guided every action of every king in the world. Every battle between nations is fought to gain land and the magic it contains. There is no crossing back into Kellen for you—except at an army's head." Teacher reached up and took Tennoc gently by the arms. "You are not solely here at your father's summoning."

Tennoc hung his head. "In truth, I have nowhere else to go. Dunnoc has betrayed me."

"I know a good deal about betrayal," murmured Teacher. "Never worry. You are safe here."

Tennoc thought of his mother, and hoped she was safer than he was.

The discovery of the guards' bodies put Gwyrfal in an uproar. "How could Tennoc have defeated three of my best men?" fretted Dunnoc. "Three men he *trusted!*"

"He had to have been warned, sire," said Daevys ar Ulvyn. "There's no other explanation, though perhaps it was his plan all along. He took them by surprise like a coward." He helped Dunnoc drink from his cup. The King shook now more than ever. His legs were growing stiff; he never left his rooms but for meals at which he presided but did not eat for fear of spilling food and drink down his front in public.

"Who could have done it? Who betrayed me?"

"We shall discover the man, sire. Or woman."

Dunnoc looked at him in alarm. "Woman? What do you mean, woman?"

"Rest easy, sire," soothed Ulvyn. "I will root out those who work against you. In the meantime, let me help you. Is this partridge to your liking, or shall I cut you a morsel of beef?"

Dunnoc huffed in exasperation. "As you please. Food is a necessary evil to me now, no more. Why is the Queen not here to wait on me?"

"Do you not recall? She said she no longer wished to attend to you." What Queen Lassanna had said was that she did not wish to attend to Dunnoc with Ulvyn hanging over her shoulder; Dunnoc would not dismiss his favorite lord, the only one who told him what really went on in his court. Hadn't Ulvyn been right about Tennoc? He must be right about Lassanna. She was the ungrateful cur's mother, after all.

"What does my Queen do with her days, since she does not deign to wait on me?"

Ulvyn held a bite of meat until the shaking stopped enough for Dunnoc to eat it. "She spends much time with your children, sire. She seems quite close to Kenver. *Quite.* They spend many hours together. At all hours."

Dunnoc choked. "What are you saying?"

"Nothing, sire. They have many interests in common, among them, Tennoc. It's only natural," he said, wiping Dunnoc's mouth. "Your lady, though not a girl, is still lively, and your son is handsome. It may be she enjoys the sight of him so often in her bower. She is still a beauty. It could not be counted as unusual that in the absence of one they loved so much as Tennoc they might, er, *find comfort* one with the other."

"Enough." Tiny flames flickered on the King's fingertips; now used to Dunnoc's diminishing control, Ulvyn sidled away. "What do you believe?" demanded Dunnoc. "What is it you believe? You must tell me!"

The little flames reflected in Ulvyn's eyes. "I believe, sire, you know already."

"My son and my wife—! They must have betrayed me to Tennoc! But how could Kenver and the Queen have discovered what we meant to do!"

Ulvyn smiled. "I shall not rest until I find the traitor. In the meantime, sire, the Princess Gwynna should no longer be exposed to such as the Queen, do you not think?"

"I must find her a husband," whispered Dunnoc. "I must find her someone to keep her away from Tennoc, someone I can trust." He looked up through rheumy eyes. "Perhaps I shall give her to you."

"I wish nothing more than Gwynna's safety and happiness, sire, and would happily marry the lady now that my own wife is dead. But hush now, we shall not speak of it."

Teacher and Tennoc worked to increase the Heir's control over his share of Tremontine magic. "You are trying too hard," Teacher said time and again. "Let it float lightly on your thoughts, like telling your eye to blink or your leg to bend. You do not ask, you command, and with little thought. You must be sure in your mind. If you are unsure, do not use magic—choose some other method. Indecision will be your undoing in all things magical."

Day by day, Tennoc grew stronger and more confident, and King Andrin grew weaker. He did not leave his bed now, and Tennoc came to him every evening to display his progress. "I would accuse you of sucking the life from me," chuckled Andrin through dry and cracked lips this night, "but in truth I believe seeing you has kept me living a little longer than otherwise." He reached for Tennoc's hand and took it in a hot, papery grasp. "Do not think too badly of me, son. I must seem heartless to one raised as a Kell, but in Tremont, these things are different. In truth it is a good thing I left your mother in Kellen so that you might be raised with honor and a name, even if neither were mine." His grasp faltered. "It is too late, I think, for us to love one another, but not too late for me to be proud of you, both as Tennoc ar Sial and Temmin of Tremont."

"Thank you, sir," said Tennoc. His voice shook, and his stomach roiled. It *was* too late to love his father—perhaps too late even to forgive him—but knowing the King was proud of him hit him in a way he did not expect.

The next morning, Andrin breathed but did not wake. He lingered for three nights. On the fourth, Tennoc awoke from a dead sleep, screaming. A white, roaring ocean broke over him. The white faded, leaving coal-red traces in the air and sparks around the edges of his vision. Hanni ran in from the next room, yellow hair wild about his head. "What ails you?"

"He's dead," Tennoc rasped. "I'm too young to be King. I don't know the people, I don't know the country. I'm not ready. Pagg help me, Hanni."

The day after he committed his father's body to the Hill, Tennoc rode down from the Keep to Tremont City for his hasty, simplified coronation, his father's reluctant lords at his back. Hanni followed behind, holding the reins of a white bull calf. They climbed the long winding switchbacks on foot up Pagg's Hill to the Temple at its top. He could have lifted himself to the top had he wished—Teacher had taught him to raise himself on a column of solid air—but he did not wish to leave his lords behind. He had lords now. What a strange thought. Would that he could depend on them.

They stopped at Father's Rock, the great flat stone that had served as Pagg's holy place in the City before Temmin the Great built the white marble Temple beside it. Tremontine banners fluttered from atop the Temple among Pagg's purple and gold streamers. A flock of burly young priests in rough white robes stood by, as did the Little Father and Pagg's Embodiment dressed in resplendent purple with gold trimmings. Teacher stood off to one side, already come by reflection. Hanni handed the reins of the bull calf to the Little Father. The young priests wrestled the animal to the ground and bound it before and behind; the entire company turned to Tennoc in expectation.

Teacher had coached him on the ceremony. Tennoc's magic lifted the bawling calf into the air; he dropped it hard atop the rock, stunning it. The Embodiment took a gold-hilted knife and slit its throat, expertly dodging the artery's spurt; the blood ran down the Rock's already-stained sides. The Little Father examined the pathways the blood took down the Father's Rock, pronounced them auspicious, and led them all into the Temple where he read the prayers and placed the crown atop Tennoc's head, proclaiming him "The Third Temmin, great-great-grandson of the Great Temmin and our true King." The company cheered, though not as lustily as they might have. It didn't matter. Andrin's magic had passed to him, and Teacher recognized him as King; they mightn't have been happy about it, but to his surprise no one questioned it.

Tennoc had no sooner led the procession back down the Hill to the gathered horses when a messenger galloped up. He jumped down from the saddle and dropped to one knee. "Sire, two travelers have come from Kellen—they appear to be noble. They've taken refuge at the Healer's House, for the man is badly hurt and not faring well. The girl is overset, and they bore something that…well, none have seen inside it but we all can smell it.

Oh, please come, Your Majesty, they are begging for you!"

"When you need me, sire, look for me in a reflection," said Teacher. "I will stand ready."

Tennoc swung himself into the saddle, and the Brothers who'd accompanied him mounted as well."I want only Hanni," he said.

"You will take us too, Your Majesty," said their stubborn leader.

"Oh, very well!" he exclaimed, and spurred his horse toward the Sister's Hill and the Healer's House at its foot.

Tennoc found the travelers from Kellen in a small, bright room. On its low bed lay a naked man covered in yellowing bruises, sores and lash marks; broken teeth showed in his open mouth, one eye must have been swollen shut not long ago, and stertorous breathing spasmed his chest. His crooked left leg had turned an ugly purple, green and black. Beside him knelt a young woman, grass and bracken tangled in her messy, dark braids. Dried blood stained her tattered dress.

The man was Sian ar Lifris; the young woman beside him was his daughter, Cariodas. As she helped the Sisters tend her father's wounds, she murmured in a steady voice that they were safe, he would be looked after now, but when she saw Tennoc she lost her composure; her great brown eyes brimmed over, and she began to shake.

"What's happened!" cried Tennoc in Kellish. "How came you to be here? Cariodas, what's happened?" He lifted her to her feet, and she stumbled into his arms.

"Your Majesty," said the elder of the Sisters, "if you know this lady, please convince her to let us care for her. She is exhausted. Make her lie herself down."

Tennoc smoothed her hair. "Cariodas," he translated, "the Sisters say you must lie down and let them take care of you."

"I'm not hurt," said Cariodas. She propped herself up on Tennoc's chest and trembled in shock and weariness. "Papa is hurt, I have to stay with him. They beat him, they've nearly killed him—oh, Tennoc!" She collapsed against him in a near-swoon. He scooped her up, carried her to the darkened room next door and laid her down on the bed.

A rangy Sister bustled after him and took over, washing Cariodas's face and hands and checking her pulses. "She is not injured, sire, but driven to the ends of endurance," said the Sister. "I doubt she's slept more than a few hours in days, or eaten at all. She is a brave, brave girl. The man with her—"

"Her father, a noble lord of Kellen."

The Sister shook her head. "Kellish ladies must be made of strong stuff.

She dragged him behind her horse on a branch sled all the way from Kellen along with that wretched chest. He will lose his leg at best, sire—I don't know how she got him here alive."

"Do what you can for him. Where is this chest?"

The tall Sister's nose wrinkled. "Sire, I'm sorry, but we could not keep it here. It is on its way as we speak to Harla's Hill, for while this lady insisted only you might open it, we could smell what it contained."

Tennoc's hair prickled. "This lady's name is Cariodas ar Lifris. Her father's name is Sian ar Lifris. They are dear to me. Watch over them, Sister."

He sprinted from the Healer's House back to his horse. "It's Cariodas, Hanni," he said as he mounted. "And her father—Lifris has been beaten near to death."

"What did they carry, sire?"

"Nothing good. We're off to Harla's Hill." Hanni blanched, but followed his master at a gallop.

They overtook the cart not far from the Temple's entrance. At first, no scent assaulted Tennoc's nose, but when they stopped the cart, it came to him—no more than a whiff, but he knew it instantly. "We will take this into the Hill, for whatever is in it belongs there."

Once at the Temple's door, the Friends of Harla emerged and helped carry the chest inside. The high priestess introduced herself as Friend Dian. "You were right to come here, Your Majesty," she said. "We will open it in a grieving room. Whoever it was must be cleansed." Tennoc knew the chest contained something quite dead, but hearing it referred to as "who" and not "what" made his skin crawl. Dian made a sign; the Friends bowed and disappeared through various passages. Tennoc and Hanni followed the chest into the small grieving room, where its bearers placed it beside the stone table and water-filled basin at the room's center. Dian gestured to the chest.

Tennoc crept up to it, more afraid than he'd ever been in his life. His hands and feet turned to ice, and sweat formed on his palms. He unfastened the clasp and with a determination he did not feel, he opened the lid.

It contained two heads, one male, one female. The man's hair was dark. The woman's hair was ash blonde, a scant few wiry strands of gray marring it. "Judging by the smell and the state of the flesh, sire, these people have been dead about three weeks," murmured Friend Dian. "Do you know them?"

Tennoc couldn't breathe; his throat closed and his chest clenched at every attempt until he got in a great gulp of air. A discreet Friend appeared from nowhere carrying a large basin, and Tennoc vomited into it. Somewhere nearby Hanni screamed in Leutish as if his eyes were being plucked from his head. Tennoc retched and retched; when he finished he slumped back on the floor, spent.

Dian handed Tennoc a wet towel and a cup of water to rinse his mouth. Beside him, Hanni lay in a wretched lump on the cold stone floor, great sobs shaking his wiry frame. "Who were they, Your Majesty?" said Dian.

"Prince Kenver and Queen Lassanna of Kellen. My brother—my best friend—and…and my mother…" Hanni crawled across the floor, and Tennoc held the man as he howled in grief. Dian put an unnoticed hand on Tennoc's head in blessing; Tennoc kept his arms tight around his old friend, and ashes filled his heart.

Temmin scrambled back from the book, knocking his chair over in his drive to get away. He knotted his fingers in his hair and pulled to keep himself from screaming, but a choking sob broke through. "How—how *dare* you—!"

"I told you, when I chose this story I did not know what would happen to your mother," said Teacher, arms folded behind.

"Uncaring, unfeeling *whoreson*!" Temmin shouted. "Pagg damn you, you *bastard*, you *block of stone*! You don't even *remember* your own mother! Get out of my sight!" Teacher didn't move. Temmin charged, and hit the wall of air he'd unconsciously expected. He staggered back. "Coward! Drop your shield! Fight me like a man, damn you!"

"You have hurt yourself, sir," said Teacher, unruffled.

Temmin blinked away blood; he must have opened up the wound at his temple. His pain mingled with Tennoc's still-lingering horror into a mounting hysteria. "Do you think I care? What of it! What do I care? My mother's in the Hill—he killed her! No, she—Ibbit—" He threw back his head and screamed.

Jenks threw the door open, knife drawn and two Guards at his heels. "What in Amma's name—" he said at Teacher's quelling gesture. "What have you done to him? Your Highness—Temmin, you're bleeding!" Jenks waved the Guards away and shut the door after them. Temmin dropped to his knees, still screaming through tears. Jenks kneeled down next to him, folded a handkerchief and held the improvised compress to his unresisting charge's forehead; Temmin's sobs diminished into disconsolate, ragged breaths as the big man stayed near, the only contact between them the handkerchief and a steadying hand on one shoulder. "What did you do to him?" said Jenks again.

"A difficult part of our current lesson. I want us to finish this story, Your Highness," Teacher added to Temmin. "It is hard for you to hear, but I strongly believe that hearing Tennoc's story may help you grieve. You are not alone in this trouble. I must return to the Keep now. Your father needs me. Amma's Day is tomorrow. I will return the day after, on Paggday."

"You'll do nothing of the kind," growled Jenks.

"I will return on Paggday," Teacher repeated and walked to the mirror in the bedchamber, leaving Temmin and his old friend crouching on the rug.

"Come now, come, sir," said Jenks, leading him to the sofa. "Hold this handkerchief while I get you a sticking plaster or two. It's just a cut above the eye, they bleed like anything, but they're not serious."

"I'm not such an idiot I don't know that," sniffed Temmin.

Jenks returned from the bathroom with the plasters. "As you say, sir. Ah, Temmin, you've opened your stitches, too, and damn it, you've ruined your shirtfront!"

"Cold water."

Jenks laughed. "You're learning."

"I pay attention," Temmin sniffed again, this time with a faint smile.

"Now tell me, what did the old crow say to upset you so?"

Temmin hesitated, but Jenks had seen Teacher do impossible things; in the end, Temmin told all. "When you feel everything the person in the story feels..." Tears filled his eyes again, but he kept his composure even as they fell. "His mother was murdered, and so was mine. When he opened the chest, it was like finding Mama's head—and yours, or maybe Alvo's."

"Nothing prepares you for the death of someone you love, sir, not even war. Some of our friends fell when your uncle and I were in Inchar, and it hurt when they died, I don't deny it. And when Pat died..." The big man trailed off and cleared his throat. "They say when someone you love dies, a piece of you goes to the Hill with them. There is a great bleeding chunk of me in the Hill with your Uncle Pat, and another with your mother."

"Teacher said you never get over it, you just get used to it."

Jenks grimaced. "I will give the old crow his due: He's right. He's often right. I don't like it, but it's so."

FOURTEEN

To Temmin's surprise, Amma's Day comforted him. He watched the farmhands herd the Estate's cattle, sheep and goats between the two sacred bonfires and helped the stablehands do the same with the horses, leading his own Jebby through himself; Alvo worked beside him but said no more than "A blessed Amma's Day to you, Your Highness." Temmin wanted to shake him.

As Duke of Whithorse it was also Temmin's duty to walk with the Reggiston Temple's Senior Mother through the cleaned and shining stables, poultry yards, goat sheds and pig pens blessing the animals. Every barn cat that could be found, every sheep dog at its master's heels received the Mother's Blessing.

They ended at the shearing shed, where the most beautiful of last year's lambs waited. It was too cold, really, for the poor thing to lose its fleece— Temmin could see his own breath—but tradition must be upheld. The expert shearer clipped the fine, creamy wool into a single unbroken sheet, and the little ewe bounded away. She would be kept in the shed wearing a wool blanket until the weather warmed, a detail that had delighted Temmin as a child. "A sheep in a wool blanket!" he'd crow to his mother every year. It still made him smile even as it reminded him Mama wasn't there to share the joke. The Mothers carefully rolled the fleece in a blue ceremonial cloth to be borne away to the Mother's Temple in Reggiston; the Mothers and Sisters would scour it, spin it and make it into clothing for the newborns in the Mother's House.

For the first time since they'd arrived, Ellika left the house. Though she wore black and dark circles still lingered under her eyes, a little of her old sparkle shone whenever she looked at her baby sister Anneya. Nurse had swaddled the poor infant in layer upon layer of white wool sacques, under-caps, bonnets, mitts, shawls and blankets until she looked more like a gigantic cocoon than a baby. Second Nurse had to carry her about; the entire bundle was too much for Nurse, though she hovered beside them, tugging the coverings up and down in open disapproval of the new addition to the nursery's staff. The baby herself, now exactly three weeks old, slept through the whole thing.

Lady Donnis, who unofficially ran the household, insisted that however things had gone on so far at the Estate no one was to dine in his room on a holiday, or indeed from now on. All attended in evening dress to eat their Amma's Day pork and lamb. Standfast Jenks, resplendent in full Tremontine red and gold uniform with a wide black ribbon round his left arm, stood out against the rows of black crape. Never in Temmin's memory had Jenks eaten in the dining room.

More remarkable than Jenks's presence was his mother's absence. Temmin sat at the table's head; Dowager Duchess Markellis came from Meadow House and sat at its foot. Temmin kept looking down the table expecting to see Mama there and finding his grandmother instead. He kept his composure during the meal and quiet conversation in the drawing room after, but he excused himself not long after the tea was brought in, and went to bed.

Temmin stared up into the canopy while scenes from his childhood played over and over in his head. He would never again give his mother an Amma's Day gift. He thought of every time he'd made her unhappy, and wished he could tell her he was sorry.

Temmin came back from the stables the next day vexed at best. Alvo showed no signs of softening, and Temmin began to wonder if he could win his friend back. What had he done that was so bad, anyway? His father had said an Heir could not be friends with a groom, but he'd beaten his father once to become a Supplicant. Compared to that, insisting on friendship with Alvo was trivial. How could Alvo have so little faith in him? Alvo was his best friend. Possibly something more—time would tell—but after his mother's death no one, not even the Gods, would ever keep him from the people he loved again, not Alvo nor…

…nor Allis.

Temmin threw himself down on his well-broken-in, faded gold sofa; behind his head, he stuffed a down pillow he'd compressed into the perfect shape over the course of his boyhood and that his mother had loathed. He missed Allis. He knew his leave had been her doing, though she'd never said so. He needed her. Maybe she'd sensed it and sent him away to keep him from doing something stupid—again. Home was safer, and frankly more comforting, but now that they'd been apart more than a week he felt her absence keenly. He needed home and Allis at the same time, and it rankled that he couldn't have them both. He should get used to it; when his time at the Temple ended at Nerr's Day, three spokes from now, they would rarely see each other until her time as Embodiment was over.

And then what? Could he make her his mistress? Not if she chose to stay at the Temple. No, he couldn't let her do that, he'd have to find a way to make her leave. Issak might stay, but not Allis. He loved Issak, but not as he loved Allis. He and Issak would always be friends; with luck they'd remain bedmates. The particular way Issak bit his neck came to mind; he shivered at the tug in his groin. No, he didn't have to worry about Issak, or Anda. Though he wouldn't see them often at the Temple, when he did it would be a reunion with a good friend.

Allis was more than a good friend. He ached for her.

A gentle throat-clearing came from the doorway to his bedchamber. "Not feeling sneaky today?" said Temmin, keeping his head on the pillow.

Teacher came into the room. "I am never 'sneaky.' I am circumspect."

"To be sure," said Temmin in a flat voice. A long silence fell. "Well?" he finally said.

"I am here to resume the story, if you wish it."

"I should burn that Pagg-damned book," growled Temmin.

"It will not burn, but you are welcome to try if you think that might alleviate your pain. You may not believe me, but I am here to help you."

Temmin put a forearm across his aching eyes. "Some help."

"I believe experiencing the grief of an ancestor who faced his mother's murder may help you cope with your own grief more than destroying a book, sir. May we at least try?"

"Just go away," Temmin said from under his arm.

The room had been silent for several minutes before Temmin sat up and looked around to find Teacher gone. Part of him was angry Teacher gave up so easily; the rest of him was just angry. "I need to hit something," he muttered.

The training salon was in its own building, low-slung and utilitarian. The Estate's Own sparred here, in a complex containing a parade grounds, the main armory, the military stables and the Guards' barracks. Temmin changed into sparring clothes—loose trousers, no shirt, boots never worn outside the salon—and found Jenks waiting for him. "Where's Fen? I expected him," said Temmin in irritation.

"He's busy elsewhere. We've never sparred, sir, and now my secret's out I thought we'd enjoy a round or two."

Temmin hesitated; Jenks stood with his hands in his pockets. He had to be at least as old as Temmin's father, but apart from countless scars his body didn't show it. His arms were corded and thick, his shoulders broad, and his chest reminded Temmin of Jebby's. "Come on, then, boy," Jenks said more loudly, taking his hands from his pockets.

"I can't hit you," exclaimed Temmin, dismayed and surly at the same time.

"Why not?"

"You're too old!"

Jenks grinned and took his stance. "There's your trouble, for I have no problem hitting you, sir. But please, royalty first."

Temmin took his stance, feinted with his left and threw a strong punch with his right. Jenks stepped to one side, moving so fast Temmin could hardly track him. He flicked aside the blow, hooked a leg around Temmin's, and pushed him over with the flat of his right. Temmin thudded to the floor. "Again," said Jenks.

Temmin got up and came at him again with a flurry of kicks and punches that Jenks either sidestepped or blocked. Temmin found an opening in Jenks's guard; they grappled. Jenks chuckled, picked him up and threw him to the floor. "Again."

Temmin threw everything he had at Jenks, but every time he ended up on the floor. The last time, Jenks had his foot on the back of Temmin's neck and one of the Prince's arms in a twist. "Tsk, sir," said Jenks, pressing down until Temmin wheezed, "you're grossly out of form, if you ever were in form." He lifted his foot and helped Temmin up. Jenks had barely broken a sweat, while Temmin's hair was dripping. Jenks handed him a towel. "D'you feel better, Your Highness?"

"Yes," he huffed, "I think I do. Thank you."

Once cleaned up and fed, Temmin did feel much better, but now he paced in his room with nothing to do. He might take a nap, but he wasn't sleepy. Books did not appeal, until the old red-bound book caught his eye. He regretted sending Teacher away and was just wishing he could use a reflection to apologize when a cool voice broke his revery. "You were wise to work out some of your frustrations with Mr Jenks."

"I'm sorry for snapping at you," said Temmin, looking up to find his advisor in the doorway again. "I'm just miserable, is all— wait, how did you know about me sparring with Jenks?"

Teacher smiled. "A shield was propped at such an angle that I could see you but you could not see me. I doubt you were looking for me in the first place."

"I wish you wouldn't do that." Temmin sat down on the couch and rubbed the heels of his palms on his forehead. "In truth, I'm glad you're here. I'm going out of my mind with nothing to do but ride and—and remember."

"Would returning to the Temple be preferable? There is no barrier to an early return, I am sure."

"No, I'm no use to anyone there. I can't keep my mind on most things longer than a few minutes."

"Shall I leave you alone, then?"

"No, no," said Temmin, leaning back. "I'm willing to take your advice. Go on." He opened the book, Teacher began to read, and the drawing room faded away.

Inside the catacombs, Tennoc stared at the two bricked-in niches. In the lefthand one, his father King Andrin the First moldered; to the right, the heads of his mother and his best friend lay, sewn into clean linen and left to rot away to bone, with Tennoc's heart beside them.

Lassanna died Queen of Kellen; Whitehorse would also lay claim to her remains, but Tennoc would keep Mama here, in the Tremontine royal chapel beside Andrin's bones—and some day, his own. Kenver's spirit would not fully rest until he lay in Gwyrfal's Hill with his ancestors; somehow Tennoc would return his stepbrother's skull to Kellish soil.

Thoughts of Gwyrfal brought thoughts of his Gwynna. She must be alone and friendless now, for Dunnoc had clearly lost his mind. Even so, madness wouldn't stop Tennoc from caving his stepfather's head in.

Tennoc thanked the Friends for their care, called for Hanni and stalked from Harla's Hill. "What now, sire?" said the servant.

"Now we go to Cariodas and find out who I'm to kill besides Dunnoc."

At the Healer's House they found Cariodas sound asleep. "Let her be, sire," said the Sister in charge. "She is fair done up. We will send a messenger when she awakes."

Cariodas slept for the better part of two days. The Sisters took Sian ar Lifris's left leg off above the knee the first night, but Harla still hovered over him; the amputation had come too late, and the putrescence was spreading throughout his body. Cariodas had just enough time to say goodbye before her father sank into a sleep everyone knew would be his last.

When Tennoc found her, she was sitting on the bed in the little room the Sisters had given her, holding a pillow to her chest and staring off into space. She'd been washed and dressed in a gray wool gown that hung from her now-thin shoulders. Tennoc wondered for a moment if she'd lost her senses, but she looked up and smiled at him from a far-away place. She dropped the pillow, rose to her feet and made her curtsey. "Lady, please don't bow to me," he said, lifting her up. "I am to blame for this." He guided her gently back to the bed, the only real seat in the room, and sat her down.

"*You* to blame?" exclaimed Cariodas. "You didn't spread lies. You didn't beat my father and drive me from Kellen. *You* didn't—didn't…" She left the sentence dangling. "You are not to blame," she finished in despair.

Tennoc sat on a stool at her feet. "Who did?"

"The King, though Daevys ar Ulvyn all but rules Kellen now."

"I cannot believe Dunnoc would listen to such a man."

Cariodas all but spat. "Who do you think urged your exile? Who do you think convinced Dunnoc to have you killed? He boasts of it outside the King's hearing. Not that it matters now."

"Tell me what happened."

Cariodas took a deep breath, her fingers flexing in the pillow's stuffing. "When they discovered the bodies of the Guards at the crossroads, the King ordered the traitor who'd warned you found. Ulvyn followed the trail back to my father. I confess…I confess I was surprised Father did it. He was never the bravest of men, but he worried for the kingdom and he saw Dunnoc's weakness. The King is far worse than when you left. He shakes openly now, and his mind is clouded. Some began to whisper he was being poisoned, and Ulvyn took advantage of it. He accused the Queen."

"*That's* why he killed her? With what proof? And why kill Kenver? Amma's heart, he is truly mad!"

Cariodas shook her head. "That's the least of it. You know how jealous the King's become. When it was discovered Father betrayed the plot against you to Kenver, Ulvyn convinced His Majesty Kenver and the Queen were—were lovers conspiring against him in your favor...and the King did as you have seen."

"I will kill him!" choked Tennoc. He sprang from the footstool, tipping it over, and paced the room as he tore at his hair. "I will kill them both, I swear I will kill them *all* for this." Cariodas huddled on the bed; in the clutches of an unseen hand, the footstool was beating itself to flinders against the opposite wall. *I'm frightening her. She should be frightened of me. Everyone should be.* He regained control over himself; the remains of the footstool dropped meekly to the floor, and he turned back to the bed. "What of Gwynna?"

"I'm sorry, Tennoc. I know you..." She faltered, and Tennoc fought down panic; was Gwynna dead as well? "King Dunnoc made Ulvyn his heir and gave Gwynna to him the very day of the execution. She fought, you should know. Ulvyn had to drag her to the marriage bed. She may still be tied to it for aught I know—he exiled us before he let her out."

Tennoc began assembling his army in his head. "And then? What happened to you and your father?"

Cariodas flinched, gripping the pillow in both hands. "They beat my father in open court the next day. They surrounded him, called him traitor. Broke his sword. Beat him before my eyes until he stopped screaming and the blood poured from him. You could—you could see the bones sticking from his leg, though I did the best I could later on to set it. They drove us from Gwyrfal with little food, no clothing but what we had on our backs, a cloak for me and a blanket for him, no escort, no way to defend ourselves, just a horse and the branch sled. And that vile, vile chest! Oh, that was almost the worst, Tennoc, knowing what it contained! They even sent riders ahead, warning people not to help us. So many times I thought Father had died in the night."

Tennoc sat down next to her and took her hand. "What did you do?"

"Ulvyn bid us to come to Tremont Keep and show you 'what Kellen does to its enemies.' The Mother's Temples gave us food and the Sisters helped me with Father—when they could. Most towns refused us entrance for fear of angering the King. There was nothing for it but to keep moving. By the time we crossed the River Cobb I was so tired and frightened I didn't even try to get help in a town—I don't speak Tremontine, and I didn't think to find anyone who spoke Old Sairish. I just tried to stay out of sight and get to you." She squeezed his hands and blinked rapidly, clearing away tears. "So. I am in your hands, sire."

"You needn't call me 'sire.' I'm not your king."

Her eyes flashed to his. "Tennoc, you've always been my king." She hung her head, blushing at her own impulsiveness. "That is, I cannot return to Kellen, Your Majesty. I would become Tremontine if you would have me as your subject."

"Lady Cariodas, any king would be proud to have you as his subject. You will always have an honored place in my court, as will your father."

"Thank you, sire, but he's dying. He won't last the night."

Tennoc left instructions that Cariodas and Lifris be given the best of everything. He sent fine clothes, rich food and a girl to serve Cariodas as maid, but Lifris never regained consciousness and died two days later. Cariodas saw him into Tremont City's Hill and came to live at the Keep.

LATE FALL'S ENDING, 62 KY
GWYRFAL, KELLEN

Six spokes after her wedding, Princess Gwynna was still kept to her rooms; armed guards stood beside her door, and she could trust none of her attendants. Her husband visited her every few days, but she saw no one else.

During his latest visit, Ulvyn once again denied her request to leave her rooms. "I am five spokes with child," she said in disgust. "How am I supposed to manage an escape? Who would help me?"

"You are impetuous, my dear," said her husband. "I would not wish anything to happen to the baby."

"I don't care what happens to it!"

"And that's why you cannot leave your rooms," he chuckled.

Gwynna tried another tack. "Can I at least see my father? He can no longer come to me."

"I might allow it," said Ulvyn, "but he won't recognize you. He spends much time talking to your late brother and stepmother."

Lassanna and Kenver on the executioner's block filled her mind's eye. Lassanna had gone first; did Kenver stare into his stepmother's eyes before his head fell into the basket beside hers? "You *dare* mention them to me?"

Ulvyn smirked. "I may dare anything with my wife."

That night, Ulvyn and five guards came to Gwynna's chambers and took her to see her father. King Dunnoc rarely left his rooms now, though his shaking had subsided. The Sisters said that in palsies like his, this signaled his final decline, though how long it would last no one could say.

The King sat swaddled in furs and blankets in a chair. No fire burned in the hearth nor candles in holders; Ulvyn carried a lantern so that they might see, but kept it out of Dunnoc's line of sight. The sole furnishing was a bed firmly attached to the wall. "How can you keep him like this?" cried Gwynna, pulling her cloak around her swelling belly against the chill. "Are you trying to kill him with cold and dark?"

"He can no longer control his magic, Lady," apologized one of his attendants. "If we have open flame in the room he'll set fire to the castle unless Prince Daevys is here to confine it, and if we leave things lying about, the King's magic will throw them at us. Sometimes the very air hardens," he added, pointing to the ugly bruise on his right cheek.

"We keep him covered in furs, as you see," hastened the other, "and there are hot stones always at his feet. Unless he throws them." A pillow from the bed flew up, bounced off the ceiling and fell in a heap before her. The first attendant shrugged ruefully and placed it back on the bed.

Gwynna squatted down beside him, her heavy belly between her knees. "It's me, Papa, it's Gwynna." Dunnoc mumbled something. "What? I can't hear you."

"Faithless woman," quavered Dunnoc. "I kill you and *now* you come back to me. Now you and Hallia both reproach me, so 'tis? You killed Hallia too, I wager, so you could get your hooks into me. Oh, Kenver, don't look at me like that, I did *try* to stop them from stealing all the cheese."

Gwynna's heart sank. "Do you know me, Papa? I'm Gwynna."

"Gwynna?" Dunnoc focused bloodshot eyes on her and poked a once-thick hand out from among the furs to prod her cheek as if to prove she was real. "Gwynna. I had a grandmother named Gwynna."

"I am her namesake, sir."

"She had black hair not red. You're not her."

"No, sir," she said with increasing effort, "I am your daughter."

"I have no children," he crooned, "none a-tall. No wife, no children, none a-tall…" He closed his eyes, still mumbling to himself in a soft voice. Gwynna sat back on the bare floor, biting her lip.

"I told you not to come," said her husband.

The next day, Daevys ar Ulvyn met with his cronies. "Do I have your support, then?" he said.

Bryth ar Brennow warmed his hands on his cup of hot wine. "You've had our support all through this, Ulvyn, though I'm left wondering what I'll gain in the end."

"Once I've taken the throne, I'll give you Brunsial, how will that be? Williard ar Sial can't hold out under siege forever. Then we shall march on Whitehorse—our armies are almost ready, and we've seen no movement yet from the Tremontine bastard. He's likely fighting his own lords over the succession. Besides, when he does move it's certain to be against Trefhallyn. He'll take Maalig by sea—he's well-loved there even now, they'll open the gates to him—and then he'll march to the relief of his uncle. But we can't do anything while Dunnoc lives."

"Dunnoc is dying already," complained a lord, frowning into his thick black beard. "Why not wait until he's dead? Is it necessary to kill him?" A murmur went up around the room.

Ulvyn smacked his fist on the trestle table before him; the men jumped. "Because most of the kingdom's magic is tied up in his crumbling bulk, and it might take him another turn of the wheel to die—perhaps more! If we are to move against Tremont it must be now, before Tennoc can consolidate his power. We must have Dunnoc's magic."

"I don't see how it matters," said the bearded lord. "Magic is defensive. We can't use it outside of Kellen, that whelp Tennoc can't use his outside of Tremont. If he can use it at all."

"That's the point," said Brennow impatiently. "If Tremont moves before us, we will be unable to defend ourselves!"

"I have Kenver's magic now as Dunnoc's heir," continued Ulvyn, "and you all have your paltry bits of power, but all of us together could not defeat Tremont in battle even on our own soil. No, we must take territory from him before he can gather his forces—win the land's allegiance, take its magic for ourselves and use it to build defenses *in Whitehorse*—and with Dunnoc's magic I can do that. Perhaps I'll give you a goodly chunk of Whitehorse instead of Brunsial, Bryth."

"Perhaps both?" smiled Brennow hopefully.

"Help me kill Dunnoc, and we'll see. If we succeed, there will be enough for all of us."

NEW YEAR'S DAY, 63 KY

King Dunnoc did not appear at the Eddin's Day celebrations for the new year: too ill, said Ulvyn, to leave his rooms. Gwynna sat at her husband's side, hugely pregnant. It was for the best that Dunnoc had not been brought down. He'd begun drooling, and his private conversations with ghosts had become even more incoherent. The Sisters said he might go on like this for spokes—perhaps years.

Her father's condition oppressed her spirits as much as the infant within her did. In the last days its squirming and kicking had subsided. Perhaps it had died. She would not cry if it was stillborn. Nevertheless, she loved children and she feared that one look at a tiny, helpless baby of her own, even one fathered by Ulvyn, would be her undoing. She had resolved not to look at it and to leave it to a wet nurse until she recovered her equilibrium.

All of this came to Gwynna's mind in an urgent rush when her water broke there on the dais, soaking the heavy brocade of her dress.

When the contractions, the fear, the pain, the pushing was over, a tiny boy nursed in Gwynna's arms just as she'd feared; his wispy white-blond hair let off the most delicious scent. "Little bit," she murmured, "you can't help what you are."

Ulvyn came to see his heir. He looked the baby over in delight, counting its fingers and toes and dandling it a while before handing it back to the birth attendant. "A strapping boy, my love! You've done well. I will name him for my father: Ennys." But Gwynna had already whispered the child's name in his tiny ear: Ardunn, a variation on "of Dunnoc," for her own father. Kellish tradition said his heart would then answer to that name and no other, despite what the world might call him.

"There is more news, lady wife," said Ulvyn. He sat down beside the bed and tried to take her hand, but she frowned and tucked it under the blankets. Ulvyn cleared his throat and composed his face. "Your father is dead. He died while you were giving birth. They tell me it was peaceful. He just stopped breathing and was gone."

A sharp pain hit her heart like the kick of a horse, and she gulped for air. She recovered her breath. "Leave me now." For once, he obliged her. Alone, she let her attendants see to the sleeping baby and turned her face to the wall. Her breasts ached—her whole body ached.

He'd been so sick. He hadn't been himself for two years at the least— since before he'd banished Tennoc—and if he'd understood what had happened to him she knew he would have wanted to die. He was still her father, and she grieved that he had not seen his grandson. Now he would be with her mother Hallia, and perhaps he might even be reconciled with Kenver and Lassanna in Harla's embrace.

More than three hundred miles to the south and east, Winter's Beginning brought a new wooden bridge on the River Cobb at Riverbend. It spanned the Cobb not far from where Tennoc and Hanni first crossed into Whitehorse more than a year before, within sight of Castle Crymavon. The Tremontines took only ten days to build it, and on Eddin's Day Tennoc led his armies across in broken cadence to the river's western shore. They marched without Tremont's contingent of Brothers; Farr's priests declined battle between kingdoms. A pity, but it meant he would not be facing Kellish Brothers in return.

Tennoc's magic drained away as soon as he'd crossed halfway over the bridge, but he paid it little mind; he'd fought every battle in the past without magic, and no battle would be fought today. They found but a small contingent of soldiers at Riverbend who surrendered after a half-hearted rattling of swords.

Tennoc met with the town's leaders to assure them there would be no looting; the army would take only its forage and no plunder. If farmers and merchants tried to resist, the Tremontines would regrettably kill them and their families, and seize everything they owned rather than the customary tenth. When he spoke to them gently but firmly in Kellish the Riverbenders smiled and bowed as if they accepted his supremacy already; Tennoc was a Kell as far as they were concerned.

Flickers of power licked at his skin again as he rode his horse among his men; he'd gained the land's allegiance here. Teacher said no one really understood how, but the land always knew whose blood line ruled it. Sometimes it seemed to choose a blood line based on brute force, sometimes based on stewardship. Thinking of Teacher made Tennoc wish the counselor was nearby; he needed good advice. Tennoc once loved Kellen, but now his instincts told him to kill every noble, wipe out every soldier he captured. Vengeance tugged at him, begging to be unleashed.

Fallik of Whitehorse reined in his horse beside Tennoc. "Mean you to besiege Crymavon, sire?"

Tennoc looked down the River Cobb to Castle Crymavon. "Not if I don't have to," he answered. "My mother's cousin Flaryn is the lady of the castle, or was—I hear Dunnoc has been busy trying to purge my relations. I recall Lady Flaryn's husband as quite devoted, but I wonder if he's done away with her to avoid trouble. My great-uncle at Brunsial has been under siege for the better part of a year."

"It'll take a few weeks to march a division down to his aid, if you intend it."

"Uncle Williard's a canny old man. He'll hang on until we get there—or more likely, until the besieging army is called back to defend Gwyrfal. Now let's go talk to my cousin, shall we?" Tennoc tapped his horse, and the armies advanced on Castle Crymavon.

When Tennoc arrived at the castle's gates, Lady Flaryn's husband had already thrown them open. "I saw your forces long before you got here, Tennoc ar Sial," said Cror ar Crymavon, "and I couldn't have defended against your war machines had I wished to."

Tennoc smiled, but he drew his lips flat. "You're wise, cousin. In my current humor I am not countenancing resistance."

Lady Flaryn ar Crymavon still lived. In her own court, the cousin Tennoc's mother had remembered as painfully shy had blossomed into an assured woman, still beautiful and like enough to Lassanna that Tennoc's heart ached at the sight of her. "Why did you not stop here in your flight from Gwyrfal, cousin?" she asked him in Kellish at dinner that night.

"I was unsure of my welcome, Lady."

"You are Clan Sial. Never doubt your welcome among your kinsmen, King of Tremont or no—especially now, after what Dunnoc has done to my dear cousin Lassa." Flaryn squeezed his hand, and her eyes welled. "I loved her, Tennoc."

"We all did," added her husband.

"What are they saying?" murmured Fallik in Tremontine.

Tennoc swallowed hard and stuffed his grief down harder. "Lady Flaryn tells us we are welcome here," he answered in pointed Old Sairish.

Cror cleared his throat and apologetically switched tongues to Old Sairish so that the Tremontines might understand him. "The King is quite ill, Tennoc. Some say he will not last out the year, but I know from sad experience that the shaking sickness can take years to kill someone. One of my liegemen died of it. It took ten years from start to finish, and Dunnoc started shaking no more than four years ago. Were you to take Kellen, now would be the time, while the country's magic is tied up in a debilitated body. Cousin, I will be blunt—I'm a plain-spoken man. Is this a simple raid? I cannot believe it is, seeing the armies at your back. You are here to take the country, yes?"

Tennoc paused. He'd turned the question over in his own mind for some time. His other lords and generals believed they were to conquer the

whole country, but he wanted Gwynna and revenge, and he chafed at prov-
ing the slanders against him. He would be revenged upon Daevys ar Ulvyn
and his allies, and Dunnoc himself, but who would succeed to the throne?
No Kellish lord seemed strong enough to hold the country together.

The Corrish might sweep down from the north. The Ulav Mountains
stood between Corland and the Duchy of Whitehorse, but only the Bay of
Kellen separated them from Kellen itself; were the Corrish to take northern
Kellen, they would then have a western border with Tremont as well. They'd
find the River Cobb far easier to cross than the Ulavs. For that matter, the
Sairish might come back to Maalig and take back all of Trefhallyn.

Tennoc wasn't altogether sure he wanted an independent Kellen. More
and more, Kellen seemed rightfully his, payment for the deaths of Lassanna
and Kenver. His hold on the violence within him slipped.

Tennoc examined the lord of the castle. Cror ar Crymavon was an
open-faced older man with little gray in his blond hair: vigorous, with
strong, shrewd blue eyes. "If I took the country, would you support me?"
said Tennoc.

"Would you leave Clan Crymavon be?"

"Have you no desire for the throne yourself?"

Lord Cror waved away the thought. "Never have I wanted more than
what I have, and to pass on what I have to my sons."

"So I might count on you to bend your knee to Tremont and come with
me on campaign against Dunnoc."

"Not bend my knee to Tremont," said Crymavon, pointing at him. He
spoke again in Kellish. "To *you*, as king of Kellen as well as Tremont. We are
kinsmen through my wife, and you are more fit to rule Kellen than Dunnoc
or any who might succeed him—especially Ulvyn. I would want two things:
assurances Clan Crymavon would remain unmolested...and that our, uh,
tradition of tax-free trading across the border into Whitehorse would remain unmolested as well," he grinned.

"O ho, my smuggling kinsman," said Tennoc, answering his grin.

"What does he say?" murmured Fallik in Tremontine again.

"He says he will follow me," answered Tennoc.

"That's good," said Fallik. "I like him."

"I like you too," smiled Cror in barely accented Tremontine. Tennoc
burst out laughing. Fallik scowled, but Cror kept refilling the Whitehorser's
cup until the scowl disappeared.

Tennoc took his armies north along the River Cobb toward Gwyrfal,

Crymavon's men joining the expedition. The Kellish towns and castles along the way were caught unawares and lightly defended. Some surrendered outright to the Hero of Maalig, others after a brief skirmish; a few chose to fight to the last. The fierce battles at the coal mines of Baltha ended in the fortress's taking, and the slaughter of Clan Baltha's men. The women and girls would be taken back into Tremont to be indentured with the other noblewomen whose clans had refused to surrender; the prices they fetched would pay for the war. Tennoc showed mercy; they would not be sold to brothels or as menials, and their terms would be kept short. When he returned he would marry them off to his own nobles to secure them in their new Kellish holdings. After indenture, the women would be grateful when they might have resisted before. They should consider themselves lucky to be alive; his mother was dead.

Tennoc's power was returning, sometimes in tiny lappings, sometimes in thick white waves; it advanced and retreated in rhythm with his victories. Gradually, Kellen was giving itself to him. Tennoc was not surprised when a scouting expedition came pelting back from the north: The Kellish armies were on the move, under Daevys ar Ulvyn and Bryth ar Brennow.

"Why would they come out from Gwyrfal?" said Fallik of Whitehorse, stabbing a hard finger at the map spread atop a camp table before Tennoc. "It's a well-defended city, thick-walled, supplied with water and open to resupply from its harbor. It would take us spokes to outfit ships to blockade Gwyrfal, if even we could. They could hold out for years."

"Not against magic," said Tennoc.

"Magic?" chuckled Crymavon. "Dunnoc has the magic here, not that he's able to use it. You're not in Tremont. You're in Kellen, cousin."

"And Kellen is in *me*, cousin." Tennoc flicked his finger. The map lifted into the air, rolled into a tube and stuffed itself back into its case. Tennoc smiled at Crymavon's blank face. "The land knows me. The ground we have taken has added itself to Tremont. When we move on to land that still recognizes the old Kellish bloodline I will lose my magic again, but here, now, at Balta I have my full power. If Dunnoc cannot fight, we will have an advantage in more than numbers."

"I still don't understand why he'd send his armies from Gwyrfal," said Fallik.

"Dunnoc and Ulvyn must feel Kellen's magic draining away. They'll want to meet me out here, before I take more land. He'll be wanting to lure me away from here to a place he still holds. I'll be wanting to stay put."

"So we stay put?"

"More or less."

Tennoc re-established contact with Teacher, who came by reflection to hold council. "You cannot rely upon me, for the magic will ebb and flow," said Teacher. "If the land leaves Tremontine control, I will be taken back to the Keep."

Tennoc sat back in the former Duke of Baltha's heavy throne, dragged from its dais to the table's head. "You would leave me?"

"It would be involuntary, I assure you. I will simply vanish, and it will take time for me to return even after you re-establish control. I must stay on Tremontine soil. Wherever you have magic, I may be. Wherever you do not have magic, I may not be. Just be prepared to fight without me and without your magic."

"Every battle I've ever fought has been with my hands, not magic," said Tennoc. "I don't trust it yet."

"Oh, you must use it at some point. Dunnoc will, and Ulvyn will use what little he has as well," said Fallik of Whitehorse.

As they spoke, Tennoc practiced delicate magical work, sending an apple zipping through the air around various obstacles. "If ground is in dispute, certainly we will both be without our magic at some point?" he said, keeping Teacher in the corner of his eye.

Teacher nodded. "And then do kings rely on their armies."

Crymavon motioned for his goblet to be refilled and took a long drink. "Shall we force them into siege?"

"No," said Tennoc. "Baltha is not easily defended against magic, and Ulvyn would surely retake the surrounding land's allegiance for Dunnoc if we retreated to the castle. We will go out to meet him, but not over-far. The valley just to the north, probably."

Fallik scratched his beard. "Do we know what forces Ulvyn is fielding?"

"Infantry and longbowmen," said Crymavon, nervously watching the apple careen through the room.

"We haven't faced Kellish longbowmen yet. What do we know of their skill?" said Fallik.

Hanni spoke from his position behind Tennoc's chair. "I, Hanni der Geelt, trained many."

"Meaning what?" said Fallik.

"Meaning they're deadly," answered Tennoc. "With apologies to my old friend, it matters only so much. We have numbers on our side across the field, and heavy cavalry as well. The advantage is ours." He brought the apple flying across the room in a blur of red and green to his hand.

The Tremontines met the Kells at Forchyll Valley, where Tennoc discovered his enemy had fielded far more men than expected; they now outnumbered the Tremontines almost two to one. Dunnoc—or Ulvyn, there was no more pretending that Dunnoc ruled any more—had obviously been preparing for war and had already called in mercenaries from the Western Isles and even Kellen's enemy Corland; mercenaries considered gold their only allegiance.

While Kellen fielded longbowmen, Tremont relied on a newer technology: the crossbow. Its range was almost as great as a longbow, but at longer distances its accuracy was not as good. On the other hand, if a crossbowman fell a spearman could take his place; anyone could fire a crossbow, but it took strength and skill to use a longbow. Ulvyn's advantage in numbers would in part be taken up protecting those archers. Tennoc knew from his own days fighting for Kellen that a shield wall would protect the vulnerable archers the entire battle; he had to breach it.

Tennoc stood on a slight prominence watching the Kells approach the wide expanse of the triangular Forchyll Valley. Snow lay in plentiful white caps on low mountains extending to the west in a double rank, making a wide pocket. A smaller mountain stood alone to the east as if guarding the valley. The trick would be to force the Kells into that pocket, stopper the entrance—and keep from getting trapped themselves.

Tennoc blew on his cold fingers, willing his magic to let the warmth penetrate his gloves; with a little more skill he could have risked heating his gauntlets, but now the chances of burning himself were still too high. Steam rose from his horse's nostrils; he could almost imagine the steam coming off the horses at the mouth of the pocket, where Fallik lay in wait with the main force of cavalry.

He should have deferred the campaign until spring. Tennoc's anger had gotten the better of him. He'd always thought of himself as peaceable. He laughed bitterly to himself: *When presented with the severed heads of those he loves, apparently a man is driven to anger.*

Tennoc breathed on his gloved hands again, but this time his magic didn't work; it flickered like a candle flame in a drafty hall. Teacher had already vanished back to Tremont Keep. Tennoc wondered if Ulvyn's magic was as unreliable. In any event, a Kellish prince's magic could not compare to a Tremontine King's. No matter. Magic wouldn't have to play into it. His battle plan avoided magic entirely.

The plan broke, as plans do and as Tennoc expected it would. Fallik's cavalry waited too long to charge the Kells, giving them time to set up the shield wall so familiar to Tennoc. The Tremontines had no such reliable protection. He gritted his teeth in frustration; he'd warned his cousin, but Fallik was both headstrong and unconvinced Tennoc knew his business despite their previous victories. Magic could puncture the shield wall, but Tennoc's power had deserted him again.

The Kellish archers launched flight after flight into his spearmen, cutting them down in their ranks. His crossbowmen's bolts rained down on the enemy, but they bounced off the wall of shields protecting the longbows. He cursed himself for using a weapon he knew little about himself, but crossbows were what the Tremontines had. It took years to train a longbowman. Tennoc swore the Tremontines would *become* longbowmen; he would kidnap babies from their cradles to train them up from childhood if he had to.

He sent word to Fallik not to move, but in vain: his cousin struck before the message reached him. Fallik had expected the bolts to soften the Kellish shield wall and so charged his men straight into a deadly barrage of arrows. The Tremontine cavalry, the pride of Whitehorse and the nation, fell back in disarray, some toward the protection of Tennoc's men in the south but a far larger contingent back the way they'd come to the west—straight into the pocket valley's mouth. A great cry arose from the Kells, and the shield wall broke. The Kellish sergeants urged their men to stay in formation, but the infantry behind the archers surged through in pursuit of the fleeing Tremontines, hoping to trap them in the pocket.

Tennoc cursed Fallik's impetuousness but blessed that of the Kells; he spurred his own cavalry detachment forward toward the opening. The reinforcements turned the retreating remnants of Fallik's men, who joined the foot soldiers behind the horses. Tennoc's cavalry cut straight into the Kellish infantry's open lines, killing vulnerable archers and foot soldiers alike. Fallik's men rallied and turned back from the pocket, trapping a mass of Kells between the Whitehorsers and the Tremontine infantry; Fallik was in the middle of the melee, still on his horse though he'd lost his lance.

An arrow struck Tennoc's horse and he went down—another cheer from the Kells. His men faltered until he rose, battle axe in hand, and charged into combat on foot. At times his magic surged, and he'd scatter enemies with a great burst of wind or batter them with a lethal barrage of stones. No flame burned on the field, or he would have thrown fire into the Kellish ranks. At times his magic failed him entirely, leaving him with just his axe.

So it went for nearly two grueling hours, Tennoc's magic rising and falling with the battle's flow, each pulse rejuvenating him, until a strong wind sent men bowling past him. Before him stood Daevys ar Ulvyn, its source. "All hail Temmin, Bastard of Tremont," he mocked.

Ulvyn shouldn't have been able to raise a wind that strong. Tennoc took in the device on his enemy's shield; a king's crown had been added to the Ulvyn coat of arms. Dunnoc was dead. He faced a King, not a Prince. His own magic was gone again, and he trembled on the edge of exhaustion.

"You look tired, Your Majesty," said Ulvyn.

"Comes of fighting instead of lounging about in the rear," answered Tennoc. Magic surged up through his feet, easing his fatigue; he held sway over the land on which he stood. Ulvyn raised his hands to his mouth again to summon the wind, but this time Tennoc expected the attack and raised a shield; the wind buffeted the solid air before him but could not break through. "King of Kellen you may be, but I am King of Tremont!" he bellowed. He blew through his hands and threw them outward; a shrieking wind flattened everything and everyone in its path. Ulvyn threw up a shield of his own, but it wavered under Tennoc's assault. Ulvyn's shock radiated back to him, and he bared his teeth.

Just then, victory cries rose from a Kellish battalion nearby; the banner of Whitehorse had fallen, and Fallik with it. He disappeared under an onslaught of Kells, each trying to get in a blow against the hated Tremontine Lord. Tennoc's own men held firm around him, though the Kells pushed fiercely in on them. Tennoc's magic vanished. He took a step back to find his dominance, and another, but his power did not return.

With each step back, Ulvyn advanced. "Have you heard? I have an heir now. Gwynna gave me a son on Eddin's Day. Propitious, don't you think, brother king?"

Tennoc stopped, as stunned as if Ulvyn had struck him. A son—a child that should have been his. A small boulder flew through the air; distracted, he ducked but it glanced his right shoulder. Numbness ghosted down his arm. He switched his battle axe to his left hand, flexing his right. "Eddin is sly, a trickster God. Don't rely on Him for your son's fortune."

"Which God rides with you today? Amma takes in by-blows, pray to Her for strength!"

"Pagg rides with me, to give me justice!" Tennoc roared. He charged; Ulvyn threw up a shield of air. Though his right arm still tingled, Tennoc took his axe in both hands and battered away. The shield shook with each blow, and Ulvyn turned pale with effort. He was older than Tennoc, just past his prime, and while he had more experience using magic he'd come into the bulk of it only in the last spoke. Magic began trickling into Tennoc's body again as he pounded at Ulvyn's shield. Rocks flew at him but dropped to the ground as they reached some invisible border. Ulvyn was losing his grip on the land's allegiance.

Power sang in Tennoc's blood now. He chose not to use it and kept hammering at the solid air surrounding his enemy like a bell, pushing Ulyvn back and back. "Do you feel your loss?" he yelled.

"Where's your gain?" panted Ulvyn; the air inside his shield was running low.

"I don't *need* magic to kill you!" The shield broke. Tennoc swung his axe once and sank it screaming into Ulvyn's skull.

Tennoc wrenched out his axe with a sickening, sucking sound and stood over the body. Gore and brains dripped from the axe, and exhaustion overtook him. With the last of his magic, he raised Ulvyn's corpse over the battlefield and amplified his voice. "Daevys ar Ulvyn, the murderer of Prince Kenver, is dead!" he boomed in Kellish, so loudly a faint echo from the mountains reached him; men nearby shrieked and fell to the ground, covering their ears. "Kells, lay down your arms or die! Tremontines," he added in their language, "obey your King and spare any Kell who surrenders!"

Ulvyn's body crashed to the ground as Tennoc dropped his axe and fell to his knees. He held his shield before him in both hands, seeing his own battered reflection in the equally battered metal. It wavered, as he'd hoped it would; a pale, intent face filled it, and Teacher swirled from the shield. "I need you," said Tennoc. He passed out.

What Temmin hated most about leaving the book's spell was its lingering after-effects; the wounds, fear, hatred, even love and desire took time to dissipate and always left him confused and disoriented. "I'd wondered how magic worked in battles. I mean, if it were me, I'd just stand out front with you and let 'em have it. I guess it doesn't work that way."

"No," said Teacher, "otherwise we would own more of Inchar than we do. Your father has no magic in any event, and my magic has been greatly eroded over the centuries."

"Eroded? Eroded how?"

Teacher sighed. "The kings of Tremont are not always wise in their use of magic. There are magical defenses at Mallik—what was once Maalig—and the other major harbors such as Ouve and Esta. The Armor of the Tremontine Kings is enchanted to make it impenetrable. There are thousands of similar enchantments, some great and some small—and some quite petty. The stones of Marsury Field, for example, where Marsury Castle once stood."

"I *knew* that had to be magic!" exclaimed Temmin. "You can't stack one atop the other and that's hardly natural, is it?"

"It is my doing," Teacher nodded.

"Why is the enchantment still there?"

"Every time I suggest removing it I am told it is tradition, a monument to a dead king. Some day perhaps I shall tell you how it came to happen. So much of my magic is bound up in your family's pride—the Antremonts are a stiff-necked race. Pride is responsible for so many of your family's problems. I would not care but for the drain on my resources. Marsury is a small spell, but the small ones add up just as the big ones do. Every time I place such an enchantment the magic needed to create it stays tied to it. It is the same for any magic user. The magic is unavailable until it is either released or the magic user loses his magic. Or dies."

"So if *you* die…"

"The defenses at the harbors fall, the King's Armor can be breached, and men may once again stack the stones of Marsury one atop the other."

"But you can't die."

"Not yet. More I may not say, and do not ask further. 'May as well build with Marsury stone.'" The old saying raised a pale smile on Teacher's oddly sensual mouth.

Temmin returned the smile. "You still seem powerful—at least as powerful as you were in the stories I've seen."

"Remember, Tremont was much smaller then. Why do you think Tremont always seems to be at war?"

Temmin's mind turned to the battle he'd just experienced; Tennoc's power grew with every chunk of Kellen he wrested from Dunnoc. "To increase our access to magic."

"The quest for power drives most of the wars of this world, but our wars in particular. It is your dynasty's very basis, this lust for magic, and it is why Tremont is rarely if ever at peace."

Temmin scratched at the stubble of his mourning braid before he remembered his stitches. "But Tennoc went to war to avenge his mother and stepbrother, and to save Gwynna."

"Did he," said Teacher, replacing the book atop the study's lectern. "We will resume tomorrow."

Even with the book's dubious distraction, Temmin chafed at inactivity. "I think we'll return to the City sooner than later," he said to Jenks the next morning.

Jenks paused in the arrangement of Temmin's cravats in a wardrobe drawer; in the sitting room, a little crash announced Fen Wallek, clearing up the early tea. Jenks winced. "I thought we might stay a little longer, surely."

"No, I want to depart on the eleventh. That gives everyone a week to prepare. I'm sure Elly and Cousin Donnis will remain for the present, so I will be returning with you, Wallek, his wife if I can wrest her from Elly's clutches, Jebby and Alvo Nollson."

"You will, will you?" said Jenks, finishing with his fussing. "And how do you intend to get Alvo to come along? What happened between you and Alvo anyway? He's bordering rude these days."

Temmin grimaced and turned away, hoping Jenks didn't see his tell-tale cheeks. No amount of Lovers' Temple training so far had conquered his propensity to blush when it came to his personal business. "We...had a fight the night before I left two years ago, and apparently he's chosen not to forgive me."

"How do you intend to coax him into coming with you?"

He was Heir of Tremont and a Supplicant of the Lovers' Temple, that's how, he said to himself. "I'll figure it out, one way or another."

Suddenly Jenks strode into the bedchamber; a manly squeak and an "Oi!" followed, and Temmin hurried out to find Jenks in the doorway to the sitting room, his thumb and forefinger pinching Fen Wallek's freckled ear. Temmin folded his arms. "Oh?"

"Oh," growled Jenks. "An eavesdropper."

"I wasn' eavesdroppin!" said the outraged valet-in-training. "I was on-ly...I needed to tell you...all right, I was eavesdroppin!" Jenks gave his ear a last pinch and let go; Fen rubbed at it. "And I dunno if I want to go back to the Keep if it's all the same, sir."

"It isn't, and you will. Jenks is coming with me, and he tells me you're tethered to him. Therefore, you're coming. See if you can get Arta away from the nursery."

"She won' go, sir, I can tell you that now. She's stuck on the little Princess as much as she's stuck on our own babe. You'll never shift 'er, not without a team of oxen."

"Then you'll have to come alone and she'll join you when she's through," said Temmin. Jenks frowned, and Fen's face drooped, but Temmin would not relent; he wanted—no, needed—his people around him. "See to it, Jenks. Get things in motion." As he stalked away Jenks said, "Eavesdropping is part of the job! Get better at it, you spotted oaf!"

Temmin headed toward the stables for his morning ride. He'd been trying the gentle approach, encouraging Alvo to come to him rather than forcing the issue, but it had been almost two weeks. Temmin didn't have time to wait for Alvo to come around. He had to get behind him and push.

He found the stocky young man in Jebby's stall. "How fortuitous. My horse and my best friend, just the two I want. Fetch a horse, Alvy, we're going riding."

Alvo froze midway through taking off his cap. "Your Highness, I have work to do."

"Balls to that. Saddle up. This is not a request." Alvo stomped off. Sometimes, thought Temmin, a man must use the tools at his disposal, and rank was such a tool.

Soon they were trotting from the yards, Temmin on Jebby and Alvo on a stubborn-faced but obedient gray. Frost covered the ground this morning; it crackled under the horses' hooves. Neither man spoke as they broke into a canter and left the road, flying over the familiar pastures and meadows surrounding the Estate and its farms.

Temmin let their course set itself as he thought over what to say and soon discovered he'd pointed them at the old hill fortress rising up from the flattest part of the lands around the Estate. The lords of Whithorse had abandoned the Freehold long ago, though he remembered it from Tennoc's story as it was in its prime. Sheep grazed where its defenses once stood, the ramparts and ditches reduced to steeply rolling ridges around the great hill. The Freehold's enclosing walls had crumbled away; on the broad, flat hilltop could still be seen the stone fortress's faint remains. After a long gallop he reined in, and Alvo did the same.

A strained silence descended, as sharp and clear as the cold air. Temmin had been taught a dozen ways to breach such a silence, but none came to him now as they began the long circumnavigation of the great rise. He settled on pointed scrutiny—often a winner—and turned a steady gaze on his old friend.

Alvo could not be called handsome; compared to Senik and Issak he was coarse, lumpy and common. His broad face had lost the childish roundness still clinging to it just two years ago, his solid cheekbones and clean-shaven jaw sharp and his neck corded with muscle. His wide, round-tipped nose had grown a bit red in the chill. The dark hair under its habitual tweed cap had more the texture of hay than silk. His best feature—expressive, honest eyes the color of freshly turned earth—stayed focused on the horizon framed by the stubborn-faced gray's ears. Coarse and common it may have been, but Temmin loved Alvo's face beyond measure.

He pressed his lips together in frustration and abandoned his tactic. "Damn it, Alvy, I deserve better than this!"

"I didn't have to come, sir," rasped Alvo.

"The Hill you didn't. I have been waiting out your sulk since I got here. I have been patient and approachable, and now I'm done. You *will* talk to me, Alvo Nollson."

"Very well, sir," Alvo answered in an even, servile voice. "My sister's husband tells me the lambing is going well, sir—"

Temmin dug his heels into Jebby's sides, rode ahead and cut Alvo off. "Hang the lambs, damn you!"

Alvo stopped, though he could have easily walked around the big chestnut blocking his way. His obstinate mouth gave a tell-tale quiver. "I shouldn't think hanging 'em is good for 'em, would you, sir?" he said, suppressed laughter in his tone.

A great grin spread over Temmin's face. "Hang whether it's good for 'em!" The two men broke out in boyish guffaws, tension driving laughter greater than the small joke was worth until tears streamed from their eyes. Temmin brought himself close facing the other direction and reached out his hand. "Oh, Alvy, how I've missed you."

"And I you, Tem," said Alvo, quietly taking it.

"I'm leaving for the City on the eleventh. I want you to come back with me."

Alvo dropped his hand. "To the Keep? What for? You're at the Temple still."

"For three more spokes. You can find something to do there for three more spokes."

"And then what? Oh, no. If I'm going to be currying horses I'd rather do it here, where I'm known and respected, instead of in a stable where I'll get treated like a rustic stooge."

"No one would dare treat you like a rustic stooge. Alvy, you're the closest thing I have to a brother." Tennoc and Kenver came to mind. "You *are* my brother. With things the way they are and me leaving the Temple soon I have no one and nothing but you."

"You have your sisters."

"Sedra's engagement will be announced as soon as mourning for Mama is over. And you've seen Elly. I don't think she's quite right in the head at present, and besides, she intends to stay here with the baby."

"What about Jenks? And that Wallek character?"

Temmin grimaced. "Jenks…that's complicated, and Fen's a good sort of fellow but he's not you."

"There's your father—"

"We hardly know one another!"

"Then start!" said Alvo. "You're lucky to have a father." He tapped the gray's sides and started off again around the Freehold at a slow walk.

Temmin followed after him. "I need you. No one else knows me as well as you do. I need you to help me stay myself. You were right, the City is changing me—and not all in bad ways—but you were wrong, too. I'll never forget my best friend and they can never keep us apart. Alvo, please." He rode far enough ahead to seize the gray's bridle, bringing them both to a halt. "My last night here before I moved away, you begged me. Now I'm begging you. Come back to the Keep with me. Be my rock."

Alvo stared at Temmin's stirrup. "I don't know if I can be near you knowing you like…that's it's not just women you like," he murmured.

"I honestly don't know about sex with me and you," said Temmin, releasing the gray's bridle. "I need more than that from you. Sex—I can get that anywhere. I can't get brothers anywhere."

"The Heir can't be brothers with a groom anyway."

Temmin smirked. "You won't be a groom. I'm making you my Master of Horse."

Alvo met his eyes in astonishment. "The Heir's Master of Horse? At the *Keep*?" he cried, pleased in spite of himself. He recovered his equilibrium. "You can't be brothers with your Master of Horse, either."

"Alvo Nollson, are you angling for a knighthood?"

Alvo's face dropped in horror. "No!"

"Because I can't give you one for at least thirty years if Amma blesses the King with long life—and here's hoping. I'm in no hurry to rule." Even the notion of his father's death brought his mother's to mind and his eyes welled, but now was not the time to indulge in grief. He laughed and dashed the tears away with the back of his glove. "The cold makes my eyes water. Listen, one thing I've learned about being the Heir is that despite all the official nonsense I can mostly do as I please. Especially compared with Temple life. Good Gods, I'll never complain again. So if I want to be best friends with my Master of Horse I'm bloody well going to be."

Pain colored Alvo's face. "You're asking something very selfish, Tem, do you even know that? You're asking me to go with you, with no hope for the future—to love you with nothing in return—"

"Will you love me if you stay here?"

"I'll always love you," Alvo said with a simplicity that drew Temmin's heart from his body.

"Then love me at the Keep. I can't give you the answer you want about more than brotherhood right now. Love and sex—you'd think my time at the Temple would have helped me understand the ways in which they're different and the same, but Gods help me if it has. I need you. Please come back with me."

Alvo contemplated the chalk horse carved into the hill rising far across the flat fields around the ruined fortress, his thoughts clear on his broad countenance as he weighed life at Whithorse—achingly far from the man he loved—versus life at the Keep—close by, but possibly filled with its own suffering. Temmin's heart tumbled as the winner became clear: "No." Alvo wheeled his horse around and uttered a curt "Gidyap!" The gray shot off across the wide plains toward the hillocks surrounding the Estate.

Temmin let him go. The wind grew colder, though the strengthening sun stood higher in the sky.

Pagg's balls.

FIFTEEN

Temmin brooded in his study, saying little to either the nervous Fen as he juggled the luncheon service or Jenks when he came to check on his disciple's work. "What did he do to put you in a mood, sir?" said Jenks.

"What did who do—Wallek? Nothing. He's fine." Fen exhaled and dropped a fork. "A little less scrutiny, Jenks," smiled Temmin, rising from the table. "It's no wonder he's dropping things with you breathing down his neck."

Jenks propelled the trainee and the luncheon cart out the door. "Sir, if you need me—for anything—just ring. *I* will answer the summons."

"I'll be all right, Jenks. Teacher will be here soon to whisk me off into his fairy tales." Jenks lifted his eyebrows but continued into the hall and closed the door behind him.

Temmin thrust his hands into his pockets. He stood with his back to the hearth, the tails of his coat over his arms, and rubbed the Inchari rug's pile with the toe of his boot, a long-standing habit. Watching the color and luster of velvet, carpet—anything with a pile—change as he pushed it one way and then the other gave him something to stare at while his mind worked on things. Alvo was his most immediate concern, but the second and much larger was whether he'd learned anything at all at the Lovers' Temple.

To be sure, he now knew ways to handle almost everyone, to read their telltale body language and expressions well enough that he might match his words and actions to their needs, for their good or his own, but when it came to anyone close to him, he failed. He struggled to remain composed and unreadable around them and while he often knew their deeper states of mind, he didn't always know what to do about them. He always knew what Alvo was thinking. Anyone could see what Alvo was thinking. He hadn't known Alvo loved him, true, but that was two years ago, when he couldn't see past his own nose. He couldn't bring Alvo round his thumb any more, though; thinking on their strained conversation at the hill fortress, he cursed himself for his clumsiness, his tactlessness, his complete lack of technique. Mathanus Postulant could have done a better job of persuasion.

It wasn't just Alvo. Allis flummoxed him down to his bootlaces. He never knew what *she* was thinking or what she wanted from him unless she chose to tell him. Granted, she was the Embodiment of a Goddess and had been training to read and not be read for more than ten years now, but as well as he knew her and loved her, he should know her heart by now. She must know his. Everyone must know his. When it came to those he deeply loved, he was as transparent as Alvo Nollson.

He'd lost the last year of his mother's life only to fail as a Supplicant.

"You look introspective this afternoon, Your Highness," said Teacher's cool voice at the bedchamber door.

"I suppose I am," said Temmin as the advisor entered the room to stand before the fire. "I am wondering if I did the right thing in taking Supplicancy. I don't seem very good at it."

Teacher's brows raised. "The Most Highs and senior clergy tell me you are doing rather well. Your petitioners are grateful, and your fellow clergy respect you. What makes you think otherwise?"

Temmin scuffed at the carpet again until a sudden awareness that he looked like an eight-year-old made him stop. "I suppose I read people well, and I like them in general—I want to help, I like helping, and yes, all right, people seem to think I've helped them," he said, thinking of poor Meggan Esterill among many others. "But it only seems to work with relative strangers, or people I know and don't really care about—no, that's not right!" He didn't scuff so much as kick at the hearth rug. "If truth be known—and I say this to you because you've never betrayed me—it's like this. The more I…I love someone, the less devotional I get. I lose my way, I can't use what I've learned, I can't veil my heart, I can't stop feeling things I'm not supposed to feel!"

"Emotions are neither right nor wrong, Your Highness. It is what we do in their grip that is right or wrong."

"So they keep telling me, but it's not true. There are things we're not supposed to feel for one another at the Temple."

"Such as?"

Temmin flicked a guilty glance at Teacher and settled his eyes back on the fine wool scrollwork beneath his feet. Unlike most people, Temmin trusted more than feared Teacher. He could never have become a Supplicant without Teacher, who could have betrayed him any number of times but never had. "I am in love with someone."

"Loving someone is not impermissible at the Temple, surely."

"Loving someone in this way is."

"Ah. Exclusive love. What have your superiors told you?"

"To seek pleasure and affection elsewhere. I have tried, believe me—I'm never at a loss for either. But..." He trailed off, watching the flowers on the rug lean first to one side and then to the other beneath his toe.

"Does the object of your affection encourage you in your love?"

"No, oh no. At least—sometimes I think she might. But she is the hardest to read of all, she's so very good at what we do, so sympathetic and compassionate, but that's hardly surprising, I suppose."

"No, it is not."

Temmin realized he'd given himself away and took his hands from his pockets. "Teacher, you must say nothing, please, I beg you."

"No one knows you love Allis?"

"*Everyone* knows!" cried Temmin, taking up a path before the fire. "Everyone *must* know! She knows, Senik knows, Issak knows, Anda knows, the Most Highs know."

"That does not mean 'everyone' knows."

"*You* knew."

"You made it quite clear who you meant."

Temmin shook his head in irritation and scrubbed at one eye until he realized he was back to being eight again. "Well. Allis began avoiding me, and I hoped it would help but it hurt so much I couldn't bear it. Then right after last Nerr's Day the Most High Beloved lectured me on it, and I did as she told me. I took many lovers, I redoubled my efforts with petitioners and I became especially diligent in my devotions. I thought I was getting better but then Mama died and now it's getting worse and I don't know what to do. I pray and pray, but They don't seem to want to help me."

"And Allis?"

"I'm fairly certain Allis sent me here." Temmin stopped his pacing, pulled a chair close to the fire, sat down and put his feet up on the fender, though his right foot kept up a nervous rhythm that sent his knee jiggling up and down. "I don't know what that means."

"Did you not want to come home?"

"No. Yes. Merciful Amma! I just want some peace!" Temmin pressed the heels of his palms into his eyes. "But *you're* here," he said in a quick exhalation. "Did Tennoc find peace?"

"Kings are never at peace," answered Teacher.

"That's why I don't understand why everyone wants to be king, though it's dawning on me that princes have no peace, either."

"Princes and paupers all find peace elusive, Your Highness."

Temmin sat back in his chair. "Well then, go ahead, read on." Teacher opened the book, and the story began again.

Tennoc awoke alone in his pavilion the next day. He'd been stripped of his armor and bloodied clothing, and lay naked on his cot under blankets and furs. A small camp stove burned nearby warming the winter air; on its hob a can of water heated. He found a towel and scrubbed dirt and blood from his body; goosebumps rose on his wet skin. He dressed in clean clothes, placed a gold circlet set with ruby cabochons upon his head and a fur-lined cloak around his shoulders, and walked outside. Men huddled near fires came to attention as Tennoc passed. He ignored them and left the camp.

Tennoc found Teacher on the rise overlooking the battlefield. Sisters and Friends both Kellish and Tremontine who'd followed their respective armies moved among the dead and wounded. Scavengers human and animal had already moved in as well, gathering weapons, armor and—in the case of the animals—flesh from the dead. Kellish prisoners were digging three large trenches to use as graves; there would be no time to get bodies to Hills before they began to stink. One trench would hold Tremontines, another Kells, and a third the mercenaries who'd fallen; once the victor had become clear, the Western Islanders and Corrishmen had fled northward.

Soldiers were trundling up to each trench with carts full of the dead; they dumped them in, Friends sprinkled salt water over them in lieu of their final baths, and the prisoners shoveled dirt atop them. In a few years the

Friends would return to take the bones back to Hills in each country. They would be with their comrades not their families, but their spirits would find rest. As long as one bone, even one tooth, rested in a Hill, so could a man's spirit.

"Where is Fallik of Whitehorse?" said Tennoc.

"Alas, we have not found him, Your Majesty," said Teacher. "I suspect there is nothing left to find. The Kells hated him—many were his incursions across the border. We found his banner and have set it aside to return to Whitehorse and Lord Gonnor. We must hope some of Fallik's bones will find their way into a Hill. However, we have found the bodies of fifteen Kellish lords, including Daevys ar Ulvyn and Bryth ar Brennow."

"Have they been buried?"

"No, sire. The men wished to do to them what had been done to Lord Fallik. I set a watch on them as I was unsure what *you* wished to do."

"Take me to them."

The bodies had been respectfully laid out on the ground, each man stripped of his armor and arranged on his back, his weapon atop his chest and his arms crossed over it. A cloth covered Ulvyn's split head. Atop Ulvyn's sword rested the battle crown of the Kells, now a mangled piece of metal; Tennoc's axe had nearly destroyed it. He picked up the twisted band. Some of the pearls, blue lapiz and jet set in the gold had been knocked out. It had been Dunnoc's crown, and the crown of many kings before him. Now it was Tennoc's. He handed it to Teacher. "Can you repair it?"

"Oh yes. What do you wish to do? Shall we bury the lords with the rest of the Kells?"

"No." Tennoc called for soldiers; he ordered the men to gather up the dead lords' weapons and banners, and set them aside.

"What are you going to do?" said Teacher. Tennoc gave no answer but ordered the soldiers to stack the bodies in a pile. "Your Majesty, what do you intend?" Teacher asked again.

Tennoc looked back at the camp and found what he was looking for: a cooking fire. He snatched at it, and flames rose in his hands. He swept his arms wide. Magic came easily now after the battle, and fire erupted in a wide arc between his hands. He threw it outward and it rushed at the bodies; the stack burst into flame and soon a sweet stench turned his stomach. "Not a single bone, a single tooth will I leave," he said in a dark voice that sounded alien even to himself. "They can wander the earth forever for what they've done."

"Their spirits may haunt you," said Teacher.

"Their deeds haunt me already."

When the fire finished its work and Tennoc dismissed it, he stirred the ashes with his foot; he found not a single scrap of tooth or bone. He walked away and left the rest of the dead to the Friends, but the weight on his heart remained. Perhaps when he reached Gwynna it would all be over and he might begin to live for more than death.

The towns and cities approaching Gwyrfal were almost glad to see the Tremontines, for the mercenaries fleeing the Forchyll Valley had overrun many of them. Tennoc made sure to go into each one with Cror ar Cryma-von and Teacher beside him to speak with the townsmen. Only once did a town resist him; he killed its men singlehandedly and sent the women and children into permanent indenture. He let enough of them escape to spread the word: this powerful new ruler showed mercy if you obeyed him but none otherwise. No resistance came after that.

"The ones responsible for your mother's murder are dead," said Teacher in a gentle voice. "You cannot hold all of Kellen responsible."

Tennoc scowled at his advisor. "Do you question my actions?"

"I wonder at your ferocity."

"*I* wonder at my forbearance."

"Your actions make a point," said Teacher, "but it is not the point I would have you make."

"Which is?"

"That life under your rule will be better than it was before."

"It will be, but only if they obey me. That is *my* point."

Gwyrfal surrendered without a struggle as soon as Tennoc approached its walls. He rode through the gates, Hanni at his side, just as they had left the city almost two years before. "Mean you first to find our Gwynna, sire?" said Hanni as they rode through the city they'd once called home.

"I have to find Ulvyn's heir first," Tennoc replied.

"We will find the child with our Gwynna, no?"

Tennoc paused. "Perhaps." But he hoped not for her sake.

"What will you do, Lady?" said one of Gwynna's attendants as they looked out over the Tremontine armies gathered before the city. It seemed to Gwynna they went on past the horizon. Daevys must be dead, or else his forces so broken up that he could not regroup. If Daevys lived, Tennoc would hunt him down. She was or would soon be a widow, free to make her own choices.

She could not see the march into the city, but she knew Tennoc would come to claim her father's throne, and possibly herself. Nothing stopped them from marrying now—in fact, everything was in favor of it. But would it still be his wish? It had been a little over a spoke since she'd birthed another man's child, after all. Had he heard? Perhaps he'd already married Cariodas, if she'd lived to reach Tremont City. She'd always been his intended, after all. Cariodas, riding out of Gwyrfal dragging her father behind her: perhaps a girl as brave as that would make him a better wife. "I will prepare to meet our conqueror, is what I shall do," Gwynna said in the end.

"Should you not continue in mourning, ma'am?" said the attendant as she helped spread out the violet gown that set off the young Queen's eyes so.

Gwynna hesitated. She would never wear mourning for Daevys. Official mourning for her father hadn't ended, but she had a purpose beyond propriety. "No. I shall meet Tennoc in colors."

When Tennoc strode into the Great Hall, Gwynna stood on the dais, her dozen ladies deliberately arrayed around her, all but her dressed in black. They mourned not for Dunnoc or Ulvyn but for their husbands; these ladies were the wives of the lords who'd fought against Tennoc at Forchyll, and now they wept for their lives and those of their children.

Tennoc approached in light armor and no helm; lords both Tremontine and Kellish followed at his back. On his head rested the battle crown of Kellen. He'd changed in the two years they'd been apart; his blue eyes beneath their straight brows were still bright, but now held a feverish, frightening look that almost made Gwynna quail. His boyish face had gone hard, he'd added muscle to his once-slender frame, and his movements, while still graceful, were no longer those of a man who loved dancing as much as battle. Her gentle lover was gone. Only the soldier was left, and she was afraid of him.

"Princess—*Queen* Gwynna," said Tennoc. He stopped before the dais but did not bow.

Gwynna held up a hand as if to ward him off. "Your Majesty, before we proceed I must beg a favor from you, a very great favor."

Tennoc stopped mid-approach. "Ask it, you know you may have anything from me," he said in a softer voice than his face would have led her to expect.

Her heart warmed again and her fear retreated. "These ladies around me are the widows of the men who fought against you. I beg you to grant clemency to them and to their children. This war was none of theirs."

Tennoc frowned. "You ask a great deal. Perhaps I shall spare the women, but any boys—"

"If they are now alive, it is clear they did not fight against you," insisted Gwynna.

"I cannot let them live to fight against me later," he said.

Gwynna descended from the dais, holding out both hands. "What if they swear on their swords that you are their king? What if they kneel to you in Pagg's Temple and swear, if they're too young to have their swords yet? You said you would not deny me, Tennoc. As we both loved my brother, do not deny me this. Spare my ladies and all their children. Let those who swear allegiance to you live unmolested. Take the males into Tremont as captives if you must, but spare them from indenture and foster them among your lords instead—raise them as you were raised here at Gwyrfal."

"As I was raised?" Tennoc's mouth twisted. "Are so many Kells bastards, then?"

Now Gwynna's anger rose. "Until my father became ill you were treated the same as Kenver and I were, Tennoc, and you cannot say otherwise." She paused, thinking of the many slights he'd endured. "Those who ill-treated you are dead, yes?"

Tennoc nodded. "You are a widow, ma'am."

"I am glad of it," she spit as a grim joy filled her. "I am heartily glad of it. Your enemies are dead, and so you must show mercy and forgive these ladies their husbands' folly. Swear to me you will spare them, and…" She blushed. "And nothing of King Dunnoc's will be denied to you."

He took her hands. "Nothing will be denied to me in any event," he said in a low voice. "Nevertheless," he added for all to hear, "I will grant your boon. These ladies and their children shall remain unmolested, but their sons young and old must come to Pagg's Temple and swear allegiance to me. Any above age seven will be taken back to Tremont as you suggest but will not be indentured. If they themselves fought against me there will be no mercy, and if they fight against me in future I will wipe their houses from this earth, down to the last girl child. I am sworn." At this, the ladies in black wept anew in grief and gratitude; one fainted, but her fellows caught her before she slumped to the ground.

Most of her ladies meant little to Gwynna; some had been real friends, but most acted as Daevys's spies. Even so, the guilt belonged to their husbands and she did not wish them dead. Besides, granting her request proved Tennoc had changed without but remained the same within: an honorable man, merciful, kind-hearted and good, the man she and her brother had always loved. She knew what happened to the houses that stood against him;

sparing the greatest of them proved he would do anything for her. She had no fear now that when she asked for mercy for her son it would be granted.

Gwynna removed the crown from her head. "Then I swear allegiance to you as King of Kellen and Tremont." She gave the circlet into his hands and made a low curtsey. He took her hand and raised her up; though her hand was steady, his trembled.

Air came back into the room. The servants began setting out the tables for the banquet to come. Formalities concluded, the assembly mingled and chattered among themselves; Gwynna's ladies retired to their grief.

Tennoc held Gwynna's hand in a strong, almost painful grip. "You will wear this crown again, you know, Gwynna," he said, his voice low and shaking. "You are all I have left. I will come to you tonight."

She blushed, terrified and exhilarated at the same time. "I wait on your pleasure, Your Majesty. I—I must attend to things now." He released her hand reluctantly.

The deposed Queen shocked the company when she next sought out Yellow Hanni among the attendants in the back of the room. He was much more weatherbeaten, though it had been just two years since she'd seen him last, and looked as troubled as she felt. Gray was just beginning to creep into his bright yellow hair. She embraced her old minder and kissed his cheek, whispering into his ear, "Has he changed so much?"

"Child of mine heart, he is broken," Hanni murmured in return. "To you it will fall to mend him."

Gwynna kept Hanni's words in mind as she waited for Tennoc that night in her bower. When he came to her, he'd taken his armor off, as well as Dunnoc's crown. He wore simple clothes and looked like her own Tennoc instead of the frightening Tremontine stranger in the Great Hall. They exchanged formal pleasantries until Gwynna excused her attendants and they were alone. "Oh, Tennoc, I am so *very* happy to see you well," she began, but before she'd taken more than a step toward him he'd crossed the space between them and seized her.

He had never touched her like this, never touched her at all apart from a surreptitious clasp of her hand as he helped her dismount and the like. His grip hurt her arms. She had time for one gasp before he pressed his mouth to hers as if he needed her breath as well as his own. She thought of drowning men who took their rescuers down with them, but she opened her mouth to him; he whimpered into it. "Gwynna," he choked as he kissed her neck, her cheeks, her eyes. "Oh, my Gwynna." Tennoc lifted her up in his arms and hurried into her bedchamber, where he set her on her feet and began forcing open the fastenings of her dress.

Gwynna stiffened. She had wanted this for so long; she had cried when Daevys and not Tennoc had been the first to unfasten her dress. This, however, was too quick for her. "Tennoc, my own love, please, calm yourself."

His hands slid down the thin chemise covering the bare skin of her back, but his movements slowed. "Just to touch you calms me," he said and kissed her again, this time more deliberately. "Tell me you love me."

"I do, I always have, but…" She'd given birth not long before; should she even be contemplating this? But to mention the birth was to remind him Ardunn was Daevys's son.

"Are you concerned I won't marry you?" he said, an unbelieving laugh in his voice. "You know I will. I would marry you tomorrow, tonight, this minute, but you deserve more than a sleepy Father and a string for a marriage cord." Gwynna's glance flicked before she could stop herself to the elaborately braided cord that had bound her to Daevys, still hanging over her bedchamber door. Tennoc turned his head, saw it himself and released her. He reached out his hand; the cord whipped across the room to him. "You don't need this any more." A ball of flame blossomed in his other hand; he dropped the cord into it and sent the resulting ashes into the fire warming her room. "Is that your trouble?"

Gwynna blanched at his display of magic; she was unused to it in his hands. Her father and brother had used it, certainly, but not so nonchalantly. Without its fastenings Gwynna's heavy dress kept slipping from her shoulder; in irritation she gave up adjusting it and simply held it there. "You… you know I bore a child, yes?" He nodded, his face clouded. "It's been just six weeks. I'm not sure…I should ask the Sisters…"

"Oh, Gwynna, I hadn't thought. I never mean to hurt you." He took her in his arms and kissed her again, and his gentleness this time melted her fear. "I will always love you, always want you. I never thought to have you at all." He slipped his fingers into the hair behind her ears. "Gwynna, may I stay with you anyway? May we just lie together—I won't force you to do anything, no, or even try to persuade you, but oh, I have been so lonely! It has been so hard, all of it has been so hard!" Then he was crying, his eyes nearly shut as he fought against tears. A sob broke from deep in his chest.

She'd always known she would lose Tennoc—he would marry Cariodas, and she would marry whomever her father chose—but losing him to exile had been worse. Watching her father lose his grip on his power, his kingdom and his mind had been worse still. Marriage to Ulvyn had broken her heart, and watching her brother's head follow their stepmother's into the executioner's basket had nearly broken her spirit. Gwynna matched his tears, and the two let their mutual grief overcome them.

They climbed onto the bed, still clothed, and held each other as they cried. When they'd recovered enough to speak, he took a cloth from a pouch at his belt, dried her eyes and nose, and then his own. They lay facing one another; she stroked his face and his hair in wonder. "I can't believe you're here."

"I swore when…" He paused, and Gwynna thought he might begin crying again. "When Cariodas came I swore I would return to you at the head of an army, and so here I am."

She gave a slight laugh. "Am I to believe this was all for me?"

"I would be lying if I said it was *all* for you, but my other motive I am sure you will approve of," he said with increasing intensity, "and that is to revenge my mother and Kenver. When things have settled I will go to Brennow and Ulvyn and level them to the ground. I will leave no child of those Houses alive. What is it, sweetheart? You've gone white."

Gwynna did her best to wipe the panic from her face. *Please don't let him ask after Ardunn.* "I don't like the thought of children dying, any child— even an Ulvyn or a Brennow."

"We don't have to talk about it now." Tennoc pulled her to him, cradling her against his chest. There had been an almost-innocent sea air tang to him before, but now he smelled darker, earthier and more masculine, mingled with a scent she'd always associated with her father—wild, unpredictable and terrifying, like lightning. He smelled of magic. "You're shaking—you're cold. Let's go to bed. Skin to skin we'd be warmer, you know," he smiled.

Gwynna *was* cold, and the idea of lying naked in the bed with a man she'd loved since girlhood warmed her in several ways. "I'd like that, but…"

"I still promise I will not persuade you to anything that might injure you or that you mightn't like. I just want to feel you beside me. Is that all right?"

They shed their clothes before the fire and slipped shivering into the bedclothes. Gwynna huddled in his embrace, his body heat smoothing away her goosebumps. He was true to his word; he did nothing but hold her. Her thigh brushed against his erection. She withdrew her leg quickly, but over time it relaxed of its own accord until it pressed against him. "Gwynna, that is unwise," he murmured. "I can control myself, but you make it difficult."

Daevys was Gwynna's sole experience of sex. He had tied her to the bedpost with the marriage cord and raped her in accordance with custom, though custom didn't call it rape and most married women went to their beds willingly or at least in resignation. Over the weeks she gave up fighting in favor of survival, and Daevys turned into a surprisingly gentle lover, if he might be called "lover." Gwynna was practical. Tennoc's return was improbable at best, but somehow she might escape Daevys if he trusted her enough to let her outside her rooms. He never had, and then had come Ardunn, and now Ulvyn was dead and here was Tennoc, his skin erasing Daevys's memory even as her breasts ached for her son. "It's all right to touch me," she whispered.

His arm was already beneath her; he slid his free hand down her back's curve, around her hip and up her side. His hand was warm and gentle, and would stop every few inches as if asking a question; her body would answer, and the hand would continue on until it asked for permission again. She gave it over and over without a word until his hand reached her milk-filled breasts. She moved it away to her belly, still loose from Ardunn's birth; Tennoc didn't seem to notice or care. A tautness crept over her.

"Gwynna," he murmured, "if we are not to go on, I must leave you."

"No, don't leave, not yet," she said, embracing him closer. His hand rested on her bottom, his hard cock just above her mound. He slid uncertainly against her until she wrapped her leg over his hip and pulled him atop her.

"You're sure?"

"I'm sure," said Gwynna, and he pushed inside her. Just knowing it was him—her Tennoc, so long forbidden and then gone—was enough to send ripples of happiness through her until frustrating, burning pain made her gasp, "Tennoc—Tennoc, stop, it hurts. I'm sorry, I'm sorry, you're hurting me."

He pulled out and rolled away, groaning. "I would never hurt you, I'm so sorry, we don't have to go on. We can do other things." Tennoc slipped his fingers between her lips to find her clitoris but removed them. "No wonder it hurt, you're dry. Did you really want this?"

"Oh yes! I can't tell you how much. So many nights I would lie awake thinking of you, and now that you're here—"

"Ssh, I have waited this long, I can wait longer."

Tennoc licked his fingers and slipped them just inside her again. He put one to each side of her clitoris and caressed her, the strokes almost lazy. At first the slowness reassured her, a sign she was not to be rushed, but as the pleasure increased her body demanded more.

A memory flashed over her of Daevys in her bed and she opened her eyes in sudden panic to find Tennoc whispering her name and looking into her face. His eyes were blue not brown, his jaw clean-shaven not bearded, he was her own, her beautiful Tennoc and not Daevys. She could not control her breathing; it matched her frantic heartbeat and the pulses of relief, delight and love that flooded her as she called out to him. When she finished, he took her into his arms and kissed her over and over while she gasped and laughed and trembled.

Gwynna's breath returned to her. "I want to try again."

"Are you sure?"

In answer, she sat up. The fire still burned in the hearth but did little to warm the room. Her nipples puckered and goosebumps rose on her arms; she giggled from nerves and the cold. She lay down atop him and he carefully arranged the bedclothes to cover them both.

This way she might control matters. If it hurt again it would be easy to stop, and she was no longer as dry so it mightn't hurt at all. She placed him at her entrance and slid down on him, her hands braced on either side of his chest. Tennoc let out a strangled cry; he twitched but stopped himself from bucking up into her, letting her set the pace. Belly to belly they moved together. She wanted him deeper, as if she might keep him with her always, but every time she tried her body reminded her the birth wasn't that long ago. There would be time. They were together now.

Tennoc didn't last long. He clutched her ass to his hips and pushed up into her as far and as hard as she would let him before he came. Though she did not join him this time, the warmth of his pleasure inside her made up for it, his happiness hers. Afterwards, he stroked her hair in drowsy contentment as they lay together, breath slowing. So this was lovemaking.

Within the quarter-hour, Tennoc was fast asleep; the new lines etched beside his mouth and between his brows disappeared as his face relaxed into the one she remembered. She herself was far from sleep; her heart was too full, and so were her breasts. She rose and threw on her chemise and a robe as she shivered near the fire. She crossed into her bower and from there into the little nursery where Ardunn and his nursemaid spent what time apart they must. The rarely-used cradle was empty; the baby and his nursemaid slept in a bed wide enough for the two of them and one other. When Ardunn could not begin the night with his mother, he slept here until she joined him. Usually the nursemaid brought him to her, but tonight she would stay with them, preferring to let Tennoc sleep. If she woke up early enough she'd rejoin him.

She shifted the blankets, settled herself into the bed, picked up her tiny son and put him to her breast. The sleepy nursemaid smiled at Gwynna.

"Will he be kind to us, my lady?" she whispered. "Will he be merciful?"

Ardunn snuffled at his mother's nipple. Gwynna smiled at him, sleepy and content as he caught it and began to nurse. "Oh, yes," she yawned. "He has always been kind to everyone, and he loves me." She fell asleep to the baby's tiny, satisfied gulps.

Tennoc was gone when Gwynna awoke, tending to what must be an endless number of details now that he'd taken Gwyrfal. Now she sat in her bower amusing her babe. Ardunn had just begun to smile, and making him do so was her chief delight.

A rustle at the now-unguarded door made her pause; she stood up with the baby in her arms. Hanni slipped inside, a finger at his lips; his usual buffoonish demeanor had turned sober. He pointed toward the nursery, shooed her in and shut the door behind them. Tears shone on Hanni's cheeks in the weak sunlight just beginning to struggle through the windowpane's thick glass; Gwynna's heart began to thump; she wondered if Ardunn could feel it as he lay against her shoulder. "What is it? Is Tennoc all right?"

"Oh, child of mine heart! Run we must, and now, if you wish to keep your son!"

"Hanni, what's happened? Daevys isn't still alive, is he?"

"Nay, nay, Ulvyn is ashes on the winds of the Forchyll Valley. It is Tennoc. He intends to kill your boy."

Gwynna's head rang as if he'd boxed her ears. Ardunn sensed her sudden fear and whimpered; she dandled him up and down. "I don't understand—" she began, but Tennoc's words came back to her, coarse and dark: *I will leave no child of that House alive.* "Ardunn is my child, not just Ulvyn's! He would never do such a thing!"

"Dear, dear one, any king would do it."

"Not Tennoc, not to a child of mine!"

"He is not our Tennoc, not since Cariodas came to us with the chest. He will do it. He plans to call you away to attend him and take the child when you are not here. I know this, for he is wanting me to do it, and I will not. I helped his mother escape injustice, and now I help you. I am yours now, just as I belonged to my dear ladies Inglatine and Lassanna. I will not serve this stranger."

Gwynna had never seen Hanni so serious, as direct as an arrow from his own bow. "What are we to do?"

"Do you trust your woman?" Hanni had a stealthy hand on his dagger and stood a little more in the doorframe than before.

The nursemaid saw none of that. She clutched at Gwynna's arm and put a protective hand on Ardunn's back. "I will help you, please let me come with you!"

"Then come," said Hanni. "They will kill you if you stay, anyway."

"Where are we going?" said Gwynna.

"We cannot leave Gwyrfal in this weather," answered Hanni. "The Mother's Temple is the closest shelter. We must hurry. Tennoc rose before dawn and is at the Brother's Temple meeting with Kellen's Eldest Brother. When he returns, it will be too late."

They spent a frantic fifteen minutes bundling the two women and the infant into warm clothing; Gwynna disguised herself in some of the nurse-maid's clothes and shoveled as much jewelry as she could into a sack. Yellow Hanni stuffed his telltale hair under a cap.

Hanni had timed their escape well; the early morning procession of vendors and entreating merchants there to see the seneschal was in full swing. Hanni hid Gwynna and the baby in a wheelbarrow covered in sacking and purloined turnips. The nursemaid walked beside him grumbling aloud to herself about the rudeness of the seneschal: "He wouldn't even *look* at our turnips!" Once clear of the castle, a two mile walk down the hilly road into the city surrounding it, they found a deserted, stinking alleyway, ditched the wheelbarrow and its turnips, and walked through the snowy streets to the Mother's Temple, where to the astonishment of the Mothers, Queen Gwynna, her child and her servant claimed and were granted asylum.

As a man, Hanni was not. "I leave you here, child of mine heart, where I know you and the little one will be safe."

"What will you do?" said Gwynna.

Hanni shrugged. "For now I go to Corland. I can stay nowhere in Tremont or Kellen—they are the same now, no? Tennoc will be angry and look for me. Perhaps I go to the Western Isles. From there?" He shrugged. "Years it is since I have seen my home in Leute. Perhaps I take a ship and go back there at last."

Tennoc returned to the castle, his step heavy but determined. He'd wrestled with himself over Ulvyn's child. Were it not Gwynna's he would have no hesitation; when a House set itself up in armed opposition to his own, he had to kill any male that might grow up to rebuild and revenge; it had gone against logic to spare the sons of the Kellish nobility, and he would never have done it had Gwynna not asked it of him.

Teacher disapproved of killing Ulvyn's son, to Tennoc's surprise, and

Hanni had advised against it as well. The infant was Gwynna's. Hanni said she loved it. How could she love it? It was of Ulvyn! No, he had to do it. In time she would have other children, their children, and remember only her hatred of Ulvyn and not the lost child.

In the end after much argument Hanni had agreed to do the necessary, but he wasn't in Tennoc's rooms when the young King returned from the Warrior's Temple, nor was he in his own rooms. Tennoc stopped a Guardsman. "Find Yellow Hanni. I need him." To a nearby servingwoman he said, "Go and fetch Her Majesty. Tell her I wish to show her some preparations I'm making for our wedding."

The servingwoman came back alone. "The Lady is not in her bower, sire."

"She must be in the nursery," he said, starting toward her rooms.

"No, sire, I looked there next and she isn't. The little one and his nursemaid aren't there, either. If it weren't winter I'd think the three of them were out in the gardens, but no one would take a wee thing like that out into the snow unless—"

By then Tennoc had run down the stairs to the main hall, where Kellish Brothers were conferring with Tremontine Guards. "All of you, fan out. You must find Yellow Hanni, the Lady Gwynna or the woman who cares for Ulvyn's son. Search everywhere!"

"What's amiss, Your Majesty?" said Cror ar Crymavon, hurrying in from the courtyard.

Tennoc's fury rose up through his body, sweeping grief, shame and pain before it. "Hanni's betrayed me."

"He's here, Lady," the Kellish Little Mother murmured.

Gwynna stood up, the baby in her arms. "Where?"

"In the Worship Hall. He is alone," added the old priestess. "He wished to bring his men inside, but the Brothers would not allow it—they are ringing the Temple even now. Quite the argument he made, too. The Eldest Brother said he understood and even sympathized with the new King's… aims… but you'd taken shelter here and they could not break Pagg's Law. Do not be deceived—if you leave the Temple, the Brothers themselves will kill the child on the new King's orders. But they will not enter these walls on such an errand."

"I'm still unsure it's wise for me to see him."

"I made him vow before the Mother that he would harm no one in this Temple were we to let him inside, with magic or anything else. It's best you see him." The Little Mother held out gnarled, gentle hands. "You may leave the little one with me."

"No. Tennoc will see the one he wishes to kill."

As she walked to the Worship Hall and its many little altars to the Mother in all Her aspects, Gwynna wished she were wearing something a bit more regal than the nursemaid's practical wool dress. Lassanna always said bearing made a Queen—usually when she returned filthy from a hunt—and Gwynna's stepmother had been about the most queenly woman Gwynna had ever known, whether laughing and covered in mud, or with her head on the block. What would Lassanna think of Tennoc now, she wondered. Gwynna straightened her back, pushed her braids over her shoulders, and marched into the Hall.

At its far end near the doors stood Tennoc. He wore armor, his helm under one arm, and his face wore those haunted lines again. "Come home, Gwynna," he said without preamble.

"Not without your vow before the Mother that my son may live."

"You know I cannot do that."

"I know nothing of the kind!" she shouted. Ardunn stirred, and she took a moment to sooth him back down before continuing in a softer voice, "All I know is you would kill my child."

"Did you love Ulvyn as you love me, then, that you would keep it?"

Gwynna thought about her late unwanted husband, how she had loathed but borne his touch in hopes of better days. "Never did I love him, and as you have seen I do not mourn him."

"Then how can you love something of his getting?"

"He's my child, whatever his getting!"

Tennoc threw down his helm; Gwynna started as the sound of the metal on marble crashed through the Temple. "*He's my enemy!* Infant or no, when he is grown he will threaten our sons!"

"We can raise him as a Tremontine," pleaded Gwynna, "and he will love you as his father and our sons as his brothers if you treat him as you will your own. It's how you yourself were raised. My father loved you as his own!"

"How did that turn out? For *any* of us?"

Gwynna held herself up as high as she could and turned Ardunn so that Tennoc could see the sleeping baby's face. "Here is the innocent you would kill. His name is Ardunn. If you insist on doing this, there will be no children of ours. I will not marry you."

A white wave of rage built on his brow. "You will marry me if I have to tie you to the bedpost!"

"Then you are no better than Ulvyn!" she shot back.

Shock replaced rage on Tennoc's face. "How can you say such a thing—he murdered Kenver and my mother!"

"And you would murder my son—Kenver's nephew and Dunnoc's grandson—all we have left of them!"

"Being in Dunnoc's line as well as Ulvyn's is why he must die. Do not pretend you don't understand this." Tennoc picked up his helm and put it on; she could no longer see his face, and this upset her most of all. "When you leave this place, madam, my men will be waiting—*I* will be waiting. The moment you leave the Temple I will ensure the safety of whatever sons I may have, by whatever woman I marry."

"Then I shall never leave."

"If he lives past infancy, he will grow to manhood and then he must leave."

"There is time enough to consider the problem," said Gwynna. Tennoc spun away and walked toward the door, and she realized these were the last moments they would spend together in this life. "You will say no good thing to me? Not even goodbye, Tennoc?"

The helm turned toward her. In the shadows it looked empty, as if no man inhabited it, and Gwynna shuddered. He said something in Tremontine she didn't understand in a voice curt, harsh and hollow, so unlike Tennoc, and then he was gone. She had no one left in the world to her but Ardunn, and she grew so hollow, so fragile, that if someone tapped her in the wrong spot she was sure to shatter.

A gentle throat-clearing came from behind her. The Kellish Little Mother stepped from the shadows. "Forgive me, my dear, but I wanted to make sure you were safe. I believe the new King to be true to his word, but…" The old priestess let the thought hang.

Gwynna wiped her eyes on the none-too-soft wool of the nursemaid's sleeve. "I wish I knew what he said at the end."

"I speak the language," murmured the Little Mother. "He said, 'My name is Temmin.'"

Temmin shook his head to clear it of Gwynna's terror and rage. "I don't like to hear my name used by someone like Tennoc."

"How so?" said Teacher.

"To kill a child—an infant?"

Teacher leaned back against the mantel. "Politics is an ugly business. There is a very real fear in any regime change that someone with perhaps a better claim—someone like Ardunn—would become a rallying point against a ruler and must be eliminated early. Your uncles have no clear claim to the throne, but they have become such rallying points. Is it so strange that Tennoc would wish to secure his position? Especially as a bastard?"

"But you told him not to do it, and he ignored you."

"There were voices against me, Cror ar Crymavon's most notably. Crymavon was not a bad man, but he considered himself practical. Tennoc wanted Ulvyn's every trace erased. He wanted revenge."

Temmin sat up straighter. "And you told him revenge was a bad idea."

"Not at all. I have been known to mete out vengeance myself now and again," said Teacher with a smile that sent a draft down Temmin's neck. "But I revenge myself on the offenders, not their families. Sadly, the kings of Tremont usually have different ideas. Remember the archer who killed King Fredrik the Last of Leute in the story of King Warin and Queen Emmae," added Teacher, reaching down to tap on the book. "Warin slaughtered his family down to the last innocent child."

"I don't want the murder of children on my conscience," muttered Temmin, thinking of his future as king.

"It is easy to avoid, sir," said Teacher. "Do not murder children."

MIDDLEMONT, THE HOME COUNTY
THE FOURTH DAY OF WINTER'S ENDING, 992 KY

A Sister midwife and her two lay assistants had taken up residence at Middlemont just in time for Twenna Shelstone's confinement. "Best send word to the King," said the Sister to Hallik the butler.

"How long will it take?" he asked.

"As long as it takes." The Sister closed the door to Twenna's bedchamber not a moment too soon for Hallik, who had no children of his own and had never heard a woman in labor. He hurried to his dayroom to write the message and call for a groom to ride to the Keep.

"Will you go?" said Winmer on presenting the message.

Harsin waved his hand. "After the baby is born. There is nothing I can do, after all. It's woman's work. And I've had my fill of Sisters and tears."

By the end, Twenna had had her fill, too. Water bathing her sweat-soaked body, hands freeing and brushing her hair, and then cool, clean sheets beneath her had never been as sweet as when she'd passed the afterbirth and was helped into her bed from the birthing chair where she'd pushed out a son.

He lay belly-down against her bare breast beneath the blanket. He'd already had his first nursing, latching onto her nipple "like a good 'un" as a midwife said approvingly, and now Twenna indulged in the sleepy new mother's favorite pastime: examining her baby. All fingers and toes accounted for; soft, golden fuzz stroked; his features searched for echoes of her mother, her father, his father. She saw few, but the midwives said babies changed from minute to minute well into their second year.

"Now you should sleep, dear, you've been up all night working very hard," soothed the Sister midwife. "We'll take the babe so you can sleep."

"So I can sleep?" exclaimed Twenna. "I won't be able to sleep *without* him!" She yawned and snuggled down further into the pillows; the baby didn't stir, but stayed splayed on her chest like a little pink frog. "Won't Harsin be surprised? He thought it would be a girl! I think he'll be happy it's a boy. Men like boys. I must think of a name." Twenna drifted off into a deep, pleased sleep.

Later she sat up in bed dressed in a pretty new nightdress, a blue ribbon matching her eyes pulling her hair from her happy face. As she had long hoped, the King arrived, his voice abrupt and clipped outside her door, and Mistress Hallik's voice agitated in response. He opened the bedchamber door with more force than was required. "Who is he?"

Joy burst over her. She hadn't seen Harsin in spokes. Now she'd given him a son, he would return to her, and the three of them could be happy. "We must pick a new name! I was thinking perhaps—"

"Name him what you please. He's none of mine."

Twenna opened her eyes wide in confusion. "What do you mean? I thought you were going to acknowledge him."

"I was going to acknowledge it when I thought it was mine."

"He *is* yours, Harsin, who else could be his father?"

"I asked you that when I came into the room, woman!"

What had happened to change him so? His red eyes glared; his dark, graying hair had come loose from its queue and now fell about his temples, covering the shorn spot where he'd cut the Queen's mourning lock. He *was* in mourning, of course, though she'd always believed his relationship with the Queen was more for show than anything else. Her Majesty was the mother of his children, though; her death had to have been a shock. The Prince and Princesses were probably upset and turning to their father more than usual. It wrung her tender heart. "Oh, Harsin, come see your little son, I hope he may ease some of your pain!"

"*You* are my current pain!" he roared, "and that child is no son of mine!"

She shrank against the pillows. "I don't understand. What are you saying?"

"All this time I've been waiting for the birth of a child who isn't mine, planning honors for you, elevating your greasy toad of a father, and for what? Betrayal! Who fathered that baby? *Who is he!*"

Twenna began to cry. "Harsin, there's never been anyone but you! Why do you not think he's your son? Yes, I know you thought it was a girl, but surely a son—"

"Teacher!" Harsin called into the next room. A black sliver with iron-colored hair and odd silvery eyes entered, and Twenna shivered as if the Black Man were drawing his fingers down her spine. "You're certain? You're certain this is not my son?"

"But how would he know?" quavered Twenna.

"Be quiet!" said Harsin. "Teacher?"

The frightening figure frowned at the lay midwife holding the baby. "I am certain."

"What?" cried Twenna. "No, no, Harsin, no, he's lying, I've never known another man, *ever*, this is our son! This is *your son!*"

"We're done here." Harsin turned on his heel, calling for Hallik as he strode out of the bedchamber. Teacher trailed behind.

The baby began to cry. "He's hungry, miss," said the lay midwife.

"In a moment, a moment!" Twenna stumbled from the bed.

"No, miss, no," said the Sister midwife, "you lost quite a bit of blood in the birth, you must stay in bed another few days until you've regained your strength!"

"I must follow him! He's wrong, that man is lying, it's Harsin's son! It's Harsin's!" She sagged into the Sister's arms and wailed.

"Shut those doors!" said Harsin from the hallway outside Twenna's apartments. "I never want to hear her voice again! Hallik! Where is Shelstone?"

"Sir Elbig is on his way, sir," answered the butler.

"I don't know any 'Sir Elbig,'" said the King.

A whiff of Elbig Shelstone's jasmine-tinged cologne hurried into the hall before he did. "Your Majesty! Felicitations on the birth of your new son, my grandson!" he beamed. "Why are you standing in the hallway? Hallik, take him in to see the little thing! He's perfect in every way, sir, resembles his father—"

"Whoever *he* is," snapped Harsin. "Do you know who Twenna's been dallying with? You must know, you're the one who put her in my way, aren't you? A pimp whoring out his own daughter." Shelstone opened his mouth in shock, but Harsin cut him off. "Was it Twenna's idea to laugh behind her hand at me? No, she's never had a single thought in her head. So whose influence did you believe more important than your King's, Shelstone? Whose favor were you currying?"

"Your Majesty!" sputtered Shelstone. "Sir, you've gone mad! I mean—sir, how can you believe these things? Twenna was a maid when you met her, and has been with no other man, I swear it! That child is yours!"

"The child is *not* his," said Teacher.

Shelstone made Amma's sign, but said, "I don't know what you'd know about it!"

Harsin turned to the butler. "Hallik, make a carriage ready to take *Mister* Shelstone and his daughter back to town immediately."

"Your Majesty, the lady is still too weak to travel," protested Mistress Hallik, who'd been hovering behind her husband. "Have pity, sir! In the time we have been here, there has been no man in the house when you yourself have not been, but even if there had been—"

"You lecture us?"

Mistress Hallik left the shelter of her husband's side and stood firm before the King, though her mouth trembled and she clutched her hands before her. "Amma commands me to, sir. I have served you from girlhood, and will serve you to my dying day even if that day is today, but I will not see a woman newly delivered of a child turned out of a house in the middle of winter!" Harsin glared at her, but she refused to drop her gaze.

"She is in the right, Your Majesty," murmured Teacher. "You may give Miss Shelstone some kindness at no cost to your consequence."

Harsin ground his teeth. "As soon as the Sister says Miss Shelstone can travel, she will leave. Send Mr Shelstone away this instant. Hallik, saddle a horse and send a groom along. The groom can take the horse to the Keep's stables once he's delivered Shelstone to his own door." He turned to the former tailor. "Elbig Shelstone, we strip you of your holding and your title. Anything in this house and at Menantola is forfeit. You will take nothing with you but the clothes on your back, and be grateful for them. Be grateful we don't have you flogged round the City! Teacher, take me home." Harsin stalked down the hallway into the rooms he used as his own when in residence.

Shelstone called after him, "You're taking Menantola from me? You can't! Your Majesty, this is a misunderstanding! Sir, you can't!" The hallway emptied as the Halliks left to attend to their tasks, Mistress Hallik wiping her eyes on her handkerchief.

Shelstone collapsed against the wall, rattling the paintings. "What am I to do?" he whimpered. "I am encumbered all around, no one to turn to, not a feather to fly with, and now…I shall go to the block! They'll indenture me! I cannot allow it, I cannot! I cannot stand in the Father's Temple to be auctioned off for debt while the whole City laughs! I cannot! Oh Gods—!" He fled to his rooms.

When Hallik and the groom came for him not half an hour later, they found him hanging from a rail in the wardrobe among his many perfectly tailored suit coats, quite dead.

SIXTEEN

Harsin sat at breakfast the next day, alone but for his eldest daughter. Ansella's robin's egg blue morning room, cheerful even in the weak winter sun, served as consolation and goad to them both; they sat silent, picking at their eggs and coffee. The butler appeared, arms full of newsprint, but set the stack before the King alone. "Affton, where are my morning papers?" asked Sedra.

"There'll be no more of that," growled her father. "I'm done with you ruining your mind. All this reading will stunt your ability to bear children."

"Papa, you know that isn't true! Many educated women—"

"Not in my house!" roared Harsin. "Not in my house! No more! I will not have the women of this family constantly disobeying me! Is your mother's death not proof enough I know best? You will obey me, Sedra. Better you should learn to bend that stiff neck now, because Brinnid of Sairland is due next year to bargain for his brother. Do you hear me? You will obey my will and then your husband's, girl, and we're both within our rights to beat you bloody otherwise!"

"May I remind you I'm not sold—excuse me, *married*—yet, sir?"

Harsin reached across the table and slapped her.

Sedra brought her hand to her cheek in shock. No one had ever hit her before, let alone her father. She was his favorite. He disapproved of her

studying and encouraged it at the same time; they talked politics at breakfast and over dinner, enthusiastic and friendly arguments that often ended
in laughter. She thought they understood one another, in spite of the dis-
agreement over Teacher, in spite of his conventional attitudes toward her
learning.

He had hit her.

She pushed her chair back, deposited her napkin beside her untouched
breakfast and left the room with measured step; her father stared after her
but didn't call her back. When she was certain she was unobserved, she
raced up the stairs to her rooms, slamming the door behind her. "Camma!
Damn you, Sinsett, where are you?"

Miss Sinsett came hurrying from Sedra's bedchamber. "Miss, what is it?
Why is your cheek so red? Let me bring you some lavender water—"

"I don't want to bathe my face. I'm going out. Lay out my new black
winter walking suit. I'll have the black mink muff and hat as well."

"Oh, but Miss, you haven't been out in at least a week. It's quite cold out,
and the snow is thick on the ground. You won't be able to get through the
woods on foot, I'm certain of it."

"Then lay out a riding suit and furs, and send a footman to the stables
to bring LeiLei here. I should have gone home with Elly!"

Dressed in warm black wool and warmer fur, Sedra stomped out of the
mudroom entrance, mounted LeiLei and galloped into the snowy King's
Woods. So, the Sairish were coming, a deal would be made, and she would
leave Tremont. She would become a figurehead and be hemmed in on all
sides, even more than she already was. No reading, no walks, just endless
nodding and smiling and the bed of an unknown man. Her worth would no
longer be measured in her abilities but in the number of children she bore.

She'd never had any real illusions as to her future; she was "the smart
one" after all, and had always known she and Ellika were destined for dip-
lomatic marriages. She'd expected it far, far sooner than this. Perhaps Papa
should have married her off more quickly; at 17 she might have been more
flexible, more biddable, than she was now at not-quite 23. When mourning
for Mama finished she'd be almost 24—perhaps older before the wedding
could be celebrated. She'd be so far away—she'd never see Tremont again.
With Mama gone, would that be so very bad?

No, it was still unsupportable, never seeing her sisters and brother
again, never wandering in these woods again, never being her own person
again. She was not made for marriage. She was made for learning and independence, for books and quiet woods.

Sedra stopped. She'd come to the place Teacher and Connin had called Mirror Clearing. Down the path before her stood the Travelers' caravans; pleasantly tangy smoke came to her nose. She reined LeiLei in. The old crone had invited her to take up where Teacher's instruction had left off. Yes, Maeve had been Sedra's unknown rival for Teacher's affections, but the chance to learn more about her family's unknown history, especially its women, was tempting. Maybe there'd be something in it to hold her up and guide her through the coming years.

And then there was Connin's invitation to consider.

Sedra tapped her heels into LeiLei's sides, and they started down the path toward the camp.

It had snowed overnight at Whithorse Estate as well, smoothing the rolling hills and long flat plains and turning the old Freehold in the distance into a white palace. Temmin rode out into the snow on Jebby. Alvo's greeting had bordered on curt, and he'd answered in kind; if that's what Alvo wanted, that's what Temmin would give him. By the time he came home on his steaming horse he was contrite, but Alvo had disappeared. Sunk in gloom, he left Jebby to the grooms, ate a lonely breakfast in the Morning Room and stomped upstairs to let Jenks fuss over his morning toilet.

"Bathed, trimmed, turned out and for what?" Temmin muttered.

"For your own good, sir. A man's outsides affect a man's insides, and that's all there is to it. Look at the old crow," Jenks continued as Teacher entered the drawing room. "Neat as a pin every time you see him. Orderly dress leads to an orderly mind."

"High and unexpected praise, Colonel," said Teacher, iron-colored brows raised, "but is my mind orderly because I am 'neat as a pin,' or am I neat as a pin because my mind is orderly?"

"One follows the other," sniffed Jenks. "I'm off, sir. Wallek needs more etiquette beaten into him." He shut the door behind him.

"Poor Wallek," murmured Teacher.

"Oh, he's all right, he has a hard head," said Temmin, his expression approaching a smile.

"And how is your head this morning?"

Temmin sank back onto the gold couch. "Troubled. I like the snow—love it—but today it's just cold white stuff. I can't seem to get much enthusiasm going about anything. My best friend won't speak to me, just when I need him the most. I'd say let's take a trip into the book to take my mind off everything, but I'm wary of what I'll find out."

"Shall we assay it anyway?" said Teacher.

"Oh, why not," groaned Temmin. He opened the book and the story continued.

Winter turned to spring and still Gwynna and the baby could not leave the Temple. Soldiers kept watch day and night in sun, rain and snow. The Brothers also kept watch to prevent the soldiers from entering, but they were protecting the sanctity of the Mother's Temple, not Ardunn; they would kill the baby themselves if Gwynna and Ardunn left their holy shelter.

Some days King Temmin stood among them—she could not call the man who'd spoken with her at the feet of the Mother that day "Tennoc." Sometimes he called to her, and sometimes she heard him. Sometimes he even sounded like Tennoc. The day came when the Mothers told her the new King had finally left Gwyrfal to turn his attention to conquering the rest of Kellen. Cror ar Crymavon was left behind with instructions to continue the watch.

Gwynna began working in the Mother's House—still a safe haven as it sat on the Temple grounds. Word arrived that Tennoc had married Cariodas. Gwynna had expected it for years, but it still cut deeply, as did later news of their first son's birth. But she had made her choice; never could she give Ardunn up. She began to hope Tennoc would grow tired of hounding her now that his dynasty was secure, especially once news of other children came. Instead, the years went by and the soldiers remained, always rotating so none might become overly sympathetic to the Mothers' most famous inmate.

Ardunn grew tall. He looked more like Dunnoc's line than Ulvyn's, with her family's gray eyes and the same calm, irreverant, loving disposition as Kenver. He was the cheerful kind of older boy who seemed to be a human climbing tree and often walked about with younger children hanging from every limb. More than once Gwynna mistook him for her brother out of the corner of her eye. More than once she thought that if he could just see Ardunn, Tennoc would love him and let him live.

Clergy came to the Mother's House to teach the children and look for postulants. Sisters checked their health, taught the girls spinning and tried to coax them into the Hearth; Scholars came to instruct the brighter boys in their letters and all the children in their numbers. Sometimes Friends came to take a child to the Hill, giving the little bodies their final baths at the House so their playmates could add their tears.

Brothers came three times a week, giving lessons in warfare to the boys and scouting them for potential postulants. Ardunn did well, so well the warrior priests gave him a real sword and talked themselves hoarse extolling the virtues of life in Farr's Temple. "I may be for a warrior's life," he would say with a wink at the nearest girl his own age, "but I won't give up the company of women."

Still, Gwynna wondered if Ardunn's one safe way out of the Mother's Temple when he came of age was to enter the Warrior's Temple. Though she racked her brains the only solution she could see to save his life was some form of priesthood, and the other Gods did not suit him.

When Ardunn was nearly eighteen King Temmin the Third of Tremont returned to Gwyrfal, the city the conquering Tremontines had renamed Greenvale. It was Fall's Ending when his entourage arrived, a few weeks before Eddin's Day—Ardunn's birthday.

"Do you think he's come for me?" Ardunn asked his mother one night. They sat by the fire in the tiny antechamber she shared with two other lay Mothers, she with a pile of smocks to mend, he with his back propped against her chair and his legs stretched out on the hearthstones.

Gwynna paused in her mending. "I honestly cannot say. He was ever a respectful man, but that was long ago when he bore a different name."

"What shall we do if he does come for me?"

"There's no escape I've ever found," she said, twirling her needle between her fingers in thought. "Else I would have taken it long ago. Outside the Temple grounds the Brothers will obey the King and kill you, no matter how much they like you themselves."

"I wish you to go without me, then."

"I will never leave you, not until I have seen you safely settled. Ardunn, have you given any further thought to the Warrior's Temple? You'd be safe there."

"I have no objection to a warrior's life, but I'm not a lover of men, and to give up all hope of a wife..." Ardunn faltered, and added with a crooked smile, "I suppose I should have no illusions about taking a wife as things stand, hey?" Gwynna's eyes prickled. She had never gone that far in her imaginings for her son; it had been hard enough to imagine him alive after the coming Eddin's Day, when he turned eighteen and would have to leave the Mother's Temple one way or another.

"If they come for us before my birthday, there will be fighting," Ardunn resumed in his calm way. "The Brothers will defend the Temple, but I don't know how many soldiers the King brought with him nor how determined he is to kill me. If he has enough men to breach the Brothers' lines, the chances are good they'll kill any boy even close to my age they find. Maybe every boy, no matter his age. That's what I'd do if I wanted to be sure. So if they come for me—now or on Eddin's Day—I will leave the Temple sword in hand to die honorably and alone. Don't cry, Mother," he said, patting her knee. "We always knew this would happen. I'm grateful you fought for me, and I've had a good life here at the Temple. I've tried to make myself useful, and perhaps Harla will be kind to me in the next world—when I am dead, please ask the King to let me rest in the Hill with my grandfathers, for I have done nothing to him that he should deny me burial rites."

Gwynna could not answer him; her hands covered her face, and she sobbed into them as she rarely allowed herself to do. Nothing had gone her way since the day Tennoc rode from Gwyrfal, and now the time had come when she might lose her one comfort, her dear Ardunn, to him. What had she done to deserve her life? What had her child done to deserve his death? She had prayed to Amma for some answer to her questions, and none had come. Perhaps this was the answer to her prayers: an end to the suspense. She controlled her tears long enough to say, "If you go out with your sword, I go out with my dagger. We die together." No amount of Ardunn's pleading, cajoling or flat-out ordering her to stay safely in the Temple would change her determination. He would try to arrange some sly way of keeping her from danger, but she would find an equally sly way to stay by his side.

Several days passed with no sign from the King, until a messenger arrived. The Temple was to expect a visitor the next day. Would it be some emisssary, or King Temmin himself? That morning, a nervous young Mother came to fetch Gwynna down to the emptied Worship Hall: the visitor stood just outside the doors.

A sharp pang stabbed at Gwynna; life had beaten most of whatever vanity she'd possessed out of her, but she had been beautiful eighteen years ago. Work had roughened her hands, for no one could afford to be idle in the Mother's House. She wore the simple undyed wool habit of a lay Mother, a blue linen veil over her head; it had been long since she'd dressed in fine clothes. She didn't have a mirror to see how she'd aged, and wondered how she would appear in her visitor's eyes. There was nothing to be done for it. She walked to the Worship Hall and stood as she had when Ardunn was a baby, at the feet of the Mother's great statue.

The doors to the antechamber opened, and a woman stepped through. She wore rich clothing trimmed in fur, and the train of her dark blue brocade dress extended a good foot behind her. A thin gold circlet set with ruby cabochons pinned a silk veil to her head; long, thick dark braids hung over her shoulders. Years and childbirth had thickened her figure somewhat, but she was still lovely, her brown eyes still bright. "Lady Gwynna, my old friend, I am happy to see you, though I wish it were not in this place."

"Cariodas!" exclaimed Gwynna, taking a step forward. "Truly…truly you are the last person I expected to see."

Cariodas smiled, a full, genuine smile tinged with sadness. "He thought perhaps I should speak to you first, that you might be less averse to me than to him."

Gwynna halted in her tracks. This was not just her old friend; this was the Queen of Tremont—Tennoc's wife. *It should have been me, it should have been me…* "What is there to speak of?"

"Oh, Gwynna, don't tell me we are to be enemies! I know how hard these years have been for you—"

"You know nothing of the kind. Is your son under threat as mine is?"

Cariodas's face stilled into sobriety. "All of my children are under threat. Any king's child is."

"Yours have more protection than the skirts of the Mother. That's all Ardunn and I have."

"Oh, Gwynna," sighed Cariodas. "Know that I want so much more for the both of you."

"Speak to your husband, then."

"I have! I have and Teacher has—oh, but perhaps you don't know him."

"The Black Man? I have seen him."

"As the King's advisor he always counsels against the murder of innocents, but Temmin—our Tennoc does not always listen. Did not always listen. I believe he is listening now." Cariodas stepped forward, hands outstretched and eyes brighter than ever. "The last glimpse I had of you was as we rode away that—that horrible day! You were crying in the open window of your bower. I could just see your face. Gwynna, we were girls together. You remember my father and I remember Kenver and Lassanna! Please say we are still friends, please!"

Gwynna willed herself not to cry. Cariodas driven out from the castle, her half-dead father sharing a rude sled with the awful chest at his feet, came to her more clearly than in any nightmare. With that hideous memory also came the years of their girlhood, the happy times at Gwyrfal full of dancing—and rivalry, for they'd both loved the same man, but they'd also loved one another.

So much time had passed—what was Cariodas to her now? Wife of the man who would kill her son and probably her in the end. *You forget yourself, Your Majesty* formed in her throat, but instead she blurted out, "Oh, Cariodas!" The Queen in all her finery rushed into the lay Mother's rough wool arms, and they held one another close. "Cariodas, save my son, please save my son!" said Gwynna when they broke apart, all restraint and pride gone.

Cariodas brushed away a tear with a bejeweled finger. "I have done what I can, please believe me. You must speak for yourself now. Please say you'll see him."

"Is he sworn?"

"He's never considered himself unsworn."

She surrendered to the inevitable. "Then I'll see him." Cariodas nodded, squeezed Gwynna's hands a last time and turned to leave. A final question rose in Gwynna's mind, and she called out, "Cariodas, has he been good to you?"

The Queen paused and looked back at her old friend, her expression so sad Gwynna wished she hadn't asked. "He's been kind. He loves our children—we have three sons and two daughters now. He visits me regularly and treats me kindly and with respect, but he's taken many other women." Her voice dropped to a whisper. "They all look like you, Gwynna. He never stopped loving you. Goodbye, my dear." Cariodas passed out of the door, the bright sunlight turning her departing form into a soft blur of blue.

Gwynna covered her mouth with both hands. Tennoc was coming, and his own wife said he still loved her. Shivers began deep in her chest, spreading out to her fingertips like tiny cramps. Fear, excitement, hatred, love—they all shook her at once, and instead of the strong woman she'd been since Ardunn's birth she was a tree hit by lightning, its bark ripped open and its heartwood exposed. The door opened again and the King stepped through.

He'd grown a beard in the Tremontine style. Gray was creeping into its sandy brown; it made him look older than his forty years. He was no longer a slender young man. His chest and shoulders had broadened, and he stood tall and easy in his furs and silks, the scabbard at his side empty. His straight brow was heavy—she remembered her father and how he'd had the same serious air about him before his mind had gone.

Tennoc examined her with his familiar, steady blue gaze, and Gwynna blushed for her plain appearance. "You look just the same," he said in a low, roughened voice. She blushed harder, pleased in spite of herself. The King turned his head slightly, as if bringing a good eye to bear on her. "I could have killed Ulvyn's son in his sleep any time these last eighteen years, you know."

"How is that?" she frowned, her pleasure brought to an abrupt end.

"Kellen is part of Tremont now. I can see into every corner of it. I've watched you both. I could have stepped through the reflection into this Temple and killed him a thousand times over."

She should have known he would watch her. The fine hairs all over her body rose thinking about it. "Why didn't you?"

"I was sworn."

"Why are you here now?"

"On Eddin's Day the boy turns eighteen. He will leave this place."

"And then?"

The King's bearded jaw worked, and he dropped his eyes, no longer regal but uncertain. "I don't know. My wife and chief counselor have urged me to speak with you before I do anything, and so I'm here." He raised his head again; the invisible crown settled back on his brow. "What does he intend?"

"Intend?" she laughed incredulously. "What *can* he intend? How can he even have dreamed a future? You said he had none, and it's easy to believe you meant it every time I see the soldiers outside still waiting for him."

"This is not what I wanted for us," said Tennoc, so quietly the soft echoes of his voice almost garbled the words.

"I daresay it wasn't what I wanted, either," she answered. "This was your doing."

"I daresay it was." He shifted suddenly, drawing himself up. "The Elder Brother here tells me Ardunn ar Ulvyn is a worthy young man. He wants the boy to join the Brothers. That would put him beyond my reach."

"Though he admires them, he does not wish to join them."

"He has not a martial spirit?"

"...Men do not inspire his devotion, shall we say," said Gwynna, bowing slightly. "The Brothers say he is as good a swordsman as any they've seen, but he feels he cannot take a vow he cannot keep even to save his life."

The King nodded slowly. "I want to see this son of yours." At Gwynna's stiffening face, he added, "I am sworn, Lady. I have neither sword nor armor."

"Only the magic of two lands to protect you," she mocked.

"I am sworn," he repeated, his voice rumbling through her body to the statue of the Mother behind her. "I wish...I wish to see the grandson of

Dunnoc ar Gwyrfal."

Which of Ardunn's ancestors did he hate more, wondered Gwynna: Dunnoc ar Gwyrfal or Daevys ar Ulvyn? He might kill Ardunn here in the Hall at the feet of the Mother, break his vow to the Gods and be damned, or he might kill Ardunn in the street and face nothing but his lords' approval. She opted for his damnation; at least she and Ardunn would get some sort of revenge. "All right, I will call for him." She walked back through the doors leading to the cloister and took her time finding a Postulant Mother to carry the message; let the King wait.

Ardunn was wearing his sword when he joined her at the doors to the Worship Hall. His serious young face was so much like Kenver's that her already-fragile heart broke open. "I've said my goodbyes, Mother. Let's see this King."

For the first time Gwynna saw him as a grown man, and she was reduced to tugging at his sleeve like a child. "Don't go at him, I beg you—let him bear the blame. He claims he is still sworn. Let him take the damnation on himself."

"Never worry, I know what to do." Ardunn strode past her into the Worship Hall, hands carefully held away from his sword hilt. She hurried to precede him, giving him a quelling look; to her surprise, he obeyed.

Gwynna bowed her head formally to the King and brought her son forward. "This is Ardunn ar Ulvyn, son of Gwynna ar Gwyrfal, grandson of Dunnoc ar Gwyrfal and nephew of Kenver ar Gwyrfal." She waited to observe the effect of this last on him, looking back and forth from his face to Ardunn's.

Ardunn made a respectful bow. "Your Majesty."

The King seemed thunderstruck. He took a step toward the boy, then another. "You are very like your uncle."

"So my mother has told me. I never knew him."

"I did, and I loved him very much," said Tennoc. "I've seen you in reflections before this. The resemblance could not be denied, but as you stand before me...you are very like," he finished, obviously unsettled. Gwynna watched him, sharp-eyed. All her agitation vanished; she focused entirely on the interplay between the man and boy. "What do you have to say for yourself?"

"Say for myself?" said Ardunn, surprised but calm. "I don't know that I have anything to say for myself, nor whether I need to say anything for myself."

"You brought your sword."

"I've been told for eighteen years I might need one, you see," said Ardunn.

The King seemed to settle in to the same calm surrounding the younger man; he joined his hands loosely before him. "What else have you been told?"

"That I am the son of a man you hated for good reason," Ardunn answered. "I never knew him nor any of his kin—as far as I'm aware, I'm the only Ulvyn left, am I not?" At Tennoc's grim nod, he continued, "I know my grandfather was your stepfather and that he loved you until he went mad. And I know you grew up under a cloud, as I have."

The King cast a shrewd glance at Gwynna, who raised her eyebrows in acknowledgement. "You are also the heir of the last King of Kellen," he said.

The boy smiled. "Strange, I thought *you* were King of Kellen."

"We are King of Tremont, which now includes Kellen."

"Then that officially makes me nobody," concluded Ardunn.

Gwynna wanted to box Ardunn's ear and tell him to curb his irreverence, but she suddenly realized Tennoc almost enjoyed her son's gentle flippancy. "You're an Ulvyn," he said.

"I cannot hold allegiance to a house that doesn't exist any more. Could I take my mother's clan name I would, but what's left of Clan Gwyrfal is too frightened to accept me. The Mother's House is the only allegiance I hold—I'm Ardunn ar Amma, I suppose. So here we are."

"Here we are," repeated the King, faintly smiling. "What has your mother told you of me?"

What would Ardunn say? She had never lied to him about the Tremontine King's resolve, but she had also couched it in political terms. In spite of hating Tennoc, she'd never been able to stop loving him either, not after a lifetime. What else had she told her son? She could not remember. "She has said little with her mouth but much otherwise," said her son, giving her a long, measuring look that made her blush. "Her heart has always been in two places, but that's what she told me of herself, not of you."

The King fidgeted, staring first at Gwynna's blushing face and then at her impudent son. "What would you do if you left the Mother's House?"

"I would serve the Mothers as protector, but I can't take vows to Farr in good conscience."

"If you took vows you would be beyond my reach."

"Oh yes, but I neither desire men nor can I turn my back on women, not well enough for me to become a priest of the Warrior without breaking my vows in any event. Nor am I particularly dedicated to the Scholar, the

Lovers, the Father or the Bloody One. I grew up in a temple, you see. Vows have great meaning for me—it's not enough that they would save my life. Amma is my Lady, but I cannot serve Her in orders."

The King fastened his hands behind his back, nodded his head and paced slowly from side to side, as if hoping for better views of the boy—really, very much a man, thought his proud mother. "I see. If you cannot serve a God, would you serve me?"

Ardunn let out a small startled noise, but before he could say more Gwynna bounded forward. "What are you suggesting? Is this a ruse to get him to leave this place?"

"Mother, this conversation is between this man and me," said Ardunn, steel in his voice, "and he needs no ruse. Whether I come out today or Eddin's Day—it doesn't matter, the end result is the same." She fell back, abashed.

"The end result," said the King. "I'm entirely unsure what that result might be now. You are not afraid of me, are you, Ardunn?"

"Perhaps I am, but if you choose to kill me I choose to face my death with honor. I will not cringe from it."

At this the King turned away. Gwynna crept up to her son's side and clutched his arm; he removed it and took her hand in his, the clasp warm and comforting. How hard to be the comforted and not the comforter. "You asked a boon of me when I took Gwyrfal, Gwynna, do you remember?" said Tennoc, his back still to them.

"I asked you not to send the wives and daughters of your enemies into indenture, and to spare the boy children," she said.

The King faced them again. "I swore that if the boys of those families would swear allegiance to me on their swords I would let them live, to go into fosterage in Tremont and be raised as Tremontines. I kept that oath and so far I have not regretted it. This boy is the son of one who took sides." He stared intently at Ardunn. "Swear allegiance to me on your sword in Pagg's Temple. Swear to come with me into Tremont and never return to Kellen. Then I will let you go."

"I've never been in Pagg's Temple—swearing there would mean nothing to me," said Ardunn. "Let me swear here before the Mother, and I will do as you say though I know nothing of Tremont nor do I speak the language."

"You're a bright young man. You'll learn." Tennoc turned to Gwynna; she vibrated in shocked hope. "Call for the senior Mothers," he said. "They will bear unimpeachable witness."

"One matter," interrupted Ardunn. "My mother. What's to become of her?"

The King bowed his head to her. "Lady? What's to become of you?"

"Am I to be allowed to accompany my son?" she said in a shaking voice.

"You are free to do as you please," said the King.

"Then I'll come."

"Then I'll swear," said Ardunn.

The Mothers soon gathered. Ardunn knelt before the King at the feet of Amma's image; his hands clasped his sword hilt and his new lord wrapped his hands round them both. In a strong voice, Ardunn swore his allegiance to Temmin of Tremont, swore away the name of Ulvyn, and placed his life at the King's disposal. He rose, saying, "I never considered anyone but you King at any event, let alone myself."

"It's not your opinion that concerns me, insolent boy," snapped the King. "It's the opinions of Kellish lords who may wish to use you as a pawn."

"Not much chance of that and never was," said Ardunn with the expansive cheerfulness of an unexpected reprieve, "though I don't regret my oath in the least. I've already said my goodbyes, though expecting a different outcome. When do we go?"

"Now. Gather your things." Ardunn bowed deeply and left for his room at a fast pace; the King dismissed the Mothers from the room.

All this had stretched poor Gwynna's endurance to the breaking point. Eighteen years of worry and grief now over—and a new era of worry begun. More immediately, gratitude, love and resentment toward the man before her sank her to the floor sobbing her thanks, her forehead on the King's feet. "No, no, Gwynna, never do that, *never*!" cried Tennoc, bending down to her. "I cannot bear you prostrating yourself before anyone, especially me." He raised her up to stand before him; his hands rested uneasy on her arms as she collected herself, but he did not remove them. "He is an extraordinary young man, Gwynna," he said in a rough voice. "Dunnoc and Kenver would be proud of him."

"Thank you." Gwynna bit at the inside of her mouth long enough to stop her tears and said, "What will you do with him?"

"I intend to take him directly to Marsury to be of use to—I suppose you'd call her my stepmother. You must have heard Mother talk of her—the Lady Inglatine, Mother's great friend who was once my father's wife. She's now styled Countess of Marsury. She's the mother of seven of my half-sisters, a most amiable old dame. I have a fine detachment of Guards there. If Ardunn does well, I'll give him a commission and a name."

A name! That meant a holding—a title! Gwynna's heart swelled; this was more than she'd ever hoped for. "I wonder—where might I live close by?"

"I hoped…how close by must you be to him?"

"As close as I can, of course," she said, worried some impediment might still arise.

Tennoc's hands tightened on her arms and he leaned down in tender, rather frightening intensity. "Live with me at Tremont Keep. Be my love."

Gwynna's heart took a joyful leap, only to hit a brick wall. "No, I won't do that to Cariodas. Let me live near my Ardunn. Forget me."

"I have not forgotten you, nor will I ever forget you," said Tennoc in a voice like tearing skin. He kissed her, and she fell into his arms as she had eighteen years ago, with a different pain and longing. The blue linen veil had fallen away, and as he whispered his repentance his breath puffed against her hair, warm in the drafty Worship Hall. "Gwynna, please, please come back to me."

She burrowed her nose in his shoulder. Tennoc smelled of silk and fur, of the outdoors, of salt air and musk and the ozone of his magic. Their one night together surged through her, and she lost her grip on her refusal. "Can you not come to me at Marsury now and again through a reflection?" she said in a small voice. "I can't, I *can't* live with you under the same roof as Cariodas and I would not have you send her away for the world—has she been a bad wife to you?"

"She has been the best wife a man could wish for. Her only flaw is that she isn't you," said Tennoc, stroking her wet cheek.

"Then give her the respect she deserves. If you leave Cariodas her dignity and if you give up your other women—yes, she told me, and quite reluctantly—if you give up your other women I would…I would welcome you to my bed in Marsury whenever you might come to me."

"I will be in Marsury every night!" he cried, hugging her close.

"You will not be there every night and you know it," she laughed. "I cannot believe I am considering such a thing!"

"You love me."

"I love you," she confessed.

Temmin rose from the book oddly comforted. "He let the boy Ardunn live? He didn't change his mind once they were in Tremont?"

"No," said Teacher. "Tennoc took Ardunn to Marsury, where he became quite the pet of the Lady Inglatine. At Marsury he trained with the Brothers and Guardsmen, served with distinction against border incursions to the far north of Barle and the Leutan border, and married Eselda, the youngest of Temmin the Bastard's daughters by Cariodas. He was never allowed to return to Kellen, but was given a holding in northern Barle. Ardunn was the first Marquess of Hawksfield, and took the name Anamma."

"Anamma? But they're still at Hawksfield—I have Anamma cousins!" exclaimed Temmin.

Teacher nodded. "Ardunn is your ancestor, just as Tennoc is. Ardunn was a charming man, perhaps the most charming of all your ancestors. I enjoyed his company very much the rare times he was at court."

"What happened to Gwynna? And Cariodas?"

"Gwynna was recognized as Royal Mistress, a court position until relatively recent times. She and Queen Cariodas never saw one another again, the Queen staying at the Keep and Gwynna staying at Marsury with Lady Inglatine until that good woman's death. She was very old when she died—eighty-three. Queen Cariodas died young, of bleeding. She had not even reached the age of fifty. One day when her moontimes were coming to an end, her moon began and never stopped. Some suspicion fell on the King, and on Gwynna."

"They didn't hurt her, did they?"

"Oh, no, no. Tennoc sincerely loved her in his way. The Sisters acquitted anyone of wrongdoing in her death. Tennoc and Gwynna both mourned her for a solid year, and when her bones were ready for the royal chapel the King had her skull set with rubies—when next you are there, look for it. Queen Cariodas was a kind, gentle woman." The royal chapel in the Hill was the last place Temmin wanted to visit, but he knew when his mother's bones were taken there he would have no choice but to look for Cariodas. "In some ways, Cariodas was the stronger of the two women," continued Teacher. "She bore a great deal, but so did Gwynna. Gwynna came to court after the Queen's death as Royal Mistress. The King would have married her but she refused even then. They lived together until Tennoc's death in the year 112. She outlived him by two years and died in the reign of Andrin the Second."

"And Yellow Hanni?"

Teacher smiled. "Even I do not know what became of Hanni der Geelt. Tennoc looked for him in reflections the rest of his life. Wherever Hanni was, it was not within the borders of the Tremont of that time. I like to think he returned to his home country and died in some plump Leutan woman's arms a very old man."

Temmin returned a faint glimmer of Teacher's smile, thinking less of Hanni's fate and more of Tennoc's journey. He wanted his own revenge, badly. How many nights had he lain awake imagining the moment when he caught Ibbit? Then again, Tennoc knew where his enemies were and had the power to take reprisals. Temmin knew his enemy but not how to get at her, nor did he know how many more of Ibbit's kind there were. The only way to make sure was to slaughter the entire Sisterhood, sweep their clergy clean and start the Temple over, let damnation fall where it may. *It's what Tennoc did in Kellen before Gwynna stopped him, after all.* "Love stopped Tennoc from killing Ardunn, and the sons of the other lords," he said at last.

"He loved Gwynna more than he loved revenge," said Teacher. "There is always something more worthy of love than revenge, Temmin. Remember that if nothing else."

The remaining days passed quickly. Temmin said his goodbyes on the eleventh, kissing Lady Donnis, his grandmother the Dowager Duchess and his sisters big and small. He'd made one last attempt the night before to coax Alvo into coming with him, but the groom almost ran away—just like the last time he'd left, thought Temmin. Even so, he told the stablemaster that Alvo should be considered the man's second in command and successor in the stable yards. "No fear o' that, sir," said the man, "Nollson's the steadiest young 'un I've got, which is no surprise knowing 'is family, Estatesmen all the way back. T'wouldn't be surprising if a Nollson helped build t'old place," he added, jerking a thumb toward the Freehold.

Though he could not call himself a happy man, as he boarded the train to the City Temmin was a steadier man than he was on arriving at Whithorse. He returned with only Jenks and Fen Wallek; just as Fen had predicted, Arta refused to leave Anneya. "How could I be leavin a little babe like that to starve?" she'd exclaimed.

"There are others what can feed it!" grumbled her husband the morning of departure.

"'Who,' not 'what,' Mr Wallek," Jenks growled back.

"Who, what—who cares, I want my wife!" said Fen, throwing his hands in the air.

"We'll keep you busy, Wallek," said Temmin. "She'll be with you before you know it."

Temmin settled back into the royal car's red plush seats and brooded on Alvo's absence. At least Jebby was returning with him. Small comforts—perhaps they'd add up. The Lovers' Temple waited as well, but it was a double-edged comfort at best.

He thought of Tennoc, longing for his Gwynna and knowing he could never have her. Temmin longed for Allis and knew he could never have her, either. Gwynna reminded Tennoc of his humanity and stopped him from damning himself. Allis could stop Temmin from doing anything except loving her, and while he longed for her love in return, he knew it would damn them both if she did.

SEVENTEEN

Twenna and the baby arrived at her father's townhouse two weeks after the birth to chaos. Burly men were coming and going with everything they could cart off. White shrouds covered the few remaining furniture pieces until the movers could fetch them as well.

Twenna's one consolation was Wendia. The loyal maid's wages had been paid till the end of the spoke, and now she held the baby as Twenna tried to save something from the wreckage. Her wardrobe was already empty, the many beautiful dresses gone, even the ones she'd owned before she'd become the King's mistress. All that remained was the periwinkle silk she had on her back.

Her jewels had long since gone back to the Keep, including the sapphires he'd said were hers forever. Elbig Shelstone's creditors had even tried to take the little gold and coral ring her dead mother had given her to celebrate her first moon blood—she'd never taken it off, ever—but she'd cried so hard and looked so pitiful clutching her hand that the lawyer supervising the household's dismantling had finally relented. "We're taking all the rest, miss, and you can't stop us. We'd take that cloak," he added, gesturing to the blue velvet, ermine-lined cloak covering her shoulders, "but we've already packed up all your other clothes and t'isn't right to let a new mother wander winter streets without a covering of some kind."

"Thanks awfully," snapped Wendia; the man had enough heart to look ashamed for five seconds.

A huge man whose nose had been broken at least twice stuck his head through the drawing room door. "Miss? There's a gentl'man 'ere to see ya."

She looked to the lawyer. "We can give you a few moments of privacy, I suppose," he said. "Nothing small enough in here to smuggle out." Wendia, the lawyer and his workmen retreated, and Percet Lord Fennows sauntered in.

"Dear me, what a ruin," he said, staring about. "You're preoccupied with the, ah, *dismantling* of your household I should think, poor girl, so I'll get straight to the point, shall I. I am sympathetic to your plight. I have a proposal for you."

"Yes, My Lord?" fidgeted Twenna. In the next room the baby was working up to the thin wail of a newborn; he must be hungry. If this took much longer, Twenna's breasts would leak; they might stain not just her chemise, but soak her corset straight through onto her one dress.

"You're a comely little thing, Twenna, always said it. As it happens, I'm between, ah, *little friends* at the moment. Come with me. I have a nice apartment in the Park District, out of the way but not horribly far from the Promenade. You'd have your own staff, of course, and I'd clothe your back and shod your foot as the saying goes, ha ha! I'm prepared to be quite generous to a girl as pretty as you, I should think."

Twenna's stomach fluttered. Take the protection of Lord Fennows? She'd been required to play the part of his friend out of loyalty to his father, but she'd never liked him, not even a little; in fact, she rather loathed him. He was always leering at her and must have thought her too stupid to catch his many insulting innuendos. Still, she was desperate. She would hear him out. "What about my son, sir? What about Nerrik?"

He barked a laugh. "Nerrik? That's what happened, eh? Spread your legs on Neya's Day, did you? Put it in the Mother's House. I know a fine one outside the City, I sponsor a child there already—er, not *my* child, you understand, it's just the decent thing to do, a 'coin for the Lady' as the saying goes, eh? It's clean and out of the way, and they'll raise the little tyke up to be a skilled craftsman or perhaps even a Father or Scholar if he's bright. You'll never have to think of it again."

"No!" said Twenna before he'd even finished speaking. "No! They can have everything else. They can't take Rikki!"

"Damn you, girl, you can't expect a fellow to take you under his protection with a baby in your arms! Girls like you don't get to keep their children, not if they want to make a living."

Twenna's despair boiled into rage. "You, sir, are not a gentleman! I'll go to the Mother's House myself before I accept the protection of a lout—a cad—a *spotty-faced prat* like you!" She fled from the room.

"And you're no lady! You'll end up on the block in the Father's Temple without your brat anyway, see if you don't, and then I'll visit you in the whorehouse you end up in!" Fennows yelled after her. "Perhaps I'll buy your indenture myself!"

Twenna joined the maid and the baby in the entryway; he was now crying so hard his little blunt tongue vibrated in his open mouth. "Thank you, Wendia, thank you so much, Amma bless you," Twenna sobbed as she took him in her arms. She ran up the stairs to her now-empty room, closed the door and sat down on the uncarpeted floor. She unfastened her bodice and guided the tiny boy onto her nipple; he complained around it until he settled down to eat.

Resting her back against the wall, she could just see out the window; snow fell in fits and starts. The grate was empty and cold, and she pulled the blue velvet cloak closer around the baby at her breast. There she stayed, rocking him on the bare floor until the workmen begged her pardon but she had to leave now, very sorry she had no place to go but that's how it was, miss, very sorry, nothing personal, only business. They chivvied her out the door and onto the front step of the house that had once been her father's; the Shelstones' former belongings, heaped on tarped wagons, were just pulling away.

Nerrik slept; Twenna pulled the cloak closed around them, grateful for its fur lining, and gazed about her in bewilderment. In the distance high above the City hovered the Keep like a giant astride the rock. Why had she ever wished to see inside it?

The snow stopped. She stepped out from under the doorway's protection and into the slushy street, toward the last resort of abandoned women and children.

The Temple of Amma was a C-shaped, white stone building tiled in clear blues from powder to midnight in mosaics and reliefs of sheep, goats, pigs, sheaves of wheat, children, mothers, looms and shuttles; its wings curved away from the Promenade, where it anchored the row of buildings leading down the Temple Green to its end at the Temple of Pagg the Father. Nestled between those wings stood the enormous Mother's House, an institutional-looking structure built around a large courtyard. By the time

Twenna reached its steps, her little boots were soaked through; they were made for carriages, not for walking winter streets.

Inside it was warm and noisy; the place smelled of cabbage, sour milk, lavender, clean laundry and children. Women and children were cleaning, carrying laundry and scurrying about. It hummed, loudly but not unpleasantly. The women wore shapeless, ugly wool dresses, high-necked and utilitarian, blue for the priestesses and gray for the laity; some carried babies on their backs or in slings across their fronts. The boy children wore dark wool breeches and smocks; the girls wore dresses much like their elders, covered in white pinafores. Twenna took Nerrik out from under her cloak. A whiff came to her nose; did Rikki need changing, or was it coming from somewhere else?

A frazzled little woman in a Mother's blue habit marched up to her. "May I help you? Are you leaving this child?"

"I…I've never been here, can you help me?"

The Mother swept a professional eye over her. "Hm. Come with me." She led the way into a cramped room off the busy main hall and shut the door; the noise seeped through the thin wood. She motioned to a chair, sat down herself behind a desk, its one short leg shimmed with a wooden block, and pulled out a thick ledger bound in blue cloth. "There is a back way, you know. Or you could have sent it with a maidservant, you didn't have to come yourself."

"I beg your pardon? Sent what?"

"The baby. You're leaving it here, aren't you?"

Twenna hugged Nerrik tight and stood up; he squeaked in his sleep. "You won't take him from me, will you? Please don't take him!"

"Gently, gently, dear!" soothed the surprised Mother, waving her back down into her chair. "We won't take him from you unless you want us to. You really won't be parted?"

"No, no, never!"

"Oh, you poor thing," sighed the Mother. She dipped a pen in the desk's inkwell. "All right then, your name?"

"Twenna Shelstone. Miss."

"Parents?"

"Elbig and Deannis. They're dead."

"Child's name?"

"Nerrik."

"His father's name?"

"I…I'm not sure."

"Last name Shelstone, then." The Mother gave her scribbling a judg-
mental squint; she passed the pen to Twenna and turned the ledger around.
"Sign here." Twenna dipped the pen and signed. The Mother blotted it,
sanded it for good measure, poured the sand into its reservoir and closed
the book. "All right then, Miss Shelstone, welcome to the Mother's House.
It's not a comfortable life," she said, looking askance at the ermine, "but
you get breakfast, luncheon, tea and dinner, and while the babe is nursing
he may sleep with you in your cell. In exchange, you are expected to work.
Cleaning, cooking, taking care of the motherless children—if you have a
great deal of milk, we may make you a wet nurse. We try to feed as many
babies on the breast as possible. It's cheaper, and here at the Mother's House
we're forced to scrimp and save where we can. Come with me, now." They
left the tiny office.

"Otherwise," the Mother continued as they marched into the main
hall, "it's the laundry for a strong young one like you. We do all the other
Temples' laundry, you know. It's our main income apart from tithes." The
Mother led her through the swarms in the main hall and down a flight of
stairs into the basement. Women and older children bustled about the huge,
warm, steamy room; it smelled pleasantly of soft soap. As comfortable as it
was now, it was probably a sight less so in the summer.

Behind a counter, a silent woman dressed in gray sized Twenna up and
gave the Mother two large bundles wrapped in white sheets. The Mother
gave a polite nod and marched Twenna back into the main hall and up five
flights of stairs to a dark but clean hallway lined in narrow doors. From behind them came snatches of lullabies and the crying of both newborns and
grown women. The Mother took a key from her apron pocket and opened
a door at the hallway's end. "This is one of the nicer rooms. You'll have a
window facing the courtyard, at least."

Twenna looked around the tiny, immaculate, colorless room: whitewashed walls; pegs for clothing; white sheets and gray wool blankets with
a thick blue stripe at the top on a neatly-made, narrow bed; gray-painted
floorboards; a small, rough rug that might have once been blue on the floor
before the bed; a basin and pitcher atop a miniature night stand; a pale un-
padded wood rocking chair; a tiny radiator beneath a window that looked
out on a gray and white sky and the wing far across the courtyard that likely
held little rooms just like the one in which they stood; and a tiny figure of
Amma in a niche above the bed's curving metal headboard.

The harried Mother dropped the two great white bundles on the bed.
"These are yours. Diapers and clothes for the little chap in this one and

clothes for you in the other one, both wrapped in spare sheets just in case he has an accident. Clean sheets once a week otherwise. You are to maintain this room exactly as it is now—a Senior Mother inspects unannounced. There's a tap at the end of the hall, cleaning supplies are in the hall closet, and you are to tend to the room on your own time. We rise at dawn and retire at sundown, regardless of the season. Key's on the nightstand, keep it with you and the door locked when you're not here. The child is never to be left unattended in this room. Please change into your uniform as soon as possible. Just lay the little one down on the bed, he can't roll off yet." The Mother marched out of the room, leaving the door open.

"Where am I to put my things?" Twenna said to no answer. Nerrik began to root and fuss against her shoulder, weak movements that nevertheless set her breasts to aching. She sat down on the bed between the two bundles and allowed herself a long, shuddering sob.

"It's not that bad," said a voice at the door. Twenna looked up. It was a woman about her own age, her chestnut hair twisted into a low, simple bun. Her snub nose sat in a face neither pretty nor plain. She wore a lay Mother's uniform, the same as the one in Twenna's bundle: ugly loose gray high-necked dress collared in white; a voluminous unbleached muslin apron tying it closer to the body; and a plain wool shawl still the color of the sheep, its ends crossed over her breast and pinned behind her. In a canvas sling before her slept a baby not much older than Rikki, or so Twenna guessed; all she could see was white-blond fuzz and an obstinate little nose exactly like its mother's.

"I've been here three spokes—since before the baby was born," the woman resumed. "A roof over your head, hot food, and it's not *too* cold in the rooms. The Mothers try to be kind when they can, and they work as hard as we do. It's not that bad, really, once you get used to it." She eyed the cape and the silk dress. "Though you had further to fall than I did."

The woman came into the room, closed the door and held out her arms. "Here, let me take the little one while you get dressed. We'll get you new boots after, those are ruined."

"He's hungry," faltered Twenna.

"Well then, let's get you settled to feed him and I'll help you put your things away, shall I." The woman took Nerrik from Twenna's arms, shooed her off the bed and set the baby squarely in the middle before she attacked the bundles. "Just take off your nice things and hang them on the pegs for now, we'll get them put away properly in a bit. My name's Meggan Esterill. At least I think it's still Esterill. I'm not sure if Gyors will make me stop using it, the divorce isn't final yet. Just call me Meggan."

Twenna hung up her blue velvet cape and her periwinkle silk dress on the pegs; she tucked her gloves into the cloak's inside pocket and let her fingers linger a moment on the cloak's soft ermine lining. All gone, all her finery gone. "Take off those petticoats," advised Meggan. "Put them away with your good things. There are petticoats in your bundle—oh, good heavens, take *all* those underthings off and save them for better times, the laundresses will ruin them! Let me play ladies maid for you. Ugh, I think your babe needs changing."

Soon they had Nerrik clean if unhappy, and Twenna re-dressed in a plain linen chemise, plain canvas maternity stays, two wool petticoats, thick black woolen stockings and the ugly gray wool dress. "See, here's how it opens to let you nurse your babe, and I see you're going to need these nursing pads. Tuck these against your nipples when you're done feeding him, it'll keep you from staining your chemise. Sit down, now," said Meggan, guiding Twenna into the rocker. She draped a heavy woolen shawl over Twenna's shoulders and handed her the agitated baby, tucking the bed's pillow under Twenna's elbow.

Twenna fumbled with the unfamiliar dress fastenings ahead of Nerrik's impending scream and guided the freed nipple into his hungry mouth. Her milk began to flow; the tension inside her ebbed, and exhaustion flooded in to take its place. "Thank you, Meggan. My name is Twenna Shelstone."

"I know who you are, Miss Shelstone. We were never introduced, but we attended several of the same gatherings over the course of my last season. Your last season too, apparently."

"Please call me Twenna." The baby in the sling began to fuss; Meggan used the remaining bundle on the bed to bolster herself into the corner, where she sat crosslegged as she nursed her own child. "What's your baby's name?" said Twenna.

"I still haven't decided. She hasn't a last name either. My husband turned me away, my lover turned me away, my father turned me away. I'm just Meggan now. I'll probably take formal vows at some point and become Mother Meggan. I don't know what else I can do—well I suppose I could remarry, but then I'd have to leave poor little no-name here and I won't, will I, little bunny?" she crooned to the tiny blond bit. "That's what I should name you—Connia. *Connia.* I hadn't thought of it before, I rather like it. It means 'little rabbit' in the old Kellish tongue, or so my great-gran always said. She called me that when I was little. *Connia. Connie.* Hm! What's your baby's name?"

Nerrik pulled off the nipple with a gasping sigh of sleepy delight and Twenna chuckled in spite of herself. "Nerrik. I call him Rikki."

"Oh, a Neya's Day babe?"

"He—he has to be," said Twenna, her own sleepy relaxation retreating. "I was at the Spectacle last year. I don't remember what happened—as far as I know I was never with anyone other than Harsin, I swear it."

"It's all right, you're not on trial here. If you told me who it was I'd never tell anyway. I didn't have to tell *my* husband, he was there when it happened in a way."

"I beg your pardon?"

Meggan fixed her with a hard, questioning eye. "Are you easily shocked? No? ...My husband doesn't like women."

"What's so shocking about that? I don't think my father likes—liked— women all that much. He never remarried after my mama died, and I'm their only child."

"No, but he did manage to get *you* on her. Gyors couldn't bear to touch me at all, but he was the oldest son. It was his duty to have children, or re- nounce his inheritance. He couldn't bear to do *that*—what gentleman wish- es to earn his living? Oh, I knew he preferred men, but you hear about mar- ried men and their lovers all the time, don't you, and *they* have children. He said he loved me, and I just thought..." She absently shook her baby's tiny hand as it clutched her finger. "I didn't think. It never occurred to me that he couldn't spare at least a little love for me. The man I knew was his *particular friend* has children by his wife. Several. Gyors went to great lengths to prove he loved me before we married, but once the cord was tied it all changed. He didn't love me at all, not even a little. He only had sex with me once, and that was in the Lovers' Temple with another man. A sweet man, the current Supplicant. The Heir, actually. How funny to think I've seen the Heir half- naked. I still think about him now and again, how kind he was to me. That was the only time Gyors could manage it."

Twenna found this extremely personal, candid talk on such indelicate topics uncomfortable, but then, coming to a Mother's House was usually the result of indelicate topics; perhaps shared experience made for less restraint in conversation here. "Then how...?"

"Oh, once we'd gone to the Temple, I decided to do as he asked and let his *particular friend* into our bed. The time at the Lovers' Temple didn't take, you see, so we tried again, this time with Pollus. My husband still couldn't perform. But later that week, Pollus came to me while Gyors was at his club..."

"…And you…?"

"'And we,'" said Meggan, her smile crooked, sad and somewhat defiant. "'And we' for a whole spoke or more, almost every day, until I got with child. Gyors knew it couldn't be his, and so here I am with little no-name—Connia. I think I really like that name."

"You never told him who the father is?"

"He said he didn't believe me, and Pollus denied it. Gyors doesn't want to know because he loves Pollus…but he knows. It's just a matter of time before they end it."

Nerrik let out a tiny snore and Twenna fumbled the unfamiliar fastenings of her bodice closed. The tears in her eyes made it more difficult than it should have been, even one-handed. "Harsin swears he's not the father, but there's never been anyone else." She thought about the golden young man whose face she could not see, but whose body she remembered against her, inside her, all around her. "Except sometimes I try to remember what happened at the Neya's Day Spectacle and maybe…I don't know!"

"A girl as beautiful as you could leave the baby here and re-marry," said Meggan, fastening up her own dress as the newly-named Connia slept in her sling. "Men come here all the time from the other duchies looking for wives—widowers looking for a free nanny and housekeeper, mostly. They try Mother's Houses far from home to avoid anyone knowing the wives they bring back, though everyone knows she must be a beggar, an orphan, a bastard or worse. As long as she behaves no one mentions it. They'll make you leave your child behind, but they'll provide for you. You'd be respectable again and mistress of your own house. You might even come here and see the baby from time to time. They encourage it, if you settle nearby and your new husband will allow it. Most women take the chance."

Twenna shook her head. "My mother is dead, my father is dead, my love has abandoned me—I have no one and nothing but Nerrik." She looked over at the beautiful clothes of her former life, hanging on the pegs; she looked down at her new rough gray wool skirts. She wanted to cry, but she couldn't wake the baby. "I shall learn to bear it here rather than be parted from him." She rocked and rocked and gave in to her tears, but the baby didn't wake up. "I'm not terribly clever, but I shall learn."

Winter's Ending turned into Spring's Beginning. Temmin's twentieth birthday came and went on the ninth of the spoke with little fanfare; the country was still in mourning, and he was in no mood to celebrate.

The Temple kept Temmin quite busy. Helping petitioners soothed his grief somewhat, but between sessions he walked through the rose marble halls seeing nothing but gray. His duties ran the gamut from coaching petitioners through the acts of love to helping heal emotional wounds. What he so often had in common with the petitioners was not eroticism but pain, now more than ever. "Does suffering always come with sex and emotions?" Temmin asked Barik Lover one day.

"It doesn't have to," he answered, "but it often does."

"Why?"

Barik considered. "Truthfully, Temmin, we don't always get to know *why* we suffer, and if we did it still wouldn't do us any good. The Gods conceal much from us, for reasons known only to Them. All we can do is accept Their guidance, and do the work given to us."

Temmin tried to do the work given to him, failed, and tried again. *I'm doing all I can do, Lord and Lady*, he prayed. *Make me stop loving her—or at least make me willing to stop loving her.* He received no answers; despite his prayers and outward humility, deep in his heart Temmin clung to Allis harder than ever. He fantasized her living at the Estate, or Middlemont, or even in the Keep itself once her time as Embodiment was over. His father had agreed never to keep a mistress under his roof, but surely Temmin and his own wife—whoever she was to be—might negotiate something different. Tennoc and Cariodas had done so, after all, and Teacher said she was content while she lived.

He supposed the King was already thinking about suitable brides and alliances; by Temmin's age, he'd already been married two years and was a father. Temmin resolved to marry a woman who would be the mother of his children and no more. True, it hadn't worked for his parents, but they fell in love. He would not. Look what came of it. Nothing but pain.

At least he was covering his tracks. Keeping an unruffled, unreadable exterior—or projecting an entirely different mien—was almost as important as reading others. Nerr was the God of actors, after all. Allis and Issak continued on as his teachers, but casual contact had faded to nothing; when it did occur it was inevitably with Issak and not Allis. He loved Issak, even more than he loved Anda, but not as he loved Allis.

Talking with someone about it never came into his head. He'd done that already. What could they say that hadn't already been said? It would just expose him to further humiliation and pain. Allis didn't return his feelings, and Temmin could not bear confronting it—not with a heart already so full of grief for his mother. He soldiered on, feeling more and more like a failure and a fraud.

Then came the rebuke.

Summoned once again to Most High Beloved Malla's chambers, Temmin exchanged cautious greetings with her. "How may I serve you, Most High?"

"Tonight we have a special class, my dear. I wish you to narrate the Sacred Eight for an incoming class of Postulants."

Rank beginners in the Most High Beloved's chambers? Most irregular, but Temmin kept his face neutral. "I am always happy to assist in teaching, Most High."

"You're always so good with the new Postulants, Temmin Supplicant," said the old woman, patting his thigh, "but the lesson is not for them."

Temmin's scalp prickled, but he presented polite attentiveness and curiosity. "I am always grateful for anything you may teach me, Most High."

"I rather doubt it this time." Malla clapped twice; the heavy gold-chased doors to her rooms opened, and sixteen Postulants—eight male, eight female—filed in. At the end of the timid procession came Senik Lover and Allis. She flicked a glance his way; he detected a minute anguish, but it resolved so quickly into her teaching face that he doubted himself.

The Postulants sat cross-legged on the carpeted floor in a respectful half-moon around the wide, low couch in the middle of the room. Allis and Senik disrobed, folding their Temple garb and setting it to one side. "Now, Temmin," said the Most High, "I would like you to narrate for the Postulants as Allis and Senik demonstrate the Sacred Eight."

Temmin struggled mightily, but his face flushed as he rose to his feet and placed himself before the half-moon. "Of course." He turned to the students, his back to the naked couple. "Sexual positions can be broken down into eight basics," he began. "Each one expresses the quality of a God. We call them the Sacred Eight."

A blush ran through the seated Postulants and several men began to fidget. "Turn so you may see both your students and your demonstrators, Temmin Supplicant," said Malla. "Define for them now the terms 'giver' and 'receiver.'"

Temmin did as he was told. There on the couch lay Allis, her full breasts splayed to each side of her body. Above her knelt Senik, stroking himself. Senik caught his eye and winked, and Temmin resisted the urge to throw him to the floor and beat his beautiful face in. "The giver is the one who penetrates," he continued. "The receiver is the one being penetrated. A man is not always the giver. There are ways for a woman to penetrate as well, sometimes manually, sometimes with devices."

"Very good," nodded Malla. "Senik, Allis, continue." Senik settled himself between Allis's legs; she let out a small gasp as he entered her and began a slow rhythm.

A fine red mist gathered in the periphery of Temmin's vision, but he kept up his narration. "When the giver is superior, we call it the Way of Pagg, for He is the Father and the Law. There are many variations on this basic position," he continued as Allis and Senik shifted; Senik took her legs over his shoulders and pushed deeper into her, his happy groan masking the sound of Temmin's grinding teeth.

"Next is the Way of Amma, for She is the Mother and the Lady of the Cattle." Senik withdrew long enough for Allis to rearrange herself on all fours, and entered her again. Temmin watched her breasts sway with each lazy thrust, at once aroused and furious. Allis slid to lie flat on the couch, Senik still inside her. "Again, many variations."

When he ran through the Eight himself, Temmin prided himself on his control; he drove his partners to release multiple times while holding his own back until the end. Now a tic pulsed at the corner of his eye, and he was not at all sure he'd make it to the end of this set without running away—or worse. He wanted to pull Senik off and pound into Allis himself until they were both senseless. He wanted to maul her breasts, to soothe her and cover her with kisses; he wanted to do anything but stand here, pretending to be calm.

Allis and Senik both stood up. Allis sat back down on the couch, her hands braced behind her; Senik kneeled between her legs and began kissing up the inside of her thighs. "This is the way of Venna, for She is the Sister and seeks union without penetration," grated Temmin. Senik reached the curly black thatch between his partner's legs, spread her lips wide and licked her. Allis let out a moan and cradled Senik's dark head in her hands, pressing his mouth closer; she threw back her head and came with a great cry, her knees rising up. Temmin suppressed most of a growl of pure frustration. The class studied the lovemakers in rapt concentration, the men all sporting erections and the women flushed and open-mouthed, but he knew Malla had heard him, and probably Allis and Senik as well.

When Allis stopped shaking, she and Senik traded places. "When the giver takes the receiver's mouth, it is the Way of Farr, for He is the proud Warrior Whose foe kneels at His feet." Temmin heard a tremor creep into his voice and despaired.

Senik's hands fisted in Allis's hair as her head rose and fell between his legs. A male Postulant gave a sudden cry and began to shiver; a wet patch spread on his trouser front. Senik looked up at the sound. "Word of advice, men: Don't touch yourselves during these demonstrations before you've learned the Patience." A nervous laugh rippled through the half-moon but for the embarrassed young man.

"Stop," Senik murmured, and Allis obeyed. He flashed a grin, displaying even, white teeth. "Even I can't last forever in such a skilled mouth!" The chuckle ran through the Postulants again. Temmin wanted to pull Senik's perfect teeth out through his ass.

Allis got up from her crouch, straddled Senik's lap and eased herself onto him, his hands spread on her flexing bottom. "Isn't that pretty?" murmured Malla as Senik helped his partner rise and fall.

"Seated positions are the way of Eddin, for He is the Wise One and loves learning," Temmin told the Postulants as calmly as he could. "In this position, one can see one's partner most clearly." Allis leaned back in Senik's arms so they could both watch as they came together and moved apart; Temmin couldn't see her hand, but knew where it was. Allis's face flushed and her breathing grew faster until she came again, Senik supporting her.

She wrapped her arms around Senik's neck. With his hands clutching her ass, Senik stood, still buried inside her; his thighs bunched and strained. As soon as he got his balance, he began to thrust. Stunned, Temmin pushed his tears as firmly back as possible but not quite far enough for his taste. "The Way of Nerr, Who finds pleasure in display. There are many variations on standing positions as well."

"Show them the supported Way of Nerr. We don't wish to tire Senik out completely," said Malla.

Temmin's hard-won self-control wobbled. "Most High, I'm not dressed for it."

The Most High Beloved waved a wrinkled hand at him. "Remove your shirt."

Temmin shucked off the embroidered tunic in resignation but instead of folding it he tossed it on the couch. He knew everyone could see his own erection, but it would have been considered odd if he weren't aroused. He placed himself at Allis's back, and she braced herself against him; her bottom pressed at the tip of his arousal, and he shifted her upward, supporting her thighs; sweat slicked her back, and she slid against his chest. She separated from him long enough to sweep her long black hair over one shoulder.

A wicked smile spread Senik's lips. His free hand grabbed Temmin's neck and pulled him close; Senik kissed him. "Thank you," he said when they parted. Temmin wanted to wipe his mouth off, but he couldn't without dropping Allis.

Senik's next thrust knocked her against Temmin's chest. "Unfortunate we're doing the Eight," hissed Senik. "You might take her in the ass at the same time otherwise." Temmin closed his eyes and clenched his teeth, hoping the Postulants would take it as a savoring of the moment—the only mercy he would get, for the sworn clergy in the room knew differently.

A few lusty pushes later, Senik withdrew; Temmin helped Allis to her feet again. As protocol dictated, she stood on her tiptoes and pulled him down into a brief kiss. Her lips were tentative, almost forlorn, and his heart twisted further; pity was far worse. "Thank you," she murmured before turning back to Senik, who reclined on his side on the wide couch.

Temmin took up his position again before the eager Postulants. *Almost done, almost done,* he repeated to himself. "The Way of Neya is side by side, for She prefers pleasure for its own sake. It allows Her lover access to all of Her—Her breasts and Her neck as well as Her sex." Allis snugged herself against Senik, both of them slick and shining in the warm room. She threw her topmost leg over his, and his cock slid home. Two or three Postulants let out tiny whines. Senik slipped his arms around her and molded her breasts, plucking and twisting the nipples; he bit at her neck as she writhed. Senik moved his topmost hand to where they were joined together, circling until Allis convulsed, screaming and shouting. For a moment, Temmin thought she stared at him before she closed her eyes and her hair covered her face.

Senik withdrew and lay flat on his back, playing with his cock as Allis caught her breath. Just as Temmin wondered whether she'd fallen asleep she rolled over and crawled atop Senik, straddling him. The end, finally. "The Way of Harla, the receiver atop the giver. For all our illusions of control—" Did he have any illusions of control any more? "—For all our illusions of control, Death rides us all." Senik lay still as Allis bounced atop him until he gripped her hips and began bucking up into her. She leaned over to kiss him, cradling his head in her hands until he rose up and up; his hips wedged into her, his head arched away from her, and he bellowed out his final release.

"That," said Temmin to his class, "is the Sacred Eight. You will memorize it. Men, you will be required to last through the entire sequence with ease, with variations, and without rushing before you take your vows. That gives you three years to learn the Patience. Women may reach their crisis as many times as they wish, though learning the Patience is considered good form. Shall I excuse them, Most High?"

Malla nodded. "You are excused, Postulants. Amuse yourselves as you wish before lights out, though I imagine some of you may want to practice while the demonstration is fresh in your minds. I remind you to keep your activities to the private areas of the Temple." The Postulants stampeded from the room.

Temmin stood before the Most High Beloved. "Am I excused as well, Most High?"

She studied him coolly. "You are excused. While I know you don't need to practice the Eight, I may say there are other disciplines you must work at more diligently—as you have been reminded before. I trust you are clear now on this matter, Temmin Supplicant?"

"Very, Most High," he bit off, all pretense at calm abandoned. He kissed her hand and retrieved his crumpled tunic from the couch, where Allis wiped the sweat from her body. He bowed. "Forgive me if I don't give the customary kiss." She gave him a serene, disinterested nod; he turned on his heel and stalked from the room. Perhaps it hadn't all been Malla's idea.

Senik caught up with him in the hall. "I don't think you and I are finished," he said.

"Oh, I very much think we are." Temmin picked up his pace.

Senik kept up. "You were rude to your superiors, including the Embodiment and the Most High."

"Senik, I strongly suggest you leave me alone," he growled.

"Oh, I very much think not."

Temmin jolted to a halt, his temper fully engaged and his face within an inch of Senik's classical nose; Allis's scent arose from the man. "I am warning you, Senik! Keep it up and you'll get a lot more than a kiss."

"You wanna fight?" said the priest, a back alley accent suddenly gracing his voice. His beautiful face turned hard as paving stones. "You wanna? Is that it? You wanna fight me?"

Temmin snorted like a bull and nearly pawed the ground. "I want to *grind you into a pulp!*"

"Then c'mon. You and me. In one of the Temple's Own training salons. There should be an empty one this time of day. C'mon." Senik leaned in, a sneer slashing his face.

Temmin paused. Strangling Senik until his crystalline blue eyes popped and his alluring lips turned purple tempted him. Senik's sense of humor always sliced a little too close to the bone, but Temmin didn't hate the man; they'd been bedmates more than once in the last two years. That demonstration was calculated to humiliate Temmin as much as possible, yes, but it had clearly been Malla's calculation, not Senik's.

Temmin could beat him in a fair fight; he had a longer reach, a more muscular physique, and possibly more training. But what would happen to Senik afterwards? He had to know that even if he beat Temmin, he'd lose once the King heard about it. It was a goad—either Senik's own or more likely more of Malla's rebuke—and Temmin decided not to give him satisfaction. "I could whip you," he said. "We both know it."

"We most certainly do not," laughed Senik. "You know nothing about where I've been and what I've done."

"And we both know that in the end I could *have* you whipped." Temmin kissed him, biting Senik's lip hard enough to draw blood; the Lover tasted of Allis. "There's your 'thank you.' Now leave me alone." He resumed his solitary walk back to his room.

"You still haven't thanked Allis," Senik called after him. Temmin resisted the urge to make a rude gesture and kept walking, his pace more moderated but his feet striking the floor harder than necessary.

Once inside his room, he knelt before the little altar in the Suppliants Chamber, lit a candle to the small entwined statues and prayed. "I've failed You. I've learned so much, but I haven't learned the detachment You require of us. I thought I'd done the right thing coming here, but I don't know if the people are prospering as the prophecy said they would. I'm trying not to love Allis. I did what I was told and turned to others but it hasn't helped. I've asked for Your help but You haven't answered me. I've given up so much for You! I set my father against me and lost the last years of my mother's life for Your sake. Can't you give me *something* in return? Some little thing? *Why* can't Allis love me? Why is she so cruel?" Tears started in his eyes. "It isn't fair." Even as the words left his lips he knew they were childish, and he cringed in shame. Jenks had told him something two years ago: *The great secret of adulthood is that there's always something wrong and life isn't fair.* Perhaps Temmin was an adult now, for the secret was no secret any more.

That night at dinner he sat among the clergy's lower ranks. He usually ate with the Most Highs and the Embodiments, but tonight he could not bring himself to do it.

After the meal, Anda slipped her arm in his. "Are you free? I miss you, let's have a good gabble in your room." In short order, he found himself stretched out on the Suppliants Chamber couch, his head in her lap, tears sliding down his temples into his ears and everything confessed. "Oh, Tem, I'm so sorry," she murmured, stroking his hair. "I heard a little about a demonstration and confess I wondered."

Temmin raised up on one elbow. "Heard what? From whom? I will murder Senik one day, I swear—"

"No, no, Senik is a gorgeous, annoying git but he's not malicious. I heard a couple of Postulants talking. They had no idea what they'd seen, but I gave them the 'class time is confidential' lecture and they slunk off with their tails between their legs. I wish you'd told me sooner, and why won't you talk to me about Allis? I know we're both busy, but I'll always make time for you—you can always talk to me."

Temmin sank back into her lap. "What is there to talk about? I love someone I'm not allowed to love. Malla told me once that if we were anyone other than who we are she would have separated us for good and all—each assigned to different ends of the country. But she's an Embodiment and I'm a Supplicant. We have to be here. We have to work together."

"When you've left the Temple you can pursue a less formal relationship."

"Not in the way I want. What I want is impossible."

"Surely *something* is better than nothing? You can still live in hope, Tem, just don't let it stop you from loving anyone else."

Temmin looked up into her round, good-natured face above her Beloved's tunic. She wore a short, boned velvet vest that supported her large breasts like a corset; he ran his fingers across its pile, turning it from silvery pink to deep rose and back. The color suited her better than her old white Supplicants garb had, but he missed it anyway. He took her hand and played with her fingers. "I wish *we* were in love, Anda."

"How would that be easier, hectic boy? You can't marry me, either."

"No, but I could keep you. I'd make you my mistress the day I'm through here. I'd even make you a countess when I become king."

Anda brought his hand to her lips and kissed it. "That might be nice, but it would never do, you know it wouldn't."

"No. It wouldn't." He covered her hand in his and gave it a squeeze. "When I become king, perhaps I'll make you a countess anyway." Temmin sat up on his knees and smoothed her hair back from her face. "Stay with me tonight, Anda. Please."

Anda stayed, and wiped away the tears from Temmin's eyes as they made love in his alcove bed.

EIGHTEEN

Meggan Esterill entered Twenna's tiny room with a perfunctory knock. "He's come again."

"Hush, Rikki just fell asleep," said Twenna, her foot rocking the baby's cradle. "Who's come?"

Meggan dropped her voice. "You know very well who. Captain Marr." She sat down beside Twenna on the bed.

Twenna tried to avoid her pointed look. "Oh…oh. He's serious, isn't he."

"Not to be put off, I'd say. This is his sixth visit in two weeks. Come, he's waiting for you in an alcove."

"Rikki just fell asleep," Twenna repeated in a weak voice.

Meggan patted her shoulder. "I'll watch him. Connia's at the nursery. They know where I am. If she needs me they'll come get me and I'll take Rikki with me. He won't die if you're not with him every single moment."

Twenna thought she might die without him, but she rose from the bed and put her apron back on, dawdling like a child trying to put off chores.

"Oh, come now. He's really a very nice man," tutted Meggan. "Good-looking enough, steady job in the Guards, and he'd marry you. The last two only wanted to keep you."

"I don't know if he'll let me take Rikki, and I'm not leaving without him."

"You'll never know if you don't go down to the alcove to see the man," insisted Meggan, shooing her toward the door.

Twenna dragged her feet down the five staircases from her room to the main hall. Captain Marr waited for her in the last alcove to the left of the dining hall door. The Mothers had no time to play chaperone; instead the open alcoves gave a bare amount of privacy while still allowing the occupants to be seen if not heard by the multitudes constantly coming and going past them.

Captain Marr nervously groomed the bottle-brush mustache growing into thick chops framing his broad, pleasant face, a style in fashion two years ago called the Heir after Prince Temmin, though Twenna remembered older men wearing their facial hair like that in her childhood. How much older was Captain Marr than she? Twenna estimated perhaps ten years at most—early thirties. There had always been something familiar about him, something protective and reassuring.

The Captain stood at Twenna's approach, dropped a glove and fumbled, trying to decide whether to pick it up or make his bow. He chose the bow. "Good day, Miss Shelstone, thank you so very much for honoring me with your company!"

"Oh, the honor is mine, Captain," she murmured, blushing.

"Please! Please, sit," he said, gesturing at a straight-backed wooden chair. "Or—is it—that's not correct, is it? This is your house, not mine, and…I'm afraid I am a Guardsman, ma'am, my manners are not perhaps as genteel as they might be." He sat down in the second chair and smiled, all muffled nerves and excitement.

Meggan was right. He seemed a kind man.

"He is thirty-one, widowed three years ago," Twenna told Meggan that night just before lights out. "He's being transferred to Hawksfield in Barle next week as commander of the garrison there, he has a ten-year-old girl named Mellit, he admires me greatly and thinks we should do very well together. Then he requested the honor of tying the marriage cord round my wrist."

"Will you give it to him?"

Twenna was silent for a moment. "I told him Rikki must come with me—he was reluctant and somewhat surprised, but I told him that was my bride price. He said he'd think on it and tell me later this week."

She was sweeping the main hall floor early the next morning after breakfast, Rikki in his sling, when Captain Marr returned. He'd shaved so closely that his chin shone; his beefy frame filled out his best uniform. Twenna winced, recognizing its lines: her father's special pattern, still in use at his old tailoring concern. Captain Marr apparently had money enough to bespeak the best; whatever else could be said about the late Elbig Shelstone, he'd been an excellent tailor.

"May I have a word, Miss Shelstone?" asked the Captain. Twenna looked to the raw-boned Mother supervising the cleaning crew; the smiling priestess nodded toward an empty alcove. Once inside, Marr dispensed with sitting and took her hands. "I will raise your son as my own. I will love you both. Please—Twenna—let me take you from this dismal place. Do me the honor of being my wife."

The Captain's warm, thick-fingered hands clasped hers in awkward sincerity. Rikki stirred and gave a faint squeak in his sling, his blue eyes blinking awake before flashing the gummy grin of a two-spokes-old at her. She looked around the main hall, at the gray, drawn women and barefoot children coming and going, as cheerful as they could be in a cold and sterile place. Life in Barle married to a stranger? Or life here among the ghostlike surplus women, unwanted children and overworked Mothers to watch her son grow up to an uncertain future? "The honor is mine," she faltered; with greater strength she added, "I accept you, Captain Marr."

"Lorrenz, please, my name is Lorrenz," he said, the bottle-brush on his upper lip quivering. He kissed her hands; the mustache tickled her knuckles, but not unpleasantly. "Oh, Twenna, you make me very happy, very happy indeed, and I shall do everything in my power to make you happy as well!"

The Mothers were nothing if not efficient. Twenna found herself packed and ready to go in two days, her gray uniform returned to the laundry and her fine clothes from her former life sold in exchange for four plain dresses, two of cotton and two of wool, and a warm wool cloak; she kept her beautiful underthings, stowed these last spokes in a paper box under her bed. The Captain paid for her to keep her sturdy gray shawl, her Mother's House underthings, her boots, Rikki's clothes, his sling and a supply of diapers. "I will buy you more when we are in Hawksfield, my dear, but this will do for now."

The young Father who worked as the Mother's Temple liaison officiated at the wedding, a small affair held in the Mother's House chapel. "Obedience, humility, fidelity," Father Nino chanted as he helped Lorrenz tie the marriage cord round her left wrist—expensive, fine silken cord, many-stranded and braided in bright colors. Lorrenz tucked the end into the sleeve of her new fawn-colored dress: "I'll not lead you through the streets by it all the way back to Hawksfield, I promise," he winked, and she smiled.

Twenna made her goodbyes in the main hall now, a carpet bag at her feet and the cheerful Rikki kicking his legs in her new husband's arms. "Don't forget me," said Meggan, kissing her cheek and hugging her with her free arm.

"How could I ever forget you!" said Twenna, kissing Meggan in return. "You're the best—no, you're the *only* real friend I've ever had! I shall write, I promise." She kissed Connia's fuzz-covered head. "Be good, little bunny." She didn't know whether to cry tears of relief or regret as they walked from the Mother's House, through the Temple and onto the street, the Captain carrying her carpet bag and she carrying Rikki re-wrapped in her woolen shawl and a blanket, a soft white bonnet trimmed in pale yellow ribbons on his round little head. Lorrenz hired a cab and they trundled off to the post house to begin their long journey northeast into Barle and Captain Marr's new command. His daughter Mellit had gone ahead with Twenna's maid Wendia, newly recalled to service; Wendia would make the garrison commander's house fit to live in before the newlyweds arrived.

"I, ah, I must be honest with you, Twenna, now that we're married," said the Captain, fidgeting against the cab's firmly-stuffed seats.

Twenna tried to ignore the cold, trembling fingers stealing over her heart. "Please, sir, I hope you shall always feel you may tell me anything."

"Well...I don't wish to mislead you as to the kind the life we shall have in Hawksfield. You see, I've done myself up very nicely," he said, indicating his uniform, "and I'm afraid I indulged myself in the matter of our marriage cord."

Twenna touched the silk at her wrist; the cold fingers around her heart paused in confusion. "I'm not sure I understand."

"What I'm trying to say is, I am not a rich man. I've presented myself perhaps as having more money than I do in an effort to impress. You are used to far, far better than I can provide. Not that I am poor, not at all," he hastened. "I just don't wish to mislead you. My pay as a commander is not magnificent, but I have a family annuity as well. You will always have a good solid roof over your head, a cook, a footman and a girl of all work not including your Wendia, but I can't afford to keep my own carriage. And I can't afford many silk dresses, though you shall have at least one. I am sorry you could not keep the one you had. You were very beautiful in it, but I thought it might contain too many memories."

Twenna cast her mind back. She hadn't worn that dress since she'd arrived at the Mother's House. When could he have seen her in it?

His Farr's knot bobbed as he cleared his throat, rippling up and down his solid neck. "Which brings me to my last confession." He held her hands between his own, so large they made hers look childlike. "I have loved you since the first moment I saw you. You would not have noticed me, but I was quite close by many times. I was one of the King's Own in His Majesty's personal escort—we're trained to fade into the background. I was already on my way to becoming Chief Commander of the King's Own itself some day. When you…when Nerrik was born, I heard you'd come to the Mother's House. I gave up my position in the King's Own and applied to become Commander at Hawksfield in the hope that you would marry me. If you would, then I wanted to take you away from here, away from bad memories and staring eyes. If you wouldn't, then I wanted to be as far away as possible, for fear I might see you again and my heart crack wide open in grief."

Astonished tears filled Twenna's eyes, and the icy fingers melted. "Lorrenz—!"

"I know you don't love me yet, but I hope some day you may…that some day you may forget the King and love me instead."

Twenna reversed their hand clasp to wrap hers around his. "I'm not very clever as you may know, Lorrenz, but I will try to be a good wife to you, and I will try so very hard to love you."

Though it was not Malla's intent, Temmin closed his face to the world. He spent more time in the less-senior clergy's beds and gave Allis no more than his polite, rather stoic regard. He declined any assignment that might lead to physical intimacy between them—indeed, any assignment that might lead to them being alone. Supplicants were not allowed to pick and choose, but now the senior clergy let him.

As he withdrew, Allis did her best to let Temmin go. He would leave at Nerr's Day anyway, and here it was almost Neya's Day. But he stuck to her heart like a burr, a ball of tiny hooks she could never remove no matter how hard she tried. She'd done quite well at hiding the depth of her love from Issak and the Most Highs, but to herself she despaired. He would be gone soon, she would stay behind in a beautiful, pink, plush prison, and they'd rarely see one another for at least ten more years.

She never thought she would tire of being Neya's Embodiment so soon; she was proud the Goddess had chosen her. Issak was her sole family since their mother died, and separation from him had been a constant anxiety until the Gods had accepted them both together. Now they need never part. They would always be safe, always have enough to eat and a fine place to live. Though it forced them into...*circumstances*...twice a year that reminded them both of childhood suffering, the Gods soothed and healed them even as They possessed and used their bodies. She'd been proud, relieved, even happy until Temmin. Falling in love had not been among Allis's fears. Her girlhood and training made it unlikely, and she'd gone years in the Lovers' Temple with many dear friends and bedmates. None had possessed her so.

She sat on the dais in the dining hall now, the night before her seasonal ordeal began again. She picked at her dinner and did her best to keep herself from seeking Temmin out among the ranks below her. Even so, his height and golden hair made him obvious among the others, and the rich embroidery of his Supplicant's tunic stood out in the sea of rose, white and red garb. Who sat with him? Some Lover whose name she couldn't recall— a recent transfer from the Temple at Maryakuspa—and the recently-sworn Justinna Beloved, who'd attended her last time and would again tomorrow. All three laughed and flirted. Jealousy flared like a fire that burned too hot for its hearth, and she sent up a prayer: *I wish to serve you, Neya. Take this burden from me. Do not desert me!*

Preparations for the twins' possession began the next day. Temmin kept his eyes averted from Allis as much as possible; outwardly she was composed, but now he sensed her fear for the first time. He wanted more than anything to spare her the coming ordeal and had to struggle to keep from throwing himself between her and the door to the Gods' Chambers. Everything he'd learned in the last two years deserted him. He didn't trust himself any more.

Neya's Day night, Temmin helped bind Issak to the frame, knowing the Beloveds did the same with Allis in the next room. The sound of worshippers entering the gardens filtered through to the Chambers as he went about his business with Barik Lover, Senik and Mathanus Lover. Temmin lit the incense; woody resins masked the bitterness of the drug it contained. The smoke flared up and he accidentally breathed in too much. Temmin stumbled back from the brazier, searching for fresh air. A dread crept into his bones, and he reeled as dark, indistinct images filled his head. Something terrible was approaching...

A few deep breaths, and Temmin cleared the poison from his system. The disturbing images faded, but the dread remained. He told himself it was his last Neya's Day, and that was all.

Temmin helped Barik and Mathanus set the heavy jeweled clamps in place on Issak's nipples and sac. At the right time, he kissed the Embodiment hard; Issak screamed into his mouth as the clamps came off until a shuddering calm came over the Embodiment, and possession's rosy glow spread from his streaming eyes. Temmin jumped back. Nerr had come.

Screams penetrated from Neya's side of the Chambers. The double doors flew open; Allis struggled against the frame, her breasts swinging from side to side. The holy light did not surround her: The Goddess had not come. "Release Me," said Nerr-in-Issak. His voice was cold. "Release her as well."

Allis fell from the frame in a writhing heap on the floor. Nerr ran to her, but instead of helping her up as Temmin expected, He kicked her square in the ribs. "What are you doing!" yelled Temmin. Barik tried to seize him before he could do something stupid, but it proved unnecessary; they were all rooted to the spot. Nerr kicked Allis again as the mortal attendants all cried out. Allis did nothing to avoid the blow, howling as she huddled naked on the floor. "What in Pagg's name are you doing!" Temmin yelled again.

Nerr stabbed a finger at him; pink stickiness filled Temmin's mouth. "You *dare* to invoke My Father's name against Me, little Prince?" He turned to Barik; the elder priest stumbled, the hold on him released. "Fetch Me a strap." The dark forebodings from the drugged incense crowded into Temmin's mind, less cloudy and more menacing. Barik came back holding a thick leather belt, split at one end into two wicked tongues; the stocky Lover trembled and kept his eyes averted as he handed it to Nerr. "You have spoiled My Sister's Embodiment and made her unfit for use, Temmin, and so this punishment falls on you," snarled the God. "You both leave Me little choice."

Temmin closed his eyes and waited for the expected blows but snapped them open at an agonized scream. Nerr was beating Allis, striking her bare back over and over, leaving deep welts where the tongues snapped and bit at her skin. Blood soon ran down her sides to the marble floor. Mathanus vomited on his own feet; Justinna huddled on the floor in incoherent shrieks. Temmin would have begged for Allis's life, but the stickiness filled his mouth; all he could do was cry. Nerr was going to kill her, to whip her to death, and it was his fault—*beat me, kill me, Lord!* he begged silently. "She bears responsibility too, never doubt it," said Nerr, raising the strap and bringing it down again. "She must bear the pain alone if she's to be of any use to My Sister."

The beating went on and on until Allis lay still in a pool of blood; her long black hair soaked in it. "Please, Lord, I think she's stopped breathing," begged Glaes Beloved. "She's of no use to Our Lady dead!"

Nerr threw down the strap. "She's not dead."

"Not dead at all," came Allis's voice. The rose-colored light spread over her; the savage cuts obliterating her pale skin began to close. "Though I would have preferred her less mauled, Brother." Neya-in-Allis stood up; the blood covering Her skin and clotting in Her hair fell away, leaving Her borrowed body pristine and whole once more.

"It was the only way to open her, and You know it. Besides, remembering the fruits of disobedience will serve her well. Now run, let Me chase You before I beat this princeling to death for his presumption." Neya laughed and took off running; somehow the door to the garden had opened, and as She entered the grounds the crowd roared. If only they knew what had just happened, Temmin thought. Nerr strolled up to him and took his chin in His hand. "Speak, boy."

The stickiness left his tongue. "How could You—how could You do such a thing? I prayed and prayed to You both, and no help came! What were we to do? You deserted us!" he cried.

"Prayed and prayed? Pride brought both of you down, not Us." Nerr seized his tunic and ripped it in two. "You are excused, Temmin Antremont. We release you a spoke early but still in Our debt. You will leave this place instantly, and not return while these Embodiments serve. You will not see them or speak with them in any way until We are done with them." The God released him and walked toward the garden door, followed by the other priests but for Justinna.

"What else can the Gods take from me?" Temmin screamed after Him. "I gave You two years of my life—I lost the last moments of my mother's life to You! Harla took her from me, and now You take Allis and Issak! *What more do You want from me?*"

The God turned. "Everything. The Gods are no one's friends, little Prince—but rejoice! The land loves you more than any of your line." He ran through the door in pursuit of His Sister.

The garden door closed, leaving Temmin alone but for the young Beloved still hunched on the floor. His gorge rose in his throat and he fought it back down. Best to help Justinna...and then leave. He stumbled, and his foot slipped in Allis's blood, drying on the floor. He cursed aloud. "No one's friends, no indeed—enemies!" Rage burst through him in a familiar tingling under his skin. The room grew brighter, hotter, the shadows sharper; blood and burning timber came to his nose. His eyes followed the scent to its source. Flames leaped in a wide arc from the incense braziers to the racks that had lately held the twins; they were well and truly ablaze.

He ran to the braziers. He'd doused Issak's incense himself, he knew he had, but the more sand he now dumped onto the two braziers the higher the flames rose until he fell back. At this rate the room would be an inferno in seconds.

Justinna still clutched herself in a crouch and gibbered, mad with fear and oblivious to the danger. Temmin shook her to no avail, scooped her up and over his shoulder, and ran for the door. He ran until he reached the hallway, where he deposited the young Beloved in the arms of a surprised Temple's Own guarding the door: "Take her to the Sisters here on duty, she's had a terrible shock!" To the other guard standing by, Temmin yelled, "The Chambers of the Gods are on fire, get help!" He ran back, casting around for anything he might use to smother the flames. He finally grabbed one of the rose silk wall hangings, ripped it from its moorings and dashed into the Chamber.

The fire was out, leaving nothing but faint smoke in the air and two piles of ash on the floor: the racks. Melted metal blobs, once the fastenings that held the wood together, hissed among the remains. Temmin backed away, shaken to the core.

A Temple's Own captain rushed in, more following at his back. "Your Highness! I thought there was a fire—?" He stared at the ash heaps, then at the ripped tunic still hanging from Temmin's shoulders. "Are you all right, sir? What happened here?"

"I don't know," whispered Temmin. "I don't—I don't... Bring round a carriage or horse of some kind—no, for once I'd prefer a carriage—something enclosed. I'm going home." The Temple's Own members took in a shocked breath all at once.

"I don't understand," said the captain, brows drawn together beneath his silver helm. "It's Neya's Day!"

"And I'm leaving," answered Temmin, his voice strengthening. "I'll be ready in ten minutes. Bring the carriage round immediately."

Temmin walked from the Temple and into the carriage so differently than he'd arrived on that dramatic Neya's Day two years ago. His eyes smarted, and shame and rage cramped every muscle.

When they reached the Keep, Temmin strode through the family's private entrance and surprised an antsy pair of footmen waiting until their duty ended and they could join the Neya's Day festivities. "Your Highness!" squeaked the one he recognized as Josip.

"Has the King gone to the Temple yet?" said Temmin.

"He's not going at all, sir," said the other footman. "He's up in his rooms, if you please, sir." Temmin took the stairs two at a time toward the Residence Wing. Below him, the footman said, "What's 'e doing here?" Where else was he to go?

Winmer opened the King's receiving room door to Temmin's sharp rap. "Your Highness!" he blinked. "What are you—"

Temmin brushed past the startled secretary. "Is he in?"

"He's in his study, sir. He will be puzzled but pleased to see you."

Harsin jerked around when Temmin opened the door. "Temmin! What's happened? Are you all right? What are you doing here on Neya's Day?"

To return in shame to the father he'd defied so gleefully—how could he bear it? How could he have been so wrong when two years ago he'd never been so sure of anything in his life? "I've come back," said Temmin, his voice breaking like a boy's.

Harsin circled around his chair to approach his son. "During a Spectacle? Nothing bad has happened, I hope?"

"Everything bad has happened." Temmin's head began to pound; he rubbed at his eyes. He searched until he found his father's brandy, poured himself a shot and downed it in a gulp. "Everything bad. I'm back." He poured and downed another brandy.

"Against your vows? *Now?* Temmin, don't drink so quickly, you'll make yourself sick."

"I don't care," he said, but he put down the decanter before pouring his third drink in as many minutes. "I—I'm not sure but I think my vows are suspended. I don't know. I'm confused." He was beginning to feel the two quickly-downed brandies. "All I know is, I've been banished from the Temple and I can't go back until Allis and Issak are no longer Embodiments."

"By whose order?" rumbled Harsin.

"Nerr Himself."

His father turned a pale shade of parchment. "What did you do?"

"I should never have gone. You were right. I was wrong...you were right." Temmin sank to his knees, wobbly but determined, and his eyes burned as he looked up at his father. "From now on, I'll listen. Tell me what to do."

EPILOGUE

Rodder Pawl looked down the long, curving ridge jutting out of the lake and shivered. What a fate it would be for his horse to lose her footing and drag him caravan and all down the steep wooded hillsides into that lake, icy blue even on this warm summer day with the air full of sharp green and warm brown smells. But the track was wide, his caravan sturdy, and his mare sure-footed. There would be no accident before he entered the walls of Gremassem.

Pawl was enjoying himself as he worked his way through the Northern Wastes. Mr Brown had set him up with the caravan, the mare and a good selection of merchandise, and he'd gone village to village as a peddler, selling, trading and gathering information. Most of the villages he passed through were Gremas and so spoke his grandmother's tongue, and the ones who weren't spoke it as a trade language. Bless his gran. She'd spoken the Gremas to him every day of his life while he was at home, and he spoke it as cleanly as if he'd been raised a deerherder. No one could guess he was bred and born in Corland. That would go a fair way to keeping him safe.

Had he known how much fun and profit there was to be had on the road, Pawl would have become a peddler sooner. But he never forgot his objective, the mission Mr Brown was paying him so very much to accomplish. He was to find his dead employer's daughter Mattisanis Ambleson: the girl herself at best, news of her at worst. Why she was so important, Mr Brown declined to say. Pawl knew it was a tricky business—that much Mr Brown had said—and that he must be careful not to let anyone know he was looking for the girl.

What kind of tricky business might now be in sight. He'd learned on his last few stops that Ruvin, the bastard brother of King Harsin, was at Gremassem. Pawl wasn't exactly sure how the missing girl might be connected to Ruvin, but it struck him nonetheless. He wondered if Mr Brown knew who Ruvin the Bastard was, and where he was; not many folks thought on him and his brothers these days.

Pawl cracked his whip lightly above his horse's head, catching the thong as cleanly as any Maryakuspan dandy, and the mare trotted onto the serpentine ridge. The road was taking them to the largest island of the dozens that dotted the huge lake. Atop the sheer rock that made up its cloverleaf shape sat an immense old castle that took up every square inch of it. Towers topped in light red stone and ringed with round windows stood at each of its many corners; all were capped with what looked like great green metal funnels. Gran had talked about this place a great deal when he was little: "Aye, the grand isle, the hall of great warriors, the home of Farr's true way, the home of the Headman of the Gremas, the pride of our people. Some day, Roddie, some day I hope you see the great towers of Gremassem rising from the Lake Laagrem, for I am old and will never see it again." *Well, here I am, Gran. Wish me peddler's luck.*

Pawl passed through the great iron gates on the ridge and finally through the huge doors into Gremassem's grand interior, a huge expanse more like a village than a courtyard. He could hear word of his arrival already shouted from person to person: "Peddler's here! He looks well-stocked! Tell the women and the warden—peddler's here!" An ostler took his horse's bridle and guided him to an open space near a long gallery; Pawl jumped down from the driver's bench, helped the ostler unhitch the mare and let him lead her off for grooming and feeding. His caravan would be safe enough from the hubbub in this quiet corner. It might even be quiet when he bedded down there that night.

He went about the wagon, opening the many little doors in its sides and arranging his wares enticingly on the shelves that dropped down from them. Times like this, when everyone was excited to see him, the smell of money was in the air and the anticipation of a good haggle was upon him,

Pawl thought of ditching Mr Brown's assignment and continuing on as a peddler, refreshing his wares through trade and the occasional trip back to Arren—where the well-connected Mr Brown would undoubtedly find him and kill him for taking coin for no work. Ah well, he'd keep looking for Miss as best he could. In the long run the pay would be better anyway.

Pawl rubbed his thin hands together and began assembling the smile that loosened many a feminine purse string—and sometimes feminine laces. He'd never counted himself as handsome, but for some reason he did well up here. He looked up, ready to charm some matron or girl, but instead encountered the steady gaze of a man in traditional Gremas clothing made in rich silks. The man's brown eyes turned down at the outside corner, giving him a melancholy appearance.

Pawl's heart skidded to a stop, then took off running. It was Mr Adrikson, the man who'd paid Pawl a gold piece to help him elope with Miss, and the man Mr Brown had warned Pawl against. Suddenly Miss's disappearance and Ruvin the Bastard's residence at Gremassem seemed more likely connected than not, and Pawl began to wonder if he shouldn't have asked for more gold than he'd gotten from Mr Brown. Should he acknowledge the man? Perhaps Mr Adrikson didn't remember him. He would remain watchful but disinterested.

Mr Adrikson sauntered up to the caravan. "You have some interesting wares, my man," he said in the Gremas.

"Thank you, sir," said Pawl, trying to keep his voice level. "Anything you might wish to examine?"

"It can be fairly said that someone will want to examine you and your wares," smiled Mr Adrikson. "You're awfully far north, Rodder Pawl," he murmured in Tremontine. "Come for another gold piece? Or perhaps you've already gotten one from someone else. You're playing some kind of game, and I am fairly sure I know what it is. I may even be playing it myself."

Pawl's insides twisted; the game was up, indeed, but perhaps he might at least find out what he came to know—if not for his employer, then for his own heart's ease. "Here is a fine pelt, sir, taken from the largest silver fox ever seen in the forests of Alavis," he said in louder Gremas. "A pelt of rare price." The two leaned their heads over it. "Mr Adrikson, sir," he whispered in Tremontine, "I'm fair sure my life is in your hands. If you're going to give me up, please just tell me, is Miss all right? Mistress is dead, you see—"

"Listen, Pawl, I think we may be of use to one another. We may have common cause—or we may not. That remains to be seen. Nevertheless, I shan't give you away if I might be sure of you. I will cover for you, and if you can be of use to me I'll even see a few coins into your purse. But you must do as I say. Are you my man?"

Pawl looked around him. The women of the castle were converging on the quiet corner of the courtyard; lounging in doorways were tall, hard-faced men with long blonde beards and long sharp swords at their sides, all of them watching him. A word from Mr Adrikson and it was certain the tip of one of those swords would press straight through his heart. Then again, if Mr Brown found out he'd turned away from his assignment—or possibly made cause with his enemy—he might end up on the point of a different sword, or worse.

But Mr Brown was in Arren, and Mr Adrikson was here. "I'm your man," said Rodder Pawl. "Tell me what to do."

.

ACKNOWLEDGMENTS

First shout-outs go to my team, very international this go-round: Canada, Spain, Austria and St Louis.

Annetta "Netta the Eddita" Ribken is my rock. She has been there for me any time I've needed an ear, a reassuring hand on my shoulder, or a slap upside the head. If you need an editor, hire her. You Will Not Be Sad. Her website: http://www.wordwebbing.com/

MCM is still Canadian. Canadians still have free health care and ISBNs, and it still annoys me. I hear that may be changing. I hope not. It's a good kind of annoyed to know at least some working people get to share in the bounty all around us. MCM typeset the paperback and formatted the ebook, which is why they're beautiful. His website: http://www.1889.ca/

Alice Fox could not play with us this time, but her terrific character studies and cover design for book one helped make this series what it is. Get better, Alice: http://alicefox.net/

Beatriz González stepped in for Alice and did a great job with the book cover, staying true to the look Alice established while still giving it her own stamp. Check out her eye-popping portfolio: http://www.beagonzalez.com

Robert Altbauer made the map, building on an incomplete atlas-style map I eked out with the help of the generous folks at the Cartographers' Guild. His portfolio: http://www.fantasy-map.net

My Non-Existent Beta Group consists of readers who've been with me a very, very long time. They suffered through a lot of alpha writing this go-round and caught some truly horrendous conflicts, canon violations and so on, not even counting typos and editing artifacts: Northwoodsman, Daniel Gudlat, Manoki, Katie, V, TheBoy, kawaiikune and my best friend Anhata. You are my patient darlings. Special thanks as always: to Daniel for help with the wiki, without which I couldn't keep canon straight; to Northwoodsman for plotting out the original Tremontine calendar, without which I literally cannot write the books; and to Manoki, without whom this series would not have been necessary.

Elizabeth Barrial of Black Phoenix Alchemy Lab makes perfumes and ritual oils that help me create. I will always be grateful to her for literally leading me by the nose out of a long, unhappy exile back into the sensual world of color, texture, scent, movement and creativity.

My mother is proud of me for writing, even though she can't read the History series. I love you, Mama, and I'll write something PG-13 you can read real soon.

I'm writing this a few hours after the Kickstarter pre-sale for this book closed. I asked for $1,500.

I got $5,250.

Last book, 48 people backed it via pre-sales at my website. This time, between website pre-sales and Kickstarter a total of 138 people backed me—nearly three times the number last time.

This book is for the backers, but three others take precedence. My beautiful girls put up with a helluva lot from their scribbling mother; Josie and Louisa, you are the best daughters a writing mother ever had. And John, my husband, I love you so much it's not even funny; thank you for loving me and supporting my work.

In alphabetical order, the backers who gave to have their names included in these acknowledgments:

Anna, aka the paradox
Alyxe Barron
Erica "Irk" Bercegeay
Blw1104
Brandon, aka V
Matthew Bryan
Wendi Burke
Katrina C.
Stormy C.
Narel Cantatrice
capriox bovidae
Catseyes
Cam Collins
Coral
Charissa Cotrill, Mayor of Freedonia
Rhel ná DecVandé

DixieHellcat
Tristan W Dixon
Andrea Doucette
Jeff Dow
TeKiesha Elliott
Patricia Engel
eric the girl
Flynnrt
Justine di Giovanni
Daniel Gudlat
Laureril
Lawrence Evalyn
Rachel Feldman, aka BCT
Garfield
Jeremy Philip Garnett
HannahP
Glenn Herbert
Nevin Hillegass
M.K. Hobson
Amanda Horetski
IridiumFlash
Samantha James
Kaleb
Kate, aka kalinkadink
Klio
Krey
Priscilla L.
David Lewis
Katherine Liu
Manoki
MCM
Sean Manning
Mel
Clare K. R. Miller
Jesper Wied Møller
Brian Moon
Briana Morey
Northwoodsman
Ofydd

Karen P-M
Becky Puritz
Rafante
Magdalena S.
Samaris
Saudadina
Scarth
Amanda Schloss
Sarah Schumacher
Jim Sheppard, aka @JeVoudraisCake
Sherinik
Chris Shull
Leslie Sinak
Timothy J Stegner
Stormy, Official Spokesmodel of MeiLinMiranda.com
Erinn Streeter
Becka Sutton
Anhata "A" Szot
TheBoy
Tolovana
Stephanie Travellyr
Vandole
Vortacist
Rachel "rho" Walmsley
Jennifer Wamsley, aka tigger
Whimbrel
Stephen Williams
Vella Williams
Brandy Winteler
Kate Woolard

...and thanks to you for reading this book.

APPENDIX I
A Map of Tremont

To view or download the full map, go to
http://www.meilinmiranda.com/images/tremontine-map-1

APPENDIX II
PRONUNCIATION

I try not to make too many names, either of places or people, tongue-twisters in these books; I DESPISE the habit of making every name a mess of apostrophes, Xs, Zs and letters that don't really belong together in an attempt to sound exotic. Nevertheless, I'd like to give you an idea how these words sound in my head. I'm not including names which are easily pronounced as-written (Temmin, for example).

The Royal Family
Antremont: AN-treh-mont
Ansella: ANN-sel-ah
Anneya: ah-NAY-yah
Mattisanis: mat-tih-SAN-nis

The Nobility
Anvalt Vonturus: ANN-valt von-TYUR-us
Sandopint: SAND-o-pinnt
Donnis Provisa: pro-VEE-sah

The Lovers' Temple
Issak: ISS-ak (not Isaac!)
Mathanus: mah-THA-nus
Glaes: GLASE

The Bastard Heir (including place names):
Lassanna of Whitehorse: lah-SAH-nah, LAH-sah in the diminutive
Tennoc ar Sial: TEN-noc ar SEE-all
Inglatine: EEN-glah-teen
Daevys ar Ulvyn: ULL-vin
Cariodas: CARR-ee-o-das
Ardunn Anamma: ah-NAH-mah
Brunsial: BRUN-see-al (Chalkhills in the present)

Gwyrfal: GWEER-fall (Greenvale in the present)
Trefhallyn: tref-HAL-inn

The Northern Wastes:
Kupar: KOO-PAR
Uole: YOLE-ee
Gremassem: greh-MAH-sem
Gremas: GREM-as
Laagrem: LAH-grem

Various Place Names
Whithorse: WIT-horse (not white horse)
Leute: LOY-teh (archaic name for Litta)
Vakale'le: vah-ka-LE'LE (the ' is a glottal stop, like Hawai'i)
Pau'a: POW'ah (same)
Maryakuspa: mar-ya-KOOS-pa
Ouve: OOV
Alzeh: AL-zeh

APPENDIX III
CALENDAR AND MONEY

The official Tremontine calendar is solar, based on an Earthlike planetary orbit and seasonal tilt. The calendar is maintained by the Scholars of the Wise One's Temple. The calendar is thus sometimes referred to as the Eddinite Calendar, especially by the Sisters of the Temple of Venna who maintain the original lunar calendar and refuse to recognize the solar calendar within the confines of their Temple.

The year is divided up into eight "spokes," delineated by the equinoxes, solstices and cross-quarter days. Every four years there is an extra day to keep the calendar in trim.

Winter's Beginning: Winter Solstice (Eddin's Day/New year's) to the cross-quarter

Winter's Ending: Approximately February 2nd (Amma's Day) to the equinox

Spring's Beginning: Spring Equinox (Pagg's Day) to the cross-quarter

Spring's Ending: Approximately May 1st (Neya's Day) to the solstice

Summer's Beginning: Summer Solstice (Nerr's Day) to the cross-quarter

Summer's Ending: Approximately August 2nd (Venna's Day) to the equinox

Fall's Beginning: Fall Equinox (Farr's Day) to the cross-quarter

Fall's Ending: Approximately November 1st (Harla's Day) to the solstice

Days of the week are seven, like ours, because I'm lazy:

Paggday: Sunday
Ammaday: Monday
Farrday: Tuesday
Eddinday: Wednesday
Nerrday: Thursday
Neyaday: Friday
Vennaday: Saturday

Money is also lazy. I don't care if it looks like Dungeons and Dragons, I have things on my mind! Important things! Like whether I remembered to eat!

1 gold = 100 silvers = 10,000 coppers

1 silver = 100 coppers

There are half-coppers as well, which I hope are self-explanatory. The average servant in Tremont City makes around 10 gold a year, so about 1g 25s a month plus room and board. Someone like Rodder Pawl—a footman in the small city of Arren—probably makes closer to 7-8g a year. Female servants make less, though ladies maids like Camma Sinsett, Iddie Clommert and the formidable Hanston make 25-30g a year. Gram the valet makes half-again as much.

www.ingramcontent.com/pod-product-compliance
Lightning Source LLC
Chambersburg PA
CBHW030248270626
47156CB00021B/192